DERBY  ARY

WITHDRAWN FROM STOCK
FOR SALE

DATE 23/8/01

THE HEADLINE BOOK OF SPY FICTION

THE HEADLINE BOOK OF SPY FICTION

Edited by Alan Williams

Copyright © 1992 Alan Williams
(original material and compilation)

The right of Alan Williams to be identified as the Editor of the Work has been asserted by him in accordance with the Copyright, Designs and Patents Act 1988.

First published in Great Britain in 1992
by HEADLINE BOOK PUBLISHING PLC

10 9 8 7 6 5 4 3 2 1

All rights reserved. No part of this publication may be reproduced, stored in a retrieval system, or transmitted, in any form or by any means without the prior written permission of the publisher, nor be otherwise circulated in any form of binding or cover other than that in which it is published and without a similar condition being imposed on the subsequent purchaser.

All character in this publication are fictitious and any resemblance to real persons, living or dead, is purely coincidental.

British Library Cataloguing in Publication Data

The Headline book of spy fiction.
I. Williams, Alan
823.0872

ISBN 0-7472-0536-1

Typeset in 11/12pt Times by
Falcon Typographic Art Ltd,
Edinburgh

Printed and bound in Great Britain by
Richard Clay Ltd, Bungay, Suffolk

HEADLINE BOOK PUBLISHING PLC
Headline House
79 Great Titchfield Street
London W1P 7FN

For Sophie

Acknowledgements

Ted Allbeury: Extract from *The Other Side of Silence* published by Grafton reprinted by permission of the Author and the Blake Friedmann Literary Agency Ltd

Eric Ambler: Extract from *The Mask of Dimitrios* reprinted by permission of Hodder & Stoughton Ltd

Desmond Bagley: Extract from *The Freedom Trap* reprinted by permission of HarperCollins Publishers Ltd

Kyril Bonfiglioli: Extract from *Don't Point that Thing at Me* reprinted by permission of A. P. Watt Ltd on behalf of Margaret Bonfiglioli

Len Deighton: Extracts from *Funeral in Berlin* and *Billion Dollar Brain* repinted by permission of the Random Century Group Ltd

Obituary of Cdr 'Biffy' Dunderdale reprinted by permission of the *Daily Telegraph*

Ian Fleming: Extracts from *Casino Royale* reprinted by permission of the Random Century Group Ltd

Michael Gilbert: *On Slay Down* reprinted by permission of Curtis Brown Ltd

Graham Greene: Extract from *The Ministry of Fear* © 1943 Francis Greene; extract from *Our Man in Havana* © 1958 Francis Greene; extract from *Travels With My Aunt* © 1969 Francis Greene; reprinted by permission of David Higham Associates Ltd

Geoffrey Household: Extract from *Rogue Male* reprinted by permission of the Author and A. M. Heath & Co. Ltd

Christopher Isherwood: Extract from *Mr Norris Changes Trains* reprinted by permission of the Random Century Group Ltd

John le Carré: Extracts from *Call for the Dead*, *The Honourable Schoolboy*, *The Spy Who Came in From the Cold* and *Tinker, Tailor, Soldier, Spy* reprinted by permission of David Higham Associates Ltd

W. Somerset Maugham: Extracts from *Miss King* and *The Traitor* reprinted by permission of William Heinemann Ltd and A. P. Watt Ltd

Nancy Mitford: Extract from *Don't Tell Alfred* reprinted by permission of the Peters Fraser & Dunlop Group Ltd

J. B. Morton ('Beachcomber'): Extract from *Captain Foulenough* reprinted by permission of the Peters Fraser & Dunlop Group Ltd

Gerald Seymour: Extract from *Harry's Game* reprinted by permission of HarperCollins Publishers Ltd

Irwin Shaw: *The Man With One Arm* Copyright © 1952 by Irwin Shaw from *Mixed Company* (Jonathan Cape) reprinted by permission of the Tessa Sayle Agency

Evelyn Waugh: Extracts from *Put Out More Flags* and *Officers and Gentlemen* reprinted by permission of the Peters Fraser & Dunlop Group Ltd

Contents

Introduction 1

Author's Note 6

SOME INTRODUCTIONS TO THE TRADE

A Mission is Proposed 9
John Buchan (from *Greenmantle*)
Enter the 'Bulldog' 13
'Sapper' (from *Bulldog Drummond*)
Colonel R 15
W. Somerset Maugham (from *Miss King*)
Rowe 17
Graham Greene (from *The Ministry of Fear*)
On Slay Down 18
Michael Gilbert
The 'Real' James Bond 26
Obituary of Commander W. A. Dunderdale (*Daily Telegraph*)

HICCUPS AND DISADVANTAGES OF THE TRADE

The Moment of Truth 31
Ian Fleming (from *Casino Royale*)
A Bad Apple 36
W. Somerset Maugham (from *The Traitor*)
A Tricky Encounter 40
Graham Greene (from *Our Man in Havana*)

MORE SERIOUS TRADECRAFT

A Grand Slam 45
John le Carré (from *Tinker, Tailor, Soldier, Spy*) *
Groundwork 50
Gerald Seymour (from *Harry's Game*) *
Brief Encounter 57
John le Carré (from *Call for the Dead*) *

HARD GRAFTING IN THE TRADE

The Man with One Arm 61
Irwin Shaw
On the Run 80
Geoffrey Household (from *Rogue Male*) *
Contact 89
John le Carré (from *The Spy Who Came in from the Cold*) *
Johnnie Vulkan 102
Len Deighton (from *Funeral in Berlin*) *

A TOUCH OF PATRIOTIC ZEAL

A Pacifists' Coven 111
John Buchan (from *Mr Standfast*)
An Atrocious Foreign Plot 113
'Sapper'
Ambrose Routed 115
Evelyn Waugh (from *Put out More Flags*) *

... AND SOME SCOUNDRELS

Captain Foulenough & Co. 123
J. B. Morton (from *Beachcomber*)
A Defector Returns 130
Nancy Mitford (from *Don't Tell Alfred*)
Facing the Music 135
Christopher Isherwood (from *Mr Norris Changes Trains*)

Contents

The Real Colonel Haki/Hakim	139
Eric Ambler (from *The Mask of Dimitrios*); Graham Greene (*from Travels with My Aunt*)	

PITFALLS, HORRORS AND GENERAL NASTINESS

'My Dear Boy'	149
Ian Fleming (from *Casino Royale*)	
'That's Not a Mugging. That's a Party . . .'	156
John le Carré (from *The Honourable Schoolboy*	
Another Touch of Nastiness	160
'Sapper' (from *Bulldog Drummond*)	

TRICKS AND GADGETS OF THE TRADE

Hints on Disguise	167
Len Deighton (from *Billion Dollar Brain*)	
An Example of the Same	168
John Buchan (from *Greenmantle*)	
The Purloined Letter	172
Edgar Allan Poe	
A Mysterious Device	188
Desmond Bagley (from *The Freedom Trap*)	
A More Dangerous Device	193
William Le Queuz (from *The Czar's Spy*)	

CAR CHASES, THEN AND NOW

Across Country, *circa* 1930	197
John Buchan (from *The Island of Sheep*)	
Death of a Rolls, *circa* 1970	206
Kyril Bonfiglioli (from *Don't Point That Thing at Me*)	

SOME VINTAGES OF THE GENRE

The Secret	213
E. Phillips Oppenheim (from *The Secret*)	

In the Picture	220
Evelyn Waugh (from *Officers and Gentlemen*)	
The Informer	223
Joseph Conrad (from *A Set of Six*)	
The Secret of the Fox Hunter	242
William Le Queux	
The Adventure of the Bruce-Partington Plans	258
Arthur Conan Doyle	
Eavesdropping	283
Erskine Childers (from *The Riddle of the Sands*)	
The Great Game	289
Rudyard Kipling (from *Kim**)	

PREMATURE DEMISES OF KIM PHILBY

Stop Press, 1981	305
Ted Allbeury (from *The Other Side of Silence*)	
Cut off in Mid-Flow	306
Alan Williams (from *Gentleman Traitor*)	

* The book fron which H. A. R. (Kim) Philby, in early youth, adopted his nickname.

Introduction

I should make it plain at once that I have never worked for the British Intelligence Service (SIS), nor was I even approached by them, despite having been in the very Cambridge college that nurtured the best vintage of spies/traitors/double-agents of this century. I even had, as my Senior Tutor, the University's chief recruiter for both MI6 and MI5. He probably passed me over because, in the long vacation of my first year, I managed to wangle my way into East Germany to play in an international tennis tournament in Leipzig (in which I lost ignominiously); in my second year I attended the International Youth Festival for Peace and Friendship in Warsaw, during which I helped smuggle a Polish dissident to the West, concealed on the luggage-rack of a train; and in my third year I went AWOL to Budapest during the 1956 Uprising. These experiences led to my first job, which was with Radio Free Europe, a staunchly anti-communist organization in Munich.

As a result of these Central European escapades, my Senior Tutor may have assumed (wrongly) that I already worked for the Russians – since this would have been entirely appropriate to the college's tradition. More likely, he may have thought that I was in the pay of the Americans, as Radio Free Europe had been set up by an organization called the Crusade for Freedom whose then President, General Lucius Clay, was not unknown to the Central Intelligence Agency.

I am not altogether sorry I missed the attentions of SIS – particularly if the experiences of my old friend and college contemporary (whom, for tact and security reasons, I shall call Neil) are at all typical. After a dazzling academic career, culminating in a Double-Starred First, Neil was looking – not very hard – for a job in journalism. With a degree like his he could afford to be choosy. About a month after his Tripos II results had appeared in *The Times* a letter arrived from a knighted gentleman with an address in Knightsbridge, inviting him to dinner. The postscript said that he wanted to discuss a 'literary project'. It was all done with a certain casual urgency and Neil got the impression that he was not expected to refuse. He duly turned up at a tiny maisonette, behind Harrod's, where he was admitted by an elegant young Indo-Chinese butler – the year being 1957, before the second Vietnam conflict had really begun.

His host was an ageing aesthete in a velvet smoking-jacket who received him in an exquisite little room with silk wallpaper and fragile Oriental *objets d'art*. Neil discovered he was the only guest. Over an extended and delicious Chinese dinner, and plying him with discreet quantities of rice-wine, Neil's titled host proposed that the time was now ripe for an in-depth biography of the new luminary on the Far Eastern stage, one Ho Chi Minh, and that Neil was just the man for the job. His host knew 'a respectable publisher' who would pay an advance of £1000 (a modest fortune in those days) for Neil to make his way to Hanoi and seek an interview with the Vietnamese leader, 'to try and make him see our point of view', as his host put it.

The interview terminated abruptly while they were sitting on a delicate, two-seater armchair together, discussing the finer points of Vietnamese post-Colonial politics, when his host gently slipped his hand between Neil's thighs. With postgraduate prudery, my friend leapt to his feet, made his apologies and left.

As luck would have it, the very next evening he went to a party in Chelsea (given, I think, by George Melly) where Neil was greeted by another Cambridge friend, the late Mark Boxer, whose first words, delivered in ringing tones, were: 'Ah Neil! I hear you've just been signed up by MI6 to go to Hanoi and meet Ho Chi Minh!' This was the last Neil heard of the assignment or of SIS. A month later he became leader-writer on an obscure newspaper in the North of England.

This true and salutary tale illustrates not only the absurd amateurism of the spy trade – at least until thirty years ago – but also that the most apparently far-fetched, even satirical, spy fiction – such as Graham Greene's immortal *Our Man in Havana* which I have included in this book – is not necessarily as far removed from reality as we might think. Indeed, it seems to confirm my long-held theory that, in many areas of creative work, fact is the *slavish follower* of fiction, instead of the other way round.

While Somerset Maugham's dry autobiographical stories of Ashenden, in the First World War, still have a totally authentic modern ring (he was the true precursor to Ian Fleming, but without the sex), what about John le Carré? Did our men in the SIS really invent those splendid neologisms, like 'lamp-lighter' and 'pavement-artist'? Or

Introduction

did they – as I am told is the case – start using them only *after* reading le Carré?

One of the delights of preparing this book has been to return to the extraordinary world of Captain 'Bulldog' Drummond: his boredom with the advent of peace (this is 1919!) and his relish for squeaky-clean fisticuffs with evil foreigners, Bolsheviks and other rich, degenerate trouble-makers. Indeed, both Drummond and his creator, H.E. McNeile – otherwise, the aptly named 'Sapper' – make Buchan's General Sir Richard Hannay seem positively mild, even 'liberal', by comparison. However, my extract from Buchan's *Mr Standfast*, in which Hannay infiltrates a nest of pacifists in the West Country during the height of the First World War, is a quaint diversion from the 'politically correct' attitudes of most modern writers. Both 'Sapper' and Buchan, if they were writing today, would surely risk falling on the wrong side of race relations legislation. The attitude of both authors towards sex is also noticeable, in the sense that it does not exist. (Both the 'Bulldog' and Hannay dispose of the matter by marrying their respective girlfriends, Phyllis and Mary, in early novels.) Both heroes would have mightily disapproved of James Bond.

For while today's spy fiction has certainly cleaned up its 'political' outlook and sex has also taken its predictable, rather dreary, toll at the expense of pace and plot – le Carré being a welcome exception – the spy novelist's predilection for cruelty and sadism remains constant and undiminished. There is little difference here between 'Sapper' and Fleming – as I hope to illustrate under the section, *Pitfalls, Horrors and General Nastiness* – though le Carré outbids them all in a brief and truly horrific extract from *The Honourable Schoolboy*.

While I claim that in most matters concerning the spyworld, fact may follow fiction, this cannot be entirely true of that arch-protagonist of the trade, the Ultimate Enemy – sadly, today, no longer the beast it was. I refer, of course, to the Soviet Secret Service, known as the Cheka, OGPU, the NKVD and the late KGB. For while most of its members – though not all, it must be said – have not been exposed to the apparently limitless output of western spy fiction, they have probably fed on the inspiration and older traditions set by J.V. Stalin and his fearful acolytes, Yagoda, Yezhov and Lavrenti Beria. For what ambitious thriller writer has ever bettered the intricately planned and bloody murder of Trotsky in his Mexican retreat in 1940? Which seamy practitioner of the spy novel would have invented the tale of the homosexual Admiralty clerk, Vassall, first blackmailed in Moscow by means of a KGB 'honey-pot' of quite revolting thoroughness? And what about the wretched Midland Bank executive in Moscow whose half-naked body, its head covered with a tracksuit hood, was found beneath the tenth-floor window of his apartment-block in the city, and whose death was initially described by the Croydon coroner as 'suicide'? And then the strange, still unexplained, saga of MI6's greatest double-agent, Oleg Penkovsky – that vain and ridiculous social-climber, obsessed with meeting the Queen? Surely he – together with his MI6 'cut-out', the luckless Chelsea 'businessman', Greville Wynne – would seem more probable in the pages of Graham Greene?

And on the subject of Greene, I think I have stumbled on a small oddity unique in spy fiction, and which I do not think has ever been spotted by literary reviewers. In 1969 Graham Greene seems to have 'borrowed' one of Eric Ambler's fictional characters – the sinister Colonel Haki, head of the Istanbul Secret Police – straight out of Ambler's seminal masterpiece, *The Mask of Dimitrios*. Green resurrected Ambler's character as the now old but equally sinister Colonel Hakim in his *Travels with My Aunt*. I have included both (or the same) portraits in this collection.

I shall conclude on another personal note. For as far as spies, and the grimmer side of espionage, are concerned, I soon made up for any missed opportunities after Cambridge. In 1962 I got my fill of both while working as a foreign correspondent in Algeria during the final showdown between the French Government and the European terrorist organization, the OAS. I had escaped a sentence of death. I was suspected of espionage by the French authorities and the Arab FLN who both complained about me bitterly to the UK Foreign Office. I was then sacked by the Fleet Street newspaper I worked for and embarked, almost penniless, on a merchant steamer round the Mediterranean on which I began my first spy novel, *Barbouze*, based on my experiences in Algeria. It was the end of 1962, and the ship docked for a few days in Beirut. Here, on my second day ashore, I met up in a bar with an old Australian colleague.

I happened to notice sitting beside me a dishevelled figure in a tweed jacket with leather patches at the elbow, suede chukka boots and – what particularly struck me at the time – odd socks. He was dozing quietly with his head on the bar-top. My Australian friend woke him abruptly and introduced him as Kim – otherwise H.A.R. Philby, the Middle East 'stringer' for the *Observer* newspaper and *The Economist*. As we were about to go to lunch, he turned to me, with his baggy eyes and famous stutter, and said, 'I know of an e-e-e-xcellent place near here where they d-d-do very good Abyssinian goat.' I was not to know at the time – nor when he disappeared ten days later, probably on a Syrian freighter, to surface after several months in Moscow – that I'd just been addressed by probably the greatest spy and double-agent of all time. He was also the only man to be a member of both the Athenaeum Club and the KGB, and the only Briton to hold the rank of Russian General, as well as the CBE and the Order of Lenin.

No writer of spy fiction would surely have dared risk his reputation with such unlikely nonsense as that? Indeed, it was five years before the true facts were painstakingly prised into the public domain – under dire threats of imprisonment for treason – by such indomitable figures as David Leitch and Murray Sayle of the *Sunday Times*.

From that moment on, spy fiction came into its own and nothing was too improbable, too fantastic, to seem perfectly believable. And here I must add yet another personal and immodest note. A few months before Philby's death in 1988, the foremost expert on international espionage, Phillip Knightley, obtained an exclusive interview with him in his Moscow flat. Here he noted, in his subsequent and definitive biography, *Philby: The Life and Views of the KGB Masterspy*, that the old scoundrel was a keen reader of western spy fiction and had all the works of such writers as le Carré and Deighton on his shelves, as well as my own book, *Gentleman Traitor*. This interest in such works posited the theory (not entirely without foundation) that Philby secretly craved to return to the West. On such a recommendation – however disingenuous – I have therefore included an extract from my book in this collection.

Finally, I should add that all the other extracts are from books which I have read over the past thirty-five years purely for pleasure and entertainment. I only hope that these extracts I have chosen will convey the same emotions to the readers of this book; that they will refresh the memories of those already familiar with the originals and stimulate those to whom the works are as yet unknown.

Author's Note

Faced with the exhilarating task of making my choice for this *Book of Spy Fiction*, and given a totally free hand – unburdened by the exigencies of expense and space – I would have started with John Buchan's *Greenmantle* – page one right through to the end; *all* of Somerset Maugham's *Ashenden* stories; the whole of Fleming's first and greatest of the Bond books, *Casino Royale*; great chunks of Ambler's *Mask of Dimitrios*; most of Greene's *Our Man in Havana*; the entire text of *The Spy Who Came in from the Cold* . . . and . . . and . . . But it would have been a very long and expensive book – or series of books . . .

Better keep to a few select *hors d'oeuvres*

SOME INTRODUCTIONS
TO THE TRADE

Let us start with Buchan: son of a Scottish clergyman he was, in turn, a successful barrister, Army officer, career diplomat and Member of Parliament, before becoming, as Lord Tweedsmuir, Governor-General of Canada. As a hobby, Buchan wrote the Richard Hannay novels in notebooks on his knee while travelling to Whitehall on the London Underground.

A Mission is Proposed

Sir Walter lay back in an armchair and spoke to the ceiling. It was the best story, the clearest and the fullest, I had ever got of any bit of the war. He told me just how and why and when Turkey had left the rails. I heard about her grievances over our seizure of her ironclads, of the mischief the coming of the *Goeben* had wrought, of Enver and his precious Committee and the way they had got a cinch on the old Turk. When he had spoken for a bit, he began to question me.

'You are an intelligent fellow, and you will ask how a Polish adventurer, meaning Enver, and a collection of Jews and gipsies should have got control of a proud race. The ordinary man will tell you that it was German organization backed up with German money and German arms. You will inquire again how, since Turkey is primarily a religious power, Islam has played so small a part in it all. The Sheikh-ul-Islam is neglected, and though the Kaiser proclaims a Holy War and calls himself Hadji Mohammed Guilliamo, and says the Hohenzollerns are descended from the Prophet, that seems to have fallen pretty flat. The ordinary man again will answer that Islam in Turkey is becoming a back number, and that Krupp guns are the new gods. Yet – I don't know. I do not quite believe in Islam becoming a back number.'

'Look at it in another way,' he went on. 'If it were Enver and Germany alone dragging Turkey into a European war for purposes that no Turk cared a rush about, we might expect to find the regular army obedient, and Constantinople. But in the provinces, where

Islam is strong, there would be trouble. Many of us counted on that. But we have been disappointed. The Syrian army is as fanatical as the hordes of the Mahdi. The Senussi have taken a hand in the game. The Persian Moslems are threatening trouble. There is a dry wind blowing through the East, and the parched grasses wait the spark. And the wind is blowing towards the Indian border. Whence comes that wind, think you?'

Sir Walter had lowered his voice and was speaking very slow and distinct. I could hear the rain dripping from the eaves of the window, and far off the hoot of taxis in Whitehall.

'Have you an explanation, Hannay?' he asked again.

'It looks as if Islam had a bigger hand in the thing than we thought,' I said. 'I fancy religion is the only thing to knit up such a scattered empire.'

'You are right,' he said. 'You must be right. We have laughed at the Holy War, the Jehad that old Von der Goltz prophesied. But I believe that stupid old man with the spectacles was right. There is a Jehad preparing. The question is, how?'

'I'm hanged if I know,' I said; 'but I'll bet it won't be done by a pack of stout German officers in *pickelhaubes*. I fancy you can't manufacture Holy Wars out of Krupp guns alone and a few staff officers and a battle-cruiser with her boilers burst.'

'Agreed. They are not fools, however much we try to persuade ourselves of the contrary. But supposing they had got some tremendous sacred sanction – some holy thing, some book or gospel or some new prophet from the desert, something which would cast over the whole ugly mechanism of German war the glamour of the old torrential raid which crumpled the Byzantine Empire and shook the walls of Vienna? Islam is a fighting creed, and the mullah still stands in the pulpit with the Koran in one hand and a drawn sword in the other. Supposing there is some Ark of the Covenant which will madden the remotest Moslem peasant with dreams of Paradise? What then, my friend?'

'Then there will be hell let loose in those parts pretty soon.'

'Hell which may spread. Beyond Persia, remember, lies India.'

'You keep to suppositions. How much do you know?' I asked.

'Very little, except the fact. But the fact is beyond dispute. I have reports from agents everywhere – pedlars in South Russia, Afghan horse-dealers, Turcoman merchants, pilgrims on the road to Mecca, sheikhs in North Africa, sailors on the Black Sea coasters, sheep-skinned Mongols, Hindu fakirs, Greek traders in the Gulf, as well as respectable consuls who use cyphers. They tell the same story. The East is waiting for a revelation. It has been promised one. Some star – man, prophecy, or trinket – is coming out of the West. The Germans know, and that is the card with which they are going to astonish the world.'

'And the mission you spoke of for me is to go and find out?'

He nodded gravely. 'That is the crazy and impossible mission.'

'Tell me one thing, Sir Walter,' I said. 'I know it is the fashion in this country if a man has special knowledge to set him to some job exactly the opposite. I know all about Damaraland, but instead of being put on Botha's staff, as I applied to be, I was kept in Hampshire mud till the campaign in German South-West Africa was over. I know a man who could pass as an Arab, but do you think they would send him to the East? They left him in my battalion – a lucky thing for me, for he saved my life at Loos. I know the fashion, but isn't this just carrying it a bit too far? There must be thousands of men who have spent years in the East and talk any language. They're the fellows for this job. I never saw a Turk in my life except a chap who did wrestling turns in a show at Kimberley. You've picked about the most useless man on earth.'

'You've been a mining engineer, Hannay,' Sir Walter said. 'If you wanted a man to prospect for gold in Barotseland you would of course like to get one who knew the country and the people and the language. But the first thing you would require in him would be that he had a nose for finding gold and knew his business. That is the position now. I believe that you have a nose for finding out what our enemies try to hide. I know that you are brave and cool and resourceful. That is why I tell you the story. Besides . . .'

He unrolled a big map of Europe on the wall.

'I can't tell you where you'll get on the track of the secret, but I can put a limit to the quest. You won't find it east of the Bosporus – not yet. It is still in Europe. It may be in Constantinople, or in Thrace. It may be farther west. But it is moving eastwards. If you are in time you may cut into its march to Constantinople. That much I can tell you. The secret is known in Germany, too, to those whom it concerns. It is in Europe that the seeker must search – at present.'

'Tell me more,' I said. 'You can give me no details and no instructions. Obviously you can give me no help if I come to grief.'

He nodded. 'You would be beyond the pale.'

'You give me a free hand.'

'Absolutely. You can have what money you like, and you can get what help you like. You can follow any plan you fancy, and go anywhere you think fruitful. We can give no directions.'

'One last question. You say it is important. Tell me just how important.'

'It is life and death,' he said solemnly. 'I can put it no higher and no lower. Once we know what is the menace we can meet it. As long as we are in the dark it works unchecked and we may be too late. The war must be won or lost in Europe. Yes; but if the East blazes up, our effort will be distracted from Europe and the great coup may fail. The stakes are no less than victory and defeat, Hannay.'

I got out of my chair and walked to the window. It was a difficult moment in my life. I was happy in my soldiering; above all, happy in the company of my brother officers. I was asked to go off into the enemy's lands on a quest for which I believed I was manifestly unfitted – a business of lonely days and nights, of nerve-racking strain, of deadly peril shrouding me like a garment. Looking out on the bleak weather I shivered. It was too grim a business, too inhuman for flesh and blood. But Sir Walter had called it a matter of life and death, and I had told him that I was out to serve my country. He could not give me orders, but was I not under orders – higher orders than my Brigadier's? I thought myself incompetent, but cleverer men than me thought me competent, or at least competent enough for a sporting chance. I knew in my soul that if I declined I should never be quite at peace in the world again. And yet Sir Walter had called the scheme madness, and said that he himself would never have accepted.

How does one make a great decision? I swear that when I turned round to speak I meant to refuse. But my answer was Yes, and I had crossed the Rubicon. My voice sounded cracked and far away.

Sir Walter shook hands with me and his eyes blinked a little.

'I may be sending you to your death, Hannay. Good God, what a damned task-mistress duty is! If so, I shall be haunted with regrets, but *you* will never repent. Have no fear of that. You have chosen the roughest road, but it goes straight to the hill-tops.'

He handed me the half-sheet of note paper. On it were written three words: 'Kasredin', 'cancer', and 'v. I'.

'That is the only clue we possess,' he said. 'I cannot construe it, but I can tell you the story. We have had our agents working in Persia and Mesopotamia for years – mostly young officers of the Indian Army. They carry their lives in their hand, and now and then one disappears, and the sewers of Bagdad might tell a tale. But they find out many things, and they count the game worth the candle. They have told us of the star rising in the west, but they could give us no details. All but one – the best of them. He had been working between Mosul and the Persian frontier as a muleteer, and had been south into the Bakhtiari hills. He found out something, but his enemies knew that he knew and he was pursued. Three months ago, just before Kut, he staggered into Delamain's camp with ten bullet holes in him and a knife slash on his forehead. He mumbled his name, but beyond that and the fact that there was a Something coming from the west he told them nothing. He died in ten minutes. They found this paper on him, and since he cried out the word 'Kasredin' in his last moments, it must have had something to do with his quest. It is for you to find out if it has any meaning.'

I folded it up and placed it in my pocket-book.

'What a great fellow! What was his name?' I asked.

Sir Walter did not answer at once. He was looking out of the window. 'His name,' he said at last, 'was Harry Bullivant. He was my son. God rest his brave soul!'

from *Greenmantle*, John Buchan

Captain Hugh 'Bulldog' Drummond speaks for himself. Having survived the horrors of the First World War, we find him bored with the 'peace' and advertising for more derring-do in the agony columns of the press. I include him with a twinge of nostalgia and regret, since his kind of thick-eared innocence seems gone forever.

Enter the 'Bulldog'

Captain Hugh Drummond, DSO MC, late of His Majesty's Royal Loamshires, was whistling in his morning bath. Being by nature of a cheerful disposition, the symptom did not surprise his servant, late private of the same famous regiment, who was laying breakfast in an adjoining room.

After a while the whistling ceased and the musical gurgle of escaping water announced that the concert was over. It was the signal for James Denny – the square-jawed ex-batman – to disappear into the back regions and get from his wife the kidneys and bacon which that most excellent woman had grilled to a turn. But on this particular morning the invariable routine was broken. James Denny seemed preoccupied, distrait.

Once or twice he scratched his head and stared out of the window with a puzzled frown. And each time, after a brief survey of the other side of Half Moon Street, he turned back again to the breakfast table with a grin.

'What's you looking for, James Denny?' The irate voice of his wife at the door made him turn round guiltily. 'Then kidneys is ready and waiting these five minutes.'

Her eyes fell on the table and she advanced into the room, wiping her hands on her apron.

'Did you ever see such a bunch of letters?' she said.

'Forty-five,' returned her husband grimly, 'and more to come.' He picked up the newspaper lying beside the chair and opened it out.

'Them's the result of that,' he continued cryptically, indicating a paragraph with a square finger, and thrusting the paper under his wife's nose.

. . . Demobilized officer (she read slowly) finding peace incredibly tedious, would welcome diversion. Legitimate, if possible; but crime, if of a comparatively humorous description, no objection. Excitement essential. Would be prepared to consider permanent job if suitably impressed by applicant for his services. Reply at once Box X10.

She pushed down the paper on a chair and stared first at her husband, and then at the rows of letters neatly arranged on the table.

'I calls it wicked,' she announced at length. 'Fair flying in the face of Providence. Crime, Denny – crime. Don't you get 'aving nothing to do with such mad pranks, my man, or you and me will be having words.' She shook an admonitory finger at him, and retired slowly to the kitchen. In the days of his youth, James Denny had been a bit wild, and there was a look in his eyes this morning – the suspicion of a glint – which recalled old memories.

A moment or two later Hugh Drummond came in. Slightly under six feet in height, he was broad in proportion. His best friend would not have called him good-looking, but he was the fortunate possessor of that cheerful type of ugliness which inspires immediate confidence in its owner. His nose had never quite recovered from the final one year in the Public Schools Heavy Weights; his mouth was not small. In fact, to be strictly accurate only his eyes redeemed his face from being what is known in the vernacular as the Frozen Limit.

Deep-set and steady, with eyelashes that many a woman had envied, they showed the man for what he was – sportsman and a gentleman. And the combination of the two is an unbeatable production.

from *Bulldog Drummond*, 'Sapper',

Hannay's contemporary, Maugham's dry, fastidious and highly professional Ashenden – sent as a secret agent to Switzerland during the First World War – has the understated ring of absolute conviction. The stories are mostly autobiographical, and Maugham was certainly way ahead of his time in detailing the minutiae of the spy's professional life. Incidentally, Ashenden's boss, Colonel R – although separated by a generation – is a dead-ringer for Fleming's M, introduced thirty years later, and probably based on the same man: possibly Sir Stewart Menzies, otherwise known throughout the SIS as C. Like Maugham, Fleming had first-hand experience as a spy, working for Naval Intelligence in the Second World War.

Colonel R

It was not till the beginning of September that Ashenden, a writer by profession who had been abroad at the outbreak of the war, managed to get back to England. He chanced soon after his arrival to go to a party and was there introduced to a middle-aged colonel whose name he did not catch. He had some talk with him. As he was about to leave, this officer came up to him and asked:

'I say, I wonder if you'd mind coming to see me. I'd rather like to have a chat with you.'

'Certainly,' said Ashenden. 'Whenever you like.'

'What about tomorrow at eleven?'

'All right.'

'I'll just write down my address. Have you a card on you?'

Ashenden gave him one and on this the colonel scribbled in pencil the name of a street and the number of a house. When Ashenden walked along next morning to keep his appointment he found himself in a street of rather vulgar red-brick houses in a part of London that had once been fashionable, but was now fallen in the esteem of the house-hunter who wanted a good address. On the house at which Ashenden had been asked to call there was a board up to announce that it was for sale, the shutters were closed and there was no sign that anyone lived in it. He rang the bell and the door was opened by a non-commissioned officer so promptly that he was startled. He was not asked his business, but led immediately into a long room at the back, once evidently a dining-room, the florid decoration of which looked oddly out of keeping with the office furniture, shabby and sparse, that was in it. It gave Ashenden the impression of a room in which the brokers had taken possession. The colonel, who was known in the Intelligence Department, as Ashenden later discovered, by the letter R, rose when he came in and shook hands with him. He was a man somewhat above the middle height, lean, with a yellow, deeply-lined face, thin grey hair and a toothbrush moustache. The thing immediately noticeable about him was the closeness with which his blue eyes were set. He only just escaped a squint. They were hard and cruel eyes, and very wary; and they gave him a cunning, shifty look. Here was a man that you could neither like nor trust at first sight. His manner was pleasant and cordial.

He asked Ashenden a good many questions and then, without further to-do, suggested that he had particular qualifications for the Secret Service. Ashenden was acquainted with several European languages and his profession was excellent cover; on the pretext that he was writing a book he could, without attracting attention, visit any neutral country. It was while they were discussing this point that R said:

'You know, you ought to get material that would be very useful to you in your work.'

'I shouldn't mind that,' said Ashenden.

'I'll tell you an incident that occurred only the other day and I can vouch for its truth. I thought at the time it would make a damned good story. One of the French ministers went down to Nice to recover from a cold and he had some very important documents with him that he kept in a despatch-case. They were very important indeed. Well, a day or two after he arrived he picked up a yellow-haired lady at some restaurant or other where there was dancing, and he got very friendly with her. To cut a long story short, he took her back to his hotel – of course it was a very imprudent thing to do – and when he came to himself in the morning the lady and the despatch-case had disappeared. They had one or two drinks up in his room and his theory is that, when his back was turned, the woman slipped a drug into his glass.'

R finished and looked at Ashenden with a gleam in his close-set eyes.

'Dramatic, isn't it?' he asked.

'Do you mean to say that happened the other day?'

'The week before last.'

'Impossible,' cried Ashenden. 'Why, we've been putting that incident on the stage for sixty years, we've written it in a thousand novels. Do you mean to say that life has only just caught up with us?'

R was a trifle disconcerted.

'Well, if necessary, I could give you names and dates, and believe me, the Allies have been put to no end of trouble by the loss of the documents that the despatch-case contained.'

'Well, sir, if you can't do better than that in the secret service,' sighed Ashenden, 'I'm afraid that as a source of inspiration to the writer of fiction it's a wash-out. We really *can't* write that story much longer.'

It did not take them long to settle things and when Ashenden rose to go he had already made careful note of his instructions. He was to start for Geneva next day. The last words that R said to him, with a casualness that made them impressive, were:

'There's just one thing I think you ought to know before you take on this job. And don't forget it. If you do well you'll get no thanks and if you get into trouble you'll get no help. Does that suit you?'

'Perfectly.'

'Then I'll wish you good-afternoon.'

from *Miss King*, W. Somerset Maugham

And a classic beginning for another R – Graham Greene's Rowe . . .

Rowe

Rowe went straight from Orthotex to the Free Mothers. He had signed a contract with Mr Rennit to pay him £50 a week for a period of four weeks to carry out investigations. Mr Rennit had explained that the expenses would be heavy – Orthotex employed only the most experienced agents – and the one agent he had been permitted to see before he left the office was certainly experienced. (Mr Rennit introduced him as A.2, but before long he was absent-mindedly addressing him as Jones.) Jones was small and at first sight insignificant, with his thin pointed nose, his soft brown hat with a stained ribbon, his grey suit which might have been quite a different colour years ago, and the pencil and pen on fasteners in the breast pocket. But when you looked a second time you saw experience: you saw it in the small, cunning, rather frightened eyes, the weak defensive mouth, the wrinkles of anxiety on the forehead – experience of innumerable hotel corridors, of bribed chambermaids and angry managers, experience of the insult which could not be resented, the threat which had to be ignored, the promise which was never kept. Murder had a kind of dignity compared with this muted secondhand experience of scared secretive passions.

from *The Ministry of Fear*, Graham Greene

I have also chosen for this first section one of the rare short stories in the spy genre, On Slay Down, *by Michael Gilbert. This hits off, in just a few pages, the donnish, port-sipping efficiency and chilling ruthlessness of two spies of the Old School – who, I suspect, are very much with us today if we knew where to look.*

On Slay Down

'The young man of today,' said Mr Behrens, 'is physically stronger and fitter than his father. He can run a mile quicker—'

'A useful accomplishment,' agreed Mr Calder.

'He can put a weight farther, can jump higher, and will probably live longer.'

'Not as long as the young lady of today,' said Mr Calder. '*They* have a look of awful vitality.'

'Nevertheless,' said Mr Behrens – he and Mr Calder, being very old friends, did not so much answer as override each other; frequently they both spoke at once – 'nevertheless he is, in one important way, inferior to the older generation. He is mentally softer—'

'Morally, too.'

'The two things go together. He has the weaknesses which go with his strength. He is tolerant – but he is flabby. He is intelligent – but he is timid. He is made out of cast iron, not steel.'

'Stop generalizing,' said Mr Calder. 'What's worrying you?'

'The future of our service,' said Mr Behrens.

Mr Calder considered the matter, at the same time softly scratching the head of his deerhound, Rasselas, who lay on the carpet beside his chair.

Mr Behrens, who lived down in the valley, had walked up, as he did regularly on Tuesday afternoons, to take tea with Mr Calder in his cottage on the hilltop.

'You're not often right,' said Mr Calder, at last.

'Thank you.'

'You could be on this occasion. I saw Fortescue yesterday.'

'Yes,' said Mr Behrens. 'He told me you had been to see him. I meant to ask you about that. What did he want?'

'There's a woman. She has to be killed.'

Rasselas flicked his right ear at an intrusive fly; then, when this proved ineffective, growled softly and shook his head.

'Anyone I know?' said Mr Behrens.

'I'm not sure. Her name, at the moment, is Lipper – Maria Lipper. She lives in Woking and is known there as Mrs Lipper, although I don't *think* she has ever been married. She has worked as a typist and filing clerk at the Air Ministry since – oh, since well before the last war.'

Both Mr Behrens and Mr Calder spoke of the 'last war' in terms of very slight derogation. It had not been *their* war.

'And how long has she been working for them?'

'Certainly for ten years, possibly more. Security got on to her in the end by selective coding, and that, as you know, is a very slow process.'

'And not one which a jury would understand or accept.'

'Oh, certainly not,' said Mr Calder. 'Certainly not. There could be no question here of judicial process. Maria is a season-ticket holder, not a commuter.'

By this Mr Calder meant that Maria Lipper was an agent who collected, piecemeal, all information which came her way, and passed it on at long intervals of months or even years. No messengers came to her. When she had sufficient to interest her masters, she would take it to a collecting point and leave it. Occasional sums of money would come to her through the post.

'It is a thousand pities,' added Mr Calder, 'that they did not get on to her a little sooner – before Operation Prometheus Unbound came off the drawing board.'

'Do you think she knows about *that*?'

'I'm afraid so,' said Mr Calder. 'I wasn't directly concerned. Buchanan was in charge. But it was her section that did the Prometheus typing, and when he found out that she had asked for an urgent contact, I think – I really think – he was justified in getting worried.'

'What is he going to do about it?'

'The contact has been short-circuited. I am taking his place. Two days from now Mrs Lipper is driving down to Portsmouth for a short holiday. She plans to leave Woking very early – she likes clear roads to drive on – and she will be crossing Salisbury Plain at six o'clock. Outside Upavon she turns off the main road. The meeting place is a barn at the top of the track. She has stipulated for a payment of £500 pounds in notes. Incidentally, she has never, before, been paid more than fifty.'

'You must be right,' said Mr Behrens. 'I imagine that I am to cover you here. Fortunately, my aunt is taking the waters at Harrogate.'

'If you would.'

'The same arrangements as usual.'

'The key will be on the ledge over the woodshed door.'

'You'd better warn Rasselas to expect me. Last time he got it into his head that I was a burglar.'

The great hound looked up at the mention of his name and grinned, showing his long white incisors.

'You needn't worry about Rasselas,' said Mr Calder. 'I'll take him with me. He enjoys an expedition. All the same, it *is* a sad commentary on the younger generation that a man of my age has to be sent out on a trip like this.'

'Exactly what I was saying. Where did you put the backgammon board?'

Mr Calder left his cottage at dusk on the following evening. He drove off in the direction of Gravesend, crossed the river by the ferry, and made a circle round London, recrossing the Thames at Reading. He drove his inconspicuous car easily and efficiently. Rasselas lay across the back seat, between a sleeping-bag and a portmanteau. He was used to road travel and slept most of the way.

At midnight the car rolled down the broad High Street of Marlborough and out on to the Pewsey Road. A soft, golden moon made a mockery of its headlights.

A mile from Upavon, Mr Calder pulled up at the side of the road and studied the 1/25,000 range map with which he had been supplied. The track leading to the barn was clearly shown. But he had marked a different, and roundabout way by which the rendezvous could be approached. This involved taking the next road to the right, following it for a quarter of a mile, then finding a field track – it was no more than a dotted line even on his large-scale map – which would take him up a small re-entrant. The track appeared to stop just short of the circular contour which marked the top of the down. Across it, as Mr Calder had seen when he examined the map, ran, in straggling gothic lettering, the words Slay Down.

The entrance to the track had been shut off by a gate and was indistinguishable from the entrance to a field. The gate was padlocked, too, but Mr Calder dealt with this by lifting it off its hinges. It was a heavy gate but he shifted it with little apparent effort. There were surprising reserves of strength in his barrel-shaped body, thick arms and plump hands.

After a month of fine weather the track, though rutted, was rock hard. Mr Calder ran up it until the banks on either side had levelled out and he guessed that he was approaching the top of the rise. There he backed his car into a thicket. For the last part of the journey he had been travelling without lights.

Now he switched off the engine, opened the car door and sat listening.

At first the silence seemed complete. Then, as the singing of the engine died in his ears, the sounds of the night reasserted themselves. A nightjar screamed; an owl hooted. The creatures of the dark, momentarily frozen by the arrival among them of this great palpitating steel-and-glass animal, started to move again. A mile away across the valley, where farms stood and people lived, a dog barked.

Mr Calder took his sleeping-bag out of the back of the car and unrolled it. He took off his coat and shoes, loosened his tie, and wriggled down into the bag. Rasselas lay down too, his nose a few inches from Mr Calder's head.

In five minutes the man was asleep. When he woke he knew what had roused him. Rasselas had growled, very softly, a little rumbling, grumbling noise which meant that something had disturbed him. It was not the growl of imminent danger. It was a tentative alert.

Mr Calder raised his head. During the time he had been asleep the wind had risen a little, and was blowing up dark clouds and sending them scudding across the face of the moon; the shadows on the bare down were horsemen, warriors with horned helmets riding horses with flying manes and tails. Rasselas was following them with his eyes, head cocked. It was as if, behind the piping of the wind, he could hear, pitched too high for human ears, the shrill note of a trumpet.

'They're ghosts,' said Mr Calder calmly. 'They won't hurt us.' He lay down and was soon asleep again.

It was five o'clock and light was coming back into the sky when he woke. It took him five minutes to dress himself and roll up his sleeping-bag. His movements seemed unhurried but he lost no time.

From the back of the car he took a Greener .25-calibre rifle and clipped on a telescopic sight which he took from a leather case. A handful of nickel-capped ammunition went into his jacket pocket. Tucking the rifle under his arm, he walked cautiously towards the brow of the hill. From the brow, a long, thin line of trees, based in scrub, led down to the barn whose red-brown roof could now just be seen over the convex slope of the hill.

Mr Calder thought that the arrangement was excellent. 'Made to measure,' was the expression he used. The scrub was thickest round the end tree of the windbreak, and here he propped up the rifle and then walked the remaining distance to the wall of the barn. He noted that the distance was thirty-three yards.

In front of the barn the path, coming up from the main road, opened out into a flat space, originally a cattle yard but now missing one wall.

She'll drive in here, thought Mr Calder. And she'll turn the car, ready to get away. They always do that. After a bit, she'll get out of the car and she'll stand, watching for me to come up the road.

When he got level with the barn he saw something that was not marked on the map. It was another track, which came across the down, and had been made quite recently by Army vehicles from the Gunnery School. A litter of ammunition boxes, empty cigarette cartons and a rusty brew can suggested that the Army had taken over the barn as a staging point for their manoeuvres. It was an additional fact. Something to be noted. Mr Calder didn't think that it affected his plans. A civilian car, coming from the road, would be most unlikely to take this track, a rough affair seamed with the marks of Bren carriers and light tanks.

Mr Calder returned to the end of the trees and spent some minutes piling a few large stones and a log into a small breast-work. He picked up the rifle and set the sights carefully to thirty-five yards. Then he sat down, with his back to the tree, and lit a cigarette. Rasselas lay down beside him.

Mrs Lipper arrived at ten to six.

She drove up the track from the road and Mr Calder was interested to see that she behaved almost exactly as he had predicted. She drove her car into the yard, switched off the engine and sat for a few minutes. Then she opened the car door and got out.

Mr Calder snuggled down behind the barrier, moved his rifle forward a little and centred the sight on Mrs Lipper's left breast.

It was at this moment that he heard the truck coming. It was, he thought, a 15 hundredweight truck and it was coming quite slowly along the rough track towards the barn.

Mr Calder laid down the rifle and rose to his knees. The truck engine had stopped. From his position of vantage he could see, although Mrs Lipper could not, a figure in battledress getting out of the truck. It was, he thought, an officer. He was carrying a light rifle and it was clear that he was after rabbits. Indeed, as Mr Calder watched, the young man raised his rifle, then lowered it again.

Mr Calder was interested, even in the middle of his extreme irritation, to see that the officer had aimed at a thicket almost directly in line with the barn.

Three minutes passed in silence. Mrs Lipper looked twice at her watch. Mr Calder lay down again in a firing position. He had decided to wait. It was a close decision, but he was used to making close decisions, and he felt certain that this one was right.

The hidden rifle spoke; Mr Calder squeezed the trigger of his own. So rapid was his reaction that it sounded like a shot and an echo. In front of his eyes Mrs Lipper folded on to the ground. She did not fall. It was quite a different movement. It was as though a puppet-master, who had previously held the strings taut, had let them drop and a puppet had tumbled to the ground, arms, legs and head disjointed.

A moment later the hidden rifle spoke again. Mr Calder smiled to himself. The timing, he thought, had been perfect. He was quietly packing away the telescopic sight, dismantling the small redoubt he had created and obliterating all signs of his presence. Five minutes later he was back in his car. He had left it facing outwards and downhill, and all he had to do was take off the handbrake and start rolling down the track. This was the trickiest moment in the whole operation. It took three minutes to lift the gate, drive the car through and replace the gate. During the whole of that time no one appeared on the road in either direction.

'And that,' said Mr Calder, some three days later to Mr Fortescue, 'was that.' Mr Fortescue was a square, sagacious-looking man, and was manager of the Westminster branch of the London and Home Counties Bank. No one seeing Mr Fortescue would have mistaken him for anything but a bank manager although, in fact, he had certain other, quite important, functions.

'I was sorry, in a way, to saddle the boy with it, but I hadn't any choice.'

'He took your shot as the echo of his?'

'Apparently. Anyway, he went on shooting.'

'You contemplated that he would find the body – either then, or later.'

'Certainly.'

'And would assume that he had been responsible – accidentally, of course.'

'I think that he should receive a good deal of sympathy. He had a perfect right to shoot rabbits. The rough shooting belongs to the School of Artillery. The woman was trespassing on War Department Property. Indeed, the police will be in some difficulty in concluding why she was there at all.'

'I expect they would have been,' said Mr Fortescue, 'if her body had been discovered.'

Mr Calder looked at him.

'You mean,' he said at last, 'that no one has been near the barn in the last four days?'

'On the contrary. One of the Troops of the Seventeenth Field Regiment, to which your intrusive Subaltern belongs, visited the barn two days later. It was their gun position. The barn itself was the troop command post.'

'Either,' said Mr Calder, 'they were very unobservant soldiers, or one is driven to the conclusion that the body had been moved.'

'I was able,' said Mr Fortescue, 'through my influence with the

Army, to attend the firing as an additional umpire, in uniform. I had plenty of time on my hands and was able to make a thorough search of the area.'

'I see,' said Mr Calder. 'Yes. It opens up an interesting field of speculation, doesn't it?'

'Very interesting,' said Mr Fortescue. 'In – er – one or two different directions.'

'Have you discovered the name of the officer who was out shooting?'

'He is a National Service boy. A Lieutenant Blaikie. He is in temporary command of C Troop of A Battery – it would normally be a Captain, but they are short of officers. His Colonel thinks very highly of him. He says that he is a boy of great initiative.'

'There I agree with you,' said Mr Calder. 'I wonder if the Army could find *me* a suit of battledress.'

'I see you as a Major,' said Mr Fortescue. 'With a 1918 Victory Medal and a 1939 Defence Medal.'

'The Africa Star,' said Mr Calder, firmly . . .

Approximately a week later Mr Calder, wearing a service dress hat half a size too large for him and a battledress blouse which met with some difficulty round the waist, was walking up the path which led to the barn. It was ten o'clock, dusk had just fallen, and around the farm there was a scene of considerable activity as C Troop, A Battery, of the Seventeenth Field Regiment settled down for the night.

Four guns were in position, two in front of, and two behind, the barn. The gun teams were digging slit trenches. Two storm lanterns hung in the barn. A sentry on the path saluted Mr Calder who inquired where he would find the Troop Commander.

'He's got his bivvy up there, sir,' said the sentry.

Peering through the dusk Mr Calder saw a truck parked on a flat space, beyond the barn and enclosed by scattered bushes. Attached to the back of the truck, and forming an extension of it, was a sheet of canvas, pegged down in the form of a tent. He circled the site cautiously.

It seemed to him to be just the right distance from the barn and to have the right amount of cover. It was the place he would have chosen himself.

He edged up to the opening of the tent and peered inside. A young Subaltern was seated on his bedroll, examining a map. His webbing equipment was hanging on a hook on the back of the truck.

Mr Calder stooped and entered. The young man frowned, drawing his thick eyebrows together; then recognized Mr Calder, and smiled.

'You're one of our umpires, aren't you, sir,' he said. 'Come in.'

'Thank you,' said Mr Calder. 'Can I squat on the bedroll?'

'I expect you've been round the gun position, sir. I was a bit uncertain about the AA defences myself. I've put the sentry on top of Slay Down. He's a bit out of touch.'

'I must confess,' said Mr Calder, 'that I haven't examined your dispositions. It was something – rather more personal I wanted a little chat about.'

'Yes, sir?'

'When you buried her—' Mr Calder scraped the turf with his heel – 'how deep did you put her?'

There was silence in the tiny tent, lit by a single bulb from the dashboard of the truck. The two men might have been on a raft, alone, in the middle of the ocean.

The thing which occurred next did not surprise Mr Calder. Lieutenant Blaikie's right hand made a very slight movement outwards, checked, and fell to his side again.

'Four foot, into the chalk,' he said.

'How long did it take you?'

'Two hours.'

'Quick work,' said Mr Calder. 'It must have been a shock to you when a night exercise was ordered exactly on this spot, with special emphasis on the digging of slit trenches and gun-pits.'

'It would have worried me more if I hadn't been in command of the exercise,' said Lieutenant Blaikie. 'I reckoned if I pitched my own tent exactly here, no one would dig a trench or a gun-pit inside it. By the way – who are you?'

Mr Calder was particularly pleased to notice that Lieutenant Blaikie's voice was under firm control.

He told him who he was and made a proposal to him.

'He was due out of the Army in a couple of months' time,' said Mr Calder to Mr Behrens, when the latter came up for a game of backgammon. 'Fortescue saw him and thought him very promising. I was very pleased with his behaviour in the tent that night. When I sprung it on him, his first reaction was to reach for the revolver in his webbing holster. It was hanging on the back of his truck. He realized that he wouldn't be able to get it out in time and decided to come clean. I think that showed decision and balance, don't you?'

'Decision and balance are *most* important,' agreed Mr Behrens. 'Your throw.'

On Slay Down, Michael Gilbert

From introductions to the signing off of the genuine article...

The 'Real' James Bond

Commander W.A, 'Biffy' Dunderdale, who has died in New York aged ninety, was a member of the Secret Service for thirty-eight years and was sometimes spoken of as the prototype of James Bond.

But where Ian Fleming's creation was extrovert and flamboyant, in love with the latest technology, Dunderdale – though one of the ablest agents of his time – really belonged in the Boys' Own Paper era of false beards and invisible ink, and was the most reticent of men.

To the end of his long life visitors to his New York apartment could get almost nothing from 'Biffy' about his past service.

The son of a Constantinople shipowner, Wilfred Albert Dunderdale was born on Christmas Eve 1899 and educated at the Gymnasium in Nicolaieff on the Black Sea. He was studying to be a naval architect in St Petersburg when the Russian Revolution broke out in 1917.

His father sent him to Vladivostok to take delivery of the first of a new class of Holland-designed submarines, built in America, and deliver it to the Black Sea.

To transport a submarine, still in five separate sections, thousands of miles by rail across a country in the throes of a revolution was asking a good deal of a seventeen-year-old boy – but young Biffy accomplished it.

The submarine was completed too late to serve in the Imperial Navy and was eventually scuttled at Sebastopol in April 1919. By then the political situation in the region was of literally Byzantine complexity.

In 1920 British warships operated in the Black Sea and the Sea of Marmora, bombarding shore installations and sending shore parties of sailors and marines.

With his knowledge of naval engineering – and of Constantinople and the Black Sea ports – his business-like pretext and his fluent Russian, German and French, Biffy Dunderdale made a superb undercover agent for the Navy.

Still only nineteen, with the honorary rank of sub-lieutenant RNVR and operating under the *nom de guerre* of 'Julius' he was twice mentioned in dispatches. In 1920 he was promoted honorary lieutenant RNVR and appointed MBE.

Dunderdale joined the Secret Service in 1921 and was at once involved in foiling one of the frequent Turkish plans to infiltrate troops into Constantinople and seize the city from the Allies. This attempt was finally frustrated by 'battleship diplomacy' when *HMS Bembow* and attendant destroyers appeared off the city waterfront.

In the autumn of 1922 British and Turkish troops confronted each other at Chanak in the Dardanelles. Fighting was only prevented by the good sense and moral courage of the Army C-in-C, Gen. Harington.

The end of the crisis brought the exile of Sultan Mohammed VI, who was taken to Malta in the battleship *Malaya*, and the downfall of Lloyd George as Prime Minister.

Dunderdale's part in these events was domestic rather than epic. He was responsible for arranging and paying for the repatriation of ex-members of the Sultan's harem who were not Turkish nationals – including one *houri* from Leamington Spa, packed off home on the Orient Express.

In 1926 he joined the SIS station in Paris where he worked with the Deuxième Bureau and established good relations with the French – particularly with Col. Gustav Bertrand, head of the French Intelligence Service. He was liaison officer in Paris with the Tsarist Supreme Monarchist Council.

Dunderdale was also on good terms with the Poles, which led to a major intelligence coup. The Poles were pioneers in breaking the Enigma machine cyphers which all three German armed forces were using, so it was imperative that British Intelligence obtain an example.

Dunderdale was 'the Third Man' at the celebrated meeting under the clock at Victoria Station on 16 August 1939 – which might have come straight out of a spy thriller – when C himself (head of the British Secret Service) met Bertrand, a member of the Paris embassy staff and Dunderdale, who had an Enigma machine in his valise.

C was on his way to a dinner and cut a conspicuous figure as he strode away, in evening dress, with the ribbon of the Legion d'Honneur in his buttonhole and the Enigma under his arm.

The day before was was declared Dunderdale was given the rank of commander RNVR. He was one of the last Englishmen to leave Paris when the Germans entered the city in June 1940.

When he reached Bordeaux an RAF Avro Anson was sent to make sure he escaped. During the war he kept his links with the

Poles and was in contact by radio with Bertrand in Vichy France, and with other members of the Deuxième Bureau who had stayed behind.

Dunderdale also had to deal with the notorious prickliness and slack security of the Gaullist Free French in London, and to fight off the attempts of Sir Claude Dansey, C's deputy, to dominate both the Free French Intelligence and the Bureau.

His success was shown by the number of different countries who honoured him. He was appointed CMG in 1942.

The Poles awarded him the Polonia Restituta in 1943 for services to the Polish Navy; he was made an officer of the American Legion of Merit in 1946 for 'Special Services'; he also held the Russian Order of St Anne and the Croix de Guerre, and was an officer of the Legion d'Honneur.

Dunderdale served with the SIS in London after the war until he retired in 1959, but his influence had declined. Perhaps he knew too many secrets and realized that his life in espionage had been an elaborate game; but he was an excellent host at his apartments in Paris and New York and his house in Surrey.

He was thrice married: first to June Morse, grand-daughter of Samuel B. Morse, inventor of the Morse Code; secondly, to Dorothy Hyde who died in 1978; and, thirdly, to Debbie Jackson of Boston, Massachusetts.

Obituary of Commander W. A. 'Biffy' Dunderdale
(*Daily Telegraph*)

HICCUPS AND DISADVANTAGES OF THE TRADE

When I first read Casino Royale *in 1955, Fleming was unknown to me, nor did I know the rules of baccarat, yet I was kept awake until four in the morning by what I consider to be one of the most riveting* tours de force *in modern fiction: James Bond at the gaming-table pitted against the French communist gangster, Le Chiffre, who is trying to win back at cards the money he has embezzled from Party funds, then lost in a reckless business venture.*

Later, Fleming was to describe his books as 'adult fairy tales'. But the Russians were not fooled. 'Shmersh' – 'Death to Spies' – was certainly no fairy tale, having been set up by Beria with the express purpose of tracking down and murdering Trotsky in Mexico in 1940. Other victims followed. Pravda *even went so far as to describe Fleming as 'a slanderer of the Soviet Union – a tool of the Cold War'.*

The Moment of Truth

Le Chiffre looked incuriously at him, the whites of his eyes, which showed all round the irises, lending something impassive and doll-like to his gaze.

He slowly removed one thick hand from the table and slipped it into the pocket of his dinner-jacket. The hand came out holding a small metal cylinder with a cap which Le Chiffre unscrewed. He inserted the nozzle of the cylinder, with an obscene deliberation, twice into each black nostril in turn, and luxuriously inhaled the benzedrine vapour.

Unhurriedly he pocketed the inhaler, then his hand came quickly back above the level of the table and gave the shoe its usual hard, sharp slap.

During this offensive pantomime Bond had coldly held the banker's gaze, taking in the wide expanse of white face surmounted by the short, abrupt cliff of reddish-brown hair, the unsmiling wet red mouth and the impressive width of the shoulders, loosely draped in a massively cut dinner-jacket.

But for the highlights on the satin of the shawl-cut lapels, he might have been faced by the thick bust of a black-fleeced Minotaur rising out of a green grass field.

Bond slipped a packet of notes on to the table without counting them. If he lost, the croupier would extract what was necessary to cover the bet, but the easy gesture conveyed that Bond didn't expect to lose and that this was only a token display from the deep funds at Bond's disposal.

The other players sensed a tension between the two gamblers and there was silence as Le Chiffre fingered the four cards out of the shoe.

The croupier slipped Bond's two cards across to him with the tip of his spatula. Bond, still with his eyes holding Le Chiffre's, reached his right hand out a few inches, glanced down very swiftly then, as he looked up again impassively at Le Chiffre, with a disdainful gesture he tossed the cards face upwards on the table.

They were a four and a five – an unbeatable nine.

There was a little gasp of envy from the table and the players to the left of Bond exchanged rueful glances at their failure to accept the two-million-franc bet.

With a hint of a shrug, Le Chiffre slowly faced his own two cards and flicked them away with his fingernail. They were two valueless knaves.

'*Le baccarat*,' intoned the croupier as he spaded the thick chips over the table to Bond.

Bond slipped them into his right-hand pocket with the unused packet of notes. His face showed no emotion but he was pleased with the success of his first coup and with the outcome of the silent clash of wills across the table.

The woman on his left, the American Mrs Du Pont, turned to him with a wry smile.

'I shouldn't have let it come to you,' she said. 'Directly the cards were dealt I kicked myself.'

'It's only the beginning of the game,' said Bond. 'You may be right the next time you pass it.'

Mr Du Pont leant forward from the other side of his wife: 'If one could be right every hand, none of us would be here,' he said philosophically.

'I would be,' his wife laughed. 'You don't think I do this for pleasure.'

As the game went on, Bond looked over the spectators leaning on the high brass rail round the table. He soon saw Le Chiffre's two gunmen. They stood behind and to either side of the banker. They looked respectable enough, but not sufficiently a part of the game to be unobtrusive.

The one more or less behind Le Chiffre's right arm was tall and funereal in his dinner-jacket. His face was wooden and grey, but his eyes flickered and gleamed like a conjurer's. His whole long body was restless and his hands shifted often on the brass rail. Bond guessed that he would kill without interest or concern for what he killed and that he would prefer strangling. He had something of Lennie in *Of Mice and Men*, but his inhumanity would not come from infantilism but from drugs. Marihuana, decided Bond.

The other man looked like a Corsican shopkeeper. He was short and very dark with a flat head covered with thickly greased hair. He seemed to be a cripple. A chunky malacca cane with a rubber tip hung on the rail beside him. He must have had permission to bring the cane into the Casino with him, reflected Bond, who knew that neither sticks nor any other objects were allowed in the rooms as a precaution against acts of violence. He looked sleek and well fed. His mouth hung vacantly half-open and revealed very bad teeth. He wore a heavy black moustache and the backs of his hands on the rail were matted with black hair. Bond guessed that hair covered most of his squat body. Naked, Bond supposed, he would be an obscene object.

The game continued uneventfully, but with a slight bias against the bank.

The third coup is the 'sound barrier' at chemin-de-fer and baccarat. Your luck can defeat the first and second tests, but when the third deal comes along it most often spells disaster. Again and again at this point you find yourself being bounced back to earth. It was like that now. Neither the bank nor any of the players seemed to be able to get hot. But there was a steady and inexorable seepage against the bank, amounting after about two hours' play to ten million francs. Bond had no idea what profits Le Chiffre had made over the past two days. He estimated them at five million and guessed that now the banker's capital could not be more than twenty million.

In fact, Le Chiffre had lost heavily all that afternoon. At this moment he only had ten million left.

Bond, on the other hand, by one o'clock in the morning, had won four million, bringing his resources up to twenty-eight million.

Bond was cautiously pleased. Le Chiffre showed no trace of emotion. He continued to play like an automaton, never speaking except when he gave instructions in a low aside to the croupier at the opening of each new bank.

Outside the pool of silence round the high table, there was the constant hum of the other tables, chemin-de-fer, roulette and trente-et-quarante, interspersed with the clear calls of the croupiers and occasional bursts of laughter or gasps of excitement from different corners of the huge *salle*.

In the background there thudded always the hidden metronome of the Casino, ticking up its little treasure of one-per-cents with each spin of a wheel and each turn of a card – a pulsing fat-cat with a zero for a heart.

It was at ten minutes past one by Bond's watch when, at the high table, the whole pattern of play suddenly altered.

The Greek at Number 1 was still having a bad time. He had lost the first coup of half a million francs and the second. He passed the third time, leaving a bank of two millions. Carmel Delane at Number 2 refused it. So did Lady Danvers at Number 3.

The Du Ponts looked at each other.

'*Banco,*' said Mrs Du Pont, and promptly lost to the banker's natural eight.

'*Un banco de quatre millions,*' said the croupier.

'*Banco,*' said Bond, pushing out a wad of notes.

Again he fixed Le Chiffre with his eye. Again he gave only a cursory look at his two cards.

'No,' he said. He held a marginal five. The position was dangerous.

Le Chiffre turned up a knave and a four. He gave the shoe another slap. He drew a three.

'*Sept à la banque,*' said the croupier, '*et cinq,*' he added as he tipped Bond's losing cards face upwards. He raked over Bond's money, extracted four million francs and returned the remainder to Bond.

'*Un banco de huit millions.*'

'*Suivi,*' said Bond.

And lost again, to a natural nine.

In two coups he had lost twelve million francs. By scraping the barrel he had just sixteen million francs left, exactly the amount of the next banco.

Suddenly Bond felt the sweat on his palms. Like snow in sunshine his capital had melted. With the covetous deliberation of the winning gambler, Le Chiffre was tapping a light tattoo on the table with his right hand. Bond looked across into the eyes of murky basalt. They held an ironical question. 'Do you want the full treatment?' they seemed to ask.

'*Suivi,*' Bond said softly.

He took some notes and plaques out of his right-hand pocket and the entire stack of notes out of his left and pushed them forward. There was no hint in his movements that this would be his last stake.

His mouth felt suddenly as dry as flock wallpaper. He looked up and saw Vesper and Felix Leiter standing where the gunman with the stick had stood. He did not know how long they had been standing there. Leiter looked faintly worried, but Vesper smiled encouragement at him.

He heard a faint rattle on the rail behind him and turned his head. The battery of bad teeth under the black moustache gaped vacantly back at him.

'*Le jeu est fait*,' said the croupier and the two cards came slithering towards him over the green baize – a green baize which was no longer smooth, but thick now, and furry and almost choking, its colour as livid as the grass on a fresh tomb.

The light from the broad satin-lined shades which had seemed so welcoming now seemed to take the colour out of his hand as he glanced at the cards. Then he looked again.

It was nearly as bad as it could have been – the king of hearts and an ace, the ace of spades. It squinted up at him like a black widow spider.

'A card.' He still kept all emotion out of his voice.

Le Chiffre faced his own two cards. He had a queen and a black five. He looked at Bond and pressed out another card with a wide forefinger. The table was absolutely silent. He faced it and flicked it away. The croupier lifted it delicately with his spatula and slipped it over to Bond. It was a good card, the five of hearts, but to Bond it was a difficult fingerprint in dried blood. He now had a count of six and Le Chiffre a count of five, but the banker having a five and giving a five, would and must draw another card and try and improve with a one, two, three or four. Drawing any other card he would be defeated.

The odds were on Bond's side, but now it was Le Chiffre who looked across into Bond's eyes and hardly glanced at the card as he flicked it, face upwards, on the table.

It was, unnecessarily, the best, a four, giving the bank a count of nine. He had won, almost slowing up.

Bond was beaten and cleaned out.

from *Casino Royale*, Ian Fleming

The other two extracts I have included here describe the spy as con-man. Malcolm Muggeridge, in his autobiography, suggested that Greene's Our Man in Havana *was based on a true incident involving a White Russian who was in Havana during the war and employed by the British to spy on U-boat movements in the Caribbean. He earned a handsome living by supplying his Whitehall masters with the serial numbers of whole fleets of U-boats which did not exist.*

Both Muggeridge and Greene were full-time Intelligence officers during the Second World War, working under the supervision of Kim Philby who was later to describe both men as 'the most useless agents I ever knew'.

A Bad Apple

When Ashenden, given charge of a number of spies working from Switzerland, was first sent there, R, wishing him to see the sort of report that he would be required to obtain, handed him the communications, a sheaf of typewritten documents, of a man known in the Secret Service as Gustav.

'He's the best fellow we've got,' said R. 'His information is always very full and circumstantial. I want you to give his reports your very best attention. Of course, Gustav is a clever little chap, but there's no reason why we shouldn't get just as good reports from the other agents. It's merely a question of explaining exactly what we want.'

Gustav, who lived at Basle, represented a Swiss firm with branches at Frankfurt, Mannheim and Cologne, and by virtue of his business was able to go in and out of Germany without risk. He travelled up and down the Rhine, and gathered material about the movement of troops, the manufacture of munitions, the state of mind of the country (a point on which R laid stress), and other matters upon which the Allies desired information. His frequent letters to his wife hid an ingenious code and the moment she received them in Basle she sent them to Ashenden in Geneva, who extracted from them the important facts and communicated these in the proper quarter. Every two months Gustav came home and prepared one of the reports that served as models to the other spies in this particular section of the Secret Service.

His employers were pleased with Gustav and Gustav had reason to be pleased with his employers. His services were so useful that he was not only paid more highly than the others, but for particular scoops had received from time to time a handsome bonus.

This went on for more than a year. Then something aroused R's quick suspicions; he was a man of an amazing alertness, not so much of mind as of instinct, and he had suddenly a feeling that some hanky-panky was going on. He said nothing definite to Ashenden (whatever R surmised he was disposed to keep to himself), but told him to go to Basle, Gustav being then in Germany, and have a talk with Gustav's wife. He left it to Ashenden to decide the tenor of the conversation.

Having arrived at Basle, and leaving his bag at the station, for he did not yet know whether he would have to stay or not, he took a tram to the corner of the street in which Gustav lived and, with a quick look to see that he was not followed, walked along to the house he sought. It was a block of flats that gave you the impression of decent poverty and Ashenden conjectured that they were inhabited by clerks and small tradespeople. Just inside the door was a cobbler's shop and Ashenden stopped.

'Does Herr Grabow live here?' he asked in his none too fluent German.

'Yes, I saw him go up a few minutes ago. You'll find him in.'

Ashenden was startled, for he had but the day before received through Gustav's wife a letter addressed from Mannheim in which Gustav, by means of his code, gave the numbers of certain regiments that had just crossed the Rhine. Ashenden thought it unwise to ask the cobbler the question that rose to his lips, so thanked him and went up to the third floor on which he knew already that Gustav lived. He rang the bell and heard it tinkle within. In a moment the door was opened by a dapper little man with a close-shaven round head and spectacles. He wore carpet slippers.

'Herr Grabow?' asked Ashenden.

'At your service,' said Gustav.

'May I come in?'

Gustav was standing with his back to the light and Ashenden could not see the look on his face. He felt a momentary hesitation and gave the name under which he received Gustav's letters from Germany.

'Come in, come in. I am very glad to see you.'

Gustav led the way into the stuffy little room, heavy with carved oak furniture, and on the large table covered with a tablecloth of green velveteen was a typewriter. Gustav was apparently engaged in composing one of his invaluable reports. A woman was sitting at the open window darning socks but, at a word from Gustav, rose, gathered up her things and left. Ashenden had disturbed a pretty picture of connubial bliss.

'Sit down, please. How very fortunate that I was in Basle! I have long wanted to make your acquaintance. I have only just this minute returned from Germany.' He pointed to the sheets of paper by the typewriter. 'I think you will be pleased with the news I bring. I have some very valuable information.' He chuckled. 'One is never sorry to earn a bonus.'

He was very cordial but, to Ashenden, his cordiality rang false. Gustav kept his eyes, smiling behind the glasses, fixed watchfully on Ashenden and it was possible that they held a trace of nervousness.

'You must have travelled quickly to get here only a few hours after your letter, sent here and then sent on by your wife, reached me in Geneva.'

'That is very probable. One of the things I had to tell you is that the Germans suspect that information is getting through by means of commercial letters and so they have decided to hold up all mail at the frontier for eight-and-forty hours.'

'I see,' said Ashenden amiably. 'And was it on that account that you took the precaution of dating your letter forty-eight hours after you sent it?'

'Did I do that? That was very stupid of me. I must have mistaken the day of the month.'

Ashenden looked at Gustav with a smile that was very thin. Gustav, a businessman, knew too well how important in his particular job was the exactness of a date. The circuitous routes by which it was necessary to get information from Germany made it difficult to transmit news quickly and it was essential to know precisely on what days certain events had taken place.

'Let me look at your passport a minute,' said Ashenden.

'What do you want with my passport?'

'I want to see when you went into Germany and when you came out.'

'But you do not imagine that my comings and goings are marked on my passport? I have methods of crossing the frontiers.'

Ashenden knew a good deal of this matter. He knew that both the Germans and the Swiss guarded the frontier with severity.

'Oh? Why should you not cross in the ordinary way? You were engaged because your connection with a Swiss from supplying necessary goods to Germany made it easy for you to travel backwards and forwards without suspicion. I can understand that you might get past the German sentries with the connivance of the Germans, but what about the Swiss?'

Gustav assumed a look of indignation.

'I do not understand you. Do you mean to suggest that I am in the service of the Germans? I give you my word of honour . . . I will not allow my integrity to be impugned.'

'You would not be the only one to take money from both sides and provide information of value to neither.'

'Do you pretend that my information is of no value? Why then have you given me more bonuses than any other agent has received? The Colonel has repeatedly expressed the highest satisfaction with my services.'

It was Ashenden's turn now to be cordial.

'Come, come, my dear fellow, do not try to ride the high horse.

You do not wish to show me your passport and I will not insist. You are not under the impression that we leave the statements of our agents without corroboration or that we are so foolish as not to keep track of their movements? Even the best of jokes cannot bear an indefinite repetition. I am, in peacetime, a humorist by profession and I tell you that from bitter experience.' Now Ashenden thought the moment had arrived to attempt his bluff; he knew something of the excellent but difficult game of poker. 'We have information that you have not been to Germany now, nor since you were engaged by us, but have sat here quietly in Basle, and all your reports are merely due to your fertile imagination.'

Gustav looked at Ashenden and saw a face expressive of nothing but tolerance and good humour. A smile slowly broke on his lips and he gave his shoulder a little shrug.

'Did you think I was such a fool as to risk my life for £50 a month? I love my wife.'

Ashenden laughed outright.

'I congratulate you. It is not everyone who can flatter himself that he has made a fool of our Secret Service for a year.'

'I had the chance of earning money without any difficulty. My firm stopped sending me into Germany at the beginning of the war, but I learned what I could from the other travellers. I kept my ears open in restaurants and beer cellars, and I read the German papers. I got a lot of amusement out of sending you reports and letters.'

'I don't wonder,' said Ashenden.

'What are you going to do?'

'Nothing. What can we do? You are not under the impression that we shall continue to pay you a salary?'

'No, I cannot expect that.'

'By the way, if it is not indiscreet, may I ask if you have been playing the same game with the Germans?'

'Oh, no,' Gustav cried vehemently. 'How can you think it? My sympathies are absolutely pro-Ally. My heart is entirely with you.'

'Well, why not?' asked Ashenden. 'The Germans have all the money in the world and there is no reason why you should not get some of it. We could give you information from time to time that the Germans would be prepared to pay for.'

Gustav drummed his fingers on the table. He took up a sheet of the now useless report.

'The Germans are dangerous people to meddle with.'

'You are a very intelligent man. And after all, even if your salary is stopped, you can always earn a bonus by bringing us news that can be useful to us. But it will have to be substantiated; in future, we pay only by results.'

'I will think of it.'

For a moment or two Ashenden left Gustav to his reflections. He lit a cigarette and watched the smoke he had inhaled fade into the air.

Gustav paused a moment. 'How long are you staying here?'

'As long as necessary. I will take a room at the hotel and let you know the number. If you have anything to say to me you can be sure of finding me in my room at nine every morning and at seven every night.'

'I should not risk coming to the hotel. But I can write.'

'Very well.'

Ashenden rose to go and Gustav accompanied him to the door.

'We part without ill-feeling then?' he asked.

'Of course. Your reports will remain in our archives as models of what a report should be.'

from *The Traitor*, W. Somerset Maugham

And from a bad apple to a decaying flower . . .

A Tricky Encounter

'Had a good flight?' the Chief asked.

'A bit bumpy over the Azores,' Hawthorne said. On this occasion he had not had time to change from his pale grey tropical suit; the summons had come to him urgently in Kingston and a car had met him at London Airport. He sat as close to the steam radiator as he could, but sometimes he couldn't help a shiver.

'What's that odd flower you're wearing?'

Hawthorne had quite forgotten it. He put his hand up to his lapel.

'It looks as though it had once been an orchid,' the Chief said with disapproval.

'Pan American gave it us with our dinner last night,' Hawthorne explained. He took out the limp mauve rag and put it in the ashtray.

'With your dinner? What an odd thing to do,' the Chief said. 'It can hardly have improved the meal. Personally I detest orchids. Decadent things. There was someone, wasn't there, who wore green ones?'

'I only put it in my button-hole so as to clear the dinner-tray. There was so little room, what with the hot cakes and champagne and the sweet salad and the tomato soup and the chicken Maryland and ice-cream . . .'

'What a terrible mixture. You should travel BOAC.'

'You didn't give me enough time, sir, to get a booking.'

'Well, the matter is rather urgent. You know our man in Havana has been turning out some pretty disquieting stuff lately.'

'He's a good man,' Hawthorne said.

'I don't deny it. I wish we had more like him. What I can't understand is how the Americans have not tumbled to anything there.'

'Have you asked them, sir?'

'Of course not. I don't trust their discretion.'

'Perhaps they don't trust ours.'

The Chief said, 'Those drawings – did you examine them?'

'I'm not very knowledgeable that way, sir. I sent them straight on.'

'Well, take a good look at them now.'

The Chief spread the drawings over his desk. Hawthorne reluctantly left the radiator and was immediately shaken by a shiver.

'Anything the matter?'

'The temperature was ninety-two yesterday in Kingston.'

'Your blood's getting thin. A spell of cold will do you good. What do you think of them?'

Hawthorne stared at the drawings. They reminded him of – something. He was touched, he didn't know why, by an odd uneasiness.

'You remember the reports that came with them,' the Chief said. 'The source was stroke three. Who is he?'

'I think that would be Engineer Cifuentes, sir.'

'Well, even he was mystified. With all his technical knowledge. These machines were being transported by lorry from the army headquarters at Bayamo to the edge of the forest. Then mules took over. General direction of those unexplained concrete platforms.'

'What does the Air Ministry say, sir?'

'They are worried, very worried. Interested too, of course.'

'What about the atomic research people?'

'We haven't shown them the drawings yet. You know what those fellows are like. They'll criticize points of detail, say the whole thing is unreliable, that the tube is out of proportion or points the wrong way. You can't expect an agent working from memory to get every detail right. I want photographs, Hawthorne.'

'That's asking a lot, sir.'

'We have got to have them. At any risk. Do you know what Savage said to me? I can tell you, it gave me a very nasty nightmare. He said that one of the drawings reminded him of a giant vacuum cleaner.'

'A vacuum cleaner!' Hawthorne bent down and examined the drawings again, and the cold struck him once more.

'Makes you shiver, doesn't it?'

'But that's impossible, sir.' He felt as though he were pleading for his own career. 'It couldn't be a vacuum cleaner, sir. Not a vacuum cleaner.'

'Fiendish, isn't it?' the Chief said. 'The ingenuity, the simplicity, the devilish imagination of the thing.' He removed his black monocle and his baby-blue eye caught the light and made it jig on the wall over the radiator. 'See this one here six times the height of a man. Like a gigantic spray. And this – what does this remind you of?'

Hawthorne said unhappily, 'A two-way nozzle.'

'What's a two-way nozzle?'

'You sometimes find them with a vacuum cleaner.'

'Vacuum cleaner again. Hawthorne, I believe we may be on to something so big that the H-bomb will become a conventional weapon.'

'Is that desirable, sir?'

'Of course it's desirable. Nobody worries about conventional weapons.'

'What have you in mind, sir?'

'I'm no scientist,' the Chief said, 'but look at this great tank. It must stand nearly as high as the forest trees. A huge gaping mouth at the top, and this pipeline – the man's only indicated it. For all we know, it may extend for miles – from the mountains to the sea perhaps. You know the Russians are said to be working on some idea – something to do with the power of the sun, sea evaporation. I don't know what it's all about, but I do know this thing is Big. Tell our man we must have photographs.'

'I don't quite see how he can get near enough . . .'

'Let him charter a plane and lose his way over the area. Not himself personally, of course, but stroke three or stroke two. Who is stroke two?'

'Professor Sanchez, sir. But he'd be shot down. They have Air Force planes patrolling all that section.'

'They have, have they?'

'To spot for rebels.'

'So they say. Do you know, I've got a hunch, Hawthorne.'

'Yes, sir?'

'That the rebels don't exist. They're purely notional. It gives the Government all the excuse it needs to shut down a censorship over the area.'

'I hope you are right, sir.'

from *Our Man in Havana*, Graham Greene

MORE SERIOUS TRADECRAFT

Some years ago I met a Czech defector who had been a high-ranking officer for his country's secret police, the STB. I showed him the following extract from Tinker, Tailor, Soldier, Spy – which I have called here 'A Grand Slam'. My friend read the piece twice, with absorbed interest, then consulted the name of the author. I told him that le Carré was a pseudonym. 'Of course,' my friend murmured,'but he is certainly a professional . . .' Then my friend went on to explain how he had, himself, organized and directed an almost identical operation in Bratislava, in 1951, against a British 'businessman' who was subsequently arrested and jailed for espionage.

A Grand Slam

First, Jim let it leak that he had a tentative lead to a high-stepping Soviet cypher clerk in Stockholm, and booked himself to Copenhagen in his old workname, Ellis. Instead, he flew to Paris, switched to his Hajek papers and landed by scheduled flight at Prague airport at ten on Saturday morning. He went through the barriers like a song, confirmed the time of his train at the terminus, then took a walk because he had a couple of hours to kill and thought he might watch his back a little before he left for Brno. That autumn there had been freak bad weather. There was snow on the ground and more falling.

In Czecho, said Jim, surveillance was not usually a problem. The security services knew next to nothing about street watching, probably because no administration in living memory had ever had to feel shy about it. The tendency, said Jim, was still to throw cars and pavement artists around like Al Capone, and that was what Jim was looking for: black Skodas and trios of squat men in trilbies. In the cold, spotting these things is marginally harder because the traffic is slow, the people walk faster and everyone is muffled to the nose. All the same, till he reached Masaryk Station, or Central as they're pleased to call it these days, he had no worries. But at

Masaryk, said Jim, he got a whisper, more instinct than fact, about two women who'd bought tickets ahead of him.

Here, with the dispassionate ease of a professional, Jim went back over the ground. In a covered shopping arcade beside Wenceslas Square he had been overtaken by three women, of whom the one in the middle was pushing a pram. The woman nearest the kerb carried a red plastic handbag and the woman on the inside was walking a dog on a lead. Ten minutes later two other women came towards him, arm in arm, both in a hurry, and it crossed his mind that, if Toby Esterhase had had the running of the job, an arrangement like this would be his handwriting; quick profile changes from the pram, back-up cars standing off with shortwave radio or bleep, with a second team lying back in case the forward party overran. At Masaryk, looking at the two women ahead of him in the ticket queue, Jim was faced with the knowledge that it was happening now. There is one garment that a watcher has neither time nor inclination to change, least of all in sub-Arctic weather, and that is his shoes. Of the two pairs offered for his inspection in the ticket queue Jim recognized one: fur-lined plastic, black, with zips on the outside and soles of thick brown composition which slightly sang in the snow. He had seen them once already that morning, in the Sterba passage, worn with different top clothes by the woman who had pushed past him with the pram. From then on, Jim didn't suspect. He knew, just as Smiley would have known.

At the station bookstall Jim bought himself a *Rude Pravo* and boarded the Brno train. If they had wanted to arrest him they would by now have done so. They must be after the branch-lines: that is to say, they were following Jim in order to house his contacts. There was no point in looking for reasons, but Jim guessed that the Hajek identity was blown and they'd primed the trap the moment he booked himself on the plane. As long as they didn't know he had flushed them, he still had the edge, said Jim; and for a moment Smiley was back in occupied Germany, in his own time as a field agent, living with terror in his mouth, naked to every stranger's glance.

He was supposed to catch the 13.08 arriving Brno 16.27. It was cancelled so he took some wonderful stopping train, a special for the football match, which called at every other lamp-post, and each time Jim reckoned he could pick out the hoods. The quality was variable. At Chocen, a one-horse place if ever he saw one, he got out and bought himself a sausage and there were no fewer than five, all men, spread down the tiny platform with their hands in their pockets, pretending to chat to one another and making damn fools of themselves.

'If there's one thing that distinguishes a good watcher from a bad one,' said Jim, 'it's the gentle art of doing damn all convincingly.'

At Svitavy two men and a woman entered his carriage and talked about the big match. After a while Jim joined the conversation; he had been reading up the form in his newspaper. It was a club replay and everyone was going crazy about it. By Brno nothing more had happened so he got out and sauntered through shops and crowded areas where they had to stay close for fear of losing him.

He wanted to lull them, demonstrate to them that he suspected nothing. He knew now that he was the target of what Toby would call a grand-slam operation. On foot they were working teams of seven. The cars changed so often he couldn't count them. The overall direction came from a scruffy green van driven by a thug. The van had a loop aerial and a chalk star scrawled high on the back where no child could reach. The cars, where he picked them out, were declared to one another by a woman's handbag on the glove-board and a passenger sun visor turned down. He guessed there were other signs but those two were good enough for him. He knew from what Toby had told him that jobs like this could cost a hundred people and were unwieldy if the quarry bolted. Toby hated them for that reason.

There is one store in Brno main square that sells everything, said Jim. Shopping in Czecho is usually a bore because there are so few retail outlets for each state industry, but this place was new and quite impressive. He bought children's toys, a scarf, some cigarettes and tried on shoes. He guessed his watchers were still waiting for his clandestine contact. He stole a fur hat and a white plastic raincoat and a carrier bag to put them in. He loitered at the men's department long enough to confirm that two women who formed the forward pair were still behind him but reluctant to come too close. He guessed they had signalled for men to take over, and were waiting. In the men's lavatory he moved very fast. He pulled the white raincoat over his overcoat, stuffed the carrier bag into the pocket and put on the fur hat. He abandoned his remaining parcels then ran like a madman down the emergency stair case, smashed open a fire door, pelted down an alley, strolled up another which was one-way, stuffed the white raincoat into the carrier bag, sauntered into another store which was just closing, and there bought a black raincoat to replace the white one. Using the departing shoppers for cover he squeezed into a crowded tram, stayed aboard till the last stop but one, walked for an hour and made the fallback with Max to the minute.

Here he described his dialogue with Max and said they nearly had a standing fight.

Smiley asked: 'It never crossed your mind to drop the job?'

'No. It did not,' Jim snapped, his voice rising in a threat.

'Although, right from the start, you thought the idea was poppy-cock?' There was nothing but deference in Smiley's tone. No edge, no wish to score; only a wish to have the truth, clear under the night sky. 'You just kept marching. You'd seen what was on your back, you thought the mission absurd, but you still went on, deeper and deeper into the jungle.'

'I did.'

'Had you perhaps changed your mind about the mission? Did curiosity draw you after all, was that it? You wanted passionately to know who the mole was, for instance? I'm only speculating, Jim.'

'What's the difference? What the hell does my motive matter in a damn mess like this?'

The half moon was free of cloud and seemed very close. Jim sat on the bench. It was bedded in loose gravel and while he spoke he occasionally picked up a pebble and flicked it backhand into the bracken. Smiley sat beside him, looking nowhere but at Jim. Once, to keep him company, he took a pull of vodka and thought of Tarr and Irina drinking on their own hilltop in Hong Kong. It must be a habit of the trade, he decided: we talk better when there's a view.

Through the window of the parked Fiat, said Jim, the word code passed off without a hitch. The driver was one of those stiff, muscle-bound Czech Magyars with an Edwardian moustache and a mouthful of garlic. Jim didn't like him but he hadn't expected to. The two back doors were locked and there was a row about where he should sit. The Magyar said it was insecure for Jim to be in the back. It was also undemocratic. Jim told him to go to hell. He asked Jim whether he had a gun and Jim said no, which was not true, but if the Magyar didn't believe him he didn't dare say so. He asked whether Jim had brought instructions for the General? Jim said he had brought nothing. He had come to listen.

Jim felt a bit nervy, he said. They drove and the Magyar said his piece. When they reached the lodge there would be no lights and no sign of life. The General would be inside. If there was any sign of life, a bicycle, a car, a light, a dog, if there was any sign that the hut was occupied, then the Magyar would go in first and Jim would wait in the car. Otherwise Jim should go in alone and the Magyar would do the waiting. Was that clear?

Why didn't they just go in together? Jim asked. Because the General didn't want them to, said the Magyar.

They drove for half an hour by Jim's watch, heading north-east at an average of thirty kilometres an hour. The track was winding and steep and tree-lined. There was no moon and he could see very little except occasionally, against the skyline, more forest, more hilltops. The snow had come from the north, he noticed; it was a point that was useful later. The track was clear but rutted by heavy lorries. They drove without lights. The Magyar had begun telling a dirty story and Jim guessed it was his way of being nervous. The smell of garlic was awful. He seemed to chew it all the time. Without warning he cut the engine. They were running downhill, but more slowly. They had not quite stopped when the Magyar reached for the handbrake and Jim smashed his head against the window post and took his gun. They were at the opening to a side-path. Thirty yards down this path lay a low wooden hut. There was no sign of life.

Jim told the Magyar what he would like him to do. He would like him to wear Jim's fur hat and Jim's coat and take the walk for him. He should take it slowly, keeping his hands linked behind his back, and walking at the centre of the path. If he failed to do either of those things Jim would shoot him. When he reached the hut he should go inside and explain to the General that Jim was indulging in an elementary precaution. Then he should walk back slowly, report to Jim that all was well, and that the General was ready to receive him. Or not, as the case might be.

The Magyar didn't seem very happy about this but he didn't have much choice. Before he got out Jim made him turn the car round and face it down the path If there was any monkey business, Jim explained, he would put on the headlights and shoot him along the beam, not once, but several times, and not in the legs. The Magyar began his walk. He had nearly reached the hut when the whole area was floodlit: the hut, the path and a large space around. Then a number of things happened at once. Jim didn't see everything because he was busy turning the car. He saw four men fall out of the trees and, so far as he could work out, one of them sandbagged the Magyar. Shooting started but none of the four paid it any attention, they were standing back while somebody took photographs. The shooting seemed to be directed at the clear sky behind the floodlights. It was very theatrical. Flares exploded, Very lights went up, even tracer, and as Jim raced the Fiat down the track he had the impression of leaving a military tattoo at its climax. He was almost clear – he really felt he *was* clear – when from the woods to his right someone opened up with a machine-gun at close quarters. The first burst shot off a back wheel and turned the car over. He saw the wheel fly over the bonnet as the car took to the ditch on the left. The ditch might have been ten foot deep but the snow let him down kindly. The car didn't burn so he lay behind it and waited, facing across the track, hoping to get a shot at the machine-gunner. The next burst came from behind him and threw him up against the car. The woods must have been crawling with troops. He knew that he had been hit twice. Both shots caught him in the right shoulder and it seemed amazing to him, as he lay there watching the tattoo, that they hadn't taken off the arm. A klaxon sounded, maybe two or three. An ambulance rolled down the track and there was still enough shooting to frighten the game for years. The ambulance reminded him of those old Hollywood fire engines, it was so upright. A whole mock battle was taking place, yet the ambulance boys stood gazing at him without a care in the world. He was losing consciousness as he heard a second car arrive, and men's voices, and more photographs were taken, this time of the right man. Someone gave orders but he couldn't tell what they were because they were given in Russian. His one thought, as they dumped him on the stretcher and the lights went out, concerned going back to London. He imagined himself in the St James's flat, with the coloured charts and the sheaf of notes, sitting in the armchair and explaining to Control how, in their old age, the two of them had walked into the biggest sucker's punch in the history of the trade. His only consolation was that they had sandbagged the Magyar, but looking back Jim wished very much he'd broken his neck for him; it was a thing he could have managed very easily, and without compunction.

from *Tinker, Tailor, Soldier, Spy*, John le Carré

I have also included a short piece from Gerald Seymour's novel, Harry's Game, *not only because it is a highly convincing and exciting story – the classic tale of a manhunt, as good in its way as Geoffrey Household's* Rogue Male *– but also because Seymour may be the only fiction writer so far to have succeeded in defeating the notorious 'yawn-factor' which dogs anyone who tries to tackle the problems of Ulster. Do not be put off. Where the IRA is concerned, Seymour has the last word . . .*

Groundwork

Meanwhile, Harry was being prepared for the awesome moment when he would leave the woods of Surrey and fly to Belfast, on his own, leaving the back-up team that now worked with him as assiduously as any heavyweight champion's.

Early on Davidson had brought him a cassette recorder, complete with four ninety-minute tapes of Belfast accents. They'd been gathered by students from Queen's University who believed they were taking part in a national phonetics study, and had taken their microphones into pubs, laundrettes, working men's clubs and supermarkets. Wherever there were groups gathered and talking in the harsh, cutting accent of Belfast, so different to the slower, more gentle Southern speech, tapes had attempted to pick up the voices and record them. The tapes had been passed to the Army press officer via a lecturer at the University, whose brother was on duty on the Brigade commander's staff, and then, addressed to a fictitious major, flown to the Ministry of Defence. The sergeant on Davidson's staff travelled to London to collect them from the dead-letter-box in the postal section of the Ministry.

Night after night Harry listened to the tapes, mouthing over the phrases and trying to lock his speech into the accents he heard. After sixteen years in the Army little of it seemed real. He learned again of the abbreviations, the slang, the swearing. He heard the way that years of conflict and alertness had stunted normal conversation; talk was kept to a minimum as people hurried away from shops once their business was done, and barely waited around for a quiet gossip. In the pubs he noticed that men lectured each other, seldom listening to replies or interested in opinions different to their own. His accent would be critical to him, the sort of thing that could awake the first inkling of suspicion that might lead to the further check he knew his cover could not sustain.

His walls, almost bare when he arrived at the big house, were soon covered by aerial photographs of Belfast. For perhaps an hour a day he was left to memorize the photographs, learn the street patterns of the geometric divisions of the artisan cottages that had been allowed to sprawl out from the centre of the city. The developers of the nineteenth century had flung together the narrow streets and their back-to-back terraces along the main roads out of the city. Most relevant to Harry were those on either side of the city's two great ribbons of the Falls and Shankill. Pictures of astonishing clarity taken from RAF cameras showed the continuous peace line, or the 'interface', as the army called it, the sheets of silvery corrugated iron that separated Protestant from Catholic in the no-man's land between the roads.

The photographs gave an idea of total calm and left no impression of the hatred, terror and bestiality that existed on the ground. The open spaces of bombed devastation in any other British city would have been marked down as clearance areas for urban improvement.

From the distance of Germany – where theorists worked out

war games in terms of divisions, tank skirmishes, limited nuclear warheads, and the possibility of chemical agents being thrown into a critical battle – it had become difficult for Harry to realize why the twenty or so thousand British soldiers deployed in the province were not able to wind up the Provisional campaign in a matter of months. When he took in the rabbit warren revealed by the reconnaissance photographs he began to comprehend the complexity of the problem. Displayed on his walls was the perfect guerilla fighting base. A maze of escape routes, ambush positions, back entries, cul-de-sacs and, at strategic crossroads, great towering blocks of flats commanding the approaches to terrorist strongholds.

It was the adventure playground, par excellence, for the urban terrorist, Davidson would say, as he fired questions at Harry till he could wheel out at will all the street names they wanted from him, so many commemorating the former greatness of British arms – Balkan, Raglan, Alma, Balaclava – their locations, and the quickest way to get there. By the second week the knowledge was there and the consolidation towards perfection was under way. Davidson and his colleagues felt now that the filing system had worked well, that this man, given the impossible brief he was working under, would do as well as any.

Also in the bedroom, and facing him as he lay in bed, was the 'tribal map' of the city. That was the army phrase, and another beloved by Davidson. It took up sixteen square feet of space, with Catholic streets marked in a gentle grass-green, the fierce loyalist strongholds in the hard orange that symbolized their heritage, and the rest in a mustard compromise. Forget that lot, Davidson had said. That had meant something in the early days when the maps were drawn up.

'Nowadays, you're in one camp or the other. There are no uncommitted. Mixed areas are three years out of date. In some it's the Prods who've run, in others the other crowd.'

It had been so simple in Sheik Othman, when Harry had lived amongst the Adeni Arabs. The business of survival had occupied him so fully that the sophistications they were teaching him now were unnecessary. And there he had been so far from the help of British troops that he had become totally self-reliant. In Belfast he knew he must guard against the feeling that salvation was always a street corner away. He must reject that and burrow his way into the community if he was to achieve anything.

Outside the privacy of his room Harry seldom escaped the enthusiasm of Davidson who personally supervised every aspect of his preparation. He followed Harry in the second week down beyond the vegetable garden to the old and battered greenhouse, yards long and with its glass roofing missing, and what was left coated in the deep moss-green compost that fell from the trees. There were no nurtured tomatoes growing here, no cosseted strawberry cuttings, only a pile of sandbags at the opposite end to the door with a circular coloured target, virgin new, propped against them. Here they re-taught Harry the art of pistol shooting.

'You'll have to have a gun over there – and not to wave about, Harry,' Davidson laughed. 'Just to have. You'd be the only physically fit male specimen in the province without one if you didn't have a firearm of some sort. It's a must, I'm afraid.'

'I didn't have one in Aden. Ridiculous, I suppose, but no one suggested it.'

He took the gun from the instructor, grey-haired, hard-faced, lined from weather, wearing a blue, all-enveloping boiler-suit and unmarked beret. He went through the precautionary drills, breaking the gun, flicking the revolving chamber that was empty, greased and black. The instructor counted out the first six shells.

Five times he reloaded the gun till the target was peppered and holed and askew.

'It's not the accuracy that counts so much with the first ones, sir,' said the older man, pulling off his ear muffs, 'it's the speed you get the first one or two away. If you're shooting straight enough for your opponent to hear them going by his ear that tends to be enough to get his head back a bit. But it's getting the first one away that matters. Gets the initiative for you. There aren't many men as will stand still and aim as you're pulling the trigger for the first one. Get 'em going back and then worry about the aim for the third and fourth shot. And try not to fire more than the first four straight off. It's nice to keep a couple just so that you have a chance to do something about it if things don't turn out that well. Remember, with this one, it's a great little gun, but it's slow to load. That's its problem. Everything else is OK.'

They went over the firing positions. Sometimes the classic right-arm-extended, sideways-on stance. 'That's if you've got all night, sir, and you don't think he's armed. Take your time and make sure. Doesn't happen that often.' Then they worked on the standard revolver-shooting posture. Legs apart, body hunched, arms extended, meeting in front of the eye line, butt held in both hands, the whole torso lunging at the target. 'You're small yourself then, sir, and you've got your whole body thrown in with the gun to get it away straight. You won't miss often from that, and if you do you'll give 'im such a hell of a fright that he won't do much about it.'

'What's he like, Chief?' Davidson said to the instructor.

'We've had better through here, sir, and we've had worse. He's quite straight but a bit slow as of now. I wouldn't worry about that. If he has to use it he'll be faster. Everyone is when it's real.'

Harry followed Davidson out of the greenhouse and they walked together up the brick and weed path amongst the vegetables. It was mild for November, the trees, huge above them, were already without their load of leaves and above the trees were the soft meandering grey clouds.

'I think it's going quite well, Harry – no, I mean very well at the moment. But I don't want to minimize anything that you're going to have to go through. It's all very well here, swotting for an exam if you like . . . but the questions themselves are very tough when you get to the actual paper. Forgive the metaphor, Harry, but it's not an easy road over there, however much we do for you here. There are some things we can iron out at this end. Accent. It's critical for immediate and long-term survival. We can spare your blushes but I think that's coming along very well. Your background knowledge is fine, details of events, names, folklore – that is all good. But there are other more complex factors, about which we cannot really do very much and which are just as vital.'

They stopped now some twenty-five yards from the house on the edge of the old tennis court. Davidson was looking for the words. Harry wasn't going to help him; that wasn't his style.

'Look, Harry. Just as important as the accent, and getting the background right, and knowing what the hullabaloo is about, is how you are going to stand up to this yourself. It's my job to send you in there as perfectly equipped as possible. Right? Well, the thing I cannot accurately gauge is how you'll soak up the punishment of just existing there. You could have an isolation problem . . . loneliness, basically. No one to confide in, not part of a local team, completely on your own. This could be a problem. I don't know the answer to it, I don't think you're liable to suffer too greatly from it – that's my reading of your file. Sorry, but we go through it most nights with a fine blade. Unless you're aware of it, and bolt it down, there'll come a time when you'll want to tell someone about yourself, however obliquely, however much at a tangent. Now you'll say never, never in a month of whatevers, but believe me it'll happen, and you have to watch it.'

Harry, searched his face, noting for the first time since he'd come to the big house the concern of the other man. Davidson went on, 'After Aden we're pretty confident in your ability to look after yourself. There's a lot in the file on that. I've no reason to disbelieve it, you've shown me none. The simple day-to-day business won't be pleasant but will be bearable. The other thing you have to consider is if you're discovered – what happens then? There is a fair chance that if they spot you we may be getting some sort of feedback as they build up information and we'll have time to shift you out in a hurry. You may notice something, a tail, a man watching you, questions being asked. Don't hang about then, just come back. What I'm getting at is difficult enough to say, but you have to face it, and you'll be better for facing it. You have to work out how you'll react if they take you alive.'

Harry grimaced weakly. The older man was fumbling about trying to say the most obvious thing of the whole operation, stumbling in his care not to scratch the varnish of morale that was coated sometimes thickly, sometimes sparsely on all these jobs.

'I think I can help you,' Harry smiled at him. 'You want to know whether I've considered the question of being taken, tortured and shot. Yes. You want to know whether I'm going to tell them all about here, you and everything else. Answer, I don't know. I think not, I hope not. But I don't know. You don't know these things and there's no absolute statement I can make that would be of any use. But I've thought of it and I know what you'd hope from me. Whether you'll get it I just don't know.'

They began to walk again. Davidson swung his right arm round behind Harry's back and slapped his far shoulder. Like a father, thought Harry, and he's scared stiff. It's always been nice and comfortable for him, sitting at a desk packing the nameless numbered men off to heaven-knows where, but this time the jungle's been creeping a bit close.

'Thank you, Harry. That was very fairly put. Very fair. There's things that have to be discussed if one's to keep these things professional. I'm grateful to you. I think your attitude is about right.' Thank God for that, Harry thought, now he's done his duty. We've had our facts-of-life talk, ready to go out into the big nasty world, and don't put your hands up little girls' skirts. God, he's relieved he's got that little lot over.

As they came to the paint-chipped back door, Davidson started again. 'You know, Harry, you haven't told us much about home, about your wife. The family. It's an aspect we haven't really had time to go into.'

'There's nothing to worry about there. Not that I know of. I suppose you never do till it's too late to be worrying about that sort of thing. She's very level. Not complicated. That sounds pretty patronizing, but I don't mean that. She's used to me going away in a hurry, at least *was* used to it when we were younger. It's not been so frequent over the last few years, but I think she's okay.'

'Did she know what you were doing in Aden?'

Harry said it slowly, thoughtfully, 'No. Not really. I didn't have time or the opportunity to write. There had been those little sods rolling grenades into the married quarters and smuggling bombs in with the food and things like that. The families went home before I became involved in the special stuff. I didn't tell her much about it when it was all over. There wasn't much to tell, not in my terms.'

'I'm sorry you had to come over here without being able to see her.'

'Inevitable. It's the way it is. She's not very service-minded. Doesn't live off married mess nights. Doesn't really get involved with the Army scene. I think I prefer it that way. She'd like me out, but I tell her earning anyone else's shilling than the Queen's isn't that easy these days. I think she understands that.'

'The postcards will start arriving soon. The first lot that you did. And you'd better do some more before you move on.' Davidson sounded anxious, wanting to do it right, thought Harry. As if there was anything he could say about – what was the word he used? – this 'aspect' of the job. Of course she'd want to know where he was, of course if she knew she would be stunned with worry. What else could she be, and what could be done about it? Nothing.

They hesitated outside the door of the big room where the work was done.

Davidson said, 'I wanted to be sure that you wouldn't be too concerned about your family while you're over there. It could be important. I once had a man . . .'

Harry cut in, 'It's not a problem. Not compared with the other ones. She'll cope.'

They went into the room where the others were waiting. Davidson thought to himself, he's a cold enough fish to succeed. It went through Harry's mind that his controller was either very thorough or on the reverse slope and going a touch soft. It was the only time the two men had anything approaching a personal conversation.

from *Harry's Game*, Gerald Seymour

There are always watchers and waiters . . .

Brief Encounter

Smiley was tired, deeply, heavily tired. He drove slowly homewards. Dinner out tonight. Something rather special. It was only lunch-time now – he would spend the afternoon pursuing Olearius across the Russian continent on his Hansa voyage. Then dinner at Quaglino's and a solitary toast to the successful murderer, to Elsa perhaps, in gratitude for ending the career of George Smiley with the life of Sam Fennan.

He remembered to collect his laundry in Sloane Street and finally turned into Bywater Street, finding a parking space about three houses down from his own. He got out carrying the brown-paper parcel of laundry, locked the car laboriously and walked all round it from habit, testing the handles. A thin rain was still falling. It annoyed him that someone had parked outside his house again. Thank goodness Mrs Chapel had closed his bedroom window, otherwise the rain would have . . .

He was suddenly alert. Something had moved in the drawing-room. A light, a shadow, a human form; something, he was certain. Was it sight or instinct? Was it the latent skill of his own tradecraft which informed him? Some fine sense or nerve, some remote faculty of perception warned him now and he heeded the warning.

Without a moment's thought he dropped his keys back into his overcoat pocket, walked up the steps to his own front door and rang the bell.

It echoed shrilly through the house. There was a moment's silence, then came to Smiley's ears the distinct sound of footsteps approaching the door, firm and confident. A scratch of the chain, a click of the Ingersoll latch and the door was opened, swiftly, cleanly.

Smiley had never seen him before. Tall, fair, handsome, thirty-five odd. A light-grey suit, white shirt and silver tie – *habillé en diplomate*. German or Swede. His left hand remained nonchalantly in his jacket pocket.

Smiley peered at him apologetically:

'Good afternoon. Is Mr Smiley in, please?'

The door was opened to its fullest extent. A tiny pause.

'Yes. Won't you come in?'

For a fraction of a second he hesitated. 'No thanks. Would you please give him this?' He handed him the parcel of laundry, walked down the steps again, to his car. He knew he was still being watched. He started the car, turned and drove into Sloane Square without a glance in the direction of his house. He found a parking space in Sloane Street, pulled in and rapidly wrote in his diary seven sets of numbers. They belonged to the seven cars parked along Bywater Street.

What should he do? Stop a policeman? Whoever he was, he was probably gone by now. Besides, there were other considerations. He locked the car again and crossed the road to a telephone kiosk. He rang Scotland Yard, got through to Special Branch and asked for Inspector Mendel. But it appeared that the Inspector, having reported back to the Superintendent, had discreetly anticipated the pleasures of retirement and left for Mitcham. Smiley got his address after a good deal of prevarication and set off once more in his car, covering three sides of a square and emerging at Albert Bridge. He had a sandwich and a large whisky at a new pub overlooking the river and a quarter of an hour later was crossing the bridge on the way to Mitcham, the rain still beating down on his inconspicuous little car. He was worried, very worried indeed.

from *Call for the Dead*, John le Carré

HARD GRAFTING IN THE TRADE

This fine story by Irwin Shaw describes perfectly the grim, dirty existence of a small-time spy in the immediate aftermath of the fall of Berlin. It sets the tone for le Carré's The Spy Who Came in from the Cold, *described by Graham Greene – accurately, I think – as 'the best spy novel ever written'.*

The Man with One Arm

'I would like complete reports on these three people,' Captain Mikhailov was saying. He pushed a slip of paper across the desk to Garbrecht, and Garbrecht glanced at the names. 'They are interpreters at the American civil affairs headquarters. The Americans have a charming habit of hiring ex-Nazis almost exclusively for those jobs, and we have found it rewarding to inquire into the pasts of such gentlemen.' Mikhailov smiled. He was a short, stocky man with a round, shielded face, and pale, unsmiling eyes, and when he smiled it was like a flower painted unconvincingly on stone.

Garbrecht recognized two of the three names. Mikhailov was right. They were Nazis. It would take some thinking out, later, though, to decide whether to expose them to Mikhailov, or exactly how far to expose them. Garbrecht watched Mikhailov unlock a drawer in his desk and take out some American marks. Methodically, Mikhailov counted the notes out in his square, machine-like hands. He locked the drawer and pushed the money across the desk to Grabrecht.

'There,' Mikhailov said, 'that will keep you until we see each other next week.'

'Yes, Captain,' Garbrecht said. He reached out and pulled the money towards him, leaving it on the top of the desk. He took out his wallet and, slowly, one by one, put the notes into the wallet. He was still slow and clumsy with things like that because he had not yet learned how to handle things deftly with his left hand, and his right hand and arm were buried behind the field hospital in the brewery 1400 miles away. Mikhailov watched him impassively, without offering aid.

Garbrecht put his wallet away and stood up. His overcoat was thrown over a chair and he picked it up and struggled to get it over his shoulders.

'Till next week,' she said.

'Next week,' Mikhailov said.

Garbrecht did not salute. He opened the door and went out.

At least, he thought, with a nervous sensation of triumph, as he went down the grimy steps past the two plain-clothes men loitering in the dark hall, at least I didn't salute the bastard. That's the third week in a row I didn't salute him.

The plain-clothes men stared at him with a common, blank, threatening look. By now he knew them too well to be frightened by them. They looked that way at everything. When they looked at a horse or a child or a bunch of flowers, they threatened it. It was merely their comfortable professional adjustment to the world around them, like Mikhailov's smile. The Russians, Garbrecht thought as he went down the street, what a people to have in Berlin!

Garbrecht walked without looking about him. The landscape of the cities of Germany had become monotonous – rubble, broken statues, neatly swept lanes between piled cracked brick, looming blank single walls, shells of buildings, half-demolished houses in which dozens of familes somehow lived. He moved briskly and energetically, like everyone else, swinging his one arm a little awkwardly to maintain his balance, but very little of what he saw around him made any impression on him. A solid numbness had taken possession of him when they cut off his arm. It was like the anaesthesia which they injected into your spine. You were conscious and you could see and hear and speak and you could understand what was being done to you, but all feeling was absent. Finally, Garbrecht knew, the anaesthesia would wear off, but for the present it was a most valuable defence.

'Lieutenant.' It was a woman's voice somewhere behind him and Garbrecht did not look around. 'Oh, Lieutenant Garbrecht.'

He stopped and turned slowly. Nobody had called him lieutenant for more than a year now. A short, blonde woman in a grey cloth coat was hurrying towards him. He looked at her, puzzled. He had never seen her before and he wondered if it were she who had called his name.

'Did you call me?' he asked as she stopped in front of him.

'Yes,' she said. She was thin, with a pale, rather pretty face. She did not smile. 'I followed you from Mikhailov's office.'

'I'm sure,' Garbrecht said, turning and starting away, 'that you have made some mistake.'

The woman fell in beside him, walking swiftly. She wore no stockings and her legs showed purple from the cold. 'Please,' she said, 'do not behave like an idiot.'

Then, in a flat, undemanding voice, she said several things to him that he had thought nobody alive remembered about him, and finally she called him by his correct name and he knew that there was no escaping it now. He stopped in the middle of the ruined street and sighed, and said, after a long time, 'Very well. I will go with you.'

There was a smell of cooking in the room. Good cooking. A roast, probably, and a heavy, strong soup. It was the kind of smell that had seemed to vanish from Germany some time around 1942, and even with all the other things happening to him Garbrecht could feel the saliva welling helplessly and tantalizingly up from the ducts under his tongue. It was a spacious room with a high ceiling that must have been at one time quite elegant. There was a bricked-up fireplace with a large, broken mirror over it. By some trick of fracture, the mirror reflected separate images in each of its broken parts and it made Garbrecht feel that something shining and abnormal was hidden there.

The girl had ushered him without formality into the room and had told him to sit down and had disappeared. Garbrecht could feel his muscles slowly curling as he sat rigidly in the half-broken wooden chair, staring coldly at the battered desk, the surprising leather chair behind the desk, the strange mirror, the ten-inch-high portrait of Lenin which was the only adornment on the wall. Lenin looked down at him from the wall, across the years, through the clumsy heroics of the lithographer, with a remote, ambiguous challenge glaring from the dark, wild eyes.

The door through which he had himself come was opened and a man entered. The man slammed the door behind him and walked swiftly across the room to the desk. Then he wheeled and faced Garbrecht.

'Well, well,' the man said, smiling, his voice hearty and welcoming, 'here you are. Here you are. Sorry to keep you waiting. Terribly sorry.' He beamed across the room, leaning forward hospitably from his position in front of the desk. He was a short, stocky man with a light, pink face, and pale, silky hair that he wore long, possibly in an attempt to hide what might be an increasing tendency to baldness. He looked like an amiable butcher's boy, growing a little old for his job, or the strong man in a tumbling act in a small-time circus, the one on the bottom that the others climbed on. Garbrecht stood up and peered at him, trying to remember if he had ever seen the man before.

'No, no,' the man said, waving his pudgy hands, 'no, we have never met. Do not trouble your brain. Sit down, sit down. Comfort first. Everything else after.' He leapt lightly across the room and almost pushed Garbrecht into his chair. 'It is a lesson I have learned from our friends, the Americans. How to slouch. Look what they've accomplished merely by spending most of their time on the base of their spines.' He laughed uproariously, as though the joke were too merry not to be enjoyed, and swept quickly across the room, with his almost leaping, light gait, and hurled himself into the large leather chair behind the desk. He continued beaming at Garbrecht.

'I want to say,' said Garbrecht, 'that I have no notion of why I was asked to come here. I merely came,' he said carefully, 'because the young lady made me curious, and I had an hour to spare, anyway, and . . .'

'Enough, enough.' The man rocked solidly back and forth in the squeaking chair. 'You came. Sufficient. Delighted. Very pleased. Have a cigarette . . .' With a sudden movement, he thrust out the brass cigarette box that lay on the desk.

'Not at the moment, thank you,' Garbrecht said, although his throat was quivering for one.

'Ah,' the fat man said, grinning. 'A rarity. Only German known to refuse a cigarette since the surrender. Still, no matter . . .' He took a cigarette himself and lighted it deftly. 'First, introductions, Lieutenant. My name. Anton Seedorf. Captain, Hermann Goering Division. I keep the title.' He grinned. 'A man saves what he can from a war.'

'I imagine,' Garbrecht said, 'you know my name.'

'Yes.' Seedorf seemed to bubble with some inward humour. 'Oh, yes, I certainly do. Yes, indeed, I've heard a great deal about you. Been most anxious to meet you. The arm,' he said, with sudden solemnity. 'Where was that?'

'Stalingrad.'

'Ah, Stalingrad,' Seedorf said heartily, as though he were speaking the name of a winter resort at which he had spent a marvellous holiday. 'A lot of good souls left there, weren't there, many good souls. A miscalculation. One of many. Vanity. The most terrible thing in the world, the vanity of a victorious army. A most interesting subject for historians – the role of vanity in military disasters. Don't you agree?' He peered eagerly at Garbrecht.

'Captain,' Garbrecht said coldly, 'I cannot remain here all afternoon.'

'Of course,' Seedorf said. 'Naturally. You're curious about why I invited you here. I understand.' He puffed swiftly on his cigarette, wreathing his pale head in smoke before the cracked mirror. He jumped up and perched himself on the desk, facing Garbrecht, boyishly. 'Well,' he said, heartily, 'it is past time for hiding anything. I know you. I know your very good record in the Party . . .'

Garbrecht felt the cold rising in his throat. It's going to be worse, he thought, worse than I expected.

'. . . promising career in the Army until the unfortunate accident at Stalingrad,' Seedorf was saying brightly, 'loyal, dependable, et cetera; there is really no need to go into it at this moment, is there?'

'No,' said Garbrecht, 'none at all.' He stood up. 'If it is all the same to you, I prefer not to be reminded of any of it. That is all past and, I hope, it will soon all be forgotten.'

Seedorf giggled. 'Now, now,' he said. 'There is no need to be so cautious with me. To a person like you or me,' he said, with a wide, genial gesture, 'it is never forgotten. To a person who has said the things we have said, who did the things we have done, for so many years, a paid Party official, a good soldier, a good German . . .'

'I am not interested any more,' Garbrecht said loudly but hopelessly, 'in being what you call a good German.'

'It is not a question,' Seedorf said, smiling widely and dousing his cigarette, 'of what you are interested in, Lieutenant. I beg your pardon. It is a question of what must be done. Simply that.'

'I am not going to do anything,' said Garbrecht.

'I beg your pardon once more.' Seedorf rocked happily back and forth on the edge of the desk. 'There are several little things that you can be very useful doing. I beg your pardon, you will do them. You work for the Russians, collecting information in the American zone. A useful fellow. You also work for the Americans, collecting information in the Russian zone.' Seedorf beamed at him. 'A prize!'

Garbrecht started to deny it, then shrugged wearily. There might be a way out, but denial certainly was not it.

'We, too, several of us, maybe more than several, could use a little information.' Seedorf's voice had grown harder, and there was only an echo of jollity left in it, like the sound of laughter dying down a distant alley on a cold night. 'We are not as large an organization at the moment as the Russians; we are not as well equipped for the time being as the Americans . . . but we are ever more . . . more

. . .' He chuckled as he thought of the word . . . 'curious. And more ambitious.'

There was silence in the room. Garbrecht stared heavily at the pale, fat head outlined against the broken mirror with its insane, multiplied reflections. If he were alone, Garbrecht knew he would bend his head and weep, as he did so often, without apparent reason, these days.

'Why don't you stop?' he asked heavily. 'What's the sense? How many times do you have to be beaten?'

Seedorf grinned. 'One more time, at least,' he said. 'Is that a good answer?'

'I won't do it,' Garbrecht said. 'I'll give the whole thing up. I don't want to get involved any more.'

'I beg your pardon,' said Seedorf happily, 'you will give up nothing. It is terrible for me to talk to a man who gave his arm for the Fatherland this way,' he said with a kind of glittering facsimile of pity, 'but I am afraid the Russians would be told your correct name and Party position from 1934 on, and they would be told of your affiliations with the Americans, and they would be told of your job as adjutant to the commanding officer of Maidanek concentration camp in the winter of 1944, when several thousand people died by orders with your name on them . . .'

Seedorf drummed his heels softly and cheerfully against the desk. 'They have just really begun on their war trials . . . and these new ones will not run ten months, Lieutenant. I beg your pardon for talking this way, and I promise you from now on we will not mention any of these matters again.' He jumped up and came across the room in his swift, round walk. 'I know how you feel,' he said softly. 'Often, I feel the same way. Quit. Quit now, once and for all. But it is not possible to quit. In a little while you will see that and you will be very grateful.'

'What is it?' Garbrecht said. 'What is it that you want me to do?'

'Just a little thing,' Seedorf said. 'Nothing at all, really. Merely report here every week and tell me what you have told the Russians and the Americans and what they have told you. Fifteen minutes a week. That's all there is to it.'

'Fifteen minutes a week.' Garbrecht was surprised that he had actually laughed. 'That's all.'

'Exactly.' Seedorf laughed. 'It won't be so bad. There's always a meal to be had here and cigarettes. It is almost like old times. There!' He stepped back, smiling widely. 'I am so happy it is settled.' He took Garbrecht's hand and shook it warmly with both his. 'Till next week,' he said.

Garbrecht looked heavily at him. Then he sighed, 'Till next week,' he said.

Seedorf held the door open for him when he went out. There was no one else in the corridor and no guards at the door, and he walked slowly down the creaking hall, through the rich smell of cooking, and on into the street and the gathering cold evening air.

He walked blankly through the broken brick wastes towards the American control post, staring straight ahead of him. Next week, he thought, I must ask him what the picture of Lenin is doing on the wall.

The office of Captain Peterson was very different from the bleak room in which Captain Mikhailov conducted his affairs. There was a clerk in the corner and an American flag on the wall, and the busy sound of American typewriters from the next room. There was a water-cooler and a warm radiator, and there was a picture of a pretty girl with a small blond child on Peterson's disordered desk. Garbrecht took his coat off and sat down in one of the comfortable looted plush chairs and waited for Peterson. The interviews with Peterson were much less of a strain than the ones with Mikhailov. Peterson was a large young man who spoke good German and, amazingly, fair Russian. He was good-natured and naïve, and Garbrecht was sure he believed Garbrecht's excellently forged papers and innocuous, false record, and Garbrecht's quiet, repeated insistence that he had been anti-Nazi from the beginning. Peterson was an enthusiast. He had been an enthusiast about the war in which he had performed quite creditably, he was an enthusiast about Germany, its scenery, its art, its future, its people whom he regarded as the first victims of Hitler. Mikhailov was different. He bleakly made no comment on the official soft tones issuing from Moscow on the subject of the German people, but Garbrecht knew that he regarded the Germans not as the first victims but as the first accomplices.

Of late, Garbrecht had to admit, Peterson had not seemed quite so enthusiastic. He had seemed rather baffled and sometimes hurt and weary. In the beginning, his naïveté had spread to cover the Russians in a rosy blanket, too. The assignments he gave to Garbrecht to execute in the Russian zone were so routine and so comparatively innocent that, if Garbrecht had had a conscience, he would have hesitated at taking payment for their fulfilment.

Peterson was smiling broadly when he came in, looking like a schoolboy who has just been promoted to the first team on a football squad. He was a tall, heavy young man with an excited, swift manner of talking. 'Glad to see you, Garbrecht,' he said. 'I was afraid I was going to miss you. I've been busy as a bartender on Saturday night, hand-carrying orders all over the place, packing, saying goodbye . . .'

'Goodbye?' Garbrecht said, shaken by a small tremor of fear. 'Where are you going?'

'Home.' Peterson pulled out three drawers from his desk and started emptying them in a swift jumble. 'The United States of America.'

'But I thought,' Garbrecht said, 'that you had decided to stay. You said your wife and child were coming over and . . .'

'I know . . .' Peterson threw a whole batch of mimeographed papers lightheartedly into the trash-basket. 'I changed my mind.' He stopped working on the drawers and looked soberly at Garbrecht. 'They're not coming here. I decided I didn't want my child to grow up in Europe.' He sat down heavily, staring over Garbrecht's head at the moulding around the ceiling. 'In fact,' he said, 'I don't think I want to hang around Europe any more myself. In the beginning I thought I could do a lot of good here. Now . . .' He shrugged. 'They'd better try someone else. I'd better go back to America and clear my head for a while. It's simpler in a war. You know who you're fighting and you have a general idea about where he is. Now . . .' Once more the shrug.

'Maybe I'm too stupid for a job like this,' he continued. 'Or maybe I expected too much. I've been here a year and everything seems to be getting worse and worse. I feel as though I'm sliding downhill all the time. Slowly, not very perceptibly . . . but downhill. Maybe Germany has always struck everybody the same way. Maybe that's why so many people have committed suicide here. I'm going to get out of here before I wake up one morning and say to myself, "By God, they have the right idea."'

Suddenly he stood up, swinging his big feet in their heavy Army shoes down to the floor with a commanding crash. 'Come on,' he said. 'I'll take you in to see Major Dobelmeir. He's going to replace me.' Peterson opened the door for Garbrecht and they went out into the anteroom with the four desks and the girls in uniform typing. Peterson led the way. 'I think the United States Army is going to begin to get its money's worth out of you now, Garbrecht,' Peterson said, without looking back. 'Dobelmeir is quite a different kettle of fish from that nice, simple young Captain Peterson.'

Garbrecht stared at the back of Peterson's head. So, he thought coldly, he wasn't so completely fooled by me, after all. Maybe it's good he's going.

But then Peterson opened the door to one of the rooms along the hall and they went in, and Garbrecht took one look at the major's leaf and the heavy, brooding, suspicious face, and he knew that he was wrong; it would have been much better if Peterson had stayed.

Peterson introduced them and the Major said, 'Sit down,' in flat, heavy-voiced German, and Peterson said, 'Good luck. I have to go now,' and left. The Major looked down at the papers on his desk and read them stolidly, for what seemed to Garbrecht like a very long time. Garbrecht felt the tension beginning again in his muscles, as it had in Seedorf's room. Everything, he thought, gets worse and worse, more and more complicated.

'Garbrecht,' the Major said without looking up, 'I have been reading your reports.' He did not say anything else, merely continued to read slowly and effortfully, his eyes covered, his heavy chin creasing in solid fat as he bent his head over the desk.

'Yes?' Garbrecht said finally, because he could no longer stand the silence.

For a moment, Dobelmeir did not answer. Then he said, 'They aren't worth ten marks, all of them together, to anybody. The United States Government ought to sue you for obtaining money on false pretences.'

'I am very sorry,' Garbrecht said hurriedly, 'I thought that that is what was wanted, and I . . .'

'Don't lie.' The Major finally lifted his head and stared fishily at him.

'My dear Major . . .'

'Keep quiet,' the Major said evenly. 'We now institute a new régime. You can do all right if you produce. If you don't, you can go find another job. Now we know where we stand.'

'Yes, sir,' said Garbrecht.

'I should not have to teach you your business at this late date,' the Major said. 'There is only one way in which an operation like this can pay for itself; only one rule to follow. All our agents must act as though the nation on which they are spying is an active enemy of the United States, as though the war has, in fact, begun. Otherwise the information you gather has no point, no focus, no measurable value. When you bring me information it must be information of an enemy who is probing our line for weak spots, who is building up various depots of supplies and troops and forces in specific places, who is choosing certain specific fields on which to fight the crucial battles. I am not interested in random, confusing gossip. I am only interested in indications of the disposition of the enemy's strength and indications of his aggressive intentions towards us. Is that clear?'

'Yes, sir,' said Garbrecht.

The Major picked up three sheets of clipped-together papers. 'This is your last report,' he said. He ripped the papers methodically in half and then once more in half and threw them on the floor. 'That is what I think of it.'

'Yes, sir,' said Garbrecht. He knew the sweat was streaming down into his collar and he knew that the Major must have noticed it and was probably sourly amused at it, but there was nothing he could do to stop it.

'This office has sent out its last chambermaid-gossip report,' the Major said. 'From now on, we will send out only useful military information, or nothing at all. I'm not paying you for the last two weeks' work. You haven't earned it. Get out of here. And don't come back until you have something to tell me.'

He bent down once more over the papers on his desk. Garbrecht stood up and slowly went out the door. He knew that the Major did not look up as he closed the door behind him.

Greta wasn't home, and he had to stand outside her door in the cold all evening because the janitress refused to recognize him and let him in. Greta did not get back till after midnight, and then she came up with an American officer in a closed car and Garbrecht had to hide in the shadows across the street while the American kissed Greta clumsily again and again before going off. Garbrecht hurried across the broken pavement of the street to reach Greta before she retreated into the house.

Greta could speak English and worked for the Americans as a typist and filing clerk, and perhaps something else, not quite so official, in the evenings. Garbrecht did not inquire too closely. Greta was agreeable enough and permitted him to use her room when he was in the American zone, and she always seemed to have a store of canned food in her cupboard, gift of her various uniformed employers, and she was quite generous and warm-hearted about the entire arrangement. Greta had been an energetic patriot before the defeat and Garbrecht had met her when she visited the hospital where he was lying with his arm freshly severed after the sombre journey back from Russia. Whether it was patriotism, pity or perversity that had moved her, Garbrecht did not know, nor did he inquire too deeply; at any rate, Greta had remained a snug anchorage in the wild years that had passed and he was fond of her.

'Hello,' he said as he came up behind her. She was struggling with the lock and turned abruptly, as though frightened.

'Oh,' she said. 'I didn't think you'd be here tonight.'

'I'm sorry,' he said. 'I couldn't get in touch with you.'

She opened the door and he went in with her. She unlocked the door of her own room, which was on the ground floor, and slammed it irritably behind her. Ah, he thought unhappily, things are bad here, too, tonight.

He sighed. 'What is it?' he said.

'Nothing,' she said. She started to undress, methodically, and without any of the usual graceful secrecy she ordinarily managed even in the small drab room.

'Can I be of any help?' Garbrecht asked.

Greta stopped pulling off her stockings and looked thoughtfully at Garbrecht. Then she shook her head and yanked at the heel of the right stocking. 'You could,' she said, contemptuously. 'But you won't.'

Garbrecht squinted painfully at her. 'How do you know?' he asked.

'Because you're all the same,' Greta said coldly. 'Weak. Quiet. Disgusting.'

'What is it?' he asked. 'What would you want me to do?' He would have preferred it if Greta had refused to tell him, but he knew he had to ask.

Greta worked methodically on the other stocking. 'You ought to get four or five of your friends, the ex-heroes of the German Army,' she said disdainfully, 'and march over to Freda Raush's house and tear her clothes off her back and shave her head and make her walk down the street that way.'

'What?' Garbrecht sat up increduously. 'What are you talking about?'

'You were always yelling about honour,' Greta said loudly. 'Your honour, the Army's honour, Germany's honour.'

'What's that got to do with Freda Raush?'

'Honour is something Germans have only when they're winning, is that it?' Greta pulled her dress savagely over her shoulders. 'Disgusting.'

Garbrecht shook his head. 'I don't know what you're talking about,' he said. 'I thought Freda was a good friend of yours.'

'Even the French,' Greta said, disregarding him, 'were braver. They shaved their women's heads when they caught them . . .'

'All right, all right,' Garbrecht said wearily. 'What did Freda do?'

Greta looked wildly at him, her hair disarranged and tumbled around her full shoulders, her large, rather fat body shivering in cold anger in her sleazy slip. 'Tonight,' she said, 'she invited the Lieutenant I was with and myself to her house . . .'

'Yes,' said Garbrecht, trying to concentrate very hard.

'She is living with an American captain.'

'Yes?' said Garbrecht, doubtfully. Half the girls Greta knew seemed to be living with American captains, and the other half were trying to. That certainly could not have infuriated Greta to this wild point of vengeance.

'Do you know what his name is?' Greta asked rhetorically. 'Rosenthal! A Jew. Freda!'

Garbrecht sighed, his breath making a hollow, sorrowful sound in the cold midnight room. He looked up at Greta who was standing over him, her face set in quivering, tense lines. She was usually such a placid, rather stupid and easy-going girl that moments like this came as a shocking surprise.

'You will have to find someone else,' Garbrecht said wearily, 'if you want to have Freda's head shaved. I am not in the running.'

'Of course,' Greta said icily. 'I knew you wouldn't be.'

'Frankly,' Garbrecht said, trying to be reasonable with her, 'I am a little tired of the whole question of the Jews. I think we ought to drop it, once and for all. It was all right for a while, but I think we've probably just about used it all up by now.'

'Ah,' Greta said, 'keep quiet. I should have known better than to expect anything from a cripple.'

They both were silent then. Greta continued undressing with contemptuous asexual familiarity, and Garbrecht slowly took his clothes off and got into bed, while Greta, in a black rayon nightgown that her American Lieutenant had got for her, put her hair up in curlers before the small, wavy mirror. Garbrecht looked at her reflection in the mirror and remembered the nervous, multiple reflections in the cracked mirror in Seedorf's office.

He closed his stinging eyes, feeling the lids trembling jumpily. He touched the folded, raw scar on his right shoulder. As long as he lived, he probably would never get over being shocked at the strange, brutal scar on his own body. And he would never get over being shocked when anybody called him a cripple. He would have to be more diplomatic with Greta. She was the only girl he was familiar with and, occasionally, there was true warmth and blessed hours of forgetfulness in her bed. It would be ridiculous to lose that over a silly political discussion in which he had no real interest at all. Girls were hard to get these days. During the war it was better.

You got a lot of girls out of pity. But pity went out at Rheims. And any German, even a whole, robust one, had a hard time competing with the cigarettes and chocolates and prestige of the victors. And for a man with one arm . . . It had been a miserable day and this was a fitting, miserable climax to it.

Greta put out the light and got aggressively into bed, without touching him. Tentatively he put his hand out to her. She didn't move. 'I'm tired,' she said. 'I've had a long day. Good night.'

In a few moments she was asleep.

Garbrecht lay awake a long time, listening to Greta snore; a wavering, troubling reflection from a street light outside played on his lids from the small mirror across the room.

As he approached the house in which Seedorf kept his headquarters, Garbrecht realized that he had begun to hurry his pace a little, that he was actually looking forward to the meeting. This was the fourth week that he had reported to the fat ex-Captain, and he smiled a little to himself as he reminded himself of how affectionately he had begun to regard Seedorf. Seedorf had not been at all demanding. He had listened with eager interest to each report of Garbrecht's meeting with Mikhailov and Dobelmeir, had chuckled delightedly here and there, slapped his leg in appreciation of one point or another, and had shrewdly and humorously invented plausible little stories, scraps of humour, to give first to the Russian, then to the American. Seedorf, who had never met either of them, seemed to understand them both far better than Garbrecht did, and Garbrecht had risen steadily in the favour of both Captain Mikhailov and Major Dobelmeir since he had given himself to Seedorf's coaching.

As Garbrecht opened the door of Seedorf's headquarters, he remembered with a little smile the sense of danger and apprehension with which he had first come there.

He did not have to wait long at all. Miss Renner, the blonde who had first talked to him on the street, opened the door to the ex-Captain's room almost immediately.

Seedorf was obviously in high spirits. He was beaming and moving up and down in front of his desk with little, mincing, almost dancing steps. 'Hello, hello,' he said warmly, as Garbrecht came into the room. 'Good of you to come.'

Garbrecht never could make out whether this was sly humour on Seedorf's part, or perfectly automatic good manners, this pretence that Garbrecht had any choice in the matter.

'Wonderful day,' Seedorf said. 'Absolutely wonderful day. Did you hear the news?'

'What news?' Garbrecht asked cautiously.

'The first bomb!' Seedorf clasped his hands delightedly. 'This afternoon at two-thirty the first bomb went off in Germany. Stuttgart! A solemn day. A day of remembrance! After 1918 it took twelve years before the Germans started any real opposition to the Allies. And now . . . less than a year and a half after the surrender . . . the first bomb! Delightful!' He beamed at Garbrecht. 'Aren't you pleased?' he asked.

'Very,' said Garbrecht diplomatically. He was not fond of bombs. Maybe for a man with two arms, bombs might have an attraction, but for him . . .

'Now we can really go to work.' Seedorf hurled himself forcefully into his leather chair behind the desk and stared piercingly out at Garbrecht. 'Until now, it hasn't meant very much. Really only developing an organization. Trying out the parts. Seeing who could work and who couldn't. Instituting necessary discipline. Practice, more than anything else. Now the manoeuvres are over. Now we move on to the battlefield!'

Professional soldiers, Garbrecht thought bitterly, his new-found peace of mind already shaken, they couldn't get the jargon of their calling out of their thinking. Manoeuvres, battlefields . . . The only accomplishment they seemed to be able to recognize was the product of explosion, the only political means they really understood and relished, death.

'Lieutenant,' Seedorf said, 'we have been testing you, too. I am glad to say,' he said oratorically, 'we have decided that you are dependable. Now you really begin your mission. Next Tuesday at noon Miss Renner will meet you. She will take you to the home of a friend of ours. He will give you a package. You will carry it to an address that Miss Renner will give you at the time. I will not hide from you that you will be in a certain danger. The package you will carry will include a timing mechanism that will go into the first bomb to be exploded in the new war against the Allies in Berlin . . .'

Seedorf seemed to be far away and his voice distant and strange. It had been too good to be true, Garbrecht thought dazedly, the easy-going, undangerous, messenger-boy life that he had thought he was leading. Merely a sly, deadly game that Seedorf had been playing, testing him.

'Captain,' he whispered, 'Captain . . . I can't . . . I can't . .'

'The beginning,' Seedorf said, ecstatically, as though he had not heard Garbrecht's interruption. 'Finally, there will be explosions day and night, all over the city, all over the country . . . The Americans will blame the Russians, the Russians will blame the Americans, they will become more and more frightened, more and more distrustful of each other. They will come to us secretly, bargain with us, bid for us against each other . . .'

It will never happen, Garbrecht said dazedly to himself, never. It is the same old thing. All during the war they told us that. The Americans would break with the British, the British with the Russians. And here they all were in what was left of Berlin: Cockneys, Tartars from Siberia, Negroes from Mississippi. Men like Seedorf were victims of their own propaganda, men who listened and finally believed their own hopes, their own lies. And, he, Garbrecht, next week, would be walking among the lounging American MPs, with the delicate, deadly machinery ticking under his arm, because of Seedorf's hallucination. Any other nation, Garbrecht thought, would be convinced. They'd look around at the ruin of their cities, at the ever-stretching cemeteries, at the marching enemy troops in the heart of their capital, and they'd say, 'No, it did not work.' But not the Germans. Goering was just dead in the Nuremberg jail, and here was this fat murderer with the jolly smile who even looked a bit like Goering, rubbing his hands and shouting, 'A day of remembrance! The first bomb has exploded!'

Garbrecht felt lost and exhausted and hopeless, sitting in the wooden chair, watching the fat man move nervously and jubilantly behind the desk, hearing the rough, good-natured voice saying, 'It took fourteen years last time, it won't take four years this time! Garbrecht, you'll be a full colonel in 1950, one arm and all.'

Garbrecht wanted to protest, say something, some word that would stop this careening, jovial, bloodthirsty, deluded lunatic, but he could get no sound out between his lips. Later on, perhaps, when he was alone, he might be able to figure some way out of this whirling trap. Not here, not in this tall, dark room, with the fat, shouting captain, the broken mirror, the sombre, incongruous, brooding picture of Lenin, Seedorf's obscure, mocking joke, that hung on the cracked wall.

'In the meantime,' Seedorf was saying, 'you continue your regular work. By God!' he laughed, 'you will be the richest man in Berlin when they all get through paying you!' His voice changed. It became low and probing. 'Do you know two men called Kleiber and Machewski who work out of Mikhailov's office?' He peered shrewdly at Garbrecht.

'No,' said Garbrecht after a moment. He knew them. They were both on Mikhailov's pay-roll and they worked in the American zone, but there was no sense in telling that, yet, to Seedorf.

'No matter,' Seedorf laughed, after an almost imperceptible pause. 'You will give their names and this address to your American Major.' He took a piece of paper from his pocket and put it down on the desk before him. 'You will tell the Major that they are Russian spies and that they can be found at this place.' He tapped the paper. 'It will be quite a haul for the Major,' Seedorf said ironically, 'and he will be sure to reward you handsomely. And he will have a very strong tendency after that to trust you with quite important matters.'

'Yes,' said Garbrecht.

'You're sure,' Seedorf said inquiringly, smiling a little at Garbrecht, 'you're sure you don't know these men?'

Then Garbrecht knew that Seedorf knew he was lying, but it was too late to do anything about it.

'I don't know them,' he said.

'I could have sworn . . .' Seedorf shrugged. 'No matter.' He got up from the desk, carrying the slip of paper, and came over to the chair where Garbrecht was sitting. 'Some day, my friend,' he said, putting his hand lightly on Garbrecht's shoulder, 'some day you will learn that you will have to trust me, too. As a matter of . . .' He laughed. 'A matter of discipline.'

He handed Garbrecht the slip of paper and Garbrecht put it in his pocket and stood up. 'I trust you, sir,' he said flatly. 'I have to.'

Seedorf laughed uproariously. 'I like a good answer,' he shouted. 'I do like a good answer.' He put his arm around Garbrecht in a brotherly hug. 'Remember,' he said, 'my first and only lesson – the one principle in being a hired informer is to tell the man who is paying you exactly what he wishes to hear. Any information must fit into theories which he already holds. Then he will trust you, pay you well, regard you as a more and more valuable employee. However . . .' and he laughed again, 'do not try to work this on me. I am different. I don't pay you . . . and therefore, I expect the truth. You will remember that?' He turned Garbrecht around quite roughly and peered into his eyes. He was not smiling now.

'Yes, sir,' said Garbrecht. 'I will remember it.'

'Good.' Seedorf pushed him towards the door. 'Now go down stairs and talk to Miss Renner. She will make all the arrangements.'

He pushed Garbrecht gently through the door and closed it sharply behind him. Garbrecht stared at the closed door for a moment, then walked slowly downstairs to Miss Renner.

Later, on the street, on his way to Mikhailov's office, he tried not to think of Seedorf's conversation or the ingenious, deadly device that even now was waiting for him on the other side of the city.

He felt like stopping and leaning his head against the cold, cracked brick wall of a gutted house he was passing, to weep and weep in the twisting, cutting wind. After so much, after all the fighting, all the death, after the operating-room in the brewery at Stalingrad, a man should be entitled to something, some peace, some security. And, instead, this onrushing dilemma, this flirtation with next week's death, this life of being scraped against every rock of the jagged year by every tide that crashed through Germany. Even numbness was no longer possible.

He shuffled on dazedly, not seeing where he was going. He stumbled over a piece of pavement that jutted crazily up from the sidewalk. He put out his hand to try to steady himself, but it was too late, and he fell heavily into the gutter. His head smashed against the concrete and he felt the hot laceration of broken stone on the palm of his hand.

He sat up and looked at his hand in the dim light. There was blood coming from the dirty, ripped wounds, and his head was pounding. He sat on the kerb, his head down, waiting for it to clear before he stood up. No escape, he thought, heavily, there never would be any escape. It was silly to hope for it. He stood up slowly and continued on his way to Mikhailov's office.

Mikhailov was crouched over his desk, the light of a single lamp making him look froglike and ugly as he sat there, without looking up at Garbrecht. '. . . Tell the man who is paying you exactly what he wishes to hear . . .' Garbrecht could almost hear Seedorf's mocking, hearty voice. Maybe Seedorf knew what he was talking about. Maybe the Russian was that foolish, maybe the American was that suspicious . . . Suddenly, Garbrecht knew what he was going to tell Mikhailov.

'Well?' Mikhailov said finally, still peering down at his desk. 'Anything important? Have you found out anything about that new man the Americans are using?'

Mikhailov had asked him to find out what he could about Dobelmeir last week, but Garbrecht had silently resolved to keep his mouth shut about the American. If he said too much, if he slipped once, Mikhailov would become suspicious, start prying, set someone on Garbrecht's trail. But now he spoke in a loud, even voice. 'Yes,' he said. 'He is a second generation German-American. He is a lawyer in Milwaukee in civilian life. He was under investigation early in the war because he was said to have contributed to the German-American Bund in 1939 and 1940.' Garbrecht saw

Mikhailov slowly raise his head and look at him, his eyes beginning to glisten with undisguised interest. It's working, Garbrecht thought, it actually is working. 'The case was never pressed,' he went on calmly with his invention, 'and he was given a direct commission late in the war and sent to Germany on special orders. Several members of his family are still alive in the British zone, Hamburg, and a cousin of his was a U-boat commander in the German Navy and was sunk off the Azores in 1943.'

'Of course,' said Mikhailov, his voice triumphant and satisfied. 'Of course. Typical.' He did not say what it was typical of, but he looked at Garbrecht with an expression that almost approached fondness.

'There are two things you might work on for the next few weeks,' Mikhailov said. 'We've asked everyone working out of this office to pick up what he can on this matter. We are quite sure that the Americans have shipped over a number of atomic bombs to Great Britain. We have reason to believe that they are being stored in Scotland, within easy distance of the airfield at Prestwick. There are flights in from Prestwick every day, and the crews are careless. I would like to find out if there are any preparations, even of the most preliminary kind, for basing a group of B-29s somewhere in that area. Skeleton repair shops, new fuel-storage tanks, new radar-warning stations, et cetera. Will you see if you can pick up anything?'

'Yes, sir,' said Garbrecht, knowing that, for Mikhailov's purpose, he would make certain to pick up a great deal.

'Very good,' said Mikhailov. He unlocked the drawer in his desk and took out the money. 'You will find a little bonus here,' he said with his mechanical smile.

'Thank you, sir,' said Garbrecht, picking up the money.

'Till next week,' Mikhailov said.

'Till next week,' said Garbrecht. He saluted and Mikhailov returned the salute as Garbrecht went out the door.

Although it was dark and cold outside, and his head was still throbbing from his fall, Garbrecht walked lightly, grinning to himself, as he moved towards the American zone.

He didn't see Dobelmeir till the next morning. 'You might be interested in these men,' he said, placing before the Major the slip of paper with the names of the men Seedorf had instructed him to denounce. 'They are paid agents for the Russians and the address is written down there, too.'

Dobelmeir looked at the names and a slow, delighted grin broke over his heavy face. 'Very, very interesting,' he said. 'Excellent.' His large hand went slowly over the crumpled paper, smoothing it out in a kind of dull caress. 'I've had some more inquiries for information about that Professor I asked you to check. Kittlinger. What did you find out?'

Garbrecht had found out, more by accident than anything else, that the Professor, an ageing, obscure physics teacher in the Berlin Medical School, had been killed in a concentration camp in 1944, but he was sure that there was no record anywhere of his death. 'Professor Kittlinger,' Garbrecht said glibly, 'was working on nuclear fission from 1934 to the end of the war. Ten days after the Russians entered Berlin, he was arrested and sent to Moscow. No word has been heard since.'

'Of course,' Dobelmeir said flatly. 'Of course.'

The atom, Garbrecht thought, with a slight touch of exhilaration, is a marvellous thing. It hangs over everything like a magic charm. Mention the atom and they will solemnly believe any bit of nonsense you feed them. Perhaps, he thought, grinning inwardly, I will become a specialist. Garbrecht, Atomic Secrets Limited. An easy, rich, overflowing, simple field.

Dobelmeir was industriously scratching down the doubtful history of Professor Kittlinger, Atomic Experimenter. For the first time since he had begun working for the Americans, Garbrecht realized that he was actually enjoying himself.

'You might be interested,' he said calmly, 'in something I picked up last night.'

Dobelmeir looked up assiduously from his desk. 'Of course,' he said gently.

'It probably doesn't amount to anything, just drunken, irresponsible raving . . .'

'What is it?' Dobelmeir leaned forward keenly.

'Three days ago a General Bryansky, who is on the Russian General Staff . . .'

'I know, I know,' said Dobelmeir impatiently. 'I know who he is. He's been in Berlin for a week now.'

'Well,' said Garbrecht, deliberately playing with Dobelmeir's impatience, 'he made a speech before a small group of officers at the Officers' Club, and later on he got quite drunk, and there are rumours about certain things that he said . . . I really don't know whether I ought to report anything as vague as this, as I said, just a rumour . . .'

'Go ahead,' Dobelmeir said hungrily. 'Let me hear it.'

'He is reported to have said that there will be war in sixty days. The atomic bomb is meaningless, he said. The Russian army can march to the Channel from the Elbe in twenty-five days. Then let the Americans use the atomic bomb on them. They will be in Paris, in Brussels, in Amsterdam, and the Americans won't dare touch them . . . Of course, I cannot vouch for this, but . . .'

'Of course he said it,' Dobelmeir said. 'Or, if he didn't, some other of those murderers did.' He leaned back wearily. 'I'll put it in the report. Maybe it'll make somebody wake up in Washington. And don't worry about reporting rumours. Very often there's more to be learned from a rumour than from the most heavily documented evidence.'

'Yes, sir,' said Garbrecht.

'I don't know,' said Dobelmeir, 'whether you heard about the bombing in Stuttgart yesterday.'

'Yes, sir. I did.'

'I have my own theory about it. There are going to be more, too, take my word for it. I think if you got to the bottom of it, you'd find our friends, the Russians, there. I want you to work on that, see what you can pick up this week . . .'

'Yes, sir,' Garbrecht said. What a wonderful man Seedorf is, Garbrecht thought. How astute, how correct in his intuition. How worthy of faith. He stood up. 'Is that all, sir?'

'That's all.' Dobelmeir handed him an envelope. 'Here's your money. You'll find two weeks' pay I held back in the beginning are added to this week's money.'

'Thank you very much, sir,' Garbrecht said.

'Don't thank me,' said the Major. 'You've earned it. See you next week.'

'Next week, sir.' Garbrecht saluted and went out.

There were two MPs standing at the door, in the clear winter sunshine, their equipment glittering, their faces bored. Garbrecht smiled and nodded at them, amused now, long in advance, as he thought of himself scornfully carrying the delicate parts of the first bomb past them, right under their noses.

He walked briskly down the street, breathing deeply the invigorating air, patting the small bulge under his coat where the money lay. He could feel the numbness that had held him for so long deserting him, but it was not pain that was taking its place, not pain at all.

The Man with One Arm, Irwin Shaw

On the Run

It was nearly ten o'clock. I walked to the King's Road and found a grill-room where I ordered about all the meat they had to be put on the bar and served to me. While I waited I entered the telephone box to call my club. I always stay there when I have to be in London, and that I should stay there this time I never doubted until the door of the box shut behind me. Then I found that I could not telephone my club.

What excuses I gave myself at the moment, I can't remember. I think I told myself that it was too late, that they wouldn't have a room, that I didn't wish to walk through the vestibule in those clothes and in that condition.

After my supper, I took a bus to Cromwell Road and put up at one of those hotels designed for gentlewomen in moderately distressed circumstances. The porter didn't much care about taking me in, but fortunately I had a couple of pound notes and they had a room with a private bath; since their regular clientèle could never afford such luxury, they were glad enough to let me the room. I gave them a false name and told them some absurd story to the effect that I had just arrived from abroad and had had my luggage stolen. To digest my meal I read a sheaf of morning and evening papers, and then went to my room.

Their water, thank God, was hot! I had the most pleasurable bath that I ever remember. I have spent a large part of my life out of reach of hot baths; yet, when I enjoy a tub at leisure, I wonder why any man voluntarily deprives himself of so cheap and satisfying a delight. It rested and calmed me more than any sleep; indeed, I had slept so much on the ship that my bath and my thoughts while lying in it had the flavour of morning rather than of night.

I understood why I had not telephoned my club. This was the first occasion on which I recognized that I had a second enemy dogging my movements – my own unjust and impossible conscience. Utterly unfair it was that I should judge myself as a potential murderer. I insist that I was always sure I could resist the temptation to press the trigger when my sights were actually on the target.

I have good reason now for a certain malaise. I have killed a man, though in self-defence. But then I had no reason at all. I may be wrong in talking of conscience; my trouble was, perhaps, merely a vision of the social effects of what I had done. This stalk of mine made it impossible for me to enter my club. How could I, for example, talk to Holy George after all the trouble I had caused him? And how could I expose my fellow members to the unpleasantness of being watched and perhaps questioned? No, I was an outlaw not because of my conscience (which, I maintain, has no right to torment me) but on the plain facts.

There was no lack of mirrors in the bathroom, and I made a

thorough examination of my body. My legs and backside were an ugly mess – I shall carry some extraordinary scars for life – but the wounds had healed, and there was nothing any doctor could do to help. My fingers still appeared to have been squashed in a railway carriage door and then sharpened with a pen-knife, but they were in fact serviceable for all but very rough or very sensitive work. The eye was the only part of me that needed attention. I didn't propose to have anyone monkeying with it – I dared not give up any freedom of movement for the sake of regular treatment or an operation – but I wanted a medical opinion and whatever lotions would do it the most good.

In the morning I changed all the foreign money in my possession, and bought myself a passable suit off the peg. Then I got a list of eye specialists and taxied round and about Harley Street until I found a man who would see me at once. He was annoyingly inquisitive. I told him that I had hurt the eye at the beginning of a long voyage and had been out of reach of medical care ever since. When he had fully opened the lid, he fumed over my neglect, folly, and idiocy, and declared that the eye had been burned as well as bruised. I agreed politely that it had and shut up; whereupon he became a doctor instead of a moralist and got down to business. He was honest enough to say that he could do nothing, that I'd be lucky if I ever perceived more than light and darkness, and that, on the whole, he recommended changing the real for a glass eye for the sake of appearance. He was wrong. My eye isn't pretty, but it functions better every day.

He wouldn't hear of my going about in dark glasses with no bandage, so I had him extend the bandages over the whole of my head. He humoured me in this, evidently thinking that I might get violent if opposed; my object was to give the impression of a man who had smashed his head rather than a man with a damaged eye. He was convinced that my face was familiar to him, and I allowed him to decide that we had once met in Vienna.

The next job was to see my solicitors in Lincoln's Inn Field's. The partner who has the entire handling of my estate is a man of about my own age and an intimate friend. He disapproves of me on only two grounds: that I refuse to sit on the board of any blasted company, and that I insist upon my right to waste money in agriculture. He doesn't mind my spending it on anything else, finding a vicarious pleasure in my travels and outlandish hobbies. He himself has a longing for a less ordered life, shown chiefly in his attitude to clothes. During the day he is sombrely and richly attired, and has even taken in recent years to wearing a black silk stock. At night he puts on tweeds, a sweater, and a tie that would frighten a newspaperman. One can't make him change for dinner. He would rather refuse an invitation.

Saul greeted me with concern rather than surprise; it was as if he had expected me to turn up in a hurry and the worse for wear. He locked the door and told his office manager we were not to be disturbed.

I assured him that I was all right and that the bandage was four times as long as was necessary. I asked what he knew and who had inquired for me.

He said that there had been a pointedly casual inquiry from Holy George, and that a few days later a fellow had come to consult him about some inconceivable tangle under the Married Women's Property Act.

'He was so perfectly the retired military man from the West of England,' said Saul, 'that I felt he couldn't be real. He claimed to be a friend and neighbour of yours and was continually referring to you. When I cross-examined him a bit, it looked as if he had mugged up his case out of a law book and was really after information. Major Quive-Smith, he called himself. Ever heard of him?'

'Never,' I replied. 'He certainly isn't a neighbour of mine. Was he English?'

'I thought so. Did you expect him not to be English?'

I said I wasn't answering any of his innocent questions, that he was, after all, an Officer of the Court, and that I didn't wish to involve him.

'Tell me this much,' he said. 'Have you been abroad in the employ of our government?'

'No, on my own business. But I have to disappear.'

'You shouldn't think of the police as tactless,' he reminded me gently. 'A man in your position is protected without question. You've been abroad so much that I don't think you have ever realized the power of your name. You're automatically trusted, you see.'

I told him that I knew as much of my own people as he did – perhaps more, since I had been an exile long enough to see them from the outside. But I had to vanish. There was a risk that I might be disgraced.

A nasty word, that. I am not disgraced, and I will not feel it.

'Can I vanish? Financially, I mean?' I asked him. 'You have my power of attorney and you know more of my affairs than I do myself. Can you go on handling my estate if I am never heard of again?'

'So long as I know you are alive.'

'What do you mean by that?'

'A postcard this time next year will do.'

'X marks my window, and this is a palm tree?'

'Quite sufficient if in your own handwriting. You needn't even sign it.'

'Mightn't you be asked for proof?' I inquired.

'No. If I say you are alive, why the devil should it ever be questioned? But don't leave me without a postcard from time to time. You mustn't put me in the position of maintaining what might be a lie.'

I told him that if he ever got one postcard, he'd probably get a lot more; it was my ever living to write the first that was doubtful.

He blew up and told me I was absurd. He mingled abuse with affection in a way I hadn't heard since my father died. I didn't think he would take my disappearance so hard; I suppose he is as fond of me, after all, as I am of him, and that's saying a lot. He begged me again to let him talk to the police. I had no idea, he insisted, of the number and the subtle beauty of the strings that could be pulled.

I could only say I was awfully sorry, and after a silence I told him I wanted £5000 pounds in cash.

He produced my deed box and accounts. I had a balance of £3000 at the bank; he wrote his own cheque for the other two. That was like him – no nonsense about waiting for sales of stock or arranging an overdraft.

'Shall we go out and lunch while the boy is at the Bank?' he suggested.

'I think I'll leave here only once,' I said.

'You might be watched? Well, we'll soon settle that.'

He sent for Peale, a grey little man in a grey little suit whom I had only seen emptying the waste-paper baskets or fetching cups of tea.

'Anybody taking an interest in us, Peale?'

'There is a person in the gardens between Remnant Street and here feeding the birds. He is not very successful with them, sir' – Peale permitted himself a dry chuckle – 'in spite of the fact that he has been there for the past week during office hours. And I understand from Pruce & Fothergill that there are two other persons in Newman's Row. One of them is waiting for a lady to come out of their offices – a matrimonial case, I believe. The other is not known to us and was observed to be in communication with the pigeon-man, sir, as soon as this gentleman emerged from his taxi.'

Saul thanked him and sent him out to fetch us some beer and a cold bird.

I asked where he watched from, having a vague picture of

Peale hanging over the parapet of the roof when he had nothing better to do.

'Good God, he doesn't watch!' exclaimed Saul, as if I had suggested a major impropriety. 'He just knows all the private detectives who are likely to be hanging around Lincoln's Inn Fields – on very good terms with them, I believe. They have to have a drink occasionally, and then they ask Peale or his counterpart in some other firm to keep his eyes open. When they see anyone who is not a member of the Trades Union, so to speak, they all know it.'

Peale came back with the lunch and a packet of information straight from the counter of the saloon bar. The bird-man had been showing great interest in our windows and had twice telephoned. The chap in Newman's Row had hailed my taxi as it drove away. He would be able to trace me back to Harley Street and to the clothes shop where, by a little adroit questioning, he could make an excuse to see the suit I discarded; my identification would be complete. It didn't much matter since the watchers already had a strong suspicion that I was their man.

Peale couldn't tell us whether another watcher had been posted in Newman's Row or whether the other exits from Lincoln's Inn Fields were watched. I was certain that they were and complained to Saul that all respectable firms of solicitors (who deal with far more scabrous affairs than the crooked) should have a back door. He replied that they weren't such fools as they looked and that Peale could take me into Lincoln's Inn or the Law Courts and lose me completely.

Perhaps I should have trusted them; but I felt that, while their tricks might be good enough to lose a single private detective, I shouldn't be allowed to escape so easily. I decided to throw off the hunt in my own way.

When I kept my gloves on to eat, Saul forgot his official discretion and became an anxious friend. I think he suspected what had happened to me, though not why it had happened. I had to beg him to leave the whole subject alone.

After lunch, I signed a number of documents to tidy up loose ends and we blocked out a plan I had often discussed with him of forming a sort of Tenants' Co-operative Society. Since I never make a penny out of the land, I thought they might as well pay rent to themselves, do their own repairs and advance their own loans, with the right to purchase their own land by instalments at a price fixed by the committee. I hope it works. At any rate Saul and my land agent will keep them from quarrelling among themselves. I have no other dependents.

Then I told him something of the fisherman and passed on the address that he had given me; we arranged for an income to be paid where it would do the most good – a discreet trust that couldn't conceivably be traced to me. It appeared to come from the estate of a recently defunct old lady who had left the bulk of her money to an institution for inoculating parrots against psittacosis, and the rest to any charitable object that Saul, as sole trustee, might direct.

There was nothing further to be done but arrange my cash in a body belt, and say goodbye. I asked him, if at any time a coroner sat on my body and brought in a verdict of suicide, not to believe it, but to make no attempt to reopen the case.

Peale walked with me across the square and into Kingsway by Gate Street. I observed that we were followed by a tall, inoffensive fellow in a dirty mackintosh and shabby felt hat, who was the bird-man. He looked the part. We also caught sight of a cheerful military man in Remnant Street, wearing a coat cut for riding and trousers narrower than were fashionable, whom Peale at once recognized as Major Quive-Smith. So I knew two at least whom I must throw off my track.

We parted at Holborn underground station and I took a shilling ticket with which I could travel to the remotest end of London. The bird-man had got ahead of me. I passed him on the level of the Central London and went down the escalator to the west-bound Piccadilly Tube. Ten seconds after I reached the platform Major Quive-Smith also appeared upon it. He was gazing at the advertisements and grinning at the comic ones, as if he hadn't been in London for a year.

I pretended I had forgotten something and shot out of the exit, up the stairs and down a corridor to the north-bound platform. No train was in. Even if there had been a train, the Major was too close behind for me to catch it and leave him standing.

I noticed that the shuttle train at the Aldwych left from the opposite side of the same platform. This offered a way of escape if ever there were two trains in at the same time.

The escalator took me back to the Central London level. The bird-man was talking to the chap in a glass-box at the junction of all the runways. I'd call him a ticket-collector but he never seems to collect any tickets; probably he is there to answer silly questions such as the bird-man was busily engaged in asking. I took the second escalator to the surface and promptly dashed down again.

The bird-man followed me, but a bit late. We passed each other about midway, he going up and I going down and both running like hell. I thought I had him, that I could reach a Central London train before he could; but he was taking no risks. He vaulted over the division on to the stationary staircase. We reached the bottom separated only by the extra speed of my moving staircase – and that was a mere ten yards. The man in the glass-box came to life and said: "Ere! You can't do that, you know!' But that didn't worry the bird-man. He was content to remain and discuss his anti-social action with the ticket-non-collector. I had already turned to the right into the Piccadilly Line and on to Major Quive-Smith's preserves.

At the bottom of the Piccadilly escalator you turn left for the north-bound trains and continue straight on for the west-bound. To the right is the exit, along which an old lady with two wide parcels was perversely trying to force her way against the stream of outcoming passengers. Major Quive-Smith was away to the left, at the mouth of the passage to the north-bound trains; so I plunged into the stream after the old lady, and was clear of it long before he was.

I ran on to the north-bound platform. An Aldwych shuttle was just pulling in, but there was no Piccadilly train. I shot under the Aldwych line, down to the west-bound platform, into the general exit, jamming him in another stream of outcoming passengers, and back to the north-bound Piccadilly. There was a train standing and the Aldwych shuttle had not left. I jumped into the Piccadilly train with the Major so far behind that he was compelled to enter another coach just as the doors were closing and just as I stepped out again. Having thus dispatched the Major to an unknown destination I got into the Aldwych shuttle which at once left on its half-mile journey.

This was all done at such a pace that I hadn't had time to think. I ought to have crossed to the west-bound Piccadilly and taken a train into the blue. But, naturally enough, I wanted to leave Holborn station as rapidly as possible, for fear of running into the bird-man or another unknown watcher if I waited. After half a minute in the Aldwych shuttle I realized that I had panicked like a rabbit in a warren. The mere couple of ferrets who had been after me had been magnified by my escape mechanism – a literal escape mechanism this, and working much faster than my mind – into an infinity of ferrets.

When we arrived at the Aldwych station and I was strolling to the lifts, I saw that it was not yet too late to return to Holborn. The bird-man would still be on the Central London level, for he might lose me if he left it for a moment. Quive-Smith couldn't have had time to telephone to anyone what had happened.

I turned back and re-entered the shuttle. The passengers were already seated in the single coach and the platform clear; but a man in a black hat and blue flannel suit got in after me. That meant that he had turned back when I had turned back.

At Holborn I remained seated to prove whether my suspicions were correct. They were. Black Hat got out, sauntered around the platform and got in again just before the doors closed. They had been far too clever for me! They had evidently ordered Black Hat to travel back and forth between Holborn and the Aldwych, and to go on travelling until either I entered that cursed coach or they gave him the signal that I had left by some other route. All I had done was to send Quive-Smith to Bloomsbury, whence no doubt he had already taken a taxi to some central clearing-point to which all news of my movements was telephoned.

As we left again for Aldwych, Black Hat was at the back of the coach and I was in the front. We sat as far away as possible from each other. Though we were both potential murderers, we felt, I suppose, mutual embarrassment. Mutual. I wish to God he had sat opposite me or shown himself in some way less human than I.

The Aldwych station is a dead end. A passenger cannot leave it except by the lift or the emergency spiral staircase. Nevertheless, I thought I had a wild chance of getting away. When the doors of the train opened I dashed on to and off the platform, round a corner to the left and up a few stairs; but instead of going ten yards farther, round to the right and so to the lift, I hopped into a little blank alley that I had noticed on my earlier walk.

There was no cover of any sort, but Black Hat did just what I hoped. He came haring up the corridor, pushing through the passengers with his eyes fixed straight ahead, and jumped for the emergency staircase. The ticket collector called him back. He shouted a question whether anyone had gone up the stairs. The ticket collector, in turn, asked was it likely. Black Hat then entered the lift and, in the time it took him to get there and to glance over the passengers, I was out of my alley and back on the platform.

The train was still in but, if I could catch it, so could Black Hat. The corridor was short, though with two right-angled twists, and he couldn't be more than five seconds behind me. I jumped on to the line and took refuge in the tunnel. There wasn't any employee of the Underground to see me except the driver and he was in his box at the front of the coach. The platform, of course, was empty.

Beyond the Aldwych station there seemed to be some fifty yards of straight tube, and then a curve, its walls faintly visible in a gleam of grey light. Where the tunnel goes, or if it ends in an old shaft after the curve, I didn't have time to find out.

Black Hat looked through the coach and saw that I wasn't in it. The train pulled out and when its roar had died away there was absolute silence. I hadn't realized that Black Hat and I would be left alone a hundred feet under London. I lay flattened against the wall in the darkest section of the tunnel.

The working of the Aldwych station is very simple. Just before the shuttle is due, the lift comes down. The departing passengers get into the train; the arriving passengers get into the lift. When the lift goes up and the train leaves, Aldwych station is deserted as an ancient mine. You can hear the drip of water and the beat of your heart.

I can still hear them, and the sound of steps and his scream and the hideous, because domestic, sound of sizzling. They echoed along that tunnel which leads lord knows where. A queer place for a soul to find itself adrift.

It was self-defence. He had a flash-light and a pistol. I don't know if he meant to use it. Perhaps he was only as frightened of me as I was of him. I crawled right to his feet and sprang at him. By God, I want to die in the open! If ever I have land again, I swear I'll never kill a creature below ground.

I lifted the bandages from my head and put them in my pocket; that expanse of white below my hat attracted too much attention to me. Then I came out, crossed the platform into the corridor and climbed a turn of the emergency stairs. As soon as the lift came down, I mingled with the departing passengers and waited for the train. When it came in, I went up in the lift with the new arrivals. I gave up my shilling ticket and received a surprised glance from the collector since the fare from Holborn was but a penny. The only alternative was to pretend I had lost my ticket and to pay; that would have meant still closer examination.

I left the station free, unwatched, unhurried, and took a bus back to the respectable squares of Kensington. Who would look for a fugitive between the Cromwell and Fulham roads? I dined at leisure, and then went to a cinema to think.

from *Rogue Male*, Geoffrey Household

Contact

Perhaps the strangest thing of all about prison was the brown-paper parcel when he left. In a ridiculous way it reminded him of the marriage service – with this ring I thee wed, with this paper parcel I return thee to society. They handed it to him and made him sign for it, and it contained all he had in the world. There was nothing else. Leamas felt it the most dehumanizing moment of the three months and he determined to throw the parcel away as soon as he got outside.

He seemed a quiet prisoner. There had been no complaints against him. The Governor, who was vaguely interested in his case, secretly put the whole thing down to the Irish blood he swore he could detect in Leamas.

'What are you going to do,' he asked, 'when you leave here?' Leamas replied, without a ghost of a smile, that he thought he would make a new start, and the Governor said that was an excellent thing to do.

'What about your family?' he asked. 'Couldn't you make it up with your wife?'

'I'll try,' Leamas had replied indifferently; 'but she's re-married.'

The probation officer wanted Leamas to become a male nurse at a mental home in Buckinghamshire and Leamas agreed to apply. He even took down the address and noted the train times from Marylebone.

'The rail's electrified as far as Great Missenden, now,' the probation officer added, and Leamas said that would be a help. So they gave him the parcel and he left. He took a bus to Marble Arch and walked. He had a bit of money in his pocket and he intended to give himself a decent meal. He thought he would walk through Hyde Park to Piccadilly, then through Green Park and St James's Park to Parliament Square, then wander down Whitehall to the Strand where he could go to the big café near Charing Cross Station and get a reasonable steak for six shillings.

London was beautiful that day. Spring was late and the parks were filled with crocuses and daffodils. A cool, cleaning wind was blowing from the south; he could have walked all day. But he still had the parcel and he had to get rid of it. The litter baskets were too small; he'd look absurd trying to push his parcel into one of those. He supposed there were one or two things he ought to take out, his wretched pieces of paper — insurance card, driving licence and his E.93 (whatever that was) in a buff OHMS envelope — but suddenly he couldn't be bothered. He sat down on a bench and put the parcel beside him, not too close, and moved a little away from it. After a couple of minutes he walked back towards the footpath, leaving the parcel where it lay. He had just reached the footpath when he heard a shout; he turned, a little sharply perhaps, and saw a man in an army mackintosh beckoning to him, holding the brown paper parcel in the other hand.

Leamas had his hands in his pockets and he left them there, and stood, looking back over his shoulder at the man in the mackintosh. The man hesitated, evidently expecting Leamas to come to him or give some sign of interest, but Leamas gave none. Instead, he shrugged and continued along the footpath. He heard another shout and ignored it, and he knew the man was coming after him. He heard the footsteps on the gravel, half running, approaching rapidly, and then a voice, a little breathless, a little aggravated:

'Here you – I say!' and then he had drawn level, so that Leamas stopped, turned and looked at him.

'Yes?'

'This is your parcel, isn't it? You left it on the seat. Why didn't you stop when I called you?'

Tall, with rather curly brown hair; orange tie and pale green shirt; a little bit petulant, a little bit of a pansy, thought Leamas. Could be a schoolmaster, ex-London School of Economics and runs a suburban drama club. Weak-eyed.

You can put it back,' said Leamas. 'I don't want it.'

The man coloured. 'You can't just leave it there,' he said, 'it's litter.'

'I bloody well can,' Leamas replied. 'Somebody will find a use for it.' He was going to move on, but the stranger was still standing in front of him, holding the parcel in both arms as if it were a baby. 'Get out of the light,' said Leamas. 'Do you mind?'

'Look here,' said the stranger, and his voice had risen a key, 'I was trying to do you a favour; why do you have to be so damned rude?'

'If you're so anxious to do me a favour,' Leamas replied, 'why have you been following me for the last half hour?'

He's pretty good, thought Leamas. He hasn't flinched but he must be shaken rigid.

'I thought you were somebody I once knew in Berlin, if you must know.'

'So you followed me for half an hour?'

Leamas's voice was heavy with sarcasm, his brown eyes never leaving the other's face.

'Nothing like half an hour. I caught sight of you in Marble Arch and I thought you were Alec Leamas, a man I borrowed some money from. I used to be in the BBC in Berlin and there was this man I borrowed some money from. I've had a bad conscience about it ever since and that's why I followed you. I wanted to be sure.'

Leamas went on looking at him, not speaking, and thought he wasn't all that good but he was good enough. His story was scarcely plausible – that didn't matter. The point was that he'd produced a new one and stuck to it after Leamas had wrecked what promised to be a classic approach.

'I'm Leamas,' he said at last. 'Who the hell are you?'

He said his name was Ashe, with an 'e' he added quickly, and Leamas knew he was lying. He pretended not to be quite sure that Leamas really was Leamas, so over lunch they opened the parcel and looked at the National Insurance card like, thought Leamas, a couple of sissies looking at a dirty postcard. Ashe ordered lunch with just a fraction too little regard for expense, and they drank some Frankenwein to remind them of the old days. Leamas began by insisting he couldn't remember Ashe, and Ashe said he was surprised. He said it in the sort of tone that suggested he was hurt. They met at a party, he said, which Derek Williams gave in his flat off the Ku-damm (he got that right), and all the press boys had been there; surely Alec remembered that? No, Leamas did not. Well surely he remembered Derek Williams from the *Observer*, that *nice* man who gave such lovely pizza parties? Leamas had a lousy memory for names, after all they were talking about '54; a lot of water had flown under the bridge since then . . . Ashe remembered (his Christian name was William, by-the-bye, most people called him Bill), Ashe remembered *vividly*. They'd been drinking stingers, brandy and crême de menthe, and were all rather tiddly, and Derek had provided some really gorgeous girls, half the cabaret from the Malkasten, *surely* Alec remembered now? Leamas thought it was probably coming back to him, if Bill would go on a bit.

Bill did go on, ad-lib no doubt, but he did it well, playing up the sex side a little, how they'd finished up in a night club with three of these girls; Alec, a chap from the political adviser's office and Bill, and Bill had been so embarrassed because he hadn't any money on him and Alec had paid, and Bill had wanted to take a girl home and Alec had lent him another tenner—

'Christ,' said Leamas, 'I remember now, of course I do.'

'I *knew* you would,' said Ashe happily, nodding at Leamas over his glass. 'Look, do let's have the other half, this is *such* fun.'

Ashe was typical of that strata of mankind which conducts its human relationships according to a principle of challenge and response. Where there was softness, he would advance; where he found resistance, retreat. Having himself no particular opinions or tastes, he relied upon whatever conformed with those of his companion. He was as ready to drink tea at Fortnum's as beer at the Prospect of Whitby; he would listen to military music in St James's Park or jazz in a Compton Street cellar; his voice would tremble with sympathy when he spoke of Sharpeville, or with indignation at the growth of Britain's coloured population. To Leamas this observably passive role was repellent; it brought out the bully in him, so that he would lead the other gently into a position where he was committed, and then himself withdraw, so that Ashe was constantly scampering back from some cul-de-sac into which Leamas had enticed him. There were moments that afternoon when Leamas was so brazenly perverse that Ashe would have been justified in terminating their conversation – especially since he was paying; but he did not. The little sad man with spectacles who sat alone at the neighbouring table, deep in a book on the manufacture of ball bearings, might have deduced, had he been listening, that Leamas was indulging a sadistic nature – or perhaps (if he had been a man of particular subtlety) that Leamas was proving to his own satisfaction that only a man with a strong ulterior motive would put up with that kind of treatment.

It was nearly four o'clock before they ordered the bill, and Leamas tried to insist on paying his half. Ashe wouldn't hear of it, paid the bill and took out his cheque-book in order to settle his debt to Leamas.

'Twenty of the best,' he said, and filled in the date on the cheque.

Then he looked up at Leamas, all wide-eyed and accommodating. 'I say, a cheque is all right with you, isn't it?'

Colouring a little, Leamas replied, 'I haven't got a bank at the moment – only just back from abroad, something I've got to fix up. Better give me a cheque and I'll cash it at your bank.'

'My dear chap, I wouldn't *dream* of it! You'd have to go to Rotherhithe to cash this one!' Leamas shrugged and Ashe laughed, and they agreed to meet at the same place on the following day, at one o'clock, when Ashe would have the money in cash.

On the following day, Leamas arrived twenty minutes late for his lunch with Ashe, and smelled of whisky. Ashe's pleasure on catching sight of Leamas was, however, undiminished. He claimed that he had, himself, only that moment arrived, he'd been a little late getting to the bank. He handed Leamas an envelope.

'Singles,' said Ashe. 'I hope that's all right?'

'Thanks,' Leamas replied, 'let's have a drink.' He hadn't shaved and his collar was filthy. He called the waiter and ordered drinks, a large whisky for himself and a pink gin for Ashe. When the drinks came, Leamas's hand trembled as he poured the soda into the glass, almost slopping it over the side.

They lunched well, with a lot to drink, and Ashe did most of the work. As Leamas had expected he first talked about himself, an old trick but not a bad one.

'To be quite frank, I've got on to rather a good thing recently,' said Ashe; 'freelancing English features for the foreign press. After Berlin I made rather a mess of things at first – the Corporation wouldn't renew the contract and I took a job running a dreary toffee-shop weekly about hobbies for the over-sixties. Can you *imagine* anything more frightful? That went under in the first printing strike – can't tell you how relieved I was. Then I went to live with my mama in Cheltenham for a time – she runs an antique shop, does very nicely thank you, as a matter of fact. Then I got a letter from an old friend, Sam Kiever his name is actually, who was starting up a new agency for small features on English life specially slanted for foreign papers. You know the sort of thing – 600 words on Morris dancing. Sam had a new gimmick, though; he sold the stuff already translated and, do you know, it makes a hell of a difference. One always imagines anyone can pay a translator or do it themselves, but if you're looking for a half column in-fill for your foreign features you don't *want* to waste time and money on translation. Sam's gambit was to get in touch with the editors direct – he traipsed round Europe like a gypsy, poor thing, but it's paid hands *down*.'

Ashe paused, waiting for Leamas to accept the invitation to speak about himself, but Leamas ignored it. He just nodded dully and said, 'Bloody good.' Ashe had wanted to order wine, but Leamas said he'd stick to whisky, and by the time the coffee came he'd had four large ones. He seemed to be in bad shape; he had the drunkard's habit of ducking his mouth towards the rim of his glass just before he drank, as if his hand might fail him and the drink escape.

Ashe fell silent for a moment.

'You don't know Sam, do you?' he asked.

'Sam?'

A note of irritation entered Ashe's voice.

'Sam Kiever, my boss. The chap I was telling you about.'

'Was he in Berlin too?'

'No. He knows Germany well, but he's never lived in Berlin. He did a bit of deviling in Bonn, freelance stuff. You might have met him. He's a dear.'

'Don't think so.' A pause.

'What do you do these days, old chap?' asked Ashe.

Leamas shrugged. 'I'm on the shelf,' he replied, and grinned a little stupidly. 'Out of the bag and on the shelf.'

'I forget what you were doing in Berlin. Weren't you one of the mysterious cold warriors?'

My God, thought Leamas, you're stepping things up a bit. Leamas hesitated, then coloured and said savagely, 'Office boy for the bloody Yanks, like the rest of us.'

'You know,' said Ashe, as if he had been turning the idea over for some time, 'you ought to meet Sam. You'd like him,' and then, all of a bother, 'I say, Alec – don't even know where to get hold of you!'

'You can't,' Leamas replied listlessly.

'I don't get you, old chap. Where are you staying?'

'Around the place. Roughing it a bit. I haven't got a job. Bastards wouldn't give me a proper pension.'

Ashe looked horrified.

'But Alec, that's awful, why didn't you *tell* me? Look, why not come and stay at my place? It's only tiny but there's room for one more if you don't mind a camp bed. You can't just live in the trees, my dear chap!'

'I'm all right for a bit,' Leamas replied, tapping at the pocket which contained the envelope. 'I'm going to get a job.' He nodded with determination. 'Get one in a week or so. Then I'll be all right.'

'What sort of job?'

'Oh, I don't know. Anything.'

'But you can't just throw yourself away, Alec! You speak German like a native, I remember you do. There must be all sorts of things you can do!'

'I've done all sorts of things. Selling encyclopaedias for some bloody American firm, sorting books in a psychic library, punching work tickets in a stinking glue factory. What the hell *can* I do?' He wasn't looking at Ashe but at the table before him, his agitated lips moving quickly. Ashe responded to his animation, leaning forward across the table, speaking with emphasis, almost triumph.

'But Alec, you need *contacts*, don't you see? I know what it's like, I've been on the breadline myself. That's when you need to *know* people. I don't know what you were doing in Berlin, I don't want to know, but it wasn't the sort of job where you could meet people who matter, was it? If I hadn't met Sam at Poznan five years ago I'd *still* be on the breadline. Look, Alec, come and stay with me for a week or so. We'll ask Sam around and perhaps one or two of the old press boys from Berlin if any of them are in town.'

'But I can't write,' said Leamas. 'I couldn't write a bloody thing.'

Ashe had his hand on Leamas's arm. 'Now don't fuss,' he said soothingly. 'Let's just take things one at a time. Where are your bits and pieces?'

'My what?'

'Your things: clothes, baggage and what not?'

'I haven't got any. I've sold what I had – except the parcel.'

'What parcel?'

'The brown-paper parcel you picked up in the park. The one I was trying to throw away.'

Ashe had a flat in Dolphin Square. It was just what Leamas had expected – small and anonymous with a few hastily assembled curios from Germany: beer mugs, a peasant's pipe and a few pieces of second-rate Nymphenburg.

'I spend the weekends with my mother in Cheltenham,' he said. 'I just use this place midweek. It's pretty handy,' he added deprecatingly. They fixed the camp bed up in the tiny drawing room. It was about four-thirty.

'How long have you been here?' asked Leamas.

'Oh – about a year or more.'

'Find it easily?'

'They come and go, you know, these flats. You put your name down and one day they ring you up and tell you you've made it.'

Ashe made tea and they drank it, Leamas sullen, like a man not used to comfort. Even Ashe seemed a little subdued. After tea Ashe said, 'I'll go out and do a spot of shopping before the shops close, then we'll decide what to do about everything. I might give Sam a tinkle later this evening – I think the sooner you two get together the better. Why don't you get some sleep – you look all in.'

Leamas nodded. 'It's bloody good of you' – he made an awkward gesture with his hand – 'all this.' Ashe gave him a pat on the shoulder, picked up his army mackintosh and left.

As soon as Leamas reckoned Ashe was safely out of the building he left the front door of the flat slightly ajar and made his way downstairs to the centre hall where there were two telephone booths. He dialled a Maida Vale number and asked for Mr Thomas's secretary. Immediately a girl's voice said, 'Mr Thomas's secretary speaking.'

'I'm ringing on behalf of Mr Sam Kiever,' Leamas said. 'He has accepted the invitation and hopes to contact Mr Thomas personally this evening.'

'I'll pass that on to Mr Thomas. Does he know where to get in touch with you?'

'Dolphin Square,' Leamas replied, and gave the address. 'Good-bye.'

After making some inquiries at the reception desk, he returned to Ashe's flat and sat on the camp bed looking at his clasped hands. After a while he lay down. He decided to accept Ashe's advice and get some rest. As he closed his eyes he remembered Liz lying beside him in the flat in Bayswater, and he wondered vaguely what had become of her.

He was wakened by Ashe, accompanied by a small, rather plump man with long, greying hair swept back and a double-breasted suit. He spoke with a slight central European accent; German perhaps, it was hard to tell. He said his name was Kiever – Sam Kiever.

They had a gin and tonic, Ashe doing most of the talking. It was just like old times, he said, in Berlin: the boys together and the night their oyster. Kiever said he didn't want to be too late; he had to work tomorrow. They agreed to eat at a Chinese restaurant that Ashe knew of – it was opposite Limehouse police station and you brought your own wine. Oddly enough, Ashe had some Burgundy in the kitchen and they took that with them in the taxi.

Dinner was very good and they drank two bottles of wine. Kiever opened up a little on the second; he'd just come back from a tour of West Germany and France. France was in a hell of a mess, de Gaulle was on the way out, and God alone knew what would happen then. With 100,000 demoralized *colonis* returning from Algeria he reckoned fascism was in the cards.

'What about Germany?' asked Ashe, prompting him.

'It's just a question of whether the Yanks can hold them.' Kiever looked invitingly at Leamas.

'What do you mean?' asked Leamas.

'What I say. Dulles gave them a foreign policy with one hand, Kennedy takes it away with the other. They're getting waspish.'

Leamas nodded abruptly and said, 'Bloody typical Yank.'

'Alec doesn't seem to like our American cousins,' said Ashe, stepping in heavily, and Kiever, with complete disinterest, murmured, 'Oh really?'

Kiever played it, Leamas reflected, very long. Like someone used to horses, he let you come to him. He conveyed to perfection a man who suspected that he was about to be asked a favour, and was not easily won.

After dinner Ashe said, 'I know a place in Wardour Street – you've been there, Sam. They do you all right there. Why don't we summon a cab and go along?'

'Just a minute,' said Leamas, and there was something in his voice which made Ashe look at him quickly. 'Just tell me something, will you? Who's paying for this jolly?'

'I am,' said Ashe quickly. 'Sam and I.'
'Have you discussed it?'
'Well – no.'
'Because I haven't got any bloody money; you know that, don't you? None to throw about, anyway.'
'Of course, Alec. I've looked after you up till now, haven't I?'
'Yes,' Leamas replied. 'Yes, you have.'

He seemed to be going to say something else, and then to change his mind. Ashe looked worried, not offended, and Kiever as inscrutable as before.

Leamas refused to speak in the taxi. Ashe attempted some conciliatory remark and he just shrugged irritably. They arrived at Wardour Street and dismounted, neither Leamas nor Kiever making any attempt to pay for the cab. Ashe led them past a shop window full of 'girlie' magazines, down a narrow alley, at the far end of which shone a tawdry neon sign: PUSSYWILLOW CLUB – MEMBERS ONLY. On either side of the door were photographs of girls, and pinned across each was a thin, hand-printed strip of paper which read *Nature Study. Members Only.*

Ashe pressed the bell. The door was at once opened by a very large man in a white shirt and black trousers.

'I'm a member,' Ashe said. 'These two gentlemen are with me.'
'See your card?'

Ashe took a buff card from his wallet and handed it over.

'Your guests pay a quid a head, temporary membership. Your recommendation, right?' He held out the card and, as he did so, Leamas stretched past Ashe and took it. He looked at it for a moment, then handed it back to Ashe.

Taking £2 from his hip pocket, Leamas put them into the waiting hand of the man at the door.

'Two quid,' said Leamas, 'for the guests,' and ignoring the astonished protests of Ashe he guided them through the curtained doorway into the dim hallway of the club. He turned to the doorman.

'Find us a table,' said Leamas, 'and a bottle of Scotch. And see we're left alone.'

The doorman hesitated for a moment, decided not to argue and escorted them downstairs. As they descended they heard the subdued moan of unintelligible music. They got a table on their own at the back of the room. A two-piece band was playing and girls sat around in twos and threes. Two got up as they came in but the big doorman shook his head.

Ashe glanced at Leamas uneasily while they waited for the whisky. Kiever seemed slightly bored. The waiter brought a bottle and three tumblers and they watched in silence as he poured a little whisky into each glass. Leamas took the bottle from the waiter and added as much again to each. This done, he leaned across the table and said to Ashe, 'Now perhaps you'll tell me what the bloody hell's going on.'

'What do you mean?' Ashe sounded uncertain. 'What *do* you mean, Alec?'

'You followed me from prison the day I was released,' he began quietly, 'with some bloody silly story of meeting me in Berlin. You gave me money you didn't owe me. You've bought me expensive meals and you're putting me up in your flat.'

Ashe coloured and said, 'If that's the—'

'Don't interrupt,' said Leamas fiercely. 'Just damn well wait till I've finished, do you mind? Your membership card for this place is made out for someone called Murphy. Is that your name?'

'No, it is not.'

'I suppose a friend called Murphy lent you his membership card?'

'No, he didn't as a matter of fact. If you must know, I come here occasionally to find a girl. I used a phony name to join the club.'

'Then why,' Leamas persisted ruthlessly, 'is Murphy registered as the tenant of your flat?'

It was Kiever who finally spoke.

'You run along home,' he said to Ashe. 'I'll look after this.'

A girl performed a striptease, a young, drab girl with a dark bruise on her thigh. She had that pitiful, spindly nakedness which is embarrassing because it is not erotic; because it is artless and undesiring. She turned slowly, jerking sporadically with her arms and legs as if she only heard the music in snatches, and all the time she looked at them with the precocious interest of a child in adult company. The tempo of the music increased abruptly and the girl responded like a dog to the whistle, scampering back and forth. Removing her brassiere on the last note, she held it above her head, displaying her meagre body with its three tawdry patches of tinsel hanging from it like old Christmas tree decorations.

They watched in silence, Leamas and Kiever.

'I suppose you're going to tell me that we've seen better in Berlin,' Leamas suggested at last, and Kiever saw that he was still very angry.

'I expect *you* have,' Kiever replied pleasantly. 'I have often been to Berlin, but I am afraid I dislike night clubs.'

Leamas said nothing.

'I'm no prude, mind, just rational. If I want a woman I know cheaper ways of finding one; if I want to dance I know better places to do it.'

Leamas might not have been listening. 'Perhaps you'll tell me why that sissy picked me up,' he suggested. Kiever nodded.

'By all means. I told him to.'

'Why?'

'I am interested in you. I want to make you a proposition, a journalistic proposition.'

There was a pause.

'Journalistic,' Leamas repeated. 'I see.'

'I run an agency, an international feature service. It pays well – very well – for interesting material.'

'Who publishes the material?'

'It pays so well, in fact, that a man with your kind of experience of . . . the international scene, a man with your background, you understand, who provided convincing, factual material, could free himself in a comparatively short time from further financial worry.'

'Who publishes the material, Kiever?' There was a threatening edge to Leamas's voice, and for a moment, just for a moment, a look of apprehension seemed to pass across Kiever's smooth face.

'International clients. I have a correspondent in Paris who disposes of a good deal of my stuff. Often I don't even know who *does* publish. I confess,' he added with a disarming smile, 'that I don't awfully care. They pay and they ask for more. They're the kind of people, you see, Leamas, who don't fuss about awkward details; they pay promptly and they're happy to pay into foreign banks, for instance, where no one bothers about things like tax.'

Leamas said nothing. He was holding his glass with both hands, staring into it.

Christ, they're rushing their fences, Leamas thought; it's indecent. He remembered some silly music-hall joke – 'This is an offer no respectable girl could accept – and besides, I don't know what it's worth.' Tactically, he reflected, they're right to rush it. I'm down and out, prison experience still fresh, social resentment strong. I'm an old horse, I don't need breaking in; I don't have to pretend they've offended my honour as an English gentleman.

On the other hand they would expect *practical* objections. They would expect him to be afraid; for his Service pursued traitors as the eye of God followed Cain across the desert. And, finally, they would know it was a gamble. They would know that inconsistency in human decision can make nonsense of the best-planned espionage approach; that cheats, liars and criminals may resist every blandishment while respectable gentlemen have been moved to appalling treasons by watery cabbage in a departmental canteen.

'They'd have to pay a hell of a lot,' Leamas muttered at last. Kiever gave him some more whisky.

'They are offering a down payment of £15,000. The money is already lodged at the Banque Cantonale in Bern. On production of a suitable identification, with which my clients will provide you, you can draw the money. My clients reserve the right to put questions to you over the period of one year on payment of another £5000. They will assist you with any . . . resettlement problems that may arise.'

'How soon do you want an answer?'

'Now. You are not expected to commit all your reminiscences to paper. You will meet my client and he will arrange to have the material . . . ghost written.'

'Where am I supposed to meet him?'

'We felt for everybody's sake it would be simplest to meet outside the United Kingdom. My client suggested Holland.'

'I haven't got my passport,' Leamas said dully.

'I took the liberty of obtaining one for you,' Kiever replied suavely; nothing in his voice or his manner indicated that he had done other than negotiate an adequate business arrangement. 'We're flying to The Hague tomorrow morning at nine forty-five. Shall we go back to my flat and discuss any other details?'

Kiever paid and they took a taxi to a rather good address not far from St James's Park.

Kiever's flat was luxurious and expensive, but its contents somehow gave the impression of having been hastily assembled. It is said there are shops in London which will sell you bound books by the yard, and interior decorators who will harmonize the colour scheme of the walls with that of a painting. Leamas, who was not particularly receptive to such subtleties, found it hard to remember that he was in a private flat and not a hotel. As Kiever showed him to his room (which looked on to a dingy inner courtyard and not on to the street) Leamas asked him:

'How long have you been here?'

'Oh, not long,' Kiever replied lightly, 'a few months, not more.'

'Must cost a packet. Still, I suppose you're worth it.'

'Thanks.'

There was a bottle of Scotch in his room and a syphon of soda on a silver-plated tray. A curtained doorway at the farther end of the room led to a bathroom and lavatory.

'Quite a little love nest. All paid for by the great Worker State?'

'Shut up,' said Kiever savagely, and added, 'If you want me, there's an intercom telephone to my room. I shall be awake.'

'I think I can manage my buttons now,' Leamas retorted. 'Then good night,' said Kiever shortly, and left the room. He's on edge, too, thought Leamas.

Leamas was awakened by the telephone at his bedside. It was Kiever.

'It's six o'clock,' he said, 'breakfast at half past.'

'All right,' Leamas replied, and rang off. He had a headache.

Kiever must have telephoned for a taxi, because at seven o'clock the doorbell rang and Kiever asked, 'Got everything?'

'I've no luggage,' Leamas replied, 'except a toothbrush and a razor.'

'That is taken care of. Are you ready otherwise?'

Leamas shrugged. 'I suppose so. Have you any cigarettes?'

'No,' Kiever replied, 'but you can get some on the plane. You'd better look through this,' he added, and handed Leamas a British passport. It was made out in his name with his own photograph mounted in it, embossed by a deep-press Foreign Office seal running across the corner. It was neither old nor new; it described Leamas as a clerk and gave his status as single. Holding it in his hand for the first time, Leamas was a little nervous. It was like getting married: whatever happened, things would never be the same again.

'What about money?' Leamas asked.

'You don't need any. It's on the firm.'

from *The Spy Who Came in from the Cold*, John le Carré

In contrast, I have included a beautiful set-piece by Len Deighton, describing the flashy, double-dealing German freelance spy, Johnny Vulkan, musing elegantly among cronies and accomplices in a West Berlin night club. Before the Wall came down, of course . . .

Johnnie Vulkan

Wednesday, 9 October

'Oh boy,' thought Johnnie Vulkan *Edelfresswelle* – a great calorific abundance of everything but faith – and quite frankly it was great. There were times when he saw himself as an untidy recluse in some village in the Bavarian woods, with ash down his waistcoat and his head full of genius, but tonight he was glad he had become what he had become. Johnnie Vulkan, wealthy, attractive and a personification of *Knallhärte* – the tough, almost violent quality that post-war Germany rewarded with admiring glances. The health cures at Worishofen had tempered him to a supple resilience and that's what you needed to stay on top in this town – this was no place for an intellectual today, whatever it may have been in the thirties.

He was glad the Englishman had gone. One could have too much of the English. They ate fish for breakfast and always wanted to know where they gave the best rate of exchange. The whole place was reflected in the coloured mirror. The women were dressed in sleek shiny gowns and the men were wearing 1000-mark suits. It looked like those advertisements for bourbon that one saw in *Life* magazine. He sipped his whisky and eased his foot on to the foot-rail of the bar. Anyone coming in would take him for an American. Not one of those crummy stringers who hung around writing groundless rumours with 'Our special correspondent in Berlin' on the dateline, but one of the Embassy people or one of the businessmen like the one sitting against the wall with the blonde. Johnny looked at the blonde again. Boy, oh boy! He could see what kind of suspender belt *she* was wearing. He flashed her a smile. She smiled back. A fifty-mark lay, he thought, and lost interest. He called the barman and ordered another bourbon. It was a new barman.

'Bourbon,' he said. He liked to hear himself saying that. 'Plenty of ice this time,' he said. The barman brought it and said, 'The right money, please, I am short of change.' The barman said it in German. It made Vulkan annoyed.

Vulkan tapped a Philip Morris on his thumbnail and noticed how brown his skin was against the white cigarette. He put the cigarette in his mouth and snapped his fingers. The bloody fool must have been half-asleep.

Along the bar there were a couple of tourists and a newspaper writer named Poetsch from Ohio. One of the tourists asked if Poetsch went across to the 'other side' very much.

'Not much,' Poetsch said. 'The Commies have me marked down on their black list.' He laughed modestly. Johnnie Vulkan said an obscene word loud enough for the barman to look up. The barman grinned at Johnnie and said, 'Mir kann keener.'*

Poetsch didn't speak German so he didn't notice.

There were lots of radio men here tonight: Americans with the

---

*Mir kann keener: you can't fool me (a typical Berliner comment).

blunt accents of their fathers who spoke strange Slav dialects over the jammed night air. One of them waved to Vulkan but didn't beckon him across. That was because they considered themselves the cultural set of the city. Really they were mental lightweights equipped with a few thousand items of cocktail-time small talk. They wouldn't know a string quartet from a string vest.

The barman lit his cigarette for him.

'Thanks,' said Johnnie. He made a mental note to cultivate the barman in the near future, not for the purpose of getting information – he hadn't sunk to that peanut circuit yet – but because it made life easier in a town like this. He sipped his bourbon and tried to think of a way to appease London. Vulkan felt glad that Dawlish's boy was heading back to London. He was all right as the English go, but you never knew where you were with him. That's because the English were amateurs – and proud of it. There were some days when Johnnie wished that he was working for the Americans. He had more in common with them, he felt.

All around there was a rumble of courteous conversation. The man with nose, moustache and spectacles that looked like a one-piece novelty was an English MP. He had the managerial voice that the English upper class used for hailing taxis and foreigners.

'But *here* in the actual city of Berlin,' the Englishman was saying, 'taxes are twenty per cent *below* your West German taxes and what's more your chaps at Bonn *waive* the four per cent on transactions. With a bit of wangling they will insure your freight free and if you bring in steel you have it carted *virtually* without charge. No businessman can afford to overlook it, old chap. What line of business you in?' The Englishman brushed both ends of his moustache and sniffed loudly.

Vulkan smiled to a man from the Jewish Documentation Section. That was a job Vulkan would enjoy, but the pay was very small, he heard. The Jewish Documentation Section in Vienna collected material about war crimes to bring ex-SS men to trial. There was plenty of work about, Vulkan thought. He looked through the tobacco smoke; he could count at least five ex-SS officers in here at this moment.

'Best thing that ever *happened* to the British motor-car industry.' The Englishman's loud voice cut the air again.

'Your Volkswagen people felt the draught in *no* time. Ha ha. Lost a source of cheap labour and found the trade union johnnies dunning them for money. What happened? *Up* went the price of the Volkswagen. Gave our chaps a chance. Say what you like, *best* thing that ever happened to the British motor-car industry, that wall.'

Johnnie fingered the British passport in his pocket. Well, the wall didn't make much difference to him. He preferred it, in fact. If the communists hadn't stopped all their riff-raff streaming across here in search of jobs, then where would they have got people to work in the factories? Johnnie knew where they would have got them: from the East. Who wanted to go swimming out on the Müggelsee and have it full of Mongolians and Ukrainians? Lot of chance there would be then of restoring East Prussia, Pomerania and Silesia to Germany. Not that Vulkan gave a damn about the 'lost territories' but some of these loud-mouths, who did, shouldn't shout about the wall so much.

There was a girl from Wedding. He wondered whether it was true what they said about her chauffeur. It was a strange place for a girl like her to live, horrible low-class district. That tiny house with the TV set over the bed. He had put that Scots colonel on to her. What was it he had said afterwards about her wanting a 21-inch model with colour and remote control? Vulkan remembered how the whole bar had laughed at the time. Vulkan blew her a kiss and wrinkled his eyes in greeting. She waved a small gold-mesh evening bag at him. She was still sexy, Vulkan thought, and in spite of all his resolution found himself sending the barman across to her with a champagne cocktail. He wrote a little note to go with it. He wrote the note with a small gold propelling pencil on the back of an engraved visiting card.

'Take dinner with me,' he wrote. He debated whether to add a query but decided that women hate indecision. Domination was the secret of success with women.

'Will join you later,' he added, before giving it to the barman.

Two more people had joined Poetsch down at the far end of the bar; a man and a girl. The man looked English. Poetsch said, 'You saw it, did you? We call it the "wall of shame", as you know. I'd like to show it to every living person in the world.'

A man called 'Colonel Wilson' winked at Vulkan. To do this, 'Colonel Wilson' had to remove a large pair of dark glasses. Around his left eye and upper cheek there was a mesh of scars. Wilson slid a cigar along the bar to Vulkan.

'Thanks, Colonel,' Vulkan called. Wilson was an ex-corporal cook who had got his scars from spluttering fat in a mess hall in Omaha. It was a good cigar. 'Colonel' wouldn't be such a fool as to give him a cheap one. Vulkan smelled it, rolled it and then decapitated it scientifically with a small, flat gold cigar-cutter that he kept in his top pocket. A gold guillotine. An amalgam of sharp steel and burnished gold. The barman lit the cigar for him.

'Always with a match,' Vulkan told him. 'A match held a quarter of an inch away from the leaf. Gas lighters never.' The barman nodded. Before Vulkan had the cigar properly alight, 'Colonel' had moved alongside him at the bar. 'Colonel Wilson' was six feet one-and-a-half inches of leathery skin encasing meaty sinew, packed dense like a well-made *Bockwurst*. His face was grey and lined; his hair trimmed to the skull. He could have made a living in Hollywood playing in the sort of film where the villains have thick lips. He ordered two bourbons.

Vulkan could hear Poetsch saying, 'Truth – I'm fond of saying – is the most potent weapon in the arsenal of freedom.' Poetsch *was* fond of saying that, Vulkan thought. He knew that 'Colonel Wilson' wanted something. He drank the bourbon quickly. 'Colonel Wilson' ordered two more. Vulkan looked at the barman and tipped his head a millimetre towards the girl from Wedding. The barman lowered his eyelids. It was one of the great things about this town, thought Vulkan, this sensitivity to signs and innuendo. He heard the English MP's voice, 'Good heavens, *no*. *We* have a few tricks left up our sleeve *I* can tell you.' The English MP chortled.

The British were deadly, Vulkan decided. He remembered his last visit there. The big hotel in Cromwell Road and the rain that never stopped for a week. A nation of inventive geniuses where there are forty different types of electrical plug, none of which works efficiently. Milk is safe on the street but young girls in danger, sex indecent but homosexuality acceptable, a land as far north as Labrador with unheated houses, where hospitality is so rare that 'landlady' is a pejorative word, where the most boastful natives in the world tell foreigners that the only British shortcoming is modesty.

Vulkan winked to the girl from Wedding. She smoothed her dress slowly and touched the nape of her neck. Vulkan turned to 'Colonel Wilson' and said, 'OK, what's on your mind?'

'I want thirty-nine Praktika cameras; with the f/2 lens.'

Vulkan reached for a piece of ice from the canister on the bar. The piano-player did a fancy cadenza and stopped playing. Vulkan put his cigar in his mouth and clapped his hands. His face scowled at the ribbon of smoke. Several people joined in the applause. Vulkan said, 'Do you?' still looking at the piano-player.

'Good price and in dollars,' said Colonel Wilson. There was no reply from Vulkan.

Wilson said, 'I know that you don't do that kind of thing for a living; but this is a special favour for a friend of mine. It's more of a memento – you know, a camera smuggled out of the East – these guys like that kind of thing.'

'What guys?' said Vulkan.
'Trade delegation,' said Wilson.
'Thirty-nine,' said Vulkan reflectively.
'It would be no trouble to you,' said Wilson. 'Just bring them with you when you come back with a Russian. You are the only guy I know who ever rides through Checkpoint Charlie with a Russian.' He laughed nervously.
'Thirty-nine must be the delegation of American radio and TV producers. Poetsch is running that, isn't he?'
'Aw,' said Wilson, 'don't go yelling it around. I told you in strict confidence. If you can deliver them before . . .'
'You told me nothing,' said Vulkan. 'I told *you*. I'm not a camera dealer, tell Poetsch that.'
'Leave P's name out of this.'
Vulkan gently blew smoke at Wilson, saying nothing.
'Don't cross me, Vulkan,' Colonel Wilson said. 'You don't want me spilling it to your British pal that I'm no longer a US Army major.'
'No longer,' said Vulkan gleefully, almost choking on his drink.
'I can make plenty of trouble,' said Wilson.
'And you can make a one-way trip through the wire,' said Vulkan quietly.
They stared at each other. Wilson swallowed to moisten his throat and turned back to his drink.
'OK Johnnie,' Wilson said over his shoulder. 'No hard feelings, eh, pal?'
Johnnie pretended not to hear and moved along the bar, calling for another bourbon.
'Two?' said the barman.
'One will be enough,' said Johnnie.
He could see Wilson's face in the mirror; it was very pale. He could see the girl from Wedding too, touching the hair at the nape of her neck like she didn't know she was straining her brassiere. She crossed her legs and smiled at his reflection.
'Poetsch,' Johnnie thought.
He had wanted to get something on Poetsch, if only to cut down his ranting at the bar. He could hear his voice now. Poetsch was saying, 'The very same people who made the great little TV film about the tunnel. The whole thing was paid for by the TV company, NBC. And what I'm saying, folks, is that those fifty-nine people who escaped owe their very freedom to our American system of unshackled enterprise and bold corporate drive . . .' There were a couple of favours Poetsch could do for Johnnie Vulkan. Johnnie

relished the idea of telling Poetsch about them; even the girl from Wedding wasn't a better prospect than that.

The lounge was beginning to fill up now. Vulkan leaned back against the bar, tensed his muscles and relaxed. It was good to feel he knew them all and that even Americans like 'Colonel Wilson' couldn't take advantage of him. Johnny Vulkan could pick out the tarts and the queens, the hustlers and the fairies. He knew all the heavies waiting assignment: from the nailers-up of notices to the nailers-up of Christs. He saw the girl from Wedding trying to catch his eye. Poetsch's crowd had grown too. There was that elderly English queer with the dyed hair and a stupid little Dresdener who thought he was going to infiltrate the Gehlen Bureau – except that Johnnie had told them all about him last week. He wondered whether Helmut had been serious about having the Dresdener killed in a traffic accident. It was possible. King was right as a code name, Vulkan decided; they acknowledged his stature by allotting it to him. Freudian. King Vulkan of Berlin.

He supposed the red-haired girl talking to Poetsch now was the one Poetsch had mentioned to him; the girl from Israeli Intelligence.

'Boy, oh boy!' thought Vulkan. 'What a town this is!' and he eased his way down the bar towards them, smiling at Poetsch.

from *Funeral in Berlin*, Len Deighton

A TOUCH OF PATRIOTIC ZEAL

Like the ineffable 'Sapper', there are some vintage morsels of Buchan which seem deliciously outrageous in these politically 'sensitive' times. His description of Richard Hannay infiltrating a nest of West Country pacifists during the First World War is one of my favourite gems of twentieth-century English literature. Likewise, Evelyn Waugh's cruel spoof on how the wicked Basil Seal does his bit for the war effort by first denouncing, and then spiriting away, his old foe, the Progressive Poet, Ambrose Silk. Unlike the third extract, by 'Sapper', both Buchan and Waugh write with splendid verisimilitude.

A Pacifists' Coven

There was an institution in Biggleswick which deserves mention. On the south of the common, near the station, stood a red-brick building called the Moot Hall, which was a kind of church for the very undevout population. Undevout in the ordinary sense, I mean, for I had already counted twenty-seven varieties of religious conviction, including three Buddhists, a Celestial Hierarch, five Latter-day Saints and about ten varieties of Mystic whose names I could never remember. The hall had been the gift of the publisher I have spoken of, and twice a week it was used for lectures and debates. The place was managed by a committee and was surprisingly popular, for it gave all the bubbling intellects a chance of airing their views. When you asked where somebody was and were told he was 'at Moot', the answer was spoken in the respectful tone in which you would mention a sacrament.

I went there regularly and got my mind broadened to cracking point. We had all the stars of the New Movements. We had Dr Chirk, who lectured on 'God', which, as far as I could make out, was a new name he had invented for himself. There was a woman, a terrible woman, who had come back from Russia with what she called a 'message of healing'. And to my joy, one night there was a great buck nigger who had a lot to say about 'Africa for the Africans'. I had a few words with him in Sesutu afterwards, and rather spoiled his visit. Some of the people were extraordinarily good, especially one jolly old fellow who talked about English folk songs and dances, and wanted us to set up a Maypole. In the debates which generally followed I began to join, very coyly at first, but presently, with some confidence. If my time at Biggleswick did nothing else it taught me to argue on my feet.

The first big effort I made was on a full-dress occasion when Launcelot Wake came down to speak. Mr Ivery was in the chair – the first I had seen of him – a plump middle-aged man, with a colourless face and nondescript features. I was not interested in him till he began to talk, and then I sat bolt upright and took notice. For he was the genuine silver-tongue, the sentences flowing from his mouth as smooth as butter and as neatly dovetailed as a parquet floor. He had a sort of man-of-the-world manner, treating his opponents with condescending geniality, deprecating all passion and exaggeration, and making you feel that his urbane statement must be right, for if he had wanted he could have put the case so much higher. I watched him, fascinated, studying his face carefully; and the thing that struck me was that there was nothing in it – nothing, that is to say, to lay hold on. It was simply nondescript, so almightily commonplace that that very fact made it rather remarkable.

Wake was speaking of the revelations of the Sukhomlinov trial in Russia, which showed that Germany had not been responsible for the war. He was jolly good at the job and put as clear an argument as a first-class lawyer. I had been sweating away at the subject and had all the ordinary case at my fingers' ends, so when I got a chance of speaking I gave them a long harangue with some good quotations I had cribbed out of the *Vossische Zeitung*, which Letchford lent me. I felt it was up to me to be extra violent for I wanted to establish my character with Wake, seeing that he was a friend of Mary and Mary would know that I was playing the game. I got tremendously applauded, far more than the chief speaker, and after the meeting Wake came up to me with his hot eyes and wrung my hand. 'You're coming on well, Brand,' he said, and then he introduced me to Mr Ivery. 'Here's a second and a better Smuts,' he said.

Ivery made me walk a bit of the road home with him. 'I am struck by your grip on these difficult problems, Mr Brand,' he told me. 'There is much I can tell you, and you may be of great value to our cause.' He asked me a lot of questions about my past, which I answered with easy mendacity. Before we parted he made me promise to come one night to supper.

from *Mr Standfast*, John Buchan

From the sublime to the ridiculous . . .

An Atrocious Foreign Plot

'Last night,' he said slowly, 'he was forgathering with a crowd of the most atrocious ragged-trousered revolutionaries it's ever been my luck to run up against.'

'We're in it, Captain, right in the middle of it,' cried the detective, slapping his leg. 'I'll eat my hat if that Frenchman isn't Franklyn – or Libstein – or Baron Darott – or any other of the blamed names he calls himself. He's the biggest proposition we've ever been up against on this little old earth, and he's done us every time. He never commits himself and, if he does, he always covers his tracks. He's a genius; he's the goods. Gee!' He whistled gently under his breath. 'If we could only lay him by the heels.'

For a while he stared in front of him, lost in his dream of pleasant anticipation; then, with a short laugh, he pulled himself together.

'Quite a few people have thought the same, Captain,' he remarked, 'and there he is – still drinking high-balls. You say he was with a crowd of revolutionaries last night. What do you mean exactly?'

'Bolshevists, Anarchists, members of the Do-no-work-and-have-all-the-money Brigade,' answered Hugh. 'But excuse me a moment. Waiter.'

A man who had been hovering round came up promptly.

'Four of 'em, Ted,' said Hugh in a rapid undertone. 'Frenchman with a beard, a Yank and two Boches. Do your best.'

'Right-o, old bean!' returned the waiter. 'But don't hope for too much.'

He disappeared unobtrusively into the restaurant, and Hugh turned with a laugh to the American who was staring at him in amazement.

'Who the devil is that guy?' asked the detective at length.

'Ted Jerningham – son of Sir Patrick Jerningham, Bt, and Lady Jerningham, of Jerningham Hall, Rutland, England,' answered Hugh, still grinning. 'We may be crude in our methods, Mr Green, but you must admit we do our best. Incidentally, if you want to know, your friend Mr Potts is at present tucked between the sheets at that very house. He went there by aeroplane this morning.' He waved a hand towards Jerry. 'He was the pilot.'

'Travelled like a bird and sucked up a plate of meat-juice at the end,' announced that worthy, removing his eyes with difficulty from a recently arrived fairy opposite. 'Who says that's nothing, Hugh: the filly across the road there, with that bangle affair round her knee?'

'I must apologize for him, Mr Green,' remarked Hugh. 'He has only recently left school and knows no better.'

But the American was shaking his head a little dazedly.

'Crude!' he murmured. 'Crude! If you and your pals, Captain, are ever out of a job, the New York police is yours for the asking.' He smoked for a few moments in silence and then, with a quick hunch of his shoulders, he turned to Drummond. 'I guess there'll be time to throw bouquets after,' he remarked. 'We've got to get busy on what your friend Peterson's little worry is; we've then got to stop it – some old how. Now, does nothing sort of strike you?' He looked keenly at the soldier. 'Revolutionaries, Bolshevists, paid agitators last night; international financiers this evening. Why, the broad outline of the plan is as plain as the nose on your face and it's just the sort of game that man would love . . .' The detective stared thoughtfully at the end of his cigar and a look of comprehension began to dawn on Hugh's face.

'Great Scott! Mr Green,' he said, 'I'm beginning to get you. What was defeating me was, why two men like Peterson and Lakington should be mixed up with last night's crowd.'

'Lakington! Who's Lakington?' asked the other quickly.

'Number Two in the combine,' answered Hugh, 'and a nasty man.'

'Well, we'll leave him out for the moment,' said the American. 'Doesn't it strike you that there are quite a number of people in this world who would benefit if England became a sort of second Russia? That such a thing would be worth money – big money? That such a thing would be worth paying through the nose for? It would have to be done properly; your small strike here, your small strike there, ain't no manner of use. One gigantic syndicalist strike all over your country – that's what Peterson's playing for, I'll stake my bottom dollar. How he's doing it is another matter. But he's in with the big financiers and he's using the tub-thumping Bolshies as tools. Gad! It's a big scheme' – he puffed twice at his cigar – 'a durned big scheme. Your little old country, Captain, is, saving one, the finest on God's earth; but she's in a funny mood. She's sick, like most of us are; maybe she's a little sicker than a good many people think. But I reckon Peterson's cure won't do any manner of good, excepting to himself and those blamed capitalists who are putting up the dollars.'

from *Bulldog Drummond*, 'Sapper'

. . . *and back again:*

Ambrose Routed

Ambrose's flat lay in the neighbourhood of the Ministry of Information; it was the top floor of a large Bloomsbury mansion where the marble stairs changed to deal. Ambrose ascended into what had once been the servants' bedrooms; it was an attic and, so called, satisfied the ascetic promptings which had affected Ambrose in the year of the great slump. There was, however, little else about the flat to suggest hardship. He had the flair of his race for comfort and for enviable possessions. There were expensive continental editions of works on architecture, there were deep armchairs, an object like an ostrich egg sculptured by Brancusi, a gramophone with a prodigious horn and a library of records – these and countless other features made the living-room dear to him. It is true that the bath was served only by a gas-burning apparatus which, at the best, gave a niggardly trickle of warm water and, at the worst, exploded in a cloud of poisonous vapours, but apparatus of this kind is the hallmark of the higher intellectuals all the world over. Ambrose's bedroom compensated for the dangers and discomforts of the bathroom. In this flat he was served by a motherly old Cockney who teased him at intervals for not marrying.

To this flat Basil came very late that night. He had delayed his arrival on purely artistic grounds. Colonel Plum might deny him the excitements of Scotland Yard and the Home Office, but there should be every circumstance of melodrama here. Basil knocked and rang for some time before he made himself heard. Then Ambrose came to the door in a dressing-gown.

'Oh God,' he said. 'I suppose you're drunk,' for no friend of Basil's who maintained a fixed abode in London could ever consider himself immune from his occasional nocturnal visits.

'Let me in. We haven't a moment to spare.' Basil spoke in a whisper. 'The police will be here at any moment.'

Slightly dazed with sleep, Ambrose admitted him. There are those for whom the word 'police' holds no terror. Ambrose was not of them. All his life he had been an outlaw and the days in Munich were still fresh in his memory when friends disappeared suddenly in the night, leaving no address.

'I've brought you this,' said Basil, 'and this and this.' He gave Ambrose a clerical collar, a black clerical vest ornamented with a double line of jet buttons and an Irish passport. 'You are Father Flanagan returning to Dublin University. Once in Ireland you'll be safe.'

'But surely there's no train at this time.'

'There's one at eight. You mustn't be found here. You can sit in the waiting-room at Euston till it comes in. Have you got a breviary?'

'Of course not.'

'Then read a racing paper. I suppose you've got a dark suit.'

It was significant both of Basil's fine urgency of manner, and of Ambrose's constitutionally guilty disposition, that he was already clothed as a clergyman before he said, 'But what have I done? Why are they after me?'

'Your magazine. It's being suppressed. They're rounding up everyone connected with it.'

Ambrose asked no more. He acccpted the fact as a pauper accepts the condition of being perpetually 'moved on'. It was something inalienable from his state; the artist's birthright.

'How did you hear about it?'

'In the War Office.'

'What am I to do about all this?' asked Ambrose helplessly. 'The flat, and the furniture and my books and Mrs Carver.'

'I tell you what. If you like I'll move in and take care of it for you until it's safe to come back.'

'Would you really, Basil?' said Ambrose, touched. 'You're being very kind.'

For some time now Basil had felt himself unfairly handicapped in his pursuit of Susie by the fact of his living with his mother. He had not thought of this solution. It had come providentially, with rapid and exemplary justice all too rare in life; goodness was being rewarded quite beyond his expectations, if not beyond his deserts.

'I'm afraid the geyser is rather a bore,' said Ambrose apologetically.

They were not far from Euston Station. Packing was the work of a quarter of an hour.

'But, Basil, I *must* have *some* clothes.'

'You are an Irish priest. What d'you think the Customs are going to say when they open a trunk full of Charvet ties and crêpe-de-Chine pyjamas?'

Ambrose was allowed one suitcase.

'I'll look after this for you,' said Basil, surveying the oriental profusion of expensive underclothes which filled the many drawers and presses of the bedroom. 'You'll have to walk to the station, you know.'

'Why, for God's sake?'

'Taxi might be traced. Can't take any chances.'

The suitcase had seemed small enough when Basil first selected it as the most priestly of the rather too smart receptacles in Ambrose's box-room; it seemed enormous as they trudged northward through the dark streets of Bloomsbury. At last they reached the classic columns of the railway terminus. It is not a cheerful place at the best of times, striking a chill in the heart of the gayest holiday-maker. Now in war time, before dawn on a cold spring morning, it seemed the entrance to a sepulchre.

'I'll leave you here,' said Basil. 'Keep out of sight until the train is in. If anyone speaks to you, tell your beads.'

'I haven't any beads.'

'Then contemplate. Go into an ecstasy. But don't open your mouth or you're done.'

'I'll write to you when I get to Ireland.'

'Better not,' said Basil, cheerfully.

He turned away and was immediately lost in the darkness. Ambrose entered the station. A few soldiers slept on benches, surrounded by their kit and equipment. Ambrose found a corner darker, even, than the general gloom. Here, on a packing-case that seemed by its smell to contain fish of a sort, he sat waiting for dawn; black hat perched over his eyes, black overcoat wrapped close about his knees, mournful and black eyes open, staring into the blackness. From the fishy freight below him water oozed slowly on to the pavement, making a little pool, as though of tears.

Mr Rampole was not, as many of his club acquaintances supposed, a bachelor, but a widower of long standing. He lived in a small but substantial house at Hampstead and there maintained in servitude a spinster daughter. On this fateful morning his daughter saw him off from the front gate as had been her habit years without number, at precisely 8.45. Mr Rampole paused on the flagged path to comment on the buds which were breaking everywhere in the little garden.

Look well at those buds, old Rampole; you will not see the full leaf.

'I'll be back at six,' he said.

Presumptuous Rampole, who shall tell what the day will bring forth? Not his daughter, who returned, unmoved by the separation, to eat a second slice of toast in the dining-room; not old Rampole, who strode at a good pace towards the Hampstead Underground.

He showed his season ticket to the man at the lift.

'I shall have to get it renewed the day after tomorrow,' he said affably, and tied a knot in the corner of his large white handkerchief to remind him of the fact.

There is no need for that knot, old Rampole; you will never again travel in the Hampstead Underground.

He opened his morning paper as he had done, five days a week, years without number. He turned first to the Deaths, then to the correspondence, then, reluctantly, to the news of the day.

Never again, old Rampole, never again.

The police raid on the Ministry of Information, like so many similar enterprises, fell flat. First, the plain-clothes men had the utmost difficulty in getting past the gatekeeper.

'Is Mr Silk expecting you?'

'We hope not.'

'Then you can't see him.'

When finally they were identified and allowed to pass, there was a confused episode in the religious department where they found only the Nonconformist minister whom, too zealously, they proceeded to handcuff. It was explained that Ambrose was unaccountably absent from duty that morning. Two constables were left to await his arrival. All through the day they sat there, casting a gloom over the religious department. The plain-clothes men proceeded to Mr Bentley's room where they were received with great frankness and charm.

Mr Bentley answered all their questions in a manner befitting an honest citizen. Yes, he knew Ambrose Silk both as a colleague at the Ministry and, formerly, as one of their authors at Rampole's. No, he had almost nothing to do with publishing these days; he was too busy with all this (an explanatory gesture which embraced the dripping sink, the Nollekens busts and the page of arabesques beside the telephone). Mr Rampole was in entire charge of the publishing firm. Yes, he thought he had heard of some magazine which Silk was starting, the *Ivory Tower*? Was that the name? Very likely. No, he had no copy. Was it already out? Mr Bentley had formed the impression that it was not yet ready for publication. The contributors? Hucklebury Squib, Bartholomew Grass, Tom Barebones-Abraham? Mr Bentley thought he had heard the names; he might have met them in literary circles in the old days. He had the idea that Barebones-Abraham was rather below normal height, corpulent, bald – yes, Mr Bentley was quite sure he was bald as an egg; he spoke with a stammer and dragged his left leg as he walked. Hucklebury Squib was a very tall young man; easily recognizable for he had lost the lobe of his left ear in extraordinary circumstances when sailing before the mast; he had a front tooth missing and wore gold earrings.

The plain-clothes men recorded these details in shorthand. This was the sort of witness they liked, circumstantial, precise, unhesitating.

When it came to Bartholomew Grass, Mr Bentley's invention

flagged. He had never seen the man. He rather thought it might be the pseudonym for a woman.

'Thank you, Mr Bentley,' said the chief of the plain-clothes men. 'I don't think we need trouble you any more. If we want you I suppose we can always find you here.'

'Always,' said Mr Bentley sweetly. 'I often, whimsically, refer to this little table as my grindstone. I keep my nose to it. We live in arduous times, Inspector.'

A posse of police went to Ambrose's flat, where all they got was a piece of his housekeeper's mind.

'Our man's got away,' they reported when they returned to their superiors.

from *Put out More Flags*, Evelyn Waugh

. . . AND SOME SCOUNDRELS

I have included 'Beachcomber' – the humorist, J.B. Morton, whom Bernard Levin described (correctly) as 'having no peer in the English language' – together with Nancy Mitford and Christopher Isherwood, to show, contrary to general belief, how far the world of the spy has reached in modern fiction and how diverse and unexpected have been some of its literary practitioners.

Captain Foulenough & Co.

'Geraldine Brazier, Belle of the Southern Command!'

Colonel Fritter's voice trembled with emotion as he gave the toast, and every officer in the mess of the 14th Loyal North-west Huntingdonshire Fusiliers knew that he referred to the loveliest WOOF in the British Army. Yet there was one man who braved the displeasure of his commanding officer and the sneers of his fellows. For Captain Roy Batter-Pudden sat in taciturn silence as the toast was drunk and heard himself called a prig. And as the port-type circulated more freely and tongues were loosed, the more silent became the Captain.

Outside the mess night fell on the market town of Cuddlingham.

Geraldine Brazier, the loveliest WOOF in the British Army, was always doing odd jobs in the camp of the Loyal North-west Huntingdonshire Fusiliers. The officers and the men trusted her implicitly and her mere presence made them happier. Nobody had any hesitation in talking to her about military matters, since she was so obviously heart and soul in her work. To see the Colonel raise his hat to her on the parade ground was to realize that respect was mingled with admiration. And the Adjutant boasted openly that none of his clerks or orderlies knew as much about his private papers as this efficient, serious-minded girl, who turned a blind eye to all attempts at flirtation. It was left to surly Captain Batter-Pudden to mutter that Geraldine was getting to know too much and was too deeply in the Colonel's confidence. But Batter-Pudden's black looks only earned him the epithet 'Curmudgeon'.

Often, when some important general arrived at Cuddlingham to inspect the battalion, the Colonel would say, half in jest, 'Oh, and sir, you really ought to see our prize WOOF.' And the general, stroking his moustache and whacking his leg with a riding-switch, would reply, 'Ha! Yes! I've heard of her. Deuced pretty poppet, they tell me.' And then Geraldine, simpering somewhat, and a blush mantling her damask cheek, would be led forward and introduced. And all ranks would cheer to the echo when the general complimented her on her looks. Yet she remained her sweet, innocent, simple self. One day, for instance, the Colonel surprised her reading a strictly private memorandum from the headquarters of his command. 'Naughty, naughty,' he said, taking it from her. 'I couldn't understand a word of it,' said Geraldine. 'What does it mean?' 'Not for little beauties,' replied the Colonel, mightily relieved.

No higher compliment could have been paid to Geraldine Brazier than when the Colonel said, one day in the mess, 'I really believe she knows where all my confidential documents are, better than I do myself.' A murmur of approbation greeted this avowal. But Captain Roy Batter-Pudden was heard to say, 'Do we know anything of her antecedents, sir?' The Colonel gaped awkwardly for a moment. Then he said, 'Isn't it enough for us that her Commandant, Mrs Cluckaway, recommended her highly?' It was evidently enough for all of them, except the sombre Batter-Pudden.

At this very moment the beautiful WOOF was making notes from a confidential memorandum that had just arrived. She worked late and, as Batter-Pudden took his way to his quarters, he was surprised to see a light coming from under the door of the Colonel's office.

When Captain Batter-Pudden saw the light under the door of the Colonel's office, and noted that the time was 11.53 p.m., he said to himself, 'How odd! How very odd! Who can be working in there at this hour?' Hoping to surprise some diligent, conscientious brother-officer, he approached the door stealthily, on tiptoe. He said to himself, 'I will fling the door open and cry "Boo!" and then laugh at his discomfiture.' For Batter-Pudden was a simple-minded man and fond of elementary jokes.

Creeping up, he laid his hand on the door-handle silently, twisted as though to the manner born, flung it wide and shouted breezily, 'Boo!' For answer, the loveliest girl he had ever seen turned swiftly to face him and he found himself challenged by the gentian-blue eyes of WOOF Geraldine Brazier.

For a long moment Batter-Pudden and the girl faced each other in silence. The Captain's thoughts raced through his head like paper-bags in a hurricane. He remembered his suspicions of this superb creature and, as he gazed at her, he found it hard to believe that she was not as innocent as a prawn. Her arched eyebrows expressed surprise at the intrusion until the Captain began to feel like some dull clod who has blundered into the boudoir of a delicately nurtured peeress. He moistened his dry lips and shifted on his feet. A slow smile irradiated Geraldine's face. She made no attempt to conceal the papers she was holding. Finally, with a gasp, Batter-Pudden said, 'You!' 'Yes,' was the reply, 'only little me, Captain.' Staggering under the impact of her beauty the soldier felt more and more foolish, like a little boy caught stealing marmalade. 'You!' he repeated as she turned her enormous eyes full on him again.

'What are you doing here?' asked Captain Batter-Pudden, greatly daring. 'Looking through these papers,' was the reply, delivered in a voice so melodious that the Captain's face assumed the famous Covent Garden gape. Spite of himself, he knew that he was on the brink of falling in love with this radiant creature. Yet he knew where his duty lay. Setting his teeth until his jaw ached, he said sternly, 'Pr-pr-private papers – my dear.' A blush like the sunset on Helvellyn mantled her cheeks. 'You musn't call me your dear,' she said in a small voice, lowering her eyes and veiling them with lashes that seemed to the Captain's fevered imagination as long as his arm. 'Tck, tck,' he replied, 'I meant nothing by it.' 'That is what you men always say,' replied the WOOF. 'This situation must be cleared up,' said the Captain. And at that moment his trained ear caught a stealthy step in the corridor.

As that stealthy step approached, there burst upon Captain Batter-Pudden the difficulty of the situation. Here he was alone at midnight in the Colonel's office with a renowned beauty. Geraldine Brazier appeared to be quite unmoved. 'Don't you realize—?' began the Captain. Duty and chivalry warred in his brain. Was he to denounce the girl? Was he to protect her by saying that it was he who had been looking at the papers? How explain her presence? After a hard struggle, duty won. The door opened and the Captain stood stiff as a ramrod. It was the Colonel! 'You!' cried the Colonel. 'You, sir!' exclaimed the Captain, and Geraldine, not knowing to whom the Colonel's cry was addressed, murmured innocently, 'You!' Embarrassment hung like a pall on the Colonel's face. He grinned foolishly. 'I just looked in, my dear,' he said. 'You mustn't call me your dear,' said Geraldine, smiling at the Captain.

The Colonel's eye fell on a litter of secret documents scattered about the table, and his face changed. 'I was just passing the time,' said Geraldine. 'I hope you have not *read* these,' said the Colonel. The Captain smiled sardonically. 'Of course, if you don't trust me,' said Geraldine sulkily. The Colonel weakened, but Batter-Pudden interposed. 'I ask myself, sir,' he said, 'why should a WOOF come to your office at midnight to study secret documents?' Duty and chivalry fought for mastery of the Colonel. Chivalry won. 'I'm sure,' he said, 'this little lady acted with the best intentions.' At that moment a stealthy step was heard outside in the corridor. 'Hide me, hide me!' cried Geraldine in a whisper. Colonel and Captain calmed her panic and awaited events. Slowly the handle of the door was turning.

The door opened, revealing the bland face of Major Horseferry. 'Ha!' he said heartily, as he observed the others. The Colonel and the Captain smiled uneasily. 'Quite a party,' said the Major, 'eh, little lady?' Geraldine was about to answer when yet another stealthy step was heard outside. And so the long night wore on. One stealthy step succeeded another, until there were twelve officers in the Colonel's office. And then Captain Batter-Pudden, addressing them all, said firmly, 'Colonel, gentlemen, brother officers, I accuse WOOF Geraldine Brazier of breaking in here to look at secret documents.' There was a gasp of amazement and the Colonel cried, 'Oh, I say, look here, I mean, what.' But Geraldine said calmly, 'I can explain everything.' 'Fire away, my dear,' said the Colonel.

'Gentlemen,' said Geraldine, 'I will refrain from pointing out that I might ask how so many officers happen to have crept quietly into this room. What was their business, apart from forcing upon me their unwelcome attentions? But, no. I will confine myself to the explanation of my own actions. Gentlemen, I was discovered here looking through various documents. I had intended to memorize a few unimportant details. Why? Because I have (and here she lowered her voice and her eyes) an old mother, lonely and impoverished. She is so proud when she knows that her daughter enjoys the confidence of the Army. She thinks I am even consulted by the War Office, and I let her think it for she has not long to live. But to make her last days happy I have to be able to quote documents of seeming importance.

Gentlemen, it is a kind of deception and one that I feel sure you will condone. And—'

At this point yet another of those damnable stealthy steps was heard outside.

An exclamation, perfectly timed, burst from the twelve officers in the Colonel's office as the door opened slowly to admit a frail old lady, leaning on a large umbrella. From beneath a mop of hair protruded a kindly face with blue spectacles twinkling above a fat nose. 'And who the devil may you be, madam?' asked the Colonel, bowing courteously. But before the dear old newcomer could answer, WOOF Geraldine's cry of 'Mater! What are you doing here?' sent a thrill through the assemblage. Sardonic, sinister, sombre Captain Roy Batter-Pudden said crabbedly, 'Yes, what, indeed, are you doing here – mater?' The old lady seemed to be overwhelmed. Her lips trembled, and when Geraldine approached and stroked that dear face and muttered, 'There, there, dearest mater,' Colonel Fritter clandestinely wiped his bloodshot eyes with his sleeve. Then silence fell as the dear old lady began to whisper to her daughter.

Those hardened soldiers, who had faced carnage and destruction with steely eyes, were softened by the sight of mother and daughter. They recalled their own mothers – all of them except Batter-Pudden whose suspicions never slept. As for Colonel Fritter, as though to give the lie to those who say that soldiers are cruel, he sobbed as strong men sob until the medals on his chest rattled like hail on the tin roof of a railway shed in mid-November. Still clinging to her enormous mother, Geraldine said, 'Gentlemen, my friends. My old sick mater has come to tell me that she does not want me to get any more documents for her. She says that my motives might be misunderstood. Ah, gentlemen, there is no sacrifice she would not make for me.' Too moved to speak, they gulped foolishly. All except Batter-Pudden who had seen mater's spurs beneath her long dress!

'Why does your mother wear spurs?' asked Batter-Pudden casually.

For a moment the girl changed colour and fear came into her eyes.

'Perhaps she came here on horseback,' suggested Colonel Fritter.
'Naturally,' said Geraldine; 'why else should she wear spurs?'
'How else could she have come?' added the Colonel fatuously.
'Is her sight bad?' asked Batter-Pudden.

Geraldine sighed, 'Alas!' she said. 'She is almost blind. Hence those blue glasses.'

'And yet she wants documents to read?'

'I read them to her,' said Geraldine.

'My dear daughter, she is so much an angel to me,' said mater, speaking for the first time in a deep, musical voice.

'Where is the horse?' asked Batter-Pudden.

'It goes home of its own accord,' replied Geraldine.

'And your mother can see to ride on a moonless night?'

'Only just. It is a great strain for her,' said Geraldine quickly.

'Gentlemen,' said Batter-Pudden, in an ominously soft voice, 'here is the position. A very old lady, half-blind and feeble, rides here on horseback on a moonless night to tell her daughter that she doesn't want any more confidential documents read to her. What was her daughter doing here at midnight?'

'What are any of us doing here at midnight?' asked a gallant subaltern.

'He's got you there, Batter-Pudden,' said the Colonel, whose sympathies in this matter were obvious.

'Of course,' said Geraldine, with a pretty pout, 'if you gentlemen don't trust me—'

'There, there, my dear,' said Colonel Fritter, 'we all trust and admire you.'

A chorus of approval came from the assembled officers.

'I wonder,' said Batter-Pudden, in a dangerously calm drawl, 'I wonder why your dear old mother has a pair of men's braces hanging below her skirt.'

Captain Batter-Pudden's words sent all eyes to Geraldine's dear old mater who, after a guilty start, said calmly, 'These braces which I wear, and which slipped have down, are a family heirloom. They were worn by my grandfather.' So saying, the old dame made shift to tuck them in under her skirt but, as she did so, a package fell to the floor. Geraldine, whose dainty foot would not have covered a grain of rice, tried to hide it by stepping on it. But Batter-Pudden was before her. He picked it up and handed it to the Colonel. It was addressed to Ludwig von Rümpelgutz! 'Rümpelgutz,' said the Colonel. 'A German, surely.' Then, as though realising what this meant, he turned to Geraldine. At that moment, with a cry (in a deep bass voice) of 'Heil, Hitler!' the old 'lady' leaped to the window, smashed it and dived through!

* * *

'That was not your mother,' said Colonel Fritter haughtily to Geraldine Brazier as Captain Batter-Pudden and several officers dashed in pursuit of Ludwig von Rümpelgutz. But the girl was no whit abashed, 'Nein,' she said savagely, 'and I his daughter am not.' 'I must ask you for your name,' said the Colonel icily. 'Dorothea Stüttgarten,' replied the pseudo-WOOF. 'You know what this means,' said the Colonel: 'the firing squad.'

With a last attempt to melt this iron soldier, the girl softly stroked his sleeve. But the Colonel flicked her hand off as though it had been a bug. 'This is no time for dalliance,' he barked. 'I place you under arrest and charge you with espionage. It grieves me to be harsh with one so beautiful, but war is war.'

Only the sobs of the girl broke the silence.

Dawn was breaking over the Tower of London when Colonel Fritter and Captain Batter-Pudden stopped their staff car at the entrance to the Bloody Tower to give the password of the day, which happened to be 'Scunthorpe'. From the car descended two blindfolded prisoners – Dorothea Stüttgarten, more beautiful than ever in her anger and mortification, and Ludwig von Rümpelgutz, minus the wig and braces, but still wearing the tell-tale spurs. Colonel Fritter handed a piece of paper and a pencil to the Orderly Officer who signed for the prisoners. He then bowed low to the girl, holding her hand rather longer than was necessary, while Batter-Pudden turned away from the cold fury of her eyes. A crowd of onlookers murmured sympathetically and, when Rümpelgutz spat at a woman who offered him a carton of 2000 cigarettes, there were cries of pity. Then the cell doors clanged on the prisoners.

Bang, bang, bang!

A volley rang out, two bodies sagged and fell. Two enemies of England had paid the last dread penalty. Far away in the officers' mess of the Loyal North-west Huntingdonshire Fusiliers, Colonel Fritter complimented Roy Batter-Pudden on having done his duty. But the Colonel did not say that he treasured in his pocket-book a fragrant handkerchief once dropped by the false WOOF. And the Captain did not say that he could not breathe her name without a catch in his throat. Conversation in the mess that night was desultory. Next day a new WOOF was sent to take the place of 'Geraldine' (as they still affectionately called her). The newcomer was so ugly that the Colonel said heartily, 'Spy or no spy, I preferred that other poor gal.'

'Hear, hear!' murmured the officers, sighing heavily.

Captain Foulenough

from *Beachcomber*, J. B. Morton

From one prototype 'honey-pot' to another – of a different kind.

A Defector Returns

As Davey and I came to the Place de la Concorde we saw that there was something going on. A mob of men in mackintoshes, armed with cameras, were jostling each other on the roadway outside the Hôtel Crillon. Mockbar leant against the wall by the revolving door of the hotel. I never can resist a crowd. 'Do let's find out who it is they are waiting for,' I said.

'It can only be some dreary film star. Nothing else attracts any interest nowadays.'

'I know. Only, if we don't wait we shall hear afterwards that something thrilling occurred and we shall be cross.' I showed him Mockbar. 'There's the enemy. He looks more like a farmer than a gossip writer.'

'Lady Wincham – how are you?' It was *The Times* correspondent. There was a moment of agony when I could remember neither his name nor Davey's. I feebly said, 'Do you know each other?' However, my embarrassment was covered by the noisy arrival of policemen on motor-bicycles.

'Who is it?' I shouted to *The Times* man.

'Hector Dexter. He has chosen Freedom. He and his wife are expected here from Orly any minute now.'

'Remind me—' I shouted.

'That American who went to Russia just before Burgess and Maclean did.'

I vaguely remembered. As everybody seemed so excited I could see that he must be very important. The noise abated when the policemen got off their bicycles. Davey said: 'You must remember, Fanny – there was a huge fuss at the time. His wife is English – your Aunt Emily knew her mother.'

More police dashed up, clearing the way for a motor. It stopped before the hotel; the journalists were held back; a policeman opened the door of the car and out of it struggled a large Teddy-bear of an American in a crumpled beige suit, a coat over his arm, holding a briefcase. He stood on the pavement, blinking and swallowing, green in the face. I felt sorry for him, he looked so ill. Some of the journalists shouted questions while others flashed and snapped away with their cameras. 'So what was it like, Heck?' 'Come on, Heck, how was the Soviet Union?' 'Why did you leave, Heck? Let's have a statement.'

Mr Dexter stood there, silent, swaying on his feet. A man pushed a microphone under his nose. 'Give us your impressions, Heck, what's the life like, out there?'

At last he opened his mouth. 'Fierce!' he said. Then he added, in a rush, 'Pardon me, gentlemen, I am still suffering from motion discomfort.' He hurried into the hotel.

'Suffering from what?' said Davey, interested.

'It means air sickness,' said *The Times* man. 'I wonder when we shall get a statement. Dexter used to be a tremendous chatterbox – he must be feeling very sick indeed to be so taciturn all of a sudden.'

A large pink knee loomed in the doorway of the motor. It was followed by a woman as unmistakably English as Dexter was American. She merely said 'Shits' to the snapping and flashing photographers. Using the *New Statesman* as a screen she ran after her husband. Her place was taken by a fat, pudding-faced lad who stood posing and grinning and chewing gum until everybody lost interest in him. I saw that Mockbar's elbows were getting into motion, followed by the rheumaticky superannuated stable-boy action of his lower limbs, the whole directed at me. 'Come on,' I said to Davey, 'we must get out of this, quick—'

Philip was invited to the Jungfleisch dinner as well as Davey and next morning he came to report. The return of the Dexters had been, of course, the sole topic of conversation. When it transpired that Davey had actually witnessed it he became the hero of the evening.

'They are puzzled, poor dears,' said Philip.

'Who – the Jungfleisches?'

'All the Americans here. Don't know how to take the news. Is it Good or Bad? What does it mean? How does Mr Khrushchev evaluate it? What will the State Department say? The agony for our friends is should they send flowers or not? You know how they can't bear not to be loved, even by Dexter – it's ghastly for them to feel they are not welcoming old Heck as they ought to – at the same time it was very, very wrong of him to leave the Western Camp and it wouldn't do for them to appear to condone. The magic, meaningless word Solidarity is one of their runes; old Heck has not been solid and that's dreadfully un-American of him. But one must remember old Heck has now chosen Freedom, he has come back to the Western Camp of his own accord and they would like to reward him for that. So they are in an utter fix. In the end it was decided that Mildred must have a dinner party for policy makers; Jo Alsop, Elsa Maxwell, Mr Gallagher and Mr Shean are all flying over for it – but most of them can't get here before the end of the week. We shan't know any more until they have been consulted. Meanwhile, there's the question of the flowers. Either you send at once or not at all; what are they to do? Davey suggested sending bunches with no cards, so that presently, if they want to, they can say, "Did you get my roses all right, Heck?"'

'Isn't Davey wonderful?'

'It went down very badly. They were sharked.'

Sir Harald Hardrada now came to give his lecture. It was very brilliant and a great success, Sir Harald being one of the few living Englishmen who, even the French allow, has a perfect mastery of their language. As they detest hearing it massacred and really do not like listening to any other, foreign lecturers are more often flattered than praised at the end of their performance (not that they know the difference). We all went to the Sorbonne where the lecture took place and then Mildred Jungfleisch gave a dinner party. The company was: Sir Harald, M. Bouche-Bontemps, the Valhuberts, the Hector Dexters, an American couple called Jorgmann, Philip and Northey, Alfred and me. The Dexters had been given a clean bill by the State Department, to the enormous relief of their compatriots in Paris. Having had enough, it seemed, of political activities, Mr Dexter was now acting as liaison between leading French and American art dealers.

Mrs Jungfleisch lived in a cheery, modernish (1920) house near the Bois de Boulogne. Its drawing-room, painted shiny white and without ornament of any sort, had an unnaturally high ceiling and stairs leading to a gallery; the effect was that of a swimming-bath. One felt that somebody might dive in at any moment, the Prime Minister of England, perhaps, or some smiling young candidate for the American throne. Almost the only piece of furniture was an enormous pouf in the middle of the room on which people had to sit with their backs to each other. As Americans do, she left a good hour between the arrival of the guests and the announcement of dinner, during which time bourbon (a kind of whisky) could be imbibed.

There was a little silence. Ice clicked in the glasses, people swallowed, Mrs Jungfleisch handed round caviar. Sir Harald turned to the opposite side of the pouf and said, 'Now, Geck, we want to hear all about Russia.'

Hector Dexter cleared his throat and intoned: 'My day-to-day experiences in the Union of Soviet Socialist Russia have been registered on a long-playing gramophone record to be issued free to all the members of the North Atlantic Treaty. This you will be able to obtain by indenting for a copy to your own ambassador to Nato. I was there, as you may know, for between nine and eight years, but after the very first week I came to the conclusion that the way of life of the Socialist Soviet citizen is not, and never could be acceptable to one who has had cognizance of the American way of life. Then it took me between nine and eight years to find some way of leaving the country by which I could safely bring Carolyn here and young Foster with me. It became all the more important for me to get out because my son Foster, aged now fifteen, is only ten points below genius and this genius would have been unavailing and supervacaneous, in other words wasted, behind the iron curtain.'

'Why? There can't be so many geniuses there?'

'There is this out-of-date, non-forward-looking view of life. They have not realized the vast potentialities, the enormous untapped wealth of the world of Art. They have this fixation on literature; they do not seem to realize that the written word has had its day – books are a completely outworn concept. We in America, one step ahead of you in Western Europe, have given up buying them altogether. You would never see a woman, or a man, reading a book in the New York subway. Now in the Moscow subway every person is doing so.'

'That's bad, Heck,' said Mr Jorgmann, heavily.

'Why is it bad?' I asked.

'Because books do not carry advertisements. The public of a great modern industrial state ought to be reading magazines or watching television. The Russians are not contemporary; they are not realist; they exude a fusty aroma of the past.'

'So young Foster is going into Art?'

'Yes, sir. By the time my boy is twenty-one, I intend he shall recognize with unerring certainty the attribution of any paint on any canvas (or wood or plaster), the marks of every known make of porcelain and every known maker of silver, the factory from which every carpet and every tapestry—'

'In short,' said Sir Harald, 'he'll be able to tell the difference between Rouault and Ford Madox Brown.'

'Not only that. I wish him to learn the art trade from the beginning to the end; he must learn to clean and crate and pack the object as well as to discover it and purchase it and resell it. From flea-market to Jayne Wrightsman's boudoir, if I may so express myself.'

'I should have thought that sort of talent could have been used in the Winter Palace?'

'There is too much prejudice against the West. The Russians do not possess correct attitudes. It was an unpleasant experience to discuss with individuals whose thinking is so lacking in objectivity that one was aware it was emotively determined and could be changed only by change of attitude. Besides, hypotheses, theories, ideas, generalizations, awareness of the existence of unanswered and/or unanswerable queries do not form part of their equipment. So such mental relationships as Carolyn here and I and young Foster Dexter were able to entertain with the citizens of Soviet Socialist Russia were very, very highly unsatisfactory.'

'But, Geck,' said naughty Sir Harald (I remembered that the Russian alphabet has no H), 'one doesn't want to say I told you so – not that I did, only any of us could have if you'd asked our advice – why on earth did you go?'

'When I first got back here some four or three weeks since, I could have found that question difficult, if not impossible, to answer. However, as soon as I arrived here in Paris I put myself in the hands of a brilliant young doctor, recommended to me by Mildred: Dr Jore. I go to him every evening when he has finished with the Supreme Commander. Now Dr Jore very, very swiftly diagnosed my disorder. It seems that at the time when I left this country some nine or eight years ago I was suffering from a Pull to the East which, in my case, was so overwhelmingly powerful that no human person could have resisted it. As soon as Dr Jore sent his report to the State Department they entirely exonerated me from any suspicion of anti-American procedure, deviation from rectitude, improbity, trimming or what have you and recognized that I was, at the time when I turned my back on the West, a very, very sick man.'

'Poor old Heck,' said the Jorgmanns.

'Another bourbon?' said Mrs Jungfleisch.

'Thank you. On the rocks.'

Sir Harald asked, 'And how does he set about curing a Pull to the East?'

'In my case, of course, I have already undergone the most efficacious cure, which is a long sojourn there. But we must prevent any recurrence of the disease. Well, the doc's treatment is this. I lie on his couch and I shut my eyes and I force myself to see New York Harbour, the Empire State building, Wall Street, Fifth Avenue and Bonwit Teller. Then very, very slowly I swivel my mental gaze until it alights on the Statue of Liberty. All this time Dr Jore and I, very, very softly, in unison, recite the Gettysburg Address. "Four score and seven years ago our fathers—"'

'Yes, yes,' said Sir Harald, almost rudely, I thought, breaking in on Mr Dexter's fervent interpretation. 'Very fine, but we all know it. It's in the *Oxford Book of Quotations*.'

Mr Dexter looked hurt; there was a little silence. Philip said, 'Did you see anything of Guy and Donald?'

'When Guy Burgess and Donald Maclean first arrived we all shared a dacha. I cannot say it was a very happy association. They did not behave as courteously to me as they ought to have. The looked-for Anglo-Saxon solidarity was not in evidence. They hardly listened to the analysis of the situation, as noted and recounted by me, in Socialist Soviet Russia; they laughed where no laughter was called for; they even seemed to shun my company. Now, I am not very conversant with the circumstances of their departure from the Western Camp, but I am inclined to think it was motivated by pure treachery. I am not overfond of traitors.'

'And how did you get away?'

'In the end very easily. After nine or eight years in the USSR, the Presidium having acquired a perfect confidence in my integrity, I was able to induce them to send me on a fact-finding mission. On arrival here, as I explained to them, the accompaniment of wife and son lending a permanent appearance to my reintegration in the Western Camp, I would easily persuade my compatriots that I had abandoned all tendency to communism. When their trust in me was completely re-established I would be in a position to send back a great deal of information, of the kind I knew they wanted, to the Kremlin.'

'Nom de nom!' said Valhubert.

Bouche-Bontemps shook with laughter: 'C'est excellent!'

Alfred and Philip exchanged looks.

The Jorgmanns exclaimed, 'That was smart of you, Heck!' Mrs Jungfleisch said, 'And now let's go and dine.'

We all stood up and, like so many geese, stretched our necks. That hour on the pouf had been absolute agony.

from *Don't Tell Alfred*, Nancy Mitford

Facing the Music

One morning, not long after this, Frl. Schroeder came shuffling into my room in great haste, to tell me that Arthur was on the telephone.

'It must be something very serious. Herr Norris didn't even say good morning to me.' She was impressed and rather hurt.

'Hullo, Arthur. What's the matter?'

'For heavens sake, my dear boy, don't ask me any questions now.'

His tone was nervously irritable and he spoke so rapidly that I could barely understand him. 'It's more than I can bear. All I want to know is, can you come here at once?'

'Well . . . I've got a pupil coming at ten o'clock.'

'Can't you put him off?'

'Is it as important as all that?'

Arthur uttered a little cry of peevish exasperation: 'Is it important? My dear William, do please endeavour to exercise your imagination. Should I be ringing you up at this unearthly hour if it wasn't important? All I beg of you is a plain answer: Yes or No. If it's a question of money, I shall be only too glad to pay you your usual fee. How much do you charge?'

'Shut up, Arthur, and don't be absurd. If it's urgent, of course I'll come. I'll be with you in twenty minutes.'

I found all the doors of the flat standing open, and walked in unannounced. Arthur, it appeared, had been rushing wildly from room to room like a flustered hen. At the moment, he was in the sitting-room, dressed ready to go out and nervously pulling on his gloves. Hermann, on his knees, rummaged sulkily in a cupboard in the hall. Schmidt lounged in the doorway of the study, a cigarette between his lips. He did not make the least effort to help and was evidently enjoying his employer's distress.

'Ah, here you are, William, at last!' cried Arthur, on seeing me. 'I thought you were never coming. Oh, dear! Is it as late as that already? Never mind about my grey hat. Come along, William, come along. I'll explain everything to you on the way.'

Schmidt gave us an unpleasant, sarcastic smile as we went out.

When we were comfortably settled on the top of a bus, Arthur became calmer and more coherent.

'First of all,' he fumbled rapidly in all his pockets and produced a folded piece of paper: 'Please read that.'

I looked at it. It was a *Vorladung* from the Political Police. Herr Arthur Norris was requested to present himself at the Alexanderplatz that morning before one o'clock. What would happen should he fail to do so was not stated. The wording was official and coldly polite.

'Good God, Arthur,' I said, 'whatever does this mean? What have you been up to now?'

In spite of his nervous alarm, Arthur displayed a certain modest pride.

'I flatter myself that my association with,' he lowered his voice and glanced quickly at our fellow passengers, 'the representatives of the Third International has not been entirely unfruitful. I am told that my efforts have even excited favourable comment in certain quarters in Moscow . . . I told you, didn't I, that I'd been in Paris? Yes, yes, of course . . . Well, I had a little mission there to fulfil. I spoke to certain highly placed individuals and brought back certain instructions . . . Never mind that now. At all events, it appears that the authorities here are better informed than we'd supposed. That is what I have to find out. The whole question is extremely delicate. I must be careful not to give anything away.'

'Perhaps they'll put you through the third degree.'

'Oh, William, how can you say anything so dreadful? You make me feel quite faint.'

'But, Arthur, surely that would be . . . I mean, wouldn't you rather enjoy it?'

Arthur giggled: 'Ha, ha. Ha, ha. I must say this, William, that even in the darkest hour your humour never fails to restore me . . . Well, well, perhaps if the examination were to be conducted by Frl. Anni, or some equally charming young lady, I might undergo it with -er- very mixed feelings. Yes.' Uneasily he scratched his chin. 'I shall need your moral support. You must come and hold my hand. And if this,' he glanced nervously over his shoulder,'interview should terminate unpleasantly, I shall ask you to go to Bayer and tell him exactly what has happened.'

'Yes, I will. Of course.'

When we had got out of the bus on the Alexanderplatz, poor Arthur was so shaky that I suggested going into a restaurant and drinking a glass of cognac. Seated at a little table we regarded the immense drab mass of the Praesidium buildings from the opposite side of the roadway.

'The enemy fortress,' said Arthur, 'into which poor little have got to venture, all alone.'

'Remember David and Goliath.'

'Oh, dear. I'm afraid the Psalmist and I have very little in common this morning. I feel more like a beetle about to be squashed by a steam-roller . . . It's a curious fact that, since my earliest years, I have had an instinctive dislike of the police. The very cut of their uniforms offends me and the German helmets are not only hideous but somehow rather sinister. Merely to see one of them filling in an official form in that inhuman copy-book handwriting gives me a sinking feeling in the stomach.'

'Yes, I know what you mean.'

Arthur brightened a little.

'I'm very glad I've got you with me, William. You have such a sympathetic manner. I could wish for no better companion on the morning of my execution. The very opposite of that odious Schmidt who simply gloats over my misfortune. Nothing makes him happier than to be in a position to say – I told you so.'

'After all, there's nothing very much they can do to you in there. They only knock women about. Remember, you belong to the same class as their masters. You must make them feel that.'

'I'll try,' said Arthur doubtfully.

'Have another cognac?'

'Perhaps I will, yes.'

The second cognac worked wonders. We emerged from the restaurant into the still, clammy autumn morning, laughing arm in arm.

'Be brave, Comrade Norris. Think of Lenin.'

'I'm afraid, ha, ha, I find more inspiration in the Marquis de Sade.'

But the atmosphere of the police headquarters sobered him considerably. Increasingly apprehensive and depressed, we wandered along vistas of stone passages with numbered doors, were misdirected up and down flights of stairs, collided with hurrying officials who carried bulging dossiers of crimes. At length we came out into a courtyard over-looked by windows with heavy iron bars.

'Oh dear, oh dear!' moaned Arthur. 'We've put our heads into the trap this time, I'm afraid.'

At this moment a piercing whistle sounded from above.

'Hullo, Arthur!'

Looking down from one of the barred windows high above was Otto.

'What did they get you for?' he shouted jocularly. Before either us could answer, a figure in uniform appeared beside him at the window and hustled him away. The apparition was as brief as it was disconcerting.

'They seem to have rounded up the whole gang,' I said, grinning.

'It's certainly very extraordinary,' said Arthur, much perturbed. 'I wonder if . . .'

We passed under an archway, up more stairs, into a honey-comb of little rooms and dark passages. On each floor were washbasins, painted a sanitary green. Arthur consulted his *Vorladung* and found the number of the room in which he was to present himself. We parted in hurried whispers.

'Good-bye, Arthur. Good luck. I'll wait for you here.'

'Thank you, dear boy . . . And supposing the worst comes to the worst, and I emerge from this room in custody, don't speak to me or make any sign that you know me unless I speak to you. It may be advisable not to involve you . . . here's Bayer's address; in case you have to go there alone.'

'I'm certain I shan't.'

'There's one more thing I wanted to say to you.' Arthur had the manner of one who mounts the steps of the scaffold.

'I'm sorry if I was a little hasty over the telephone this morning. I was very much upset . . . If this were to be our last meeting for some time, I shouldn't like you to remember it against me.'

'What rubbish, Arthur. Of course I shan't. Now run along, and let's get this over.'

He pressed my hand, knocked timidly at the door and went in.

I sat down to wait for him, under a blood-red poster advertising the reward for betraying a murderer. My bench shared by a fat Jewish slum lawyer and his client, a tearful little prostitute.

'All you've got to remember,' he kept telling her, 'is that you never saw him again after the night of the sixth.'

'But they'll get it out of me somehow,' she sobbed. 'I know they will. It's the way they look at you. And then they ask you a question so suddenly. You've no time to think.'

It was nearly an hour before Arthur reappeared. I could see at once from his face that the interview hadn't been so bad as he'd anticipated. He was in a great hurry.

'Come along, William. Come along. I don't care to stay here any longer than I need.'

Outside in the street he hailed a taxi and told the chauffeur to drive to the Hotel Kaiserhof, adding, as he nearly always did:

'There's no need to drive too fast.'

from Mr Norris Changes Trains, Christopher Isherwood

As for the extracts from Ambler and Greene, describing the same fictitious character – the atrocious Colonel Haki/Hakim, head of the Istanbul secret police – the pieces are separated by a thirty-year time-span; yet this is surely the greatest compliment one great writer has ever paid another in the history of English literature.

The Real Colonel Haki/Hakim

It was in the late afternoon of his last day there and he was sitting at the end of the vine-covered terrace out of earshot of the gramophone when he saw a large chauffeur-driven touring car lurching up the long dusty road to the villa. As it roared into the courtyard below, the occupant of the rear seat flung the door open and vaulted out before the car came to a standstill.

He was a tall man with lean, muscular cheeks whose pale tan

contrasted well with a head of grey hair cropped Prussian fashion. A narrow frontal bone, a long beak of a nose and thin lips gave him a somewhat predatory air. He could not be less than fifty, Latimer thought, and studied the waist below the beautifully cut officer's uniform in the hope of detecting the corsets.

He watched the tall officer whip a silk handkerchief from his sleeve, flick some invisible dust from his immaculate patent-leather riding boots, tilt his cap raffishly and stride out of sight. Somewhere in the villa, a bell pealed.

Colonel Haki, for this was the officer's name, was an immediate success with the party. A quarter of an hour after his arrival Madame Chávez, with an air of shy confusion clearly intended to inform her guests that she regarded herself as hopelessly compromised by the Colonel's unexpected appearance, led him on to the terrace and introduced him. All smiles and gallantry, he clicked heels, kissed hands, bowed, acknowledged the salutes of the naval officers and ogled the businessmen's wives. The performance so fascinated Latimer that, when his turn came to be introduced, the sound of his own name made him jump. The Colonel pump-handled his arm warmly.

'Damned pleased indeed to meet you, old boy,' he said.

'*Monsieur le Colonel parle bien anglais*,' explained Madame Chávez.

'*Quelques mots*,' said Colonel Haki.

Latimer looked amiably into a pair of pale grey eyes. 'How do you do?'

'Cheerio – all – the – best,' replied the Colonel with grave courtesy, and passed on to kiss the hand of, and to run an appraising eye over, a stout girl in a bathing costume.

It was not until late in the evening that Latimer spoke to the Colonel again. The Colonel had injected a good deal of boisterous vitality into the party: cracking jokes, laughing loudly, making humorously brazen advances to the wives and rather more surreptitious ones to the unmarried women. From time to time his eye caught Latimer's and he grinned deprecatingly. 'I've got to play the fool like this – it's expected of me,' said the grin; 'but don't think I like it.' Then, long after dinner, when the guests had begun to take less interest in the dancing and more in the progress of a game of mixed strip poker, the Colonel took him by the arm and walked him on to the terrace.

'You must excuse me, Mr Latimer,' he said in French, 'but I should very much like to talk with you. Those women – phew!' He slid a cigarette case under Latimer's nose. 'A cigarette?'

'Thank you'

Colonel Haki glanced over his shoulder. 'The other end of the terrace is more secluded,' he said; and then, as they began to walk: 'you know, I came up here today specially to see you. Madame told me you were here and really I could not resist the temptation of talking with the writer whose works I so much admire.'

Latimer murmured a non-committal appreciation of the compliment. He was in a difficulty, for he had no means of knowing whether the Colonel was thinking in terms of political economy or detection. He had once startled and irritated a kindly old don who had professed interest in his 'last book', by asking the old man whether he preferred his corpses shot or bludgeoned. It sounded affected to ask which set of books was under discussion.

Colonel Haki, however, did not wait to be questioned. 'I get all the latest *romans policiers* sent to me from Paris,' he went on. 'I read nothing but *romans policiers*. I would like you to see my collection. Especially I like the English and American ones. All the best of them are translated into French. French writers themselves, I do not find sympathetic. French culture is not such as can produce a *roman policier* of the first order. I have just added your *Une Pelle Ensanglantée* to my library. Formidable! But I cannot quite understand the significance of the title.'

Latimer spent some time trying to explain in French the meaning of 'to call a spade a bloody shovel' and to translate the play on words which had given (to those readers with suitable minds) the essential clue to the murderer's identity in the very title.

Colonel Haki listened intently, nodding his head and saying: 'Yes, I see it clearly now,' before Latimer had reached the point of the explanation.

'Monsieur,' he said when Latimer had given up in despair, 'I wonder whether you would do me the honour of lunching with me one day this week. I think,' he added mysteriously, 'that I may be able to help you.'

Latimer did not see in what way he could be helped by Colonel Haki but said that he would be glad to lunch with him. They arranged to meet at the Pera Palace Hotel three days later.

It was not until the evening before it that Latimer thought very much more about the luncheon appointment. He was sitting in the lounge of his hotel with the manager of his bankers' Istanbul branch.

Collinson, he thought, was a pleasant fellow but a monotonous companion. His conversation consisted almost entirely of gossip about the doings of the English and American colonies in Istanbul.

'Do you know the Fitzwilliams' he would say. 'No? A pity, you'd like them. Well the other day . . .' As a source of information about Kemal Ataturk's economic reforms he had proved a failure.

'By the way,' said Latimer after listening to an account of the goings-on of the Turkish-born wife of an American car salesman, 'do you know of a man named Colonel Haki?'

'Haki? What made you think of him?'

'I'm lunching with him tomorrow.'

Collinson's eyebrows went up. '*Are* you, by Jove! ' He scratched his chin. 'Well I know *of* him.' He hesitated. 'Haki's one of those people you hear a lot about in this place but never seem to get a line on. One of the people behind the scenes, if you get me. He's got more influence than a good many of the men who are supposed to be at the top at Ankara. He was one of the Gazi's own particular men in Anatolia in 1919, a deputy in the Provisional Government. I've heard stories about him then. Bloodthirsty devil, by all accounts. There was something about torturing prisoners. But then both sides did that and I dare say it was the Sultan's boys that started it. I heard, too, that he can drink a couple of bottles of Scotch at a sitting and stay stone cold sober. Don't believe that though. How did you get on to him?'

Latimer explained. 'What does he do for a living?' he added. 'I don't understand these uniforms.'

Collinson shrugged. 'Well, I've *heard* on good authority that he's the head of the secret police, but that's probably just another story. That's the worst of this place. Can't believe a word they say in the Club. Why, only the other day . . .'

It was with rather more enthusiasm than before that Latimer went to his luncheon appointment the following day. He had judged Colonel Haki to be something of a ruffian and Collinson's vague information had tended to confirm that view.

The Colonel arrived, bursting with apologies, twenty minutes late, and hurried his guest straight into the restaurant. 'We must have a whisky-soda immediately, ' he said and called loudly for a bottle of 'Johnnie'.

During most of the meal he talked about the detective stories he had read, his reactions to them, his opinions of the characters and his preference for murderers who shot their victims. At last, with an almost empty bottle of whisky at his elbow and a strawberry ice in front of him, he leaned forward across the table.

'I think, Mr Latimer,' he said again, 'that I can help you.'

For one wild moment Latimer wondered if he were going to be

offered a job in the Turkish secret service; but he said: 'That's very kind of you.'

'It was my ambition,' continued Colonel Haki, 'to write a good *roman policier* of my own. I have often thought that I could do so if I had the time. That is the trouble – the time. I have found that out. But . . .' He paused impressively.

Latimer waited. He was always meeting people who felt that they could write detective stories if they had the time.

'But,' repeated the Colonel, 'I have the plot prepared. I would like to make you a present of it.'

Latimer said that it was very good indeed of him.

The Colonel waved away his thanks. 'Your books have given me so much pleasure, Mr Latimer. I am glad to make you a present of an idea for a new one. I have not the time to use it myself and, in any case,' he added magnanimously, 'you would make better use of it than I should.'

Latimer mumbled incoherently.

'The scene of the story,' pursued his host, his grey eyes fixed on Latimer's, 'is an English country house belonging to the rich Lord Robinson. There is a party for the English weekend. In the middle of the party Lord Robinson is discovered in the library sitting at his desk – shot through the temple. The wound is singed. A pool of blood has formed on the desk and it has soaked into a paper. The paper is a new Will which the Lord was about to sign. The old Will divided his money equally between six persons, his relations, who are at the party. The new Will, which he has been prevented from signing by the murderer's bullet, leaves all to one of those relations. Therefore' – he pointed his ice-cream spoon accusingly – 'one of the five other relations is the guilty one. That is logical, is it not?'

Latimer opened his mouth, then shut it again and nodded.

Colonel Haki grinned triumphantly. 'That is the trick.'

'The trick?'

'The Lord was murdered by none of the suspects, but by the butler whose wife had been seduced by this Lord! What do you think of that, eh?'

'Very ingenious.'

His host leaned back contentedly and smoothed out his tunic. 'It is only a trick, but I am glad you like it. Of course, I have the whole plot worked out in detail. The *flic* is a High Commissioner of Scotland Yard. He seduces one of the suspects, a very pretty woman, and it is for her sake that he solves the mystery. It is quite artistic. But, as I say, I have the whole thing written out.'

'I should be very interested,' said Latimer with sincerity, 'to read your notes.'

from *The Mask of Dimitrios*, Eric Ambler

Two police cars blocked our way outside the Pera Palace. An elderly man who carried a walking stick crooked over his left arm was reaching with a stiff right leg towards the ground as we drew up. My driver told me in a tone of awe, 'That is Colonel Hakim.' The Colonel wore a very English suit of grey flannel with chalk stripes, and he had a small grey moustache. He looked like any veteran member of the Army and Navy alighting at his club.

'Very important man,' my driver told me. 'Very fair to Greeks.'

I went past the Colonel into the hotel. The receptionist was standing in the entrance presumably to welcome him; I was of so little importance that he wouldn't shift to let me by. I had to walk round him and he didn't answer my goodnight. A lift took me up to the fifth floor. When I saw a light under my aunt's door, I tapped and went in. She was sitting upright in bed wearing a bed-jacket and she was reading a paperback with a lurid cover.

'I've been seeing Istanbul,' I told her.

'So have I.' The curtains were drawn back and the lights of the city lay below us. She put her book down. The jacket showed a naked young woman lying in bed with a knife in her back, regarded by a man with a cruel face in a red fez. The title was *Turkish Delight*. 'I have been absorbing local atmosphere,' she said.

'Is the man in the fez the murderer?'

'No, he's the policeman. A very unpleasant type called Colonel Hakim.'

'How very odd because . . .'

'The murder takes place in this very Pera Palace but there are a good many details wrong, as you might expect from a novelist. The girl is loved by a British secret agent, a tough sentimental man called Amis, and they have dinner together on her last night at Abdullah's – you remember we had lunch there ourselves. They have a love scene too in Santa Sophia and there is an attempt on Amis's life at the Blue Mosque. We might almost have been doing a literary pilgrimage.'

'Hardly literary,' I said.

'Oh, you're your father's son. He tried to make me read Walter Scott, especially *Rob Roy*, but I much prefer, this. It moves a great deal quicker and there are fewer descriptions.'

'Did Amis murder her?'

'Of course not, but he is suspected by Colonel Hakim who has very cruel methods of interrogation,' my aunt said with relish.

The telephone rang. I answered it.

'Perhaps it's General Abdul at last,' she said, 'though it seems a little late for him to ring.'

'This is the reception speaking. Is Miss Bertram there?'

'Yes, what is it?'

'I am sorry to disturb her, but Colonel Hakim wishes to see her.'

'At this hour? Quite impossible. Why?'

'He is on the way up now.' He rang off.

'Colonel Hakim is on the way to see you,' I said.

'Colonel Hakim?'

'The real Colonel Hakim. He's a police officer too.'

'A police officer?' Aunt Augusta said. 'Again? I begin to think I am back in the old days. With Mr Visconti. Henry, will you open my suitcase? The green one. You'll find a light coat there. Fawn with a fur collar.'

'Yes, Aunt Augusta, I have it here.'

'Under the coat in a cardboard box you will find a candle – a decorated candle.'

'Yes, I see the box.'

'Take out the candle, but be careful because it's rather heavy. Put it on my bedside table and light it. Candlelight is better for my complexion.'

It was extraordinarily heavy and I nearly dropped it. It probably had some kind of lead weight at the bottom, I thought, to hold it steady. A big brick of scarlet wax which stood a foot high, it was decorated on all four sides with scrolls and coats of arms. A great deal of artistry had gone into moulding the wax which would melt away only too quickly. I lit the wick. 'Now turn out the light,' my aunt said, adjusting her bed-jacket and puffing up her pillow. There was a knock on the door and Colonel Hakim came in.

He stood in the doorway and bowed. 'Miss Bertram?' he asked.

'Yes. You are Colonel Hakim?'

'Yes. I am sorry to call on you so late without warning.' He spoke English with only the faintest intonation. 'I think we have a mutual acquaintance, General Abdul. May I sit down?'

'Of course. You'll find that chair by the dressing-table the most comfortable. This is my nephew, Henry Pulling.'

'Good evening, Mr Pulling. I hope you enjoyed the dancing at the West Berlin Hotel. A convivial spot unknown to most tourists. May I turn on the light, Miss Bertram?'

'I would rather not. I have weak eyes and I always prefer to read by candlelight.'

'A very beautiful candle.'

'They make them in Venice. The coats of arms belong to their four greatest doges. Don't ask me their names. How is General Abdul? I had been hoping to meet him again.'

'I am afraid General Abdul is a very sick man.' Colonel Hakim hooked his walking stick over the mirror before he sat down. He leant his head forward to my aunt at a slight angle, which gave him an air of deference, but I noticed that the real reason was a small hearing-aid that he carried in his right ear. 'He was a great friend of you and Mr Visconti, was he not?'

'The amount you know,' my aunt said with an endearing smile.

'Oh, it's my disagreeable business,' the Colonel said, 'to be a Nosey Harker.'

'Parker.'

'My English is rusty.'

'You had me followed to the West Berlin Hotel?' I asked.

'Oh no, I suggested to the driver that he should take you there,' Colonel Hakim said. 'I thought it might interest you and hold your attention longer than it did. The fashionable night clubs here are very banal and international. You might just as well be in Paris or London except that in those cities you would see a better show. Of course I told the driver to take you somewhere else first. One never knows.'

'Tell me about General Abdul,' my aunt said impatiently. 'What is wrong with him?'

Colonel Hakim leant forward a little more in his chair and lowered his voice as though he were confiding a secret. 'He was shot,' he said, 'while trying to escape.'

'Escape?' my aunt exclaimed. 'Escape from whom?'

'From me,' Colonel Hakim said with shy modesty and he fiddled at his hearing-aid. A long silence followed his words. There seemed nothing to say. Even my aunt was at a loss. She sat back against the cushions with her mouth a little open. Colonel Hakim took a tin out of his pocket and opened it. 'Excuse me,' he said, 'eucalyptus and menthol. I suffer from asthma.' He put a lozenge into his mouth and sucked. There was silence again until my aunt spoke.

'Those lozenges can't do you much good,' she said.

'I think it is only the suggestion. Asthma is a nervous disease. The lozenges *seem* to alleviate it, but only perhaps because I believe they alleviate it.' He panted a little when he spoke. 'I am always apt to get an attack when I am at the climax of a case.'

from *Travels with My Aunt*, Graham Greene

PITFALLS, HORRORS AND GENERAL NASTINESS

While torture and murder have been (together or separately) enduring staples of spy fiction, le Carré said dismissively of Bond that 'he is indifferent to pain . . .'. I think the next extract conclusively demonstrates the contrary. Indeed, there can be few readers – especially male *readers – who do not feel a genuine 'crawling of the skin' as they read of Bond's ordeal.*

'My Dear Boy'

It was a large bare room, sparsely furnished in cheap French 'art nouveau' style. It was difficult to say whether it was intended as a living- or dining-room for a flimsy-looking mirrored sideboard, sporting an orange crackle-ware fruit dish and two painted wooden candlesticks, took up most of the wall opposite the door and contradicted the faded pink sofa ranged against the other side of the room.

There was no table in the centre under the alabasterine ceiling light, only a small square of stained carpet with a futurist design in contrasting browns.

Over by the window was an incongruous-looking throne-like chair in carved oak with a red velvet seat, a low table on which stood an empty water carafe and two glasses, and a light armchair with a round cane seat and no cushion.

Half-closed venetian blinds obscured the view from the window, but cast bars of early sunlight over the few pieces of furniture and over part of the brightly papered wall and the brown stained floorboards.

Le Chiffre pointed at the cane chair.

'That will do excellently,' he said to the thin man. 'Prepare him quickly. If he resists, damage him only a little.'

He turned to Bond. There was no expression on his large face and his round eyes were uninterested. 'Take off your clothes. For every effort to resist, Basil will break one of your fingers. We are serious people and your good health is of no interest to us. Whether you live or die depends on the outcome of the talk we are about to have.'

He made a gesture towards the thin man and left the room.

The thin man's first action was a curious one. He opened the clasp-knife he had used on the hood of Bond's car, took the small armchair and with a swift motion he cut out its cane seat.

Then he came back to Bond, sticking the still open knife, like a fountain pen, in the vest pocket of his coat. He turned Bond round to the light and unwound the flex from his wrists. Then he stood quickly aside and the knife was back in his right hand.

'*Vite*.'

Bond stood chafing his swollen wrists and debating with himself how much time he could waste by resisting. He only delayed an instant. With a swift step and a downward sweep of his free hand, the thin man seized the collar of his dinner jacket and dragged it down, pinning Bond's arms back. Bond made the traditional counter to this old policeman's hold by dropping down on one knee but, as he dropped, the thin man dropped with him and, at the same time, brought his knife round and down behind Bond's back. Bond felt the back of the blade pass down his spine. There was the hiss of a sharp knife through cloth and his arms were suddenly free as the two halves of his coat fell forward.

He cursed and stood up. The thin man was back in his previous position, his knife again at the ready in his relaxed hand. Bond let the two halves of his dinner jacket fall off his arms on to the floor.

'*Allez*,' said the thin man with a faint trace of impatience.

Bond looked him in the eye and then slowly started to take off his shirt.

Le Chiffre came quietly back into the room. He carried a pot of what smelt like coffee. He put it on the small table near the window. He also placed beside it on the table two other homely objects, a three-foot-long carpet-beater in twisted cane and a carving-knife.

He settled himself comfortably on the throne-like chair and poured some of the coffee into one of the glasses. With one foot he hooked forward the small armchair whose seat was now an empty circular frame of wood, until it was directly opposite him.

Bond stood stark naked in the middle of the room, bruises showing livid on his white body, his face a grey mask of exhaustion and knowledge of what was to come.

'Sit down there.' Le Chiffre nodded at the chair in front of him.

Bond walked over and sat down.

The thin man produced some flex. With this he bound Bond's wrists to the arms of the chair and his ankles to the front legs.

He passed a double strand across his chest, under the armpits and through the chair-back. He made no mistakes with the knots and left no play in any of the bindings. All of them bit sharply into Bond's flesh. The legs of the chair were broadly spaced and Bond could not even rock it.

He was utterly a prisoner, naked and defenceless.

His buttocks and the underpart of his body protruded through the seat of the chair towards the floor.

Le Chiffre nodded to the thin man who quietly left the room and closed the door.

There was a packet of Gauloises on the table and a lighter. Le Chiffre lit a cigarette and swallowed a mouthful of coffee from the glass. Then he picked up the cane carpet-beater and, resting the handle comfortably on his knee, allowed the flat trefoil base to lie on the floor directly under Bond's chair.

He looked Bond carefully, almost caressingly, in the eyes. Then his wrist sprang suddenly upwards on his knee.

The result was startling.

Bond's whole body arched in an involuntary spasm. His face contracted in a soundless scream and his lips drew right away from his teeth. At the same time his head flew back with a jerk, showing the taut sinews of his neck. For an instant, muscles stood out in knots all over his body and his toes and fingers clenched until they were quite white. Then his body sagged and perspiration started to bead all over his skin. He uttered a deep groan.

Le Chiffre waited for his eyes to open.

'You see, dear boy?' He smiled a soft, fat smile. 'Is the position quite clear now?'

A drop of sweat fell off Bond's chin on to his naked chest.

'Now let us get down to business and see how soon we can be finished with this unfortunate mess you have got yourself into.' He puffed cheerfully at his cigarette and gave an admonitory tap on the floor beneath Bond's chair with his horrible and incongruous instrument.

'My dear boy,' Le Chiffre spoke like a father, 'the game of Red Indians is over, quite over. You have stumbled by mischance into a game for grown-ups and you have already found it a painful experience. You are not equipped, my dear boy, to play games with adults and it was very foolish of your nanny in London to have sent you out here with your spade and bucket. Very foolish indeed and most unfortunate for you.

'But we must stop joking, my dear fellow, although I am sure you would like to follow me in developing this amusing little cautionary tale.'

He suddenly dropped his bantering tone and looked at Bond sharply and venomously.

'Where is the money?'

Bond's bloodshot eyes looked emptily back at him.

Again the upward jerk of the wrist and again Bond's whole body writhed and contorted.

Le Chiffre waited until the tortured heart eased down its laboured pumping and until Bond's eyes dully opened again.

'Perhaps I should explain,' said Le Chiffre. 'I intend to continue attacking the sensitive parts of your body until you answer my question. I am without mercy and there will be no relenting. There is no one to stage a last-minute rescue and there is no possibility of escape for you. This is not a romantic adventure story in which the villain is finally routed and the hero is given a medal and marries the girl. Unfortunately these things don't happen in real life. If you continue to be obstinate, you will be tortured to the edge of madness and then the girl will be brought in and we will set about her in front of you. If that is still not enough, you will both be painfully killed and I shall reluctantly leave your bodies and make my way abroad to a comfortable house which is waiting for me. There I shall take up a useful and profitable career and live to a ripe and peaceful old age in the bosom of the family I shall doubtless create. So you see, my dear boy, that I stand to lose nothing. If you hand the money over, so much the better. If not, I shall shrug my shoulders and be on my way.'

He paused and his wrist lifted slightly on his knee. Bond's flesh cringed as the cane surface just touched him.

'But you, my dear fellow, can only hope that I shall spare you further pain and spare your life. There is no other hope for you but that. Absolutely none.

'Well?'

Bond closed his eyes and waited for the pain. He knew that the beginning of torture is the worst. There is a parabola of agony. A crescendo leading up to a peak and then the nerves are blunted and react progressively less until unconsciousness and death. All he could do was to pray for the peak, pray that his spirit would hold out so long and then accept the long free-wheel down to the final blackout.

He had been told by colleagues who had survived torture by the Germans and the Japanese that towards the end there came a wonderful period of warmth and languor leading into a sort of sexual twilight where pain turned to pleasure and where hatred and fear of the torturers turned to a masochistic infatuation. It was the supreme test of will, he had learnt, to avoid showing this form of punch-drunkenness. Directly it was suspected they would either kill you at once and save themselves further useless effort or let you recover sufficiently so that your nerves had crept back to the other side of the parabola. Then they would start again.

He opened his eyes a fraction.

Le Chiffre had been waiting for this and, like a rattlesnake, the cane instrument leapt up from the floor. It struck again and again so that Bond screamed and his body jangled in the chair like a marionette.

Le Chiffre desisted only when Bond's tortured spasms showed a trace of sluggishness. He sat for a while sipping his coffee and frowning slightly like a surgeon watching a cardiograph during a difficult operation.

When Bond's eyes flickered and opened he addressed him again, but now with a trace of impatience.

'We know that the money is somewhere in your room,' he said. 'You drew a cheque to cash for forty million francs and I know that you went back to the hotel to hide it.'

For a moment Bond wondered how he had been so certain.

'Directly you left for the night club,' continued Le Chiffre, 'your room was searched by four of my people.'

The Muntzes must have helped, reflected Bond.

'We found a good deal in childish hiding-places. The ballcock in the lavatory yielded an interesting little code-book and we found some more of your papers taped to the back of a drawer. All the furniture has been taken to pieces and your clothes and the curtains and bedclothes have been cut up. Every inch of the room has been searched and all the fittings removed. It is most unfortunate for you that we didn't find the cheque. If we had, you would now be comfortably in bed, perhaps with the beautiful Miss Lynd, instead of this.' He lashed upwards.

Through the red mist of pain, Bond thought of Vesper. He could imagine how she was being used by the two gunmen. They would be making the most of her before she was sent for by Le Chiffre. He thought of the fat wet lips of the Corsican and the slow cruelty of the thin man. Poor wretch to have been dragged into this. Poor little beast.

Le Chiffre was talking again.

'Torture is a terrible thing,' he was saying as he puffed at a fresh cigarette, 'but it is a simple matter for the torturer, particularly when the patient,' he smiled at the word, 'is a man. You see, my dear Bond, with a man it is quite unnecessary to indulge in refinements. With this simple instrument, or with almost any other object, one can cause a man as much pain as is possible or necessary. Do not believe what you read in novels or books about the war. There is nothing worse. It is not only the immediate agony, but also the thought that your manhood is being gradually destroyed and that, at the end, if you will not yield, you will no longer be a man.

'That, my dear Bond, is a sad and terrible thought – a long chain of agony for the body and also for the mind, and then the final screaming moment when you will beg me to kill you. All that is inevitable unless you tell me where you hid the money.'

He poured some more coffee into the glass and drank it down, leaving brown corners to his mouth.

Bond's lips were writhing. He was trying to say something. At last he got the word out in a harsh croak: 'Drink,' he said and his tongue came out and swilled across his dry lips.

'Of course, my dear boy, how thoughtless of me.' Le Chiffre poured some coffee into the other glass. There was a ring of sweat drops on the floor all round Bond's chair.

'We must certainly keep your tongue lubricated.'

He laid the handle of the carpet-beater down on the floor between his thick legs and rose from his chair. He went behind Bond and, taking a handful of his soaking hair in one hand, he wrenched Bond's head sharply back. He poured the coffee down Bond's throat in small mouthfuls so that he would not choke. Then he released his head so that it fell forward again on his chest. He went back to his chair and picked up the carpet-beater.

Bond raised his head and spoke thickly.

'Money no good to you.' His voice was a laborious croak. 'Police trace it to you.'

Exhausted by the effort, his head sank forward again. He was a little, but only a little, exaggerating the extent of his physical collapse. Anything to gain time and anything to defer the next searing pain.

'Ah, my dear fellow, I had forgotten to tell you.' Le Chiffre smiled wolfishly. 'We met after our little game at the Casino and you were such a sportsman that you agreed we would have one more run through the pack between the two of us. It was a gallant gesture. Typical of an English gentleman.

'Unfortunately, you lost and this upset you so much that you decided to leave Royale immediately for an unknown destination. Like the gentleman you are, you very kindly gave me a note explaining the circumstances so that I would have no difficulty in cashing your cheque. You see, dear boy, everything has been thought of and you need have no fears on my account.' He chuckled fatly.

'Now shall we continue? I have all the time in the world and, truth to tell, I am rather interested to see how long a man can stand this particular form of . . . er . . . encouragement.' He rattled the harsh cane on the floor.

So that was the score, thought Bond, with a final sinking of the heart. The 'unknown destination' would be under the ground or under the sea or, perhaps more simple, under the crashed Bentley. Well, if he had to die anyway, he might as well try it the hard way. He had no hope that Mathis or Leiter would get to him in time, but at least there was a chance that they would catch up with Le Chiffre before he could get away. It must be getting on for seven. The car might have been found by now. It was a choice of evils, but the longer Le Chiffre continued the torture the more likely he would be revenged.

Bond lifted his head and looked Le Chiffre in the eyes.

The china of the whites was now veined with red. It was like looking at two blackcurrants poached in blood. The rest of the wide face was yellowish except where a thick black stubble covered the moist skin. The upward edges of black coffee at the corners of the mouth gave his expression a false smile and the whole face was faintly striped by the light through the venetian blinds.

'No,' he said flatly, '. . . you.'

Le Chiffre grunted and set to work again with savage fury. Occasionally he snarled like a wild beast.

After ten minutes Bond had fainted, blessedly.

Le Chiffre at once stopped. He wiped some sweat from his face with a circular motion of his disengaged hand. Then he looked at his watch and seemed to make up his mind.

He got up and stood behind the inert, dripping body. There was no colour in Bond's face or anywhere on his body above the waist. There was a faint flutter of his skin above the heart. Otherwise he might have been dead.

Le Chiffre seized Bond's ears and harshly twisted them. Then he leant forward and slapped his cheeks hard several times. Bond's head rolled from side to side with each blow. Slowly his breathing became deeper. An animal groan came from his lolling mouth.

Le Chiffre took a glass of coffee and poured some into Bond's mouth and threw the rest in his face. Bond's eyes slowly opened.

Le Chiffre returned to his chair and waited. He lit a cigarette and contemplated the spattered pool of blood on the floor beneath the inert body opposite.

Bond groaned again pitifully. It was an inhuman sound. His eyes opened wide and he gazed dully at his torturer.

Le Chiffre spoke.

'That is all, Bond. We will now finish with you. You understand? Not kill you, but finish with you. And then we will have in the girl and see if something can be got out of the remains of the two of you.'

He reached towards the table.

'Say goodbye to it, Bond.'

from Casino Royale, Ian Fleming

For his part, John le Carré actually outbids Fleming for sheer, unmitigated horror in this brief scene from The Honourable Schoolboy, *in which a wretched, boozy ex-pat banker in Hong Kong is 'punished' by Chinese gangsters for his indiscretions during a night on the tiles. The horror is all the more shocking for being unspecific. The* Bulldog Drummond *extract, on the other hand, leaves nothing to the imagination and succeeds in being as harmless as something from* The Boy's Own Paper.

'That's Not a Mugging. That's a Party . . .'

Lifting the receiver Jerry nursed the idiotic hope it might be Lizzie, but it wasn't.

'Get your ass down here fast,' Luke promised. 'And Stubbsie will *love* you. *Move* it. I'm doing you the favour of our career.'

'Where's here?' Jerry asked.

'Downstairs, you ape.'

He rolled the girl off him but she still didn't wake.

The roads glittered with the unexpected rain and a thick halo ringed the moon. Luke drove as if they were in a jeep, in high gear with hammer changes on the corners. Fumes of whisky filled the car.

'What have you got, for Christ's sake?' Jerry demanded. 'What's going on?'

'Great meat. Now shut up.'

'I don't want meat. I'm suited.'

'You'll want this one. *Man*, you'll want this one.'

They were heading for the harbour tunnel. A flock of cyclists without lights lurched out of a side turning and Luke had to mount the central reservation to avoid them. Look for a damn great building site, Luke said. A patrol car overtook them, all lights flashing. Thinking he was going to be stopped, Luke lowered his window.

'We're *press*, you idiots,' he screamed. 'We're *stars*, hear me?'

Inside the patrol car as it passed they had a glimpse of a Chinese sergeant and his driver, and an august-looking European perched in the back like a judge. Ahead of them, to the right of the carriageway, the promised building site sprang into view, a cage of yellow girders and bamboo scaffolding alive with sweating coolies. Cranes, glistening in the wet, dangled over them like whips. The floodlighting came from the ground and poured wastefully into the mist.

'Look for a low place, just near,' Luke ordered, slowing down to sixty. 'White. Look for a white place.'

Jerry pointed to it, a two-storey complex of weeping stucco, neither new nor old, with a twenty-foot bamboo-stand by the entrance, and an ambulance. The ambulance stood open and the three drivers lounged in it, smoking, watching the police who milled around the forecourt as if it were a riot they were handling.

'He's giving us an hour's start over the field.'

'Who?'

'Rocker. Rocker is. Who do you think?'

'Why?'

'Because he hit me, I guess. He loves me. He loves you too. He said to bring you specially.'

'Why?'

The rain fell steadily.

'*Why? Why? Why?*' Luke echoed, furious. 'Just hurry!'

The bamboos were out of scale, higher than the wall. A couple of orange-clad priests were sheltering against them, clapping cymbals. A third held an umbrella. There were flower stalls, mainly marigolds, and hearses, and from somewhere out of sight the sounds of leisurely incantation. The entrance lobby was a jungle swamp reeking of formaldehyde.

'Big Moo's special envoy,' said Luke.

'Press,' said Jerry.

The police nodded them through, not looking at their cards.

'Where's the Superintendent?' said Luke.

The smell of formaldehyde was awful. A young sergeant led them. They pushed through a glass door to a room where old men and women, maybe thirty of them, mostly in pyjama suits, waited phlegmatically as if for a late train, under shadowless neon lights and an electric fan. One old man was clearing out his throat, snorting on to the green tiled floor. Only the plaster wept. Seeing the giant *kwailos* they stared in polite amazement. The pathologist's office was yellow. Yellow walls, yellow blinds, closed. An airconditioner that wasn't working. The same green tiles, easily washed down.

'Great *smell*,' said Luke.

'Like home.' Jerry agreed.

Jerry wished it was battle. Battle was easier. The sergeant told them to wait while he went ahead. They heard the squeak of trolleys, low voices, the clamp of a freezer door, the low hiss of rubber soles. A volume of *Gray's Anatomy* lay next to the telephone. Jerry turned the pages, staring at the illustrations. Luke perched on a chair. An assistant in short rubber boots and overalls brought tea. White cups, green rims, and the Hong Kong monogram with a crown.

'Can you tell the sergeant to hurry, please?' said Luke. 'You'll have the whole damn town here in a minute.'

'Why us?' said Jerry again.

Luke poured some tea on to the tiled floor and while it ran into the gutter he topped up the cup from his whisky flask. The sergeant returned, beckoning quickly with his slender hand. They followed him back through the waiting room. This way there was no door, just a corridor, and a turn like a public lavatory, and they were there. The first thing Jerry saw was the trolley chipped to hell. There's nothing older or more derelict than worn-out hospital equipment, he thought. The walls were covered in green mould, green stalactites hung from the ceiling, a battered spittoon was filled with used tissues. They clean out the noses, he remembered, before they pull down the sheet to show you. It's a courtesy so that you aren't shocked. The fumes of formaldehyde made his eyes run. A Chinese pathologist was sitting at the window, making notes on a pad. A couple of attendants were hovering, and more police. There seemed to be a general sense of apology around. Jerry couldn't make it out. The Rocker was ignoring them. He was in a corner, murmuring to the august-looking gentleman from the back of the patrol car, but the corner wasn't far away and Jerry heard 'slur on our reputation' spoken twice in an indignant, nervous tone. A white sheet covered the body, with a blue cross on it made in two equal lengths. So that they can use it either way round, Jerry thought. It was the only trolley in the room. The only sheet. The rest of the exhibition was inside the two big freezers with the wooden doors, walk-in size, big as a butcher's shop. Luke was going out of his mind with impatience.

'Jesus, Rocker!' he called across the room. 'How much longer you going to keep the lid on this? We got work to do.'

No one bothered with him. Tired of waiting, Luke yanked back the sheet. Jerry looked and looked away. The autopsy room was next door and he could hear the sound of sawing, like the snarling of a dog.

No wonder they're all so apologetic, Jerry thought stupidly. *Bringing a roundeye corpse to a place like this*.

'Jesus *Christ*,' Luke was saying. 'Holy *Christ*. Who did it to him? How do you *make* those marks? That's a Triad thing. *Jesus*.'

The dampened window gave on to the courtyard. Jerry could see the bamboo rocking in the rain and the liquid shadows of an ambulance delivering another customer, but he doubted whether any of them looked like this. A police photographer had appeared and there were flashes. A telephone extension hung on the wall. The Rocker was talking into it. He still hadn't looked at Luke, or at Jerry.

'I want him out of here,' the august gentleman said.

'Soon as you like,' said the Rocker. He returned to the telephone. 'In the Walled City, sir . . . Yes, sir . . . In an alley, sir. Stripped. Lot of alcohol . . . The forensic pathologist recognized him immediately, sir. Yes sir, the bank's here already, sir.' He rang off. 'Yes sir, no sir, three bags full, sir,' he growled. He dialled a number.

Luke was making notes. 'Jesus,' he kept saying in awe. 'Jesus. They must have taken *weeks* to kill him. Months.'

In actual fact, they had killed him twice, Jerry decided. Once to make him talk and once to shut him up. The things they had done to him first were all over his body, in big and small patches, the way fire hits a carpet, eats holes, then suddenly gives up. Then there was the thing round his neck, a different, faster death altogether. They had done that last, when they didn't want him any more.

Luke called to the pathologist. 'Turn him over, will you? Would you mind please turning him over, *sir*.'

The Superintendent had put down the phone.

'What's the story?' said Jerry, straight at him. 'Who is he?'

'Name of Frost,' the Rocker said, staring back with his dropped eye. 'Senior official of the South Asian and China Trustee Department.'

'Who killed him?' Jerry asked.

'Yeah, who did it? That's the point,' said Luke, writing hard.

'Mice,' said the Rocker.

'Hong Kong has no Triads, no communists and no Kuomintang. Right, Rocker?'

'And no whores,' the Rocker growled.

The august gentleman spared the Rocker further reply.

'A vicious case of mugging,' he declared, over the policeman's shoulder. 'A filthy, vicious mugging exemplifying the need for public vigilance at all times. He was a loyal servant of the bank.'

'That's not a mugging,' said Luke, looking at Frost again. 'That's a *party*.'

'He certainly had some damned odd friends,' the Rocker said, still staring at Jerry.

'What's that supposed to mean?' said Jerry.

'What's the story so far?' said Luke.

'He was on the town till midnight. Celebrating in the company of a couple of Chinese males. One cathouse after another. Then we lose him. Till tonight.'

'The bank's offering a reward of $50,000,' said the august man.

'Hong Kong or US?' said Luke, writing.

The august man said 'Hong Kong' very tartly.

'Now you boys go easy,' the Rocker warned. 'There's a sick wife in Stanley Hospital, and there's kids—'

'And there's the reputation of the bank,' said the august man.

'That will be our first concern,' said Luke.

They left half an hour later, still ahead of the field.

'Thanks,' said Luke to the Superintendent.

'For nothing,' said the Rocker. His dropped eyelid, Jerry noticed, leaked when he was tired.

We've shaken the tree, thought Jerry, as they drove away.

from *The Honourable Schoolboy*, John le Carré

'Sapper' may be more graphic but he's not necessarily so chilling . . .

Another Touch of Nastiness

It was half an hour before Drummond decided that it was safe to start exploring. The moon still shone fitfully through the trees but, since the two car watchers were near the road on the other side of the house, there was but little danger to be apprehended from them. First he took off his shoes and, tying the laces together, he slung them round his neck. Then, as silently as he could, he commenced to scramble upwards.

It was not an easy operation; one slip and nothing could have stopped him slithering down and finally crashing into the garden below, with a broken leg, at the very least, for his pains. In addition, there was the risk of dislodging a slate, an unwise proceeding in a house where most of the occupants slept with one eye open. But at last he got his hands over the ridge of the roof, and in another moment he was sitting straddle-wise across it.

The house, he discovered, was built on a peculiar design. The ridge on which he sat continued at the same height all round the top of the roof and formed, roughly, the four sides of a square. In the middle the roof sloped down to a flat space from which stuck up a glass structure, the top of which was some five or six feet below his level. Around it was a space quite large enough to walk in comfort; in fact, on two sides there was plenty of room for a deck chair. The whole area was completely screened from view, except to anyone in an aeroplane. And what struck him still further was that there was no window that he could see anywhere on the inside of the roof. In fact, it was absolutely concealed and private. Incidentally, the house had originally been built by a gentleman of doubtful sanity who spent his life observing the spots in Jupiter through a telescope and, having plunged himself and his family into complete penury, sold the house and observatory complete for what he could get. Lakington, struck with its possibilities for his own hobby, bought it on the spot; and from that time Jupiter spotted undisturbed.

With the utmost caution Hugh lowered himself to the full extent of his arms; then he let himself slip the last two or three feet on to the level space around the glass roof. He had no doubt in his mind that he was actually above the secret room and, on tip-toe, he stole round looking for some spot from which he could get a glimpse below. At the first inspection he thought his time had been wasted; every pane of glass was frosted and, in addition, there seemed to be a thick blind of some sort drawn across from underneath, of the same type as is used by photographers for altering the light.

A sudden rattle close to him made him start violently, only to curse himself for a nervous ass the next moment, and lean forward eagerly. One of the blinds had been released from inside the room and a pale, diffused light came filtering out into the night from the side of the glass roof. He was still craning backwards and forwards to try to find some chink through which he could see when, with a kind of uncanny deliberation, one of the panes of glass slowly opened. It was worked on a ratchet from inside, and Hugh bowed his thanks to the unseen operator below. Then he leant forward cautiously and peered in . . .

The whole room was visible to him and his jaw tightened as he took in the scene. In an armchair, smoking as unconcernedly as ever, sat Peterson. He was reading a letter and occasionally underlining some point with a pencil. Beside him on a table was a big ledger and, every now and then, he would turn over a few pages and make an entry. But it was not Peterson on whom the watcher above was concentrating his attention; it was Lakington – and the thing beside him on the sofa.

Lakington was bending over a long bath full of some light-brown liquid from which a faint vapour was rising. He was in his shirt sleeves and on his hands he wore what looked like rubber gloves, stretching right up to his elbows. After a while he dipped a test-tube into the liquid and, going over to a shelf, he selected a bottle and added a few drops to the contents of the tube. Apparently satisfied with the result, he returned to the bath and shook in some white powder. Immediately the liquid commenced to froth and bubble and, at the same moment, Peterson stood up.

'Are you ready?' he said, taking off his coat and picking up a pair of gloves similar to those the other was wearing.

'Quite,' answered Lakington abruptly. 'We'll get him in.'

They approached the sofa and Hugh, with a kind of fascinated horror, forced himself to look. For the thing that lay there was the body of the dead Russian, Ivolsky.

The two men picked him up and, having carried the body to the bath, they dropped it into the fuming liquid. Then, as if it was the most normal thing in the world, they peeled off their long gloves and stood watching. For a minute or so nothing happened and then gradually the body commenced to disappear. A faint, sickly smell came through the open window and Hugh wiped the sweat off his forehead. It was too horrible, the hideous deliberation of it all. And whatever vile tortures the wretched man had inflicted on others in Russia, yet it was through him that his dead body lay there in the bath, disappearing slowly and relentlessly . . .

Lakington lit a cigarette and strolled over to the fireplace.

'Another five minutes should be enough,' he remarked. 'Damn that cursed soldier!'

Peterson laughed gently and resumed the study of his ledger.

'To lose one's temper with a man, my dear Henry, is a sign of inferiority. But it certainly is a nuisance that Ivolsky is dead. He could talk more unmitigated drivel to the minute than all the rest of 'em put together . . . I really don't know who to put in the Midland area.'

He leaned back in his chair and blew out a cloud of smoke. The light shone on the calm, impassive face; with a feeling of wonder that was never far absent from his mind when he was with Peterson, Hugh noted the high, clever forehead, the firmly moulded nose and chin, the sensitive, humorous mouth. The man lying back in the chair watching the blue smoke curling up from his cigar might have been a great lawyer or an eminent divine; some well-known statesman, perhaps, or a Napoleon of finance. There was power in every line of his figure, in every movement of his hands. He might have reached to the top of any profession he had cared to follow . . . Just as he had reached the top in his present one . . . Some kink in the brain, some little cog wrong in the wonderful mechanism, and a great man had become a great criminal. Hugh looked at the bath; the liquid was almost clear.

'You know my feelings on the subject,' remarked Lakington, taking a red velvet box out of a drawer in the desk. He opened it lovingly and Hugh saw the flash of diamonds. Lakington let the stones run through his hands, glittering with a thousand flames, while Peterson watched him contemptuously.

'Baubles,' he said scornfully. 'Pretty baubles. What will you get for them?'

'Ten, perhaps fifteen thousand,' returned the other. 'But it's not the money I care about; it's the delight in having them and the skill required to get them.'

Peterson shrugged his shoulders.

'Skill which would give you hundreds of thousands if you turned it into proper channels.'

Lakington replaced the stones and threw the end of his cigarette into the grate.

'Possibly, Carl, quite possibly. But it boils down to this, my friend, that you like the big canvas with broad effects; I like the miniature and the well-drawn etching.'

'Which makes us a very happy combination,' said Peterson, rising and walking over to the bath. 'The pearls, don't forget, are your job. The big thing' – he turned to the other, and a trace of excitement came into his voice – 'the big thing is mine.' Then with his hands in his pockets he stood staring at the brown liquid. 'Our friend is nearly cooked, I think.'

'Another two or three minutes,' said Lakington, joining him. 'I must confess I pride myself on the discovery of that mixture. Its only drawback is that it makes murder too easy . . .'

The sound of the door opening made both men swing round instantly; then Peterson stepped forward with a smile.

'Back, my dear? I hardly expected you so soon.'

Irma came a little way into the room and stopped with a sniff of disgust.

'What a horrible smell!' she remarked. 'What on earth have you been doing?'

'Disposing of a corpse,' said Lakington. 'It's nearly finished.'

The girl threw off her opera cloak and, coming forward, peered over the edge of the bath.

'It's not my ugly soldier?' she cried.

'Unfortunately not,' returned Lakington grimly; and Peterson laughed.

'Henry is most annoyed, Irma. The irrepressible Drummond has scored again.'

from *Bulldog Drummond*, 'Sapper'

TRICKS AND GADGETS OF THE TRADE

On such matters as disguise and technology, Deighton is typically the most exact and up-to-date, while William Le Queux, writing at the beginning of the century, seems the most far-fetched – until we remember the CIA's plan (never executed) for assassinating Fidel Castro.

Buchan also takes sublime refuge in disguise, again from the classic Greenmantle. (Incidentally, is it my imagination – or is it Hannay's – that we are treated here to a whiff of more than just incense, in the 'Rosy Hours' dive in Constantinople?)

I have also included in this section the first spy story ever written: Edgar Allan Poe's The Purloined Letter, *first published in a New York magazine in 1842.*

Hints on Disguise

'Why did you change over the eggs in that package?'

'I told you, Harvey, the package of eggs was stolen from my baggage on the way to London Airport.'

'Tell me about that again.'

'I already told you. It was the same man who followed me from the doctor's surgery. Full face. Black horn-rimmed spectacles. Medium height.'

Harvey said, 'You said projecting ears, bad teeth, long hair, sounded like an Englishman who wanted to be taken for a Yank, bad breath. You gave me a long description.'

'That's right, the horn-rimmed spectacles were adapted to make his ears project. He was an American who put flat Cockney vowel sounds into his American accent to sound like an Englishman assuming an American accent. He used a hair-piece to cover a bald patch on top of his head. (It didn't come near the hair line so if he hadn't kept tapping it, no one would have noticed it.) He blacked out a couple of his front teeth with stage cosmetic and made his breath smell with chemical – oldest trick in the business to prevent people looking you in the face close to. He stole the baggage after it had been through customs.' I paused.

Harvey was grinning. 'Yes,' he said. 'It was me.'

I went on. 'I'd say he was a transit airline passenger on a refuelling stop who got off his aeroplane, changed into a pair of overalls in the toilet, drove off with a van-load of baggage, took what he wanted and was back on his plane well within the time his flight was called, to continue his journey without even going through customs. Not bad for someone who had just barn-stormed around after leaving college.'

Harvey laughed and said, 'Elevator shoes, contact lenses to change the eye colour, dirtied fingernails and a trace of colouring on the lips to make the face seem pale. You forgot all those.'

from *Billion Dollar Brain*, Len Deighton

And from a modern master of disguises to a past master...

An Example of the Same

We walked straight through the café, which was empty, and down the dark passage till we were stopped by the garden door. I knocked and it swung open. There was the bleak yard, now puddled with snow, and a blaze of light from the pavilion at the other end. There was a scraping of fiddles, too, and the sound of human talk. We paid the negro at the door and passed from the bitter afternoon into a garish saloon.

There were forty or fifty people there, drinking coffee and sirops and filling the air with the fumes of latakia. Most of them were Turks in European clothes and the fez, but there were some German officers and what looked like German civilians – Army Service Corps clerks, probably, and mechanics from the Arsenal. A woman in cheap finery was tinkling at the piano and there were several shrill females with the officers. Peter and I sat down modestly in the nearest corner, where old Kuprasso saw us and sent us coffee. A girl who looked like a Jewess came over to us and talked French, but I shook my head and she went off again.

Presently a girl came on the stage and danced, a silly affair, all a clashing of tambourines and wriggling. I have seen native women do the same thing better in a Mozambique kraal. Another sang a German song, a simple, sentimental thing about golden hair and rainbows, and the Germans present applauded. The place was so tinselly and common that, coming to it from weeks of rough travelling, it made me impatient. I forgot that, while for the others it might be a vulgar little dancing-hall, for us it was as perilous as a brigands' den.

Peter did not share my mood. He was quite interested in it, as he was interested in everything new. He had a genius for living in the moment.

I remember there was a drop-scene on which was daubed a blue lake with very green hills in the distance. As the tobacco smoke grew thicker and the fiddles went on squealing, this tawdry picture began to mesmerize me. I seemed to be looking out of a window at a lovely summer landscape where there were no wars or dangers. I seemed to feel the warm sun and to smell the fragrance of blossom from the islands. And then I became aware that a queer scent had stolen into the atmosphere.

There were braziers burning at both ends to warm the room and the thin smoke from these smelt like incense. Somebody had been putting a powder in the flames, for suddenly the place became very quiet. The fiddles still sounded, but far away like an echo. The lights went down, all but a circle on the stage, and into that circle stepped my enemy of the skin cap.

He had three others with him. I heard a whisper behind me and the words were those which Kuprasso had used the day before. These bedlamites were called the Companions of the Rosy Hours, and Kuprasso had promised great dancing.

I hoped to goodness they would not see us, for they had fairly given me the horrors. Peter felt the same and we both made ourselves very small in that dark corner. But the newcomers had no eyes for us.

In a twinkling the pavilion changed from a common saloon, which might have been in Chicago or Paris, to a place of mystery – yes, and of beauty. It became the garden-house of Suliman the Red, whoever that sportsman may have been. Sandy had said that the ends of the earth converged there and he had been right. I lost all consciousness of my neighbours – stout German, frock-coated Turk, frowsy Jewess – and saw only strange figures leaping in a circle of light, figures that came out of the deepest darkness to make big magic.

The leader flung some stuff into the brazier and a great fan of blue light flared up. He was weaving circles, and he was singing something shrill and high, whilst his companions made a chorus with their deep monotone. I can't tell you what the dance was. I had seen the Russian ballet just before the war, and one of the men in it reminded me of this man. But the dancing was the least part of it. It was neither sound nor movement nor scent that wrought the spell, but something far more potent. In an instant I found myself reft away from the present, with its dull dangers, and looking at a world all young and fresh and beautiful. The gaudy drop-scene had vanished. It was a window I was looking from, and I was gazing at the finest landscape on earth, lit by the pure clean light of morning.

It seemed to be part of the veld but like no veld I had ever seen. It was wider and wilder and more gracious. Indeed, I was looking at my first youth. I was feeling the kind of immortal light-heartedness which only a boy knows in the dawning of his days. I had no longer any fear of these magic-makers. They were kindly wizards who had brought me into fairyland.

Then slowly from the silence there distilled drops of music. They came like water falling a long way into a cup, each the essential quality of pure sound. We, with our elaborate harmonies, have forgotten the charm of single notes. The African natives know it, and I remember a learned man once telling me that the Greeks had the same art. Those silver bells broke out of infinite space, so exquisite and perfect that no mortal words could have been fitted to them. That was the music, I expect, that the morning stars made when they sang together.

Slowly, very slowly, it changed. The glow passed from blue to purple, and then to an angry red. Bit by bit the notes spun together till they had made a harmony – a fierce, restless harmony. And I was conscious again of the skin-clad dancers beckoning out of their circle.

There was no mistake about the meaning now. All the daintiness and youth had fled, and passion was beating in the air – terrible, savage passion, which belonged neither to day nor night, life nor death, but to the half-world between them. I suddenly felt the dancers as monstrous, inhuman, devilish. The thick scents that floated from the brazier seemed to have a tang of new-shed blood. Cries broke from the hearers – cries of anger and lust and terror. I heard a woman sob and Peter, who is as tough as any mortal, took tight hold of my arm.

I now realized that these Companions of the Rosy Hours were the only thing in the world to fear. Rasta and Stumm seemed feeble simpletons by contrast. The window I had been looking out of was changed to a prison wall – I could see the mortar between the massive blocks. In a second these devils would be smelling out their enemies like some foul witch-doctors. I felt the burning eyes of their leader looking for me in the gloom. Peter was praying audibly beside me and I could have choked him. His infernal chatter would reveal us, for it seemed to me that there was no one in the place except us and the magic-workers.

Then suddenly the spell was broken. The door was flung open and a great gust of icy wind swirled through the hall, driving clouds of ashes from the braziers. I heard loud voices without and a hubbub began inside. For a moment it was quite dark, and then some one lit one of the flare lamps by the stage. It revealed nothing but the common squalor of a low saloon – white faces, sleepy eyes and frowsy heads. The drop-scene was there in all its tawdriness.

The Companions of the Rosy Hours had gone. But at the door stood men in uniform. I heard a German a long way off murmur, 'Enver's bodyguards,' and I heard him distinctly; for, though I could not see clearly, my hearing was desperately acute. That is often the way when you suddenly come out of a swoon.

The place emptied like magic. Turk and German tumbled over each other, while Kuprasso wailed and wept. No one seemed to stop them, and then I saw the reason. Those guards had come for us. This must be Stumm at last. The authorities had tracked us down and it was all up with Peter and me.

A sudden revulsion leaves a man with low vitality. I didn't seem to care greatly. We were done, and there was an end of it. It was Kismet, the act of God, and there was nothing for it but to submit. I hadn't a flicker of a thought of escape or resistance. The game was utterly and absolutely over.

A man who seemed to be a sergeant pointed to us and said something to Kuprasso, who nodded. We got heavily to our feet and stumbled towards them. With one on each side of us we crossed the yard, walked through the dark passage and the empty shop, and out into the snowy street. There was a closed carriage waiting which they motioned us to get into. It looked exactly like the Black Maria.

Both of us sat still, like truant schoolboys, with our hands on our knees. I didn't know where I was going and I didn't care. We seemed to be rumbling up the hill and then I caught the glare of lighted streets.

'This is the end of it, Peter,' I said.

'*Ja*, Cornelis,' he replied, and that was all our talk.

By and by – hours later it seemed – we stopped. Some one opened the door and we got out, to find ourselves in a courtyard with a huge dark building around. The prison, I guessed, and I wondered if they would give us blankets, for it was perishing cold.

We entered a door and found ourselves in a big stone hall. It was quite warm, which made me more hopeful about our cells. A man in some kind of uniform pointed to the staircase, up which we plodded wearily. My mind was too blank to take clear impressions, or in any way to forecast the future. Another warder met us and took us down a passage till we halted at a door. He stood aside and motioned us to enter.

I guessed that this was the governor's room and we should be put through our first examination. My head was too stupid to think and I made up my mind to keep perfectly mum. Yes, even if they tried thumbscrews. I had no kind of a story but I resolved not to give anything away. As I turned the handle I wondered idly what kind of sallow Turk or bulging-necked German we should find inside.

It was a pleasant room with a polished wood floor and a big fire burning on the hearth. Beside the fire a man lay on a couch, with a little table drawn up beside him. On that table was a small glass of milk and a number of Patience cards spread in rows.

I stared blankly at the spectacle, till I saw a second figure. It was the man in the skin-cap, the leader of the dancing maniacs. Both Peter and I backed sharply at the sight and then stood stock still.

For the dancer crossed the room in two strides and gripped both of my hands.

'Dick, old man,' he cried, 'I'm most awfully glad to see you again!'

from *Greenmantle*, John Buchan

The Purloined Letter

Nil sapientiae odiosius acumine nimio.
SENECA

At Paris, just after dark one gusty evening in the autumn of 18—, I was enjoying the twofold luxury of meditation and a meerschaum, in company with my friend, C. Auguste Dupin, in his little back library, or book-closet, *au troisième*, No. 33 Rue Dunôt, Faubourg St Germain. For one hour at least we had maintained a profound silence; while each, to any casual observer, might have seemed intently and exclusively occupied with the curling eddies of smoke that oppressed the atmosphere of the chamber. For myself, however, I was mentally discussing certain topics which had formed matter for conversation between us at an earlier period of the evening; I mean the affair of the Rue Morgue and the mystery attending the murder of Marie Rogêt. I looked upon it, therefore, as something of a coincidence when the door of our apartment was thrown open and admitted our old acquaintance, Monsieur G—, the Prefect of the Parisian police.

We gave him a hearty welcome for there was nearly half as much of the entertaining as of the contemptible about the man, and we had not seen him for several years. We had been sitting in the dark and Dupin now arose for the purpose of lighting a lamp, but sat down again, without doing so, upon G.'s saying that he had called to consult us, or rather to ask the opinion of my friend, about some official business which had occasioned a great deal of trouble.

'If it is any point requiring reflection,' observed Dupin, as he forbore to enkindle the wick, 'we shall examine it to better purpose in the dark.'

'That is another of your odd notions,' said the Prefect, who had the fashion of calling everything 'odd' that was beyond his comprehension, and thus lived amid an absolute legion of 'oddities'.

'Very true,' said Dupin, as he supplied his visitor with a pipe and rolled towards him a comfortable chair.

'And what is the difficulty now?' I asked. 'Nothing more in the assassination way, I hope?'

'Oh no; nothing of that nature. The fact is, the business is *very* simple indeed and I make no doubt that we can manage it sufficiently well ourselves; but then I thought Dupin would like to hear the details of it, because it is so excessively *odd*.'

'Simple and odd,' said Dupin.

'Why, yes; and not exactly that either. The fact is, we have all been a good deal puzzled because the affair *is* so simple, and yet baffles us altogether.'

'Perhaps it is the very simplicity of the thing which puts you at fault,' said my friend.

'What nonsense you *do* talk!' replied the Prefect, laughing heartily.

'Perhaps the mystery is a little *too* plain,' said Dupin.

'Oh, good heavens! Who ever heard of such an idea?'

'A little *too* self-evident.'

'Ha! ha! ha! – ha! ha! ha! – ho! ho! ho!' roared our visitor, profoundly amused. 'Oh, Dupin, you will be the death of me yet!'

'And what, after all, *is* the matter on hand?' I asked.

'Why, I will tell you,' replied the Prefect, as he gave a long, steady and contemplative puff, and settled himself in his chair. 'I will tell you in a few words; but, before I begin, let me caution you that this is an affair demanding the greatest secrecy, and that I should most probably lose the position I now hold were it known that I confided it to any one.'

'Proceed,' said I.

'Or not,' said Dupin.

'Well, then; I have received personal information, from a very high quarter, that a certain document of the last importance has been purloined from the royal apartments. The individual who purloined it is known; this beyond a doubt; he was seen to take it. It is known, also, that it still remains in his possession.'

'How is this known?' asked Dupin.

'It is clearly inferred,' replied the Prefect, 'from the nature of the document and from the non-appearance of certain results which would at once arise from its passing *out* of the robber's possession – that is to say, from his employing it as he must design in the end to employ it.'

'Be a little more explicit,' I said.

'Well, I may venture so far as to say that the paper gives its holder a certain power in a certain quarter where such power is immensely valuable.' The Prefect was fond of the cant of diplomacy.

'Still I do not quite understand,' said Dupin.

'No? Well, the disclosure of the document to a third person, who shall be nameless, would bring in question the honour of a personage of most exalted station; this fact gives the holder of the document an ascendancy over the illustrious personage whose honour and peace are so jeopardized.'

'But this ascendancy,' I interposed, 'would depend upon the robber's knowledge of the loser's knowledge of the robber. Who would dare—'

'The thief,' said G., 'is the Minister D—, who dares all things, those unbecoming as well as those becoming a man. The method of the theft was not less ingenious than bold. The document in question – a letter, to be frank – had been received by the personage robbed while alone in the royal boudoir. During its perusal she was suddenly interrupted by the entrance of the other exalted personage from whom especially it was her wish to conceal it. After a hurried and vain endeavour to thrust it in a drawer, she was forced to place it, open as it was, upon a table. The address, however, was uppermost and, the contents thus unexposed, the letter escaped notice. At this juncture enters the Minister D. His lynx eye immediately perceives the paper, recognizes the handwriting of the address, observes the confusion of the personage addressed, and fathoms her secret. After some business transactions, hurried through in his ordinary manner, he produces a letter somewhat similar to the one in question, opens it, pretends to read it and then places it in close juxtaposition to the other. Again he converses, for some fifteen minutes, upon the public affairs. At length, in taking leave, he takes also from the table the letter to which he had no claim. Its rightful owner saw but, of course, dared not call attention to the act in the presence of the third personage who stood at her elbow. The minister decamped, leaving his own letter – one of no importance – upon the table.'

'Here, then,' said Dupin to me, 'you have precisely what you demand to make the ascendancy complete – the robber's knowledge of the loser's knowledge of the robber.'

'Yes,' replied the Prefect, 'and the power thus attained has, for some months past, been wielded, for political purposes, to a very dangerous extent. The personage robbed is more thoroughly convinced, every day, of the necessity of reclaiming her letter. But this, of course, cannot be done openly. In fine, driven to despair, she has committed the matter to me.'

'Than whom,' said Dupin, amid a perfect whirlwind of smoke, 'no more sagacious agent could, I suppose, be desired or even imagined.'

'You flatter me,' replied the Prefect, 'but it is possible that some such opinion may have been entertained.'

'It is clear,' said I, 'as you observe, that the letter is still in the possession of the minister since it is this possession, and not any employment of the letter, which bestows the power. With the employment the power departs.'

'True,' said G., 'and upon this conviction I proceeded. My first care was to make thorough search of the minister's hotel; and here my chief embarrassment lay in the necessity of searching without his knowledge. Beyond all things, I have been warned of the danger which would result from giving him reason to suspect our design.'

'But,' said I, 'you are quite *au fait* in these investigations. The Parisian police have done this thing often before.'

'Oh, yes, and for this reason I did not despair. The habits of the minister gave me, too, a great advantage. He is frequently absent from home all night. His servants are by no means numerous. They sleep at a distance from their master's apartment and, being chiefly Neapolitans, are readily made drunk. I have keys, as you know, with which I can open any chamber or cabinet in Paris. For three months a night has not passed, during the greater part of which I have not been engaged, personally, in ransacking the D— Hotel. My honour is interested and, to mention a great secret, the reward is enormous. So I did not abandon the search until I had become fully satisfied that the thief is a more astute man than myself. I fancy that I have investigated every nook and corner of the premises in which it is possible that the paper can be concealed.'

'But is it not possible,' I suggested, 'that although the letter may be in possession of the minister, as it unquestionably is, he may have concealed it elsewhere than upon his own premises?'

'This is barely possible,' said Dupin. 'The present peculiar condition of affairs at court, and especially of those intrigues in which

D. is known to be involved, would render the instant availability of the document – its susceptibility of being produced at a moment's notice – a point of nearly equal importance with its possession.'

'Its susceptibility of being produced?' said I.

'That is to say, of being *destroyed*,' said Dupin.

'True,' I observed, 'the paper is clearly then upon the premises. As for its being upon the person of the minister, we may consider that as out of the question.'

'Entirely,' said the Prefect. 'He has been twice waylaid, as if by footpads, and his person rigorously searched under my own inspection.'

'You might have spared yourself this trouble,' said Dupin. 'D., I presume, is not altogether a fool and, if not, must have anticipated these waylayings, as a matter of course.'

'Not *altogether* a fool,' said G., 'but then he is a poet, which I take to be only one remove from a fool.'

'True,' said Dupin, after a long and thoughtful whiff from his meerschaum, 'although I have been guilty of certain doggerel myself.'

'Suppose you detail,' said I, 'the particulars of your search.'

'Why, the fact is, we took our time, and we searched *everywhere*. I have had long experience in these affairs. I took the entire building, room by room; devoting the nights of a whole week to each. We examined, first, the furniture of each apartment. We opened every possible drawer; and I presume you know that, to a properly trained police agent, such a thing as a "secret" drawer is impossible. Any man is a dolt who permits a "secret" drawer to escape him in a search of this kind. The thing is *so* plain. There is a certain amount of bulk – of space – to be accounted for in every cabinet. Then we have accurate rules. The fiftieth part of a line could not escape us. After the cabinets we took the chairs. The cushions we probed with the fine long needles you have seen me employ. From the tables we removed the tops.'

'Why so?'

'Sometimes the top of a table, or other similarly arranged piece of furniture, is removed by the person wishing to conceal an article; then the leg is excavated, the article deposited within the cavity and the top replaced. The bottoms and tops of bedposts are employed in the same way.'

'But could not the cavity be detected by sounding?' I asked.

'By no means if, when the article is deposited, a sufficient wadding of cotton be placed around it. Besides, in our case, we were obliged to proceed without noise.'

'But you could not have removed – you could not have taken to pieces *all* articles of furniture in which it would have been possible to make a deposit in the manner you mention. A letter may be compressed into a thin spiral roll, not differing much in shape or bulk from a large knitting-needle, and in this form it might be inserted into the rung of a chair, for example. You did not take to pieces all the chairs?'

'Certainly not; but we did better – we examined the rungs of every chair in the hotel and, indeed, the jointings of every description of furniture, by the aid of a most powerful microscope. Had there been any traces of recent disturbance we should not have failed to detect it instantly. A single grain of gimlet-dust, for example, would have been as obvious as an apple. Any disorder in the gluing – any unusual gaping in the joints – would have sufficed to insure detection.'

'I presume you looked to the mirrors, between the boards and the plates, and you probed the beds and the bedclothes, as well as the curtains and carpets.'

'That of course; and when we had absolutely completed every particle of the furniture in this way, then we examined the house itself. We divided its entire surface into compartments, which we numbered, so that none might be missed; then we scrutinized each individual square inch throughout the premises, including the two houses immediately adjoining, with the microscope, as before.'

'The two houses adjoining!' I exclaimed; 'you must have had a great deal of trouble.'

'We had; but the reward offered is prodigious.'

'You include the *grounds* about the houses?'

'All the grounds are paved with brick. They gave us comparatively little trouble. We examined the moss between the bricks and found it undisturbed.'

'You looked among D.'s papers, of course, and into the books of the library?'

'Certainly; we opened every package and parcel; we not only opened every book, but we turned over every leaf in each volume, not contenting ourselves with a mere shake, according to the fashion of some of our police officers. We also measured the thickness of every book-*cover*, with the most accurate admeasurement, and applied to each the most jealous scrutiny of the microscope. Had any of the bindings been recently meddled with, it would have been utterly impossible that the fact should have escaped observation. Some five or six volumes, just from the hands of the binder, we carefully probed, longitudinally, with the needles.'

'You explored the floors beneath the carpets?'

'Beyond doubt. We removed every carpet and examined the boards with the microscope.'

'And the paper on the walls?'

'Yes.'

'You looked into the cellars?'

'We did.'

'Then,' I said, 'you have been making a miscalculation and the letter is *not* upon the premises, as you suppose.'

'I fear you are right there,' said the Prefect. 'And now, Dupin, what would you advise me to do?'

'To make a thorough research of the premises.'

'That is absolutely needless,' replied G. 'I am not more sure that I breathe than I am that the letter is not at the hotel.'

'I have no better advice to give you,' said Dupin. 'You have, of course, an accurate description of the letter?'

'Oh, yes!' And here the Prefect, producing a memorandum-book, proceeded to read aloud a minute account of the internal, and especially of the external, appearance of the missing document. Soon after finishing the perusal of this description, he took his departure, more entirely depressed in spirits than I had ever known the good gentleman before.

In about a month afterwards he paid us another visit and found us occupied very nearly as before. He took a pipe and a chair and entered into some ordinary conversation. At length I said:

'Well, but G., what of the purloined letter? I presume you have at last made up your mind that there is no such thing as overreaching the Minister?'

'Confound him, say I – yes; I made the re-examination, however, as Dupin suggested – but it was all labour lost, as I knew it would be.'

'How much was the reward offered, did you say?' asked Dupin.

'Why, a very great deal – a *very* liberal reward – I don't like to say how much, precisely; but one thing I *will* say, that I wouldn't mind giving my individual cheque for 50,000 francs to any one who could obtain me that letter. The fact is, it is becoming of more and more importance every day; and the reward has been lately doubled. If it were trebled, however, I could do no more than I have done.'

'Why, yes,' said Dupin, drawlingly between the whiffs of his meerschaum. 'I really – think, G., you have not exerted yourself – to the utmost in this matter. You might – do a little more, I think, eh?'

'How? In what way?'

'Why – puff, puff – you might – puff, puff – employ counsel in the matter, eh? Puff, puff, puff. Do you remember the story they tell of Abernethy?'

'No; hang Abernethy!'

'To be sure! Hang him and welcome. But, once upon a time a certain rich miser conceived the design of sponging upon this Abernethy for a medical opinion. Getting up, for this purpose, an ordinary conversation in a private company, he insinuated his case to the physician, as that of an imaginary individual.

'"We will suppose," said the miser, "that his symptoms are such and such; now, doctor, what would *you* have directed him to take?"'

'"Take!" said Abernethy, "why, take *advice*, to be sure."'

'But,' said the Prefect, a little discomposed, '*I* am *perfectly* willing to take advice and to pay for it. I would *really* give 50,000 francs to any one who would aid me in the matter.'

'In that case,' replied Dupin, opening a drawer and producing a cheque-book, 'you may as well fill me up a cheque for the amount mentioned. When you have signed it, I will hand you the letter.'

I was astounded. The Prefect appeared absolutely thunder-stricken. For some minutes he remained speechless and motionless, looking incredulously at my friend with open mouth and eyes that seemed starting from their sockets; then, apparently recovering himself in some measure, he seized a pen and, after several pauses and vacant stares, finally filled up and signed a cheque for 50,000 francs, and handed it across the table to Dupin. The latter examined it carefully and deposited it in his pocket-book; then, unlocking an *escritoire*, took thence a letter and gave it to the Prefect. This functionary grasped it in a perfect agony of joy, opened it with a trembling hand, cast a rapid glance at its contents and then, scrambling and struggling to the door, rushed at length unceremoniously from the room and from the house, without having uttered a syllable since Dupin had requested him to fill up the cheque.

When he had gone, my friend entered into some explanations.

'The Parisian police,' he said, 'are exceedingly able in their way. They are persevering, ingenious, cunning and thoroughly versed in the knowledge which their duties seem chiefly to demand. Thus, when G. detailed to us his mode of searching the premises at the Hotel D., I felt entire confidence in his having made a satisfactory investigation – so far as his labours extended.'

'So far as his labours extended?' said I.

'Yes,' said Dupin. 'The measures adopted were not only the best of their kind, but carried out to absolute perfection. Had the letter been deposited within the range of their search, these fellows would, beyond a question, have found it.'

I merely laughed – but he seemed quite serious in all that he said.

'The measures then,' he continued, 'were good in their kind and well executed; their defect lay in their being inapplicable to the case and to the man. A certain set of highly ingenious resources are, with the Prefect, a sort of Procrustean bed, to which he forcibly adapts his designs. But he perpetually errs by being too deep or too shallow for the matter in hand; and many a schoolboy is a better reasoner than he. I knew one about eight years of age whose success at guessing in the game of "even and odd" attracted universal admiration. This game is simple and is played with marbles. One player holds in his hand a number of these toys and demands of another whether that number is even or odd. If the guess is right, the guesser wins one; if wrong, he loses one. The boy to whom I allude won all the marbles of the school. Of course he had some principle of guessing; this lay in mere observation and admeasurement of the astuteness of his opponents. For example, an arrant simpleton is his opponent and, holding up his closed hand, asks, "Are they even or odd?" Our schoolboy replies, "Odd," and loses; but upon the second trial he wins, for he then says to himself: "The simpleton had them even upon the first trial, and his amount of cunning is just sufficient to make him have them odd upon the second; I will therefore guess odd." He guesses odd, and wins. Now, with a simpleton a degree above the first, he would have reasoned thus: "This fellow finds that in the first instance I guessed odd and, in the second, he will propose to himself, upon the first impulse, a simple variation from even to odd, as did the first simpleton; but then a second thought will suggest that this is too simple a variation and, finally, he will decide upon putting it even as before. I will therefore guess even." He guesses even, and wins. Now this mode of reasoning in the schoolboy, whom his fellows termed "lucky" – what, in its last analysis, is it?'

'It is merely,' I said, 'an identification of the reasoner's intellect with that of his opponent.'

'It is,' said Dupin. 'And, upon inquiring of the boy by what means he effected the *thorough* identification in which his success consisted, I received answer as follows. "When I wish to find out how wise, or how stupid, or how good, or how wicked is any one, or what are his thoughts at the moment, I fashion the expression of my face, as accurately as possible, in accordance with the expression of his, and then wait to see what thoughts or sentiments arise in my mind or heart as if to match or correspond with the expression." This response of the schoolboy lies at the bottom of all the spurious profundity which has been attributed to Rochefoucault, to La Bougive, to Machiavelli and to Campanella.'

'And the identification,' I said, 'of the reasoner's intellect with that of his opponent, depends, if I understand you aright, upon the accuracy with which the opponent's intellect is admeasured.'

'For its practical value it depends upon this,' replied Dupin; 'and the Prefect and his cohort fail so frequently, first by default of his identification and, secondly, by ill admeasurement, or rather through non-admeasurement, of the intellect with which they are engaged. They consider only their *own* ideas of ingenuity and, in searching for anything hidden, advert only to the modes in which *they* would have hidden it. They are right in this much – that their own ingenuity is a faithful representative of that of the *mass*; but when the cunning of the individual felon is diverse in character from their own, the felon foils them, of course. This always happens when it is above their own, and very usually when it is below. They have no variation of principle in their investigations; at best, when urged by some unusual emergency – by some extraordinary reward – they extend or exaggerate their old modes of *practice*, without touching their principles.

'What, for example, in this case of D. has been done to vary the principle of action? What is all this boring, and probing, and sounding, and scrutinizing with the microscope, and dividing the surface of the building into registered square inches – what is it all but an exaggeration *of the application* of the one principle or set of principles of search, which are based upon the one set of notions regarding human ingenuity, to which the Prefect, in the long routine of his duty, has been accustomed? Do you not see he has taken it for granted that *all* men proceed to conceal a letter – not exactly in a gimlet-hole bored in a chairleg but, at least, in *some* out-of-the-way hole or corner suggested by the same tenor of thought which would urge a man to secrete a letter in a gimlet-hole bored in a chairleg? And do you not see also that such *recherchés* nooks for concealment are adapted only for ordinary occasions and would be adopted only by ordinary intellects; for, in all cases of concealment, a disposal of the article concealed – a disposal of it in this *recherché* manner – is, in the very first instance, presumable and presumed; and thus its discovery depends, not at all upon the acumen, but altogether upon the mere care, patience and determination of the seekers; and where the case is of importance – or, what amounts to the same thing in political eyes, when the reward is of magnitude – the qualities in question have *never* been known to fail. You will now understand what I meant in suggesting that, had the purloined letter been hidden anywhere within the limits of the Prefect's examination – in other words, had the principle of its concealment been comprehended within the principles of the Prefect – its discovery would have been a matter altogether beyond question. This functionary, however, has been thoroughly mystified. The remote source of his defeat lies in the supposition that the Minister is a fool because he has acquired renown as a poet. All fools are poets; this the Prefect feels. He is merely guilty of a *non distributio medii* in thence inferring that all poets are fools.'

'But is this really the poet?' I asked. 'There are two brothers, I know, and both have attained reputation in letters. The minister I believe has written learnedly on the Differential Calculus. He is a mathematician and no poet.'

'You are mistaken. I know him well; he is both. As poet *and* mathematician, he would reason well. As mere mathematician, he could not have reasoned at all and thus would have been at the mercy of the Prefect.'

'You surprise me,' I said, 'by these opinions which have been contradicted by the voice of the world. You do not mean to set at naught the well-digested idea of centuries. The mathematical reason has long been regarded as the reason *par excellence*.'

'"*Il y a parir*,"' replied Dupin, quoting from Chamfort, '"*que toute die publique, toute convention reue, est une sottise, car elle a convenue au plus grand nombre*." The mathematicians, I grant you, have done their best to promulgate the popular error to which you allude and which is none the less an error for its promulgation as truth. With an art worthy of a better cause, for example, they have insinuated the term "analysis" into application to algebra. The French are the originators of this particular deception; but if a term is of any importance – if words derive any value from applicability – then "analysis" conveys "algebra" about as much as, in Latin, "*ambitus*" implies "ambition", "*religo*" "religion", or "*homines honesti*" a set of *honourable* men.'

'You have a quarrel on hand, I see,' said I, 'with some of the algebraists of Paris; but proceed.'

'I dispute the availability, and thus the value, of that reason which is cultivated in any especial form other than the abstractly logical. I dispute, in particular, the reason educed by mathematical study. The mathematics are the science of form and quantity; mathematical reasoning is merely logic applied to observation upon form and quantity. The great error lies in supposing that even the truths of what is called *pure* algebra are abstract or general truths. And this error is so egregious that I am confounded at the universality with which it has been received. Mathematical axioms are *not* axioms of general truth. What is true of *relation* – of form and quantity – is often grossly false in regard to morals, for example. In this latter science it is very usually *un*true that the aggregated parts are equal to the whole. In chemistry also the axiom fails. In the consideration of motive it fails; for two motives, each of a given value, have not necessarily a value, when united, equal to the sum of their values apart. There are numerous other mathematical truths which are only truths within the limits of *relation*. But the mathematician argues from his *finite truths*, through habit, as if they were of an absolutely general applicability – as the world indeed imagines them to be. Bryant, in his very learned *Mythology*, mentions an analogous source of error when he says that "although the Pagan fables are not believed, yet we forget ourselves continually, and make inferences from them as existing realities." With the algebraists, however, who are Pagans themselves, the "Pagan fables" *are* believed and the inferences are made, not so much through lapse of memory as through an unaccountable addling of the brains. In short, I never yet encountered the mere mathematician who could be trusted out of equal roots, or one who did not clandestinely hold it as a point of his faith that $x^2 + px$ was absolutely and unconditionally equal to q. Say to one of these gentlemen, by way of experiment, if you please, that you believe occasions may occur where $x^2 + px$ is not altogether equal to q and, having made him understand what you mean, get out of his reach as speedily as convenient for, beyond doubt, he will endeavour to knock you down.

'I mean to say,' continued Dupin, while I merely laughed at his last observations, 'that if the Minister had been no more than a mathematician, the Prefect would have been under no necessity of giving me this cheque. I knew him, however, as both mathematician and poet, and my measures were adapted to his capacity, with reference to the circumstances by which he was surrounded. I knew him as a courtier, too, and as a bold *intriguant*. Such a man, I considered, could not fail to be aware of the ordinary political modes of action. He could not have failed to anticipate – and events have proved that he did not fail to anticipate – the waylayings to which he was subjected. He must have foreseen, I reflected, the secret investigations of his premises. His frequent absences from home at night, which were hailed by the Prefect as certain aids to his success, I regarded only as *ruses*, to afford opportunity for thorough search to the police and thus the sooner to impress them with the conviction to which G., in fact, did finally arrive – the conviction that the letter was not upon the premises. I felt, also, that the whole train of thought, which I was at some pains in detailing to you just now, concerning the invariable principle of political action in searches for articles concealed – I felt that this whole train of thought would necessarily pass through the mind of the Minister. It would imperatively lead him to despise all the ordinary *nooks* of concealment. *He* could not, I reflected, be so weak as not to see that the most intricate and remote recess of his hotel would be as open as his commonest closets to the eyes, to the probes, to the gimlets and to the microscopes of the Prefect. I saw, in fine, that he would be driven, as a matter of course, to *simplicity*, if not deliberately induced to it as a matter of choice. You will remember, perhaps, how desperately the Prefect laughed when I suggested, upon our first interview, that it was just possible this mystery troubled him so much on account of its being so *very* self-evident.'

'Yes,' said I, 'I remember his merriment well. I really thought he would have fallen into convulsions.'

'The material world,' continued Dupin, 'abounds with very strict analogies to the immaterial; and thus some colour of truth has been given to the rhetorical dogma, that metaphor, or simile, may be made to strengthen an argument as well as to embellish a description. The principle of the *vis inertiae*, for example, seems to be identical in physics and metaphysics. It is not more true in the former that a large body is, with more difficulty, set in motion than a smaller one and that its subsequent *momentum* is commensurate with this difficulty, than it is, in the latter, that intellects of the vaster capacity, while more forcible, more constant and more eventful in their movements than those of inferior grade, are yet the less readily moved, more embarrassed and full of hesitation in the first few steps of their progress. Again, have you ever noticed which of the street signs, over the shop doors, are the most attractive of attention?'

'I have never given the matter a thought,' I said.

'There is a game of puzzles,' he resumed, 'which is played upon a map. One party playing requires another to find a given word – the name of town, river, state, or empire – any word, in short, upon the motley and perplexed surface of the chart. A novice in the game generally seeks to embarrass his opponents by giving them the most minutely lettered names; but the adept selects such words as stretch, in large characters, from one end of the chart to the other. These, like the over-largely lettered signs and placards of the street, escape observation by dint of being excessively obvious; and here the physical oversight is precisely analogous with the moral inapprehension by which the intellect suffers to pass unnoticed those considerations which are too obtrusively and too palpably self-evident. But this is a point, it appears, somewhat above or beneath the understanding of the Prefect. He never once thought it probable, or possible, that the Minister had deposited the letter immediately beneath the nose of the whole world by way of best preventing any portion of that world from perceiving it.

'But the more I reflected upon the daring, dashing and discriminating ingenuity of D.; upon the fact that the document must always have been *at hand*, if he intended to use it to good purpose; and upon the decisive evidence, obtained by the Prefect, that it was not hidden within the limits of that dignitary's ordinary search – the more satisfied I became that, to conceal this letter, the Minister had resorted to the comprehensive and sagacious expedient of not attempting to conceal it at all.

'Full of these ideas, I prepared myself with a pair of green spectacles and called one fine morning, quite by accident, at the Ministerial hotel. I found D. at home, yawning, lounging and dawdling, as usual, and pretending to be in the last extremity of *ennui*. He is, perhaps, the most really energetic human being now alive – but that is only when nobody sees him.

'To be even with him, I complained of my weak eyes and lamented the necessity of the spectacles, under cover of which I cautiously and thoroughly surveyed the whole apartment while seemingly intent only upon the conversation of my host.

'I paid especial attention to a large writing-table near which he sat and upon which lay, confusedly, some miscellaneous letters and other papers, with one or two musical instruments and a few books. Here, however, after a long and very deliberate scrutiny I saw nothing to excite particular suspicion.

'At length my eyes, in going the circuit of the room, fell upon a trumpery filigree card-rack of pasteboard that hung dangling by a dirty blue ribbon from a little brass knob just beneath the middle of the mantelpiece. In this rack, which had three or four compartments, were five or six visiting cards and a solitary letter. This last was much soiled and crumpled. It was torn nearly in two, across the middle – as if a design, in the first instance, to tear it entirely up as worthless, had been altered or stayed in the second. It had a large black seal, bearing the D. cipher *very* conspicuously, and was addressed, in a diminutive female hand, to D., the minister, himself. It was thrust carelessly and even, as it seemed, contemptuously, into one of the uppermost divisions of the rack.

'No sooner had I glanced at this letter than I concluded it to be that of which I was in search. To be sure, it was, to all appearance, radically different from the one of which the Prefect had read us so minutely a description. Here the seal was large and black, with the D. cipher; there it was small and red, with the ducal arms of the S—family. Here, the address, to the Minister, was diminutive and feminine; there the superscription, to a certain royal personage, was markedly bold and decided; the size alone formed a point of correspondence. But, then, the *radicalness* of these differences, which was excessive – the dirt, the soiled and torn condition of the paper, so inconsistent with the *true* methodical habits of D. and so suggestive of a design to delude the beholder into an idea of the worthlessness of the document – these things, together with the hyperobtrusive situation of this document, full in the view of every visitor and thus exactly in accordance with the conclusions to which I had previously arrived – these things, I say, were strongly corroborative of suspicion in one who came with the intention to suspect.

'I protracted my visit as long as possible and, while I maintained a most animated discussion with the Minister upon a topic which I knew well had never failed to interest and excite him, I kept my attention really riveted upon the letter. In this examination, I committed to memory its external appearance and arrangement in the rack and also fell, at length, upon a discovery which set at rest whatever trivial doubt I might have entertained. In scrutinizing the edges of the paper I observed them to be more *chafed* than seemed necessary. They presented the *broken* appearance which is manifested when a stiff paper, having been once folded and pressed with a folder, is refolded in a reversed direction, in the same creases or edges which had formed the original fold. This discovery was sufficient. It was clear to me that the letter had been turned as a glove, inside out, re-directed and re-sealed. I bade the Minister good-morning and took my departure at once, leaving a gold snuff-box upon the table.

'The next morning I called for the snuff-box, when we resumed, quite eagerly, the conversation of the preceding day. While thus engaged, however, a loud report, as if of a pistol, was heard immediately beneath the windows of the hotel and was succeeded by a series of fearful screams and the shoutings of a terrified mob. D. rushed to a casement, threw it open and looked out. In the meantime I stepped to the card-rack, took the letter, put it in my pocket and replaced it by a facsimile (so far as regards externals) which I had carefully prepared at my lodgings – imitating the D. cipher, very readily – by means of a seal formed of bread.

'The disturbance in the street had been occasioned by the frantic behaviour of a man with a musket. He had fired it among a crowd of women and children. It proved, however, to have been without ball and the fellow was suffered to go his way as a lunatic or a drunkard. When he had gone, D. came from the window, whither I had followed him immediately upon securing the object in view. Soon afterward I bade him farewell. The pretended lunatic was a man in my own pay.'

'But what purpose had you,' I asked, 'in replacing the letter by a facsimile? Would it not have been better, at the first visit, to have seized it openly and departed?'

'D.,' replied Dupin, 'is a desperate man and a man of nerve. His hotel, too, is not without attendants devoted to his interests. Had I made the wild attempt you suggest, I might never have left the Ministerial presence alive. The good people of Paris might have heard of me no more. But I had an object apart from these considerations. You know my political prepossessions. In this matter, I act as a partisan of the lady concerned. For eighteen months the Minister has had her in his power. She has now him in hers – since, being unaware that the letter is not in his possession, he will proceed with his exactions as if it was. Thus will he inevitably commit himself, at once, to his political destruction. His downfall, too, will not be more precipitate than awkward. It is all very well to talk about the *facilis descensus Averni*; but in all kinds of climbing, as Catalani said of singing, it is far more easy to get up than to come down. In the present instance I have no sympathy – at least no pity – for him who descends. He is that *monstrum horrendum*, an unprincipled man of genius. I confess, however, that I should like very well to know the precise character of his thoughts when, being defied by her whom the Prefect terms "a certain personage", he is reduced to opening the letter which I left for him in the card-rack.'

'How? Did you put anything particular in it?'

'Why – it did not seem altogether right to leave the interior blank – that would have been insulting. D., at Vienna once, did me an evil turn which I told him, quite good-humouredly, that I should remember. So, as I knew he would feel some curiosity in regard to the identity of the person who had outwitted him, I thought it a pity not to give him a clue. He is well acquainted with my MS and I just copied into the middle of the blank sheet the words

> Un dessein si funeste,
> S'il n'est digne d'Atrée, est digne de Thyeste.
>
> They are to be found in Crébillon's "Atrée".'
>
> *The Purloined Letter*, Edgar Allan Poe

From disguise and deceit to the gadgets that make espionage the boffin's showcase . . .

A Mysterious Device

He slid open a drawer of his desk and drew out a battery-powered shaver which he pushed across to me. 'The washroom's two doors along the corridor,' he said. 'What do you want me to look at?'

I hesitated. I couldn't very well ask Nordlinger to keep his mouth shut no matter what he found. That would be asking him to betray the basic tenets of his profession, which he certainly wouldn't do. I decided to plunge and take a chance, so I dug the metal box from my pocket, took off the tape which held the lid on and shook out the gadget. I laid it before him. 'What's that, Lee?'

He looked at it for a long time without touching it, then he said, 'What do you want to know about it?'

'Practically everything,' I said. 'But to begin with – what nationality is it?'

He picked it up and turned it around. If anyone could tell me anything about it, it was Commander Lee Nordlinger. He was an electronics officer at Keflavik Base and ran the radar and radio systems, both ground-based and airborne. From what I'd heard he was damned good at his job.

'It's almost certainly American,' he said. He poked his finger at it. 'I recognize some of the components – the resistors, for instance, are standard and are of American manufacture.' He turned it around again. 'And the input is standard American voltage and at fifty cycles.'

'All right,' I said. 'Now – what is it?'

'That I can't tell you right now. For God's sake, you bring in a lump of miscellaneous circuitry and expect me to identify it at first crack of the whip. I may be good but I'm not that good.'

'Then can you tell me what it's not?' I asked patiently.

'It's no teenager's transistor radio, that's for sure,' he said, and frowned. 'Come to that, it's like nothing I've ever seen before.' He tapped the odd-shaped piece of metal in the middle of the assembly. 'I've never seen one of these, for example.'

'Can you run a test on it?'

'Sure.' He uncoiled his lean length from behind the desk. 'Let's run a current through it and see if it plays "The Star-Spangled Banner".'

'Can I come along?'

'Why not?' said Nordlinger lightly. 'Let's go to the shop.' As we walked along the corridor he said, 'Where did you get it?'

'It was given to me,' I said uncommunicatively.

He gave me a speculative glance but said no more. We went through swing doors at the end of the corridor and into a large room which had long benches loaded with electronic gear. Lee signalled to a petty officer who came over. 'Hi, Chief; I have something here I want to run a few tests on. Have you a test bench free?'

'Sure, Commander.' The petty officer looked about the room. 'Take number five; I guess we won't be using that for a while.'

I looked at the test bench; it was full of knobs and dials and screens which meant less than nothing. Nordlinger sat down. 'Pull up a chair and we'll see what happens.' He attached clips to the terminals on the gadget then paused. 'We already know certain things about it. It isn't part of an airplane; they don't use such a heavy voltage. And it probably isn't from a ship for roughly the same reason. So that leaves ground-based equipment. It's designed to plug into the normal electricity system on the North American continent – it could have been built in Canada. A lot of Canadian firms use American-manufactured components.'

I jogged him along. 'Could it come from a TV set?'

'Not from any TV I've seen.' He snapped switches. 'A 110 volts – fifty cycles. Now, there's no amperage given so we have to be careful. We'll start real low.' He twisted a knob delicately and a fine needle on a dial barely quivered against the pin.

He looked down at the gadget. 'There's a current going through now but not enough to give a fly a heart attack.' He paused, and looked up. 'To begin with, this thing is crazy; an alternating current with these components isn't standard. Now, let's see – first we have what seems to be three amplification stages, and that makes very little sense.'

He took a probe attached to a lead. 'If we touch the probe here we should get a sine wave on the oscilloscope . . .' He looked up, '. . . which we do. Now we see what happens at this lead going into this funny-shaped metal ginkus.'

He gently jabbed the probe and the green trace on the oscilloscope jumped and settled into a new configuration. 'A square wave,' said Nordlinger. 'This circuit up to here is functioning as a chopper –

which is pretty damn funny in itself for reasons I won't go into right now. Now let's see what happens at the lead going *out* of the ginkus and into this mess of boards.'

He touched down the probe and the oscilloscope trace jumped again before it settled down. Nordlinger whistled. 'Just look at that spaghetti, will you?' The green line was twisted into a fantastic waveform which jumped rhythmically and changed form with each jump. 'You'd need a hell of a lot of Fourier analysis to sort that out,' said Nordlinger. 'But whatever else it is, it's pulsed by this metal dohickey.'

'What do you make of it?'

'Not a damn thing,' he said. 'Now I'm going to try the output stage; on past form this should fairly tie knots into that oscilloscope – maybe it'll blow up.' He lowered the probe and we looked expectantly at the screen.

I said, 'What are you waiting for?'

'I'm waiting for nothing.' Nordlinger looked at the screen blankly. 'There's no output.'

'Is that bad?'

He looked at me oddly. In a gentle voice he said, 'It's impossible.'

I said, 'Maybe there's something broken in there.'

'You don't get it,' said Nordlinger. 'A circuit is just what it says – a circle. You break the circle anywhere you get no current flow anywhere.' He applied the probe again. 'Here there's a current of a pulsed and extremely complex form.' Again the screen jumped into life. 'And here, in the same circuit, what do we get?'

I looked at the blank screen. 'Nothing?'

'Nothing,' he said firmly. He hesitated. 'Or, to put it more precisely, nothing that can show on this test rig.' He tapped the gadget. 'Mind if I take this thing away for a while?'

'Why?'

'I'd like to put it through some rather more rigorous tests. We have another shop.' He cleared his throat and appeared to be a little embarrassed. 'Uh . . . you won't be allowed in there.'

'Oh – secret stuff.' That would be in one of the areas to which Fleet's pass would give access. 'All right, Lee; you put the gadget through its paces and I'll go and shave. I'll wait for you in your office.'

'Wait a minute,' he said. 'Where did you get it, Alan?'

I said, 'You tell me what it does and I'll tell you where it came from.'

He grinned. 'It's a deal.'

I left him disconnecting the gadget from the test rig and went back to his office where I picked up the electric shaver. Fifteen minutes later I felt a lot better after having got rid of the hair. I waited in Nordlinger's office for a long time – over an hour and a half – before he came back.

He came in carrying the gadget as thought it was a stick of dynamite and laid it gently on his desk. 'I'll have to ask you where you got this,' he said briefly.

'Not until you tell me what it does,' I said.

He sat behind his desk and looked at the complex of metal and plastic with something like loathing in his eyes. 'It does nothing,' he said flatly. 'Absolutely nothing.'

'Come off it,' I said. 'It must do *something*.'

'Nothing!' he repeated. 'There is no measurable output.' He leaned forward and said softly, 'Alan, out there I have instruments that can measure any damn part of the electromagnetic spectrum from radio waves of such low frequency, you wouldn't believe possible, right up to cosmic radiation – and there's nothing coming out of this contraption.'

'As I said before – maybe something has broken.'

'That cat won't jump; I tested everything.' He pushed at it and it moved sideways on the desk. 'There are three things I don't like about this. Firstly, there are components in here that are not remotely like anything I've seen before, components of which I don't even understand the function. I'm supposed to be pretty good at my job and that, in itself, is enough to disturb me. Secondly, it's obviously incomplete – it's just part of a bigger complex – and yet I doubt if I would understand it even if I had everything. Thirdly – and this is the serious one – it shouldn't work.'

'But it isn't working,' I said.

He waved his hand distractedly. 'Perhaps I put it wrong. There should be an output of some kind. Good Christ, you can't keep pushing electricity into a machine – juice that gets used up – without getting something out. That's impossible.'

I said, 'Maybe it's coming out in the form of heat.'

He shook his head sadly. 'I got mad and went to extreme measures. I pushed a thousand watts of current through it in the end. If the energy output was in heat then the goddamn thing would have glowed like an electric heater. But no – it stayed as cool as ever.'

'A bloody sight cooler than you're behaving,' I said.

He threw up his hands in exasperation. 'Alan, if you were a mathematician and one day you came across an equation in which two and two made five without giving a nonsensical result then you'd feel exactly as I do. It's as though a physicist were confronted by a perpetual motion machine which works.'

'Hold on,' I said. 'A perpetual motion machine gets something for nothing – energy usually. This is the other way round.'

'It makes no difference,' he said. 'Energy can neither be created nor destroyed.' As I opened my mouth he said quickly, 'And don't start talking about atomic energy. Matter can be regarded as frozen, concentrated energy.' He looked at the gadget with grim eyes. 'This thing is destroying energy.'

Destroying energy! I rolled the concept around my cerebrum to see what I could make of it. The answer came up fast – nothing much. I said, 'Let's not go overboard. Let's see what we have. You put an input into it and you get out . . .'

'Nothing,' said Nordlinger.

'Nothing you can measure,' I corrected. 'You may have some good instrumentation here, Lee, but I don't think you've got the whole works. I'll bet that there's some genius somewhere who not only knows what's coming out of there but has an equally involved gadget that can measure it.'

'Then I'd like to know what it is,' he said. 'Because it's right outside my experience.'

I said, 'Lee, you're a technician, not a scientist. You'll admit that?'

'Sure; I'm an engineer from way back.'

'That's why you have a crew-cut - but this was designed by a long-hair.' I grinned. 'Or an egghead.'

'I'd still like to know where you got it.'

'You'd better be more interested in where it's going. Have you got a safe – a really secure one?'

'Sure.' He did a double-take. 'You want *me* to keep *this*?'

'For forty-eight hours,' I said. 'If I don't claim it in that time you'd better give it to your superior officer, together with all your forebodings, and let him take care of it.'

Nordlinger looked at me with a cold eye. 'I don't know but what I shouldn't give it to him right now. Forty-eight hours might mean my neck.'

'You part with it now and it will be my neck,' I said grimly.

He picked up the gadget. 'This is American and it doesn't belong here at Keflavik. I'd like to know where it does belong.'

'You're right about it not belonging here,' I said. 'But I'm betting it's Russian – and they want it back.'

'For God's sake!' he said. 'It's full of American components.'

'Maybe the Russians learned a lesson from Macnamara on

cost-effectiveness. Maybe they're shopping in the best market. I don't give two bloody hoots if the components were made in the Congo – I still want you to hold on to it.'

He laid the gadget on his desk again very carefully.

'OK – but I'll split the difference; I'll give you twenty-four hours. And even then you don't get it back without a full explanation.'

from The Freedom Trap, Desmond Bagley

A More Dangerous Device

Suddenly, while the Privy Councillor lay back in his chair pulling thoughtfully at his cigar, there was a bright, blood-red flash, a dull report and a man's short agonized cry. Startled, I leaned around the corner of the deck-house, when, to my abject horror, I saw under the electric rays the Czar's Privy Councillor lying sideways in his chair with part of his face blown away. Then the hideous truth in an instant became apparent. The cigar which Oberg had pressed upon him down in the saloon had exploded, and the small missile concealed inside the diabolical contrivance had passed upwards into his brain.

from The Czar's Spy, William Le Queux

CAR CHASES, THEN AND NOW

Like casual sex, the statutory car chase is an inevitable feature of the modern spy story. I have included a vintage chase – from Buchan's The Island of Sheep, *first published in 1935 – and one of the most grotesquely comic, from the late and lamentably neglected Kyril Bonfiglioli's* Don't Point That Thing at Me *(1972), which* The Times Literary Supplement *described as being '. . . at least of Hammett-Chandler weight, and in many ways surpassing them'.*

Across Country, *circa* 1930

There was no time to waste, so I plunged at once into my story.

'Anna, my dear,' I said, 'we've never met before, but when I was young I knew your grandfather in South Africa and he made me and another man, whose name is General Hannay, promise to stand by your father if trouble came. Your father is in great danger – has been for a long time – and now it's worse than ever. That's why he hasn't been to see you for so long. That's why you're called Smith here, when your real name is Haraldsen. That's why his letters to you always come through a bank. Now *you* are also in danger. These people Bletso, who came this morning and say they're your cousins, are humbugs. Their letter from your father is a fake. They come from your father's enemies and they want to get you into their power. Your friends discovered the danger and sent me down to bring you away. I'm only just in time. Will you trust me and do what I ask you?'

That extraordinary child's face did not change. She heard me with the same uncanny composure, her eyes never leaving mine. Then she turned to Miss Margesson and smiled. 'What a lark, Margie!' was all she said.

But Miss Margesson didn't take it that way. She looked scared and flustered.

'What a ridiculous story!' she said. 'Say it's nonsense, Anna. Your name's Smith, all right.'

'No, it isn't,' was the placid answer. 'It's Haraldsen. Sorry, Margie dear, but I couldn't tell that even to you.'

'But—but—' Miss Margesson stammered in her uneasiness. 'You know nothing about this man – you never saw him before. How do you know he's speaking the truth? Your cousins had a letter from your father and Miss Barlock, who is very shrewd, saw nothing wrong with it. They looked most respectable people.'

'I didn't like them much,' said Anna, and again I had a gleam of hope. 'The woman had ugly eyes behind her specs. And I never heard of any English cousins.'

'But, darling, listen to me,' Miss Margesson cried. 'You never heard of this man either. How do you know he comes from your father? How do you know he is speaking the truth? If you have any doubt, let us go together to Miss Barlock and tell her that you don't want to go on any cruise and want to stay here till the end of the term. In the meantime you can get in touch with your father.'

'That sounds good sense,' I said; 'but it won't do. Your father's enemies now know where you are. They are very clever people and quite unscrupulous. If you don't go away with the Bletsos, they'll find ways and means of carrying you off long before your father can interfere.'

'Rubbish,' said Miss Margesson rudely. 'Do you expect me to believe this melodrama? You look honest, but you may be half-witted. What's your profession?'

'Not one for the half-witted,' I said. 'I'm what they call a merchant banker,' and I told her the name of my firm. That was a lucky shot for Miss Margesson had a cousin in our employ and I was able to tell her all about him. I think that convinced her of my bona fides.

'But what do you propose to do with Anna?' she demanded.

'Take her straight to her father.' That I had decided was the only plan. The girl would be in perpetual danger in London, now that our enemies had got on her trail.

'Do you know where he is?' she asked.

'Yes,' I said, 'and if we start at once I can get her there before midnight.'

Then it suddenly occurred to me that I had one convincing piece of evidence at my disposal.

'Anna,' I said, 'I can tell you something that must persuade you. You had a letter from your father on your birthday three days ago?'

She nodded.

'And it didn't come from London enclosed in a bank envelope. It came from Scotland.'

'Yes,' she said, 'it came from Scotland. He didn't put any address on it, but I noticed that it had a Scotch postmark. That excited me, for I have always wanted to go to Scotland.'

'Well, it was that letter of your father's that gave his enemies the clue. One of them spotted the address in a Scotch post office. Your father's friend, Lord Clanroyden, was worried, and he sent me here at once. Doesn't that prove that I'm telling the truth?' I looked towards Miss Margesson.

Her scepticism was already shaken. 'I don't know what to think,' she cried. 'I can't take any responsibility—'

Then that astonishing child simply took charge.

'You needn't, Margie dear,' she said. 'Hop back into the house and carry on. I'm going with Mr Lombard. I believe in him. I'm going to Scotland to my father.'

'But her things are not packed,' put in Miss Margesson. 'She can't leave like this—'

'I'm afraid we can't stand on the order of our going,' I said. 'It's now just twelve o'clock, and any moment the Bletsos may turn up and make trouble. We can send for Anna's things, and in two days everything will be explained to Miss Barlock. *You* must keep out of the business altogether. The last you saw of Anna and me was in the garden and you know nothing of our further movements. But you might do me a great kindness and send this wire in the afternoon. It's to Lord Clanroyden – you've heard of him? – he's Anna's father's chief standby. He told me to bring Anna to London, but that's too dangerous now. I want him to know that we have gone to Scotland.' I scribbled a telegram on a leaf from my pocket-book.

Miss Margesson was a good girl and she seemed to share Anna's conviction. She hugged and kissed the child. 'Write to me soon,' she said, 'for I shall be very anxious,' and ran into the house.

'Now for the road,' I said. 'My car is at the front door. I'll pick you up in the main avenue out of sight of the house. Can you get there without being seen? And bring some sort of coat. Pinch another girl's if you can't find your own. The thicker the better, for it will be chilly before we get to Laverlaw.'

I picked up Anna in the avenue all right and we swung out of the lodge gates at precisely a quarter past twelve. Then I saw something which I didn't much like. Just outside the gates a car was drawn up, a very powerful car of foreign make, coloured yellow and black. It looked to me like a Stutz. The only occupant was a chauffeur in uniform who was reading a newspaper. He glanced sharply at me and, for a moment, seemed about to challenge us. When we had passed I looked back and saw that he had started the car and was moving in the direction of the village. I guessed that this was the Bletsos' car, and that the man had gone to seek his master. He did not look quite like an ordinary chauffeur.

That was the start of our journey. My plan was to get into the Great North Road as soon as possible – Stamford seemed the best point to join it at – and then to let the Bentley rip on the best highway in England. I didn't see how we could be seriously pursued even if that confounded chauffeur had spotted our departure. But I was all in a dither to reach Laverlaw that night. This young Lochinvar business was rather out of my usual line, and I wanted to get it over.

Well, we got to Stamford without mishap and after that we did a spell of over sixty to the hour. The morning had been hot and bright, but the wind had shifted and I thought we might soon run into dirty weather. At first I had kept looking back to see if we were followed, but there was no sign of a black and yellow car and, after a little, I forgot about it. Lunch was our next problem and, as there was a lot of traffic on the road, I feared that if we looked for it in a good hotel we should be hung up. I consulted Anna and she said that she didn't care what she ate as long as there was enough of it, for she was very hungry. So we drew up at a little place, half pub and half tea-house, at the foot of a long hill just short of Newark. While my petrol tank was being filled we had a scratch meal, beer and sandwiches for me, while Anna's fancy was coffee and buns, of which she accounted for a surprising quantity. I also bought two pounds of chocolates and a box of biscuits, which turned out to be a lucky step.

We were just starting when I happened to cast my eyes back up the hill. I have a good long-distance eyesight and there, at the top, about half a mile away, I saw a car which was unpleasantly like the Stutz I had seen at Brewton. A minute later I lost it, for some traffic got in the way, but I saw it again, not a quarter of a mile off. There could be no mistake about the wasp-like thing, and I didn't think it likely that another car of the same make and colour would be on the road that day.

If its occupants had glasses – and they were pretty certain to have – they must have spotted us. I drove the Bentley as hard as I dared and tried to think out our position. They knew, of course, what our destination was. They certainly had the pace of us for I had heard wonderful stories of what a Stutz could do in that line – and this was probably super-charged – so it wasn't likely that we could shake them off. If we stopped for the night in any town we should be at the mercy of people whose cleverness Clanroyden had put very high, and somehow or other they would get the better of me. A halt of that kind I simply dared not risk. The road before us for the next hundred miles or so was through a populous country and I didn't believe that they would try a hold-up on it. That would be too risky with so many cars on the road and they would not want trouble with the police or awkward inquiries. But I had driven a good deal back and forward to Scotland and I knew that, to get to Laverlaw, I must pass through some lonely country. Then would be their chance. I couldn't stand up against the toothy young man and the formidable-looking chauffeur. I would be left in a ditch with a broken head and Anna would be spirited away.

My chief feeling was a firm determination to go all out to get to Laverlaw. I couldn't outwit or outpace them, so I must trust to luck. Every mile was bringing us nearer safety and, if it was bringing us nearer the northern moorlands, I must shut down on the thought. At first I was afraid of scaring Anna but, when I saw her face whipped into colour by the wind and her bright enjoying eyes, I considered that there was no danger of that.

'You remember the car we saw at the school gates?' I said. 'The black and yellow thing? I've a notion that it's behind us. You might keep an eye on it, for I want both of mine for this bus.'

'Oh, are we being chased?' she cried. 'What fun!' And after that she sat with her head half screwed round and issued regular bulletins.

Beyond Bawtry we got into the rain, a good steady north-country downpour. We also got into a tangle of road repairs where we had to wait our turn at several single-track patches. At the last of these the Stutz was in the same queue and I managed to get a fairly good view of it. There was no mistake about it. I saw the chauffeur in his light-grey livery coat, the same fellow who had stared at us at Brewton. The others in the back of the car were, of course, invisible.

Beyond Pontefract the rain became a deluge and it was clear from the swimming roads that a considerable weight of water had already fallen. It was now between four and five and, from constant hang-ups, we were making poor speed. The Stutz had made no attempt to close on us, though it obviously had the greater pace, and I thought I knew the reason. Its occupants had argued as I had done. They didn't want any row in this populous countryside, but they knew I was making for Laverlaw and they knew that, to get there, I must pass through some desolate places. Then their opportunity would come.

In a big village beyond Boroughbridge they changed their tactics. 'The Wasp is nearly up on us,' Anna informed me, and I suddenly heard a horn behind me, the kind of terrifying thing that they fix on French racing cars. The street was fairly broad, and it could easily pass. I saw their plan. They meant to get ahead of me and wait for me. Soon several routes across the Border would branch off and they wanted to make certain that I did not escape them. I groaned, for the scheme I had been trying to frame was now knocked on the head.

And then we had a bit of unexpected luck. Down a side street came a tradesman's van, driven by one of those hatless youths whom every motorist wants to see hanged, as an example, for they are the most dangerous things on the road. Without warning it clipped over the bows of the Stutz. I heard shouting and a grinding of brakes, but I had no time to look back and it was Anna who reported what happened. The Stutz swung to the left, mounted the pavement and came to rest with its nose almost inside the door of a shop. The van-driver lost his head, skidded, hit a lamp-post, slewed round and crashed into the Stutz's off-front wing. There was a very pretty mix-up.

'Glory be,' Anna cried, 'that has crippled the brute. Well done the butcher's boy!'

But she reported that, so far as she could see, the Stutz had not been damaged seriously. Only the van, which had lost a wheel. But there was a crowd, and a policeman with a note-book, and I thought that the whole business might mean a hold-up of a quarter of an hour. I had a start again and I worked the Bentley up to a steady eighty on a beautiful stretch of road. My chief trouble was the weather, for the rain was driving so hard that the visibility was rotten and I could see little in front of me and Anna little behind.

I had to make up my mind on the route, for Scotch Corner was getting near. If I followed the main North Road by Darlington and Durham I would be for the next hundred miles in a thickly settled country. But that would take me far from Laverlaw and I would have the long Tweed valley before I got to it. If I turned left by Brough to Appleby I should have to cross desolate moorlands which would give the Stutz just the kind of country it wanted. I remembered a third road which ran through mining villages where there would be plenty of people about. It was a perfectly good road, though the map marked most of it second-class. Besides, it was possible that the Stutz didn't know about it and, if I had a sufficient start, might assume that I had gone by either Darlington or Brough. Anyhow, unless it caught me up soon, it would be at fault. Clearly it was my best chance.

But Fate, in the shape of the butcher's boy, had not done its work thoroughly. The rain stopped, the weather cleared, there was a magnificent red sunset over Teesdale and, just as I was swinging into my chosen road with an easier mind, Anna reported that the Wasp was coming into view.

That, as they say, fairly tore it. I had not diverted the hounds and the next half-hour was a wild race, for I wanted to get out of empty country into the colliery part. I broke every rule of decent driving but I managed to keep a mile or so ahead. The Stutz was handicapped by the softness of the surface after the rain and by not knowing the road as I knew it. It was beginning to grow dark and, to the best of my knowledge, what there was of a moon would not rise till the small hours. My only hope was that it might be possible, somewhere in the Tyne valley, to give the pursuers the slip. I had tramped a good deal there, in the days when I was keen about Hadrian's Wall, and knew the deviousness of the hill roads.

I reached the mining country without mishap and the lights of the villages and the distant glow of ironworks gave me a comforting sense of people about and therefore of protection. Beyond Consett the dark fell and I reflected uneasily that we were now getting into a wild moorland patch which would last till we dropped down on the Tyne. Somehow I felt that the latter event would not happen unless I managed to create a diversion. I could see the great headlights of the Stutz a mile behind, but I was pretty certain that, when it saw its chance, it would accelerate and overhaul us. I realized desperately that in the next ten minutes I must find some refuge or be done in.

Just then we came to a big hill which shut off any view of us from behind. I saw a bright light in front and a big car turned in from a side-road and took our road a little ahead of us. That seemed to give me a chance. On the left there was a little road, which looked as if it led to a farm-house, and which turned a corner of a fir wood. If I turned up that the Stutz, topping the hill behind us, would see the other car far down the hill and believe it to be ours . . . There was no time to waste so I switched off our lights and moved into the farm road, till we were in the lee of the firs. We had scarcely got there when, out of the corner of my eye, I saw the glow of the Stutz's lights over the crest, and I had scarcely shut off my engine when it went roaring down the hill fifty yards away.

'Golly,' said Anna, 'this is an adventure! Where is the chocolate, Mr Lombard? We've had no tea, and I'm very hungry.'

While she munched chocolate I started the engine and, after passing two broken-hinged gates, we came to a little farm. There was nobody about except an old woman who explained to me that we were off the road, which was obvious enough, and gave us big glasses of milk warm from the cow. I had out the map (luckily I had a case of them in the car with me) and I saw that a thin red line, which meant some sort of road, continued beyond the farm and seemed to lead ultimately to the Tyne valley. I must chance its condition, for it offered some sort of a plan. I reasoned that the Stutz would continue down the hill and might go on for miles before it spotted that the other car was not ours. It would come back and fossick about to see which side-road we had taken, but there were several in the area and it would take a little time to discover our tracks on farm road. If it got thus far, the woman at the farm would report our coming and say that we had gone back to the main road. I made a great pretence to her of being in a hurry to return to that road. But, when she had shut the door behind us, we crossed a tiny stack yard, found the continuation of the track trickling through a steep meadow and, very carefully shutting every gate behind us, slipped down into a hollow where cattle started away from our lights and we had to avoid somnolent sheep.

The first part was vile but, in the end, it was joined by another farm-track and the combination of the two made a fair road, stony, but with a sound bottom. My great fear was of ditching in one of the moorland runnels. After a little it was possible to increase the speed and, though I had often to stop and examine the map, in half an hour we had covered a dozen miles. We were in a lonely bit of country, with no sign of habitation except an occasional roadside cottage and the lights from a hillside farm, and we passed through many plantations of young firs. Here, I thought, was a place to get a little sleep, for Anna was nodding with drowsiness and I was feeling pretty well done up. So we halted at the back of a fir clump and I made a bed for Anna with the car rugs – not much of a bed for, the weather in the south having been hot, I had only brought summer wraps. We both had some biscuits and chocolate, but the child went to sleep with her mouth full, snuggled against my side, and I wasn't long in following. I was so tired that I didn't want to smoke.

I woke about four. Every little pool left by the rain was flushed rose-pink with the reflection of the sky, and I knew that that meant dirty weather. I roused Anna and we laved our faces in the burn, and had another go at the biscuits. The air was cold and raw, and we would have given pounds for hot coffee. The whole place was as quiet as a churchyard, not even a bird whistled or a sheep bleated, and both of us felt a bit eerie. But the sleep had done us good and I was feeling pretty confident that we had puzzled the Stutz. It must have spent a restless night if it had been prospecting the farm roads in north Durham. My plan now was to make straight for Laverlaw and trust to luck.

We weren't long in getting to the Tyne valley near Hexham. The fine morning still held, but the mist was low on the hills and I counted on a drizzle in an hour or two. Anna looked chilly and I decided that we must have a better breakfast. We were on a good road now and I kept my eye lifting for an inconspicuous pub. Presently I found one a little off the road and its smoking chimney showed us that the folk were out of bed. I turned into its yard, which was on the side away from the road, and Anna and I stumbled into the kitchen, for we were both as stiff as pokers. The landlord was a big, slow-spoken Northumbrian, and his wife was a motherly creature who gave us hot water to wash in and a comb for Anna's hair. She promised, too, bacon and eggs in a quarter of an hour and, in the meantime, I bought some cans of petrol to fill up my tank. It was while the landlord was on this job that, to stretch my legs, I took a stroll around the inn to where I had a view of the highroad.

I got a nasty jar, for there was the sound of a big car and the Stutz came racing past. I guessed what had happened. It had lost us right enough in the Durham moorlands, but its occupants had argued that we must be making for Laverlaw and that, if we had tangled ourselves up in by-roads, we must have made poor speed during the night. They would therefore get ahead of us and watch the road junctions for the north. There was one especially that I remembered well, where the road up the North Tyne forked from the main highway over the Cheviots by the Carter Bar. Both were possible, and there was no third by which a heavy car could make fair going. Their strategy was sound enough. If we hadn't turned into that pub for breakfast we should have been fairly caught and, if I hadn't seen them pass, in another hour we should have been at their mercy.

Yet, after the first scare, I didn't feel downhearted. I felt somehow that we had the game in our hands and had got over the worst snags. I said nothing about the Stutz to Anna and we peacefully ate an enormous breakfast. Then I had a word with the landlord about the countryside and he told me a lot about the side-ways into the upper glens of Tyne. At eight o'clock we started again in a drizzle, and soon I turned off the main highway to the left by what I had learned was one of the old drove-roads.

All morning we threaded our way in a maze of what must be about the worst roads in Britain. I had my map and my directions from the inn, but often I had to stop and ask the route at the little moorland farms. Anna must have opened fifty gates and there were times when I thought we were bogged for good. I can tell you it was a tricky business, but I was beginning to enjoy myself for I felt that we had won and Anna was in wild spirits. The sight of bent and heather intoxicated her, and she took to singing and reciting poems. The curlews especially she hailed as old friends, and shouted a Danish poem about them . . .

Well, that's about the end of my story. We never met the Stutz again and, for all I know, it is still patrolling the Carter Bar. But I was taking no risks, and when we got into the main road up the Tyne to Liddesdale I didn't take the shortest way to Laverlaw, which would have been by Rule Water, or by Hermitage and the Slitrig. You see, I had a fear that the Stutz, if it found no sign of us on the Carter or Bellingham roads, might have the notion of keeping watch on the approaches nearer Laverlaw. So I decided to come in on you from the side where it wouldn't expect us. The sun came out after midday and it was a glorious afternoon. Lord, I think we must have covered half the Border. We went down Liddel to Langholm, and up the Esk to Eskdalemuir, and so into Ettrick. For most of the way we saw nothing but sheep and an odd baker's van.

from *The Island of Sheep*, John Buchan

Death of a Rolls, *circa* 1970

To complete my skimpy breakfast, and to celebrate the victory of virtue over dullness, I opened a bottle of the twelve-year-old Scotch and was just raising it to my lips when I saw the powder-blue Buick. It was coming out of an *arroyo* ahead of us, coming fast, engine howling in a low gear, coming straight for our nearside. Our offside was barely a yard from a sheer drop of hundreds of feet – it was a fair cop. I'd had my life. Jock – I've told you how fast he could be when necessary – wrenched the wheel over to the left, stood on the brakes, snatched first gear before the Rolls stalled and was turning right as the Buick hit us. The Buick man had known nothing of the strength of a vintage Rolls Royce, nor of Jock's fighting brain; our radiator gutted his car's side with a ghastly shriek of metal and the Buick span like a top, ending up poised on the shoulder of the road, its rear end impossibly extended over the precipice. The driver, face contorted with who knows what emotion, was fighting frantically with the door handle, his features a mask of nasty blood. Jock got out, ponderously strolled over to him and stared, looked up and down the road, went to the front of the mangled Buick, found a handhold and heaved enormously. The Buick tilted, started to go very slowly; Jock had time to get to the window again and give the driver a friendly grin before the nose went up and slid out of sight, slowly still. The driver showed us all his teeth in a silent scream before he went; we heard the Buick bounce three times, amazingly loudly, but never a thread of the driver's scream – those Buicks must be better soundproofed than you'd think. I believe, but I am not sure even now, that it was friendly Mr Braun – who was once again proving to me the statistical improbability of death in an aircraft accident.

I was surprised – and pardonably proud – to find that throughout the episode I had not lost my grip on the Scotch bottle. I had my drink and, since the circumstances were exceptional, offered the bottle to Jock.

'That was a bit vindictive, Jock,' I said reprovingly.

'Lost my temper,' he admitted. 'Bloody road hog.'

'He might easily have done us a mischief,' I agreed. Then I told him about things, especially like powder-blue Buicks and the dreadful – is that word really so worn out? – the dreadful danger I was – we were – in, despite my recent brief and lovely courtship with the phantasms of success, safety and happy-ever-after. (It seemed hard to believe that I could have been dallying, so few minutes before, with so patently tinsel a mental mistress as safety.) My eloquence ran to such heights of bitter self-mockery that I heard myself, aghast, telling Jock to leave me, to get out from under before the great axe fell.

'Bollocks,' I'm happy to say, was his response to that suggestion. (But 'happy to say' is not true either; his loyalty served me but briefly and him but shabbily – you might say that his 'bollocks' were the death of him.)

When the whisky had somewhat soothed our nerves we corked the bottle and got out of the car to examine its wounds. An Anglia driver would have done this first, of course, raging at fate, but we Rolls owners are made of sterner stuff. The radiator was scarred, weeping a little on to the baking road; a headlamp and sidelamp were quite ruined; the offside mudguard was heavily crumpled but still not quite so much that it would flay the tire. The show was, if necessary, on the road. I went back into the car and thought, while Jock fussed over the damage. I may have sipped a little at the whisky bottle and who shall blame me?

No one passed along the road, in either direction. A grasshopper stridulated endlessly; I minded this at first but soon learned to live with it. Having thought, I checked my thinking both ways from the ace. The result came out the same again and again. I didn't like it, but there you are, aren't you?

We sent the Rolls over the precipice. I am not ashamed to say that I wept a little to see all that beauty, that power and grace and history, being tossed into an arid canyon like a cigar end chucked down a lavatory pan. Even in death the car was elegant; it described great majestic curves as it rebounded in an almost leisurely way from boulder to boulder and came to rest, far below us, wedged upside-down in the throat of a deep crevasse, its lovely underparts bared to the sex of sunshine for a few seconds before a hundred tons of scree, dislodged by its passage, roared down and covered it.

The death of the Buick driver had been nothing compared with this; human death in reality seems poor stuff to a devoted television watcher, but who amongst you, seasoned readers, has seen a Rolls Royce Silver Ghost die on its back? I was inexpressibly moved. Jock seemed to sense this in his rough way for he moved closer to me and uttered words of comfort.

'It was insured full comprehensive, Mr Charlie,' he said.

'Yes, Jock,' I answered gruffly, 'you read my thoughts, as usual. But what is more to the point, just now, is how easily could the Rolls be salvaged?'

He brooded down into the shimmering, rock-strewn haze.

'How are you getting down there?' he began. 'This side's all avalanches and the other side's a cliff. Very dodgy.'

'Right.'

'Then you got to get it out of that crack, haven't you?'

'Right again.'

'*Dead* dodgy.'

'Yes.'

'And then you got to get it back up here, right?'

'Right.'

'Have to close this road a couple of days while the tackle's working, I reckon.'

'That's what I thought.'

'Mind you, if it was some stupid mountaineering twit stuck down there, or some old tart's puppy dog, they'd have him up before you could cough, wouldn't they, but this is only an old jam jar, isn't it? You'd have to want it real bad – or want something in it real bad – before you'd go slummocking down there.' He nudged me and winked enormously. He was never very good as winking, it contorted his face horribly. I nudged him back. We smirked.

Then we trudged up the road, Jock carrying our one suitcase now holding essentials for both of us, which he was supposed to have salvaged with wonderful presence of mind as the Rolls teetered on the very brink of the precipice.

'Whither Mortdecai?' about summed up my thought on that baking, dusty road. It is hard to think constructively once the fine, white grit of New Mexico has crept up your trouser legs and joined the sweat of your crotch. All I could decide was that the stars in their courses were hotly anti-Mortdecai and that, noble sentiments aside, I was well rid of what was probably the most conspicuous motor car on the North American subcontinent.

On the other hand, pedestrians are more conspicuous in New Mexico than most motor cars, a fact I realized when a car swept past us going in the direction we had come from; all its occupants goggled at us as though we were Teenage Things from Outer Space. It was an official car of some sort, a black-and-white Oldsmobile Super 88, and it did not stop – why should it? To be on foot in the United States is only immoral, not illegal. Unless you're a bum, of course. It's just like in England, really: you can wander abroad and lodge in the open air so long as you've a home to go to; it's only an offence if you *haven't* one – on the same principle that ensures you cannot borrow money from a bank unless you don't need any.

After what seemed a great many hours we found a patch of shade afforded by some nameless starveling trees and, without a word spoken, we sank down in their ungenerous umbrage.

'When a car passes going in our direction, Jock, we shall leap to our feet and hail it.'

'All right, Mr Charlie.'

With that we both fell asleep instantly.

from *Don't Point That Thing at Me*, Kyril Bonfiglioli

SOME VINTAGES OF THE *GENRE*

Here I have chosen some seminal examples of spy fiction, including an extract from the classic The Riddle of the Sands *by Erskine Childers, who wrote at the time of publication in 1903 that it was intended as a propaganda tract to warn of a German plan to invade England by means of barges operating out of the low-lying channels and sandbanks of the Frisian Islands. After serving as a naval officer in the First World War, Childers – who was half-Irish – threw in his lot with the Irish Republican cause and, having set up the Sinn Fein Intelligence network in Dublin, fell foul of the newly established Irish Free State, was charged with treason and executed by firing-squad in 1922. He thus joins a long line of spy writers – from Maugham and Fleming, to le Carré and Allbeury – who had first-hand experience of the spy trade, although with less apocalyptic results.*

But first, some other examples of classic spy writing, from writers best known for fiction in other fields . . .

The Secret

'We are now,' Guest declared, 'in this position. In Hamburg I discovered the meeting place of the No. 1 Branch of the Waiters' Union, and the place itself is now under our control. In that room at the Café Suisse will be woven the final threads of the great scheme. How are we to get there? How are we to penetrate its secrets?'

'We must see the room first,' I remarked.

'And then there is the question of ourselves,' Guest continued. 'We are both nominally dead men. But none the less, our friends leave little to chance. You may not have noticed it, but I knew very well that we were followed home today from the café. Every moment of ours will be spied upon. Is the change in our appearance sufficient?'

I looked at myself in the little gilt mirror over the mantelpiece. Perhaps because I looked, thinking of myself as I had been in the days before these strange happenings had come into my life, I answered his question promptly.

'I cannot believe,' I said, 'that any one would know me for Hardross Courage. I am perfectly certain, too, that I should not recognize in you today the Leslie Guest who died at Saxby.'

'I believe that you are right,' Guest admitted. 'At any rate, it is one of those matters which we must leave to chance. Only keep your identity always before you. At the Café Suisse, we shall be watched every moment of the day. Remember that you are a German-American of humble birth. Remember that always.'

I nodded.

'I am not an impulsive person,' I answered. 'I am used to think before I speak. I shall remember. But there is one thing I am afraid of, Guest. It must also have occurred to you. Now that the Café Suisse is in the hands of strangers, will not your friends change their meeting place?'

'I think not,' Guest answered slowly. 'I know a little already about that room. It has a hidden exit, by way of the cellar, into a court, every house of which is occupied by foreigners. A surprise on either side would be exceedingly difficult. I do not think that our friends will be anxious to give up the place, unless their suspicions are aroused concerning us. You see their time is very close at hand now. This, at any rate, is another of the risks which we must run.'

'Very well,' I answered. 'You see the time?'

Guest nodded.

'I am going to explain to you exactly,' he said, 'what you have to do.'

'Right,' I answered.

'The parcel on the sofa there,' he said, 'contains a second-hand suit of dress clothes. You will put them on, over them your old black overcoat which we bought at Hamburg, and your bowler hat. At four o'clock precisely, you will call at the offices of the German Waiters' Union, at No. 13, Old Compton Street, and ask for Mr Hirsch. Your name is Paul Schmidt. You were born in Offenbach, but went to America at the age of four. You were back in Germany for two years at the age of nineteen, and you have served your time at Mayence. You have come to England with an uncle, who has taken a small restaurant in Soho and who proposes to engage you as head-waiter. You will be enrolled as a member of the Waiter's Union, as a matter of course; but, when that has been arranged, you write on a slip of paper these words, and pass them to Mr Hirsch: '"I, too, have a rifle"!'

I was beginning to get interested.

'"I, too, have a rifle",' I repeated. 'Yes! I can remember that; but I shall be talking like a poll-parrot, for I shan't have the least idea what it means.'

'You need not know much,' Guest answered. 'Those words are your passport into the No. 1 Branch of the Waiters' Union, whose committee, by the bye, meets at the Café Suisse. If you are asked why you wish to join, you need only say because you are a German!'

'Right,' I answered. 'I'll get into the clothes.'

Guest gave me a few more instructions while I was changing and by four o'clock punctually I opened the swing door of No. 13, Old Compton Street. The place consisted of a waiting-room, very bare and very dirty; a counter, behind which two or three clerks were very busy writing in ponderous, well-worn ledgers, and an inner door. I made my way towards one of the clerks and inquired in my best German if I could see Mr Hirsch.

The clerk – he was as weedy a looking youth as ever I had seen – pointed with ink-stained finger to the benches which lined the room.

'You wait your turn,' he said, and waved me away.

I took my place behind at least a dozen boys and young men, whose avocation was unmistakable. Most of them were smoking either cigarettes or a pipe, and most of them were untidy and unhealthy-looking. They took no notice of me but sat watching the door to the inner room which opened and shut with wonderful rapidity. Every time one of their number came out, another took his place. It came to my turn sooner than I could have believed possible.

I found myself in a small office, untidy, barely furnished and thick with tobacco smoke. Its only occupant was a stout man, with flaxen hair and beard, and mild blue eyes. He was sitting in his shirt sleeves and smoking a very black cigar.

'Well?' he exclaimed, almost before I had crossed the threshold.

'My name is Paul Schmidt,' I said, 'and I should like to join the Waiters' Union.'

'Born?'

'Offenbach!'

'Age?'

'Thirty!'

'Working?'

'Café Suisse!'

'Come from?'

'America!'

He tossed me a small handbook.

'Half-a-crown,' he said, holding out his hand.

I gave it him. I was beginning to understand why I had not been kept very long waiting.

'Clear out!' he said. 'No questions, please. The book tells you everything!'

I looked him in the face.

'I, too, have a rifle,' I said boldly.

I found, then, that those blue eyes were not so mild as they seemed. His glance seemed to cut me through and through.

'You understand what you are saying?' he asked.

'Yes!' I answered. 'I want to join the No. 1 Branch.'

'Why?'

'Because I am a German,' I answered.

'Who told you about it?'

'A waiter named Hans in the Manhattan Hotel, New York.' I lied with commendable promptitude.

'Have you served?' he asked.

'At Mayence, eleven years ago,' I answered.

'Where did you say that you were working?' he asked.

'Café Suisse!' I said.

It seemed to me that he had been on the point of entering my name in a small ledger, which he had produced from one of the drawers by his side, but my answer apparently electrified him. His eyes literally held mine. He stared at me steadily for several moments.

'How long have you been there?' he asked. 'I do not recognize you.'

'I commence today,' I said. 'My uncle has just taken the café. He will make me his head-waiter.'

'Has your uncle been in the business before?' he asked.

'He kept a saloon in Brooklyn,' I answered.

'Made money at it?'

'Yes!'

'Were you with him?'

'No! I was at the Manhattan Hotel.'

'Your uncle will not make a fortune at the Café Suisse,' he remarked.

'I do not think,' I answered, 'that he will lose one.'

'Does he know what you propose?'

I shook my head.

'The fatherland means little to him,' I answered. 'He has lived in America too long.'

'You are willing to buy your own rifle?' he asked.

'I would rather not,' I answered.

'We sell them for a trifle,' he continued. 'You would not mind ten shillings.'

'I would rather pay nothing,' I answered, 'but I will pay ten shillings if I must.'

He nodded.

'I cannot accept you myself,' he said. 'We know too little about you. You must attend before the committee tonight.'

'Where?' I asked.

'At the Café Suisse,' he answered. 'We shall send for you! Till then!'

'Till then,' I echoed, backing out of the room.

That night I gravely perambulated the little café in my waiter's clothes and endeavoured to learn from Karl my new duties. There were a good many people dining there but, towards ten o'clock, the place was almost empty. Just as the hour was striking, Mr Kauffman, who had been dining with Mr Hirsch, rose from his place and, with a key in his hand, made his way towards the closed door.

He was followed by Mr Hirsch and seven other men, all of whom had been dining at the long central table which easily accommodated a dozen or more visitors. There was nothing at all remarkable about the nine men who shambled their way through the room. They did not in the least resemble conspirators. Hirsch, who was already smoking a huge pipe, touched me on the shoulder as he passed.

'We shall send for you presently,' he declared. 'Your case is coming before the committee.'

I began checking some counterfoils at the desk but, before I had been there five minutes, the door of the inner room was opened and Mr Hirsch appeared upon the threshold. He caught my eye and beckoned to me solemnly. I crossed the room, ascended the step and found myself in what the waiters called the club-room. Mr Hirsch carefully closed the door behind me.

The first thing that surprised me was that, although I had seen nine men ascend the three stairs and enter the room, there was now, besides myself and Hirsch, only one other person present. That other person was sitting at the head of the table and he was of distinctly a different class from Hirsch and his friends. He was a young man, fair and well built, and as obviously a soldier as though he were wearing his uniform. His clothes were well cut, his hands shapely and white. Some instinct told me what to do. I stood to the salute and I saw a glance of satisfaction pass between the two men.

'Your name is Paul Schmidt?' the man at the table asked me.

'Yes, sir!' I answered.

'You served at Mayence?'

'Yes, sir!'

'Under?'

'Colonel Hausman, sir, thirteenth regiment.'

'You have your papers?'

I passed over the little packet which Guest had given me. My questioner studied them carefully, glancing up every now and then at me. Then he folded them up and laid them upon the table.

'You speak German with an English accent,' he remarked, looking at me keenly.

'I have lived nearly all my life in America,' I reminded him.

'You are sure,' he said, 'that you understand the significance of your request to join the No. 1 Branch of the Waiters' Union?'

'Quite sure, sir,' I told him.

'Stand over there for a few minutes,' he directed, pointing to the furthest corner of the room.

I obeyed and he talked with Hirsch for several moments in an undertone. Then he turned once more to me.

'We shall accept you, Paul Schmidt,' he said gravely. 'You will come before the committee with us now.'

I saluted, but said nothing. Hirsch pushed away the table and, stooping down, touched what seemed to be a spring in the floor. A slight crack was instantly disclosed, which gradually widened until it disclosed a ladder. We descended and found ourselves in a dry cellar, lit with electric lights. Seven men were sitting round a small table, in the furthest corner of the place. Their conversation was suspended as we appeared and my interlocutor, leaving Hirsch and myself in the background, at once plunged into a discussion with them. I, too, should have followed him, but Hirsch laid his hand upon my arm.

'Wait a little,' he whispered. 'They will call us up.'

'Who is he?' I asked, pointing to the tall military figure bending stiffly down at the table.

'Call him Captain X,' Hirsch answered softly. 'He does not care to be known here!'

'But how did he get into the room upstairs?' I asked. 'I never saw him in the restaurant.'

Hirsch smiled placidly.

'It is well,' he said, 'my young friend, that you do not ask too many questions!'

The man whom I was to call Captain X turned now and beckoned to me. I approached and stood at attention.

'I have accepted this man Paul Schmidt, as a member of the No.

1 Branch of the Waiters' Union,' he announced. 'Paul Schmidt, listen attentively, and you will understand in outline what the responsibilities are that you have undertaken.'

There was a short silence. The men at the table looked at me and I looked at them. I was not in any way ill-at-ease, but I felt a terrible inclination to laugh. The whole affair seemed to me a little ludicrous. There was nothing in the appearance of these men or the surroundings in the least impressive. They had the air of being unintelligent middle-class tradesmen of peaceable disposition, who had just dined to their fullest capacity and were enjoying a comfortable smoke together. They eyed me amicably and several of them nodded in a friendly way. I was forced to say something, or I must have laughed outright.

'I should like to know,' I said, 'what is expected of me.'

An exceedingly fat man beckoned me to stand before him.

'Paul Schmidt,' he said, 'listen to me! You are a German born?'

'Without doubt,' I answered.

'The love of your fatherland is still in your heart?'

'Always!' I answered fervently.

'Also with all of us,' he answered. 'You have lived in America so long, that a few words of explanation may be necessary. So!'

Now this man's voice, unimpressive though his appearance was, seemed somehow to create a new atmosphere in the place. He spoke very slowly, and he spoke as a man speaks of the things which are sacred to him.

'It is within the last few years,' he said, 'that all true patriots have been forced to realize one great and very ugly truth. Our country is menaced by an unceasing and untiring enmity. Wherever we have turned, we have met with its influence; whatever schemes for legitimate expansion our Kaiser and his great counsellors may have framed, have been checked, if not thwarted, by our sleepless and relentless foe. No longer can we, the great peace-loving nation of the world, conceal from ourselves the coming peril. England has declared herself our sworn enemy!'

A little murmur of assent came from the other men. I neither spoke nor moved.

'There is but one end possible,' he continued slowly. 'It is war! It must come soon! Its shadow is all the time darkening the land. So we, who have understood the signs, remind one another that the Power who strikes the first blow is the one who assures for herself the final success!'

Again he was forced to pause, for his breath was coming quickly.

He lifted his long glass and solemnly drained its contents. All the time, over its rim, his eyes held mine.

'So!' he exclaimed, setting it down with a little grunt of satisfaction. 'It must be, then, Germany who strikes, Germany who strikes in self-defence. My young friend, there are in this country today 290,000 young countrymen of yours and mine who have served their time, and who can shoot. Shall these remain idle at such a time? No! We then have been at work. Clerks, tradesmen, waiters and hairdressers, each have their society, each have their work assigned to them. The forts which guard this great city may be impregnable from without, but from within – well, that is another matter. Listen! The exact spot where we shall attack is arranged and plans of every fort which guard the Thames are in our hands. The signal will be – the visit of the British fleet to Kiel! Three days before, you will have your company assigned to you, and every possible particular. Yours it will be, and those of your comrades, to take a glorious part in the coming struggle! I drink with you, Paul Schmidt, and you, my friends, to that day!'

from *The Secret*, E. Phillips Oppenheim

In the Picture

Guy went to the carpark and found a lorry going in for rations. The road ran along the edge of the sea. The breeze was full of flying sand. On the beaches young civilians exposed hairy bodies and played ball with loud, excited cries. Army lorries passed in close procession, broken here and there by new, tight-shut limousines bearing purple-lipped ladies in black satin.

'Drop me at the Cecil,' said Guy, for he had other business in Alexandria besides Ivor Claire. He wished to make his Easter duties and preferred to do so in a city church, rather than in camp. Already, without deliberation, he had begun to dissociate himself from the Army in matters of real concern.

Alexandria, ancient asparagus bed of theological absurdity, is now somewhat shabbily furnished with churches. Guy found what he sought in a side street, a large unobtrusive building attached to a school, it seemed, or a hospital. He entered into deep gloom.

A fat youth in shorts and vest was lethargically sweeping the aisle. Guy approached and addressed him in French. He seemed not to hear. A bearded, skirted figure scudded past in the darkness. Guy pursued and said awkwardly:

'*Excusez-moi, mon père. Y-at-il un prêtre qui parle Anglais ou Italien?*'

The priest did not pause.

'*Français*,' he said.

'*Je veux me confesser en français si c'est nécessaire. Mais je préfère beaucoup Anglais ou Italien, si c'est possible.*'

'*Anglais*,' said the hasty priest. '*Par-là.*'

He turned abruptly into the sacristy, pointing as he went towards a still darker chapel. Khaki stockings and Army boots protruded from the penitents' side of the confessional. Guy knelt and waited. He knew what he had to say. The mutter of voices in the shadows seemed to be prolonged inordinately. At length a young soldier emerged and Guy took his place. A bearded face was just visible through the grille; a guttural voice blessed him. He made his confession and paused. The dark figure seemed to shrug off the triviality of what he had heard.

'You have a rosary? Say three decades.'

He gave the absolution.

'Thank you, father, and pray for me.' Guy made to go but the priest continued:

'You are here on leave?'

'No, father.'

'You have been here long?'

'A few weeks.'

'You have come from the desert?'

'No, father.'

'You have just come from England? You came with new tanks?'

Suddenly Guy was suspicious. He was shriven. The priest was no longer bound by the seal of confession. The grille still stood between them. Guy still knelt, but the business between them was over. They were man and man now in a country at war.

'When do you go to the desert?'

'Why do you ask?'

'To help you. There are special dispensations. If you are going at once into action I can give you communion.'

'I'm not.'

Guy rose and left the church. Beggars thronged him. He walked a few steps towards the main street where the trams ran, then turned back. The boy with the broom had gone. The confessional was empty. He knocked on the open door of the sacristy. No one came. He entered and found a clean tiled floor, cupboards, a sink, no priest. He left the church and stood once more among the beggars, undecided. The transition from the role of penitent to that of investigating officer was radical. He could not now remember verbatim what had occurred. The questions had been impertinent;

were they necessarily sinister? Could he identify the priest? Could he, if called to find a witness, identify the young soldier?

Two palm trees in a yard separated the church from the clergy-house. Guy rang the bell and presently the fat boy opened the door, disclosing a vista of high white corridor.

'I would like to know the name of one of your fathers.'

'The fathers have this moment gone to rest. They have had very long ceremonies this morning.'

'I don't want to disturb him – merely to know his name. He speaks English and was hearing confessions in the church two minutes ago.'

'No confessions now until three o'clock. The fathers are resting.'

'I have been to confession to this father. I want to know his name. He speaks English.'

'I speak English. I do not know what father you want.'

'I want his name.'

'You must come at three o'clock, please, when the fathers have rested.'

Guy turned away. The beggars settled on him. He strode into the busy street and the darkness of Egypt closed on him in the dazzling sunlight. Perhaps he had imagined the whole incident and, if he had not, what profit was there in pursuit? There were priests in France working for the Allies. Why not a priest in Egypt, in exile, doing his humble bit for his own side? Egypt teemed with spies. Every troop movement was open to the scrutiny of a million ophthalmic eyes. The British order of battle must be known in minute detail from countless sources. What could that priest accomplish except perhaps gain kinder treatment for his community if Rommel reached Alexandria? Probably the only result, if Guy made a report, would be an order forbidding HM forces to frequent civilian churches.

Ivor Claire's nursing-home overlooked the Municipal Gardens. Guy walked there through the crowded streets so despondently that the touts looking at him despaired and let him pass unsolicited.

He found Claire in a wheeled-chair on his balcony.

'*Much* better,' he said in answer to Guy's inquiry. 'They are all very pleased with me. I may be able to get up to Cairo next week for the races.'

'Colonel Tommy is getting a little restive.'

'Who wouldn't be at Sidi Bishr? Well, he knows where to find me when he wants me.'

'He seems rather to want you now.'

'Oh, I don't think I'd be much use to him until I'm fit, you know. My troop is in good hands. When Tommy kindly relieved me of Corporal-Major Ludovic my anxieties came to an end. But we must keep in touch. I can't have you doing a McTavish on me.'

'Two flaps since you went away. Once we were at two hours' notice for three days.'

'I know. Greek nonsense. When there's anything really up I shall hear from Julia Stitch before Tommy does. She is a mine of indiscretion. You know she's here?'

'Half X Commando spend their evenings with her.'

'Why don't you?'

'Oh, she wouldn't remember me.'

'My dear Guy, she remembers everyone. Algie has some sort of job keeping his eye on the King. They're very well installed. I thought of moving in on them but one can't be sure that Julia will give an invalid quite all he needs. There's rather too much coming and going, too – generals and people. Julia pops in most mornings and brings me the gossip.'

Then Guy recounted that morning's incident in the church.

'Not much to shoot a chap on,' said Claire. 'Even a clergyman.'

'Ought I to do anything about it?'

'Ask Tommy. It might prove a great bore, you know. Everyone is a spy in this country.'

'That's rather what I thought.'

from *Officers and Gentlemen*, Evelyn Waugh

The Informer

Mr X came to me, preceded by a letter of introduction from a good friend of mine in Paris, specifically to see my collection of Chinese bronzes and porcelain.

My friend in Paris is a collector, too. He collects neither porcelain, nor bronzes, nor pictures, nor medals, nor stamps, nor anything that could be profitably dispersed under an auctioneer's hammer. He would reject, with genuine surprise, the name of a collector. Nevertheless, that's what he is by temperament. He collects acquaintances. It is delicate work. He brings to it the patience, the passion, the determination of a true collector of curiosities. His collection does not contain any royal personages. I don't think he considers them sufficiently rare and interesting; but, with that exception, he has met with, and talked to, everyone worth knowing on any conceivable ground. He observes them, listens to them, penetrates them, measures them and puts the memory away in the galleries of his mind. He has schemed, plotted and travelled all over

Europe in order to add to his collection of distinguished personal acquaintances.

As he is wealthy, well connected and unprejudiced, his collection is pretty complete, including objects (or should I say subjects?) whose value is unappreciated by the vulgar, and often unknown to popular fame. Of those specimens my friend is naturally the most proud.

He wrote to me of X: 'He is the greatest rebel (*révolté*) of modern times. The world knows him as a revolutionary writer whose savage irony has laid bare the rottenness of the most respectable institutions. He has scalped every venerated head, and has mangled at the stake of his wit every received opinion and every recognized principle of conduct and policy. Who does not remember his flaming red revolutionary pamphlets? Their sudden swarmings used to overwhelm the powers of every Continental police like a plague of crimson gadflies. But this extreme writer has been also the active inspirer of secret societies, the mysterious unknown No. I of desperate conspiracies suspected and unsuspected, matured or baffled. And the world at large has never had an inkling of that fact! This accounts for him going about amongst us to this day, a veteran of many subterranean campaigns, standing aside now, safe within his reputation of merely the greatest destructive publicist that ever lived.'

Thus wrote my friend, adding that Mr X was an enlightened connoisseur of bronzes and china, and asking me to show him my collection.

X turned up in due course. My treasures are disposed in three large rooms without carpets and curtains. There is no other furniture than the *étagères* and the glass cases whose contents shall be worth a fortune to my heirs. I allow no fires to be lighted, for fear of accidents, and a fireproof door separates them from the rest of the house.

It was a bitter cold day. We kept on our overcoats and hats. Middle-sized and spare, his eyes alert in a long, Roman-nosed countenance, X walked on his neat little feet, with short steps, and looked at my collection intelligently. I hope I looked at him intelligently, too. A snow-white moustache and imperial made his nut-brown complexion appear darker than it really was. In his fur coat and shiny tall hat that terrible man looked fashionable. I believe he belonged to a noble family and could have called himself Vicomte X de la Z if he chose. We talked nothing but bronzes and porcelain. He was remarkably appreciative. We parted on cordial terms.

Where he was staying I don't know. I imagine he must have been a lonely man. Anarchists, I suppose, have no families – not, at any rate, as we understand that social relation. Organization into families may answer to a need of human nature but, in the last instance, it is based on law and therefore must be something odious and impossible to an anarchist. But, indeed, I don't understand anarchists. Does a man of that – of that – persuasion still remain an anarchist when alone, quite alone and going to bed, for instance? Does he lay his head on the pillow, pull his bedclothes over him and go to sleep with the necessity of the *bombardement général*, as the French slang has it, of the general blow-up, always present to his mind? And, if so, how can he? I am sure that if such a faith (or such a fanaticism) once mastered my thoughts I would never be able to compose myself sufficiently to sleep or eat or perform any of the routine acts of daily life. I would want no wife, no children; I could have no friends, it seems to me; and, as to collecting bronzes or china, that, I should say, would be quite out of the question. But I don't know. All I know is that Mr X took his meals in a very good restaurant which I frequented also.

With his head uncovered, the silver top-knot of his brushed-up hair completed the character of his physiognomy, all bony ridges and sunken hollows, clothed in a perfect impassiveness of expression. His meagre brown hands, emerging from large white cuffs, came and went, breaking bread, pouring wine and so on, with quiet mechanical precision. His head and body above the tablecloth had a rigid immobility. This firebrand, this great agitator, exhibited the least possible amount of warmth and animation. His voice was rasping, cold and monotonous in a low key. He could not be called a talkative personality; but, with his detached calm manner, he appeared as ready to keep the conversation going as to drop it at any moment.

And his conversation was by no means commonplace. To me, I own, there was some excitement in talking quietly across a dinner-table with a man whose venomous pen-stabs had sapped the vitality of at least one monarchy. That much was a matter of public knowledge. But I knew more. I knew of him from my friend – as a certainty what the guardians of social order in Europe had at most only suspected, or dimly guessed at.

He had had what I may call his underground life. And as I sat, evening after evening, facing him at dinner, a curiosity in that direction would naturally arise in my mind. I am a quiet and peaceable product of civilization and know no passion other than the passion for collecting things which are rare, and must remain exquisite even if approaching to the monstrous. Some Chinese bronzes are monstrously precious. And here (out of my friend's collection), here I had before me a kind of rare monster. It is true that this monster was polished and in a sense even exquisite. His beautiful unruffled manner was that. But then he was not of bronze. He was not even Chinese, which would have enabled one to contemplate him calmly across the gulf of racial difference. He was alive and European; he had the manner of good society, wore a coat and hat like mine, and had pretty near the same taste in cooking. It was too frightful to think of.

One evening he remarked, casually, in the course of conversation, 'There's no amendment to be got out of mankind except by terror and violence.'

You can imagine the effect of such a phrase out of such a man's mouth upon a person like myself, whose whole scheme of life had been based upon a suave and delicate discrimination of social and artistic values. Just imagine! Upon me, to whom all sorts and forms of violence appeared as unreal as the giants, ogres and even-headed hydras whose activities affect, fantastically, the course of legends and fairy-tales!

I seemed suddenly to hear above the festive bustle and clatter of the brilliant restaurant the mutter of a hungry and seditious multitude.

I suppose I am impressionable and imaginative. I had a disturbing vision of darkness, full of lean jaws and wild eyes, amongst the hundred electric lights of the place. But somehow this vision made me angry, too. The sight of that man, so calm, breaking bits of white bread, exasperated me. And I had the audacity to ask him how it was that the starving proletariat of Europe, to whom he had been preaching revolt and violence, had not been made indignant by his openly luxurious life. 'At all this,' I said, pointedly, with a glance round the room and at the bottle of champagne we generally shared between us at dinner.

He remained unmoved.

'Do I feed on their toil and their heart's blood? Am I a speculator or a capitalist? Did I steal my fortune from a starving people? No! They know this very well. And they envy me nothing. The miserable mass of the people is generous to its leaders. What I have acquired has come to me through my writings; not from the millions of pamphlets distributed gratis to the hungry and the oppressed, but from the hundreds of thousands of copies sold to the well-fed bourgeois. You know that my writings were at one time the rage, fashion – the thing to read with wonder and horror, to turn your eyes up at my pathos . . . or else to laugh in ecstasies at my wit.'

'Yes,' I admitted. 'I remember, of course; and confess frankly that I could never understand that infatuation.'

'Don't you know yet,' he said, 'that an idle and selfish class loves to see mischief being made, even if it is made at its own expense? Its own life being all a matter of pose and gesture, it is unable to realize the power and the danger of a real movement and of words that have no sham meaning. It is all fun and sentiment. It is sufficient, for instance, to point out the attitude of the old French aristocracy towards the philosophers whose words were preparing the Great Revolution. Even in England, where you have some common sense, a demagogue has only to shout loud enough and long enough to find some backing in the very class he is shouting at. You, too, like to see mischief being made. The demagogue carries the amateurs of emotion with him. Amateurism in this, that and the other thing is a delightfully easy way of killing time, and feeding one's own vanity – the silly vanity of being abreast with the ideas of the day after tomorrow. Just as good and otherwise harmless people will join you in ecstasies over your collection without having the slightest notion in what its marvellousness really consists.'

I hung my head. It was a crushing illustration of the sad truth he advanced. The world is full of such people. And that instance of the French aristocracy before the Revolution was extremely telling, too. I could not traverse his statement, though its cynicism – always a distasteful trait – took off much of its value in my mind. However, I admit I was impressed. I had the need to say something which would not be in the nature of assent and yet would not invite discussion. 'You don't mean to say,' I observed, airily, 'that extreme revolutionists have ever been actively assisted by the infatuation of such people?'

'I did not mean exactly that by what I said just now. I generalized. But since you ask me, I may tell you that such help has been given to revolutionary activities, more or less consciously, in various countries. And even in this country.'

'Impossible!' I protested with firmness. 'We don't play with fire to that extent.'

'And yet you can better afford it than others, perhaps. But let me observe that most women, if not always ready to play with fire, are generally eager to play with a loose spark or so.'

'Is this a joke?' I asked, smiling.

'If it is, I am not aware of it,' he said, woodenly. 'I was thinking of an instance. Oh! mild enough in a way . . .'

I became all expectation at this. I had tried many times to approach him on his underground side, so to speak. The very word had been pronounced between us. But he had always met me with his impenetrable calm.

'And at the same time,' Mr X continued, 'it will give you a notion of the difficulties that may arise in what you are pleased to call underground work. It is sometimes difficult to deal with them. Of course there is no hierarchy amongst the affiliated. No rigid system.'

My surprise was great, but short-lived. Clearly, amongst extreme anarchists there could be no hierarchy; nothing in the nature of a law of precedence. The idea of anarchy ruling among anarchists was comforting, too. It could not possibly make for efficiency.

Mr X startled me by asking, abruptly, 'You know Hermione Street?'

I nodded doubtful assent. Hermione Street has been, within the last three years, improved out of any man's knowledge. The name exists still, but not one brick or stone of the old Hermione Street is left now. It was the old street he meant, for he said:

'There was a row of two-storied brick houses on the left, with their backs against the wing of a great public building – you remember. Would it surprise you very much to hear that one of these houses was, for a time, the centre of anarchist propaganda and of what you would call underground action?'

'Not at all,' I declared. Hermione Street had never been particularly respectable, as I remembered it.

'The house was the property of a distinguished government official,' he added, sipping his champagne.

'Oh, indeed!' I said, this time not believing a word of it.

'Of course he was not living there,' Mr X continued. 'But from ten till four he sat next door to it, the dear man, in his well-appointed private room in the wing of the public building I've mentioned. To be strictly accurate, I must explain that the house in Hermione Street did not really belong to him. It belonged to his grown-up children – a daughter and a son. The girl, a fine figure, was by no means vulgarly pretty. To more personal charm than mere youth could account for, she added the seductive appearance of enthusiasm, of independence, of courageous thought. I suppose she put on these appearances as she put on her picturesque dresses and for the same reason: to assert her individuality at any cost. You know, women would go to any length almost for such a purpose. She went to a great length. She had acquired all the appropriate gestures of anger, of indignation against the anti-humanitarian vices of the social class to which she belonged herself. All this sat on her striking personality as well as her lightly original costumes. Very slightly original; just enough to mark a protest against the philistinism of the overfed taskmasters of the poor. Just enough, and no more. It would not have done to go too far in that direction – you understand. But she was of age, and nothing stood in the way of her offering her house to the revolutionary workers.'

'You don't mean it!' I cried.

'I assure you,' he affirmed, 'that she made that very practical gesture. How else could they have got hold of it? The cause is not rich. And, moreover, there would have been difficulties with any ordinary house-agent who would have wanted references and so on. The group she came in contact with while exploring the poor quarters of the town (you know the gesture of charity and personal service which was so fashionable some years ago) accepted with gratitude. The first advantage was that Hermione Street is, as you know, well away from the suspect part of the town, specially watched by the police.

'The ground floor consisted of a little Italian restaurant, of the flyblown sort. There was no difficulty in buying the proprietor out. A woman and a man, belonging to the group, took it on. The man had been a cook. The comrades could get their meals there, unnoticed amongst the other customers. This was another advantage. The first floor was occupied by a shabby Variety Artists' Agency – an agency for performers in inferior music-halls, you know. A fellow called Bomm, I remember. He was not disturbed. It was rather favourable than otherwise to have a lot of foreign-looking people, jugglers, acrobats, singers of both sexes, and so on, going in and out all day long. The police paid no attention to new faces, you see. The top floor happened, most conveniently, to stand empty then.'

X interrupted himself to attack impassively, with measured movements, a *bombe glacée* which the waiter had just set down on the table. He swallowed carefully a few spoonfuls of the iced sweet and asked me, 'Did you ever hear of Stone's Dried Soup?'

'Hear of *what*?'

'It was,' X pursued, evenly, 'a comestible article once rather prominently advertised in the dailies, but which never, somehow, gained the favour of the public. The enterprise fizzled out, as you say here. Parcels of their stock could be picked up at auctions at considerably less than a penny a pound. The group bought some of it and an agency for Stone's Dried Soup was started on the top floor. A perfectly respectable business. The stuff, a yellow powder of extremely unappetizing aspect, was put up in large square tins, of which six went to a case. If anybody ever came to give an order it was, of course, executed. But the advantage of the powder was this, that things could be concealed in it very conveniently. Now and then a special case got put on a van and sent off to be exported abroad under the very nose of the policeman on duty at the corner. You understand?'

'I think I do,' I said, with an expressive nod at the remnants of the *bombe* melting slowly in the dish.

'Exactly. But the cases were useful in another way, too. In the basement, or in the cellar at the back, rather, two printing-presses were established. A lot of revolutionary literature of the most inflammatory kind was got away from the house in Stone's Dried Soup cases. The brother of our anarchist young lady found some occupation there. He wrote articles, helped to set up type and pull off the sheets, and generally assisted the man in charge, a very able young fellow called Sevrin.

'The guiding spirit of that group was a fanatic of social revolution. He is dead now. He was an engraver and etcher of genius. You must have seen his work. It is much sought after by certain amateurs now. He began by being revolutionary in his art, and ended by becoming a revolutionist, after his wife and child had died in want and misery. He used to say that the bourgeois, the smug, overfed lot, had killed them. That was his real belief. He still worked at his art and led a double life. He was tall, gaunt and swarthy, with a long, brown beard and deep-set eyes. You must have seen him. His name was Horne.'

At this I was really startled. Of course, years ago, I used to meet Horne about. He looked like a powerful, rough gipsy, in an old top hat, with a red muffler round his throat and buttoned up in a long, shabby overcoat. He talked of his art with exaltation and gave one the impression of being strung up to the verge of insanity. A small group of connoisseurs appreciated his work. Who would have thought that this man . . . Amazing! And yet it was not, after all, so difficult to believe.

'As you see,' X went on, 'this group was in a position to pursue its work of propaganda and the other kind of work, too, under very advantageous conditions. They were all resolute, experienced men of a superior stamp. And yet we became struck at length by the fact that plans prepared in Hermione Street almost invariably failed.'

'Who were "we"?' I asked, pointedly.

'Some of us in Brussels – at the centre,' he said, hastily. 'Whatever vigorous action originated Hermione Street seemed doomed to failure. Something always happened to baffle the best planned manifestations in every part of Europe. It was a time of general activity. You must not imagine that all our failures are of a loud sort, with arrests and trials. That is not so. Often the police work quietly, almost secretly, defeating our combinations by clever counter-plotting. No arrests, no noise, no alarming of the public mind and inflaming the passions. It is a wise procedure. But at that time the police were too uniformly successful from Mediterranean to the Baltic. It was annoying and began to look dangerous. At last we came to the conclusion that there must be some untrustworthy elements amongst the London groups. And I came over to see what could be done quietly.

'My first step was to call upon our young Lady Amateur of anarchism at her private house. She received me in a flattering way. I judged that she knew nothing of the chemical and other operations going on at the top of the house in Hermione Street. The printing of anarchist literature was the only "activity" she seemed to be aware of there. She was displaying very strikingly the usual signs of severe enthusiasm and had already written many sentimental articles with ferocious conclusions. I could see she was enjoying herself hugely, with all the gestures and grimaces of deadly earnestness. They suited her big-eyed, broad-browed face and the good carriage of her shapely head, crowned by a magnificent lot of brown hair done in an unusual and becoming style. Her brother was in the room, too, a serious youth, with arched eyebrows and wearing a red necktie, who struck me as being absolutely in the dark about everything in the world, including himself. By and by a tall young man came in. He was clean-shaved with a strong bluish jaw and something of the air of a taciturn actor or of a fanatical priest: the type with black eyebrows – you know. But he was very presentable indeed. He shook hands at once vigorously with each of us. The young lady came up to me and murmured sweetly, "Comrade Sevrin".

'I had never seen him before. He had little to say to us, but sat down by the side of the girl and they fell at once into earnest conversation. She leaned forward in her deep armchair and took her nicely rounded chin in her beautiful white hand. He looked attentively into her eyes. It was the attitude of love-making, serious, intense, as if on the brink of the grave. I suppose she felt it necessary to round and complete her assumption of advanced ideas, of revolutionary lawlessness, by making believe to be in love with an anarchist. And this one, I repeat, was extremely presentable, notwithstanding his fanatical black-browed aspect. After a few stolen glances in their direction, I had no doubt that he was in earnest. As to the lady, her gestures were unapproachable, better than the very thing itself in the blended suggestion of dignity, sweetness, condescension, fascination, surrender and reserve. She interpreted her conception of what that precise sort of love-making should be with consummate art. And so far, she, too, no doubt, was in earnest. Gestures – but so perfect!

'After I had been left alone with our Lady Amateur I informed her guardedly of the object of my visit. I hinted at our suspicions. I wanted to hear what she would have to say, and half expected some perhaps unconscious revelation. All she said was, "That's serious," looking delightfully concerned and grave. But there was a sparkle in her eyes which meant plainly, "How exciting!" After all, she knew little of anything except of words. Still, she undertook to put me in communication with Horne, who was not easy to find unless in Hermione Street, where I did not wish to show myself just then.

'I met Horne. This was another kind of a fanatic altogether. I exposed to him the conclusion we in Brussels had arrived at, and pointed out the significant series of failures. To this he answered with irrelevant exaltation:

"I have something in hand that shall strike terror into the heart of these gorged brutes".

'And then I learned that, by excavating in one of the cellars of the house, he and some companions had made their way into the vaults under the great public building I have mentioned before. The blowing up of a whole wing was a certainty as soon as the materials were ready.

'I was not so appalled at the stupidity of that move as I might have been had not the usefulness of our centre in Hermione Street become already very problematical. In fact, in my opinion it was much more of a police trap by this time than anything else.

'What was necessary now was to discover what, or rather who, was wrong, and I managed at last to get that idea into Horne's head. He glared, perplexed, his nostrils working as if he were sniffing treachery in the air.

'And here comes a piece of work which will no doubt strike you as a sort of theatrical expedient. And yet what else could have been done? The problem was to find out the untrustworthy member of the group. But no suspicion could be fastened on one more than another. To set a watch upon them all was not very practicable. Besides, that proceeding often fails. In any case, it takes time, and the danger was pressing. I felt certain that the premises in Hermione Street would be ultimately raided, though the police had evidently such confidence in the informer that the house, for the time being, was not even watched. Horne was positive on that point. Under the circumstances it was an unfavourable symptom. Something had to be done quickly.

'I decided to organize a raid myself upon the group. Do you understand? A raid of other trusty comrades personating the police. A conspiracy within a conspiracy. You see the object of it, of course. When apparently about to be arrested I hoped the informer would betray himself in some way or other; either by some unguarded act or simply by his unconcerned demeanour, for instance. Of course there was the risk of complete failure and the no lesser risk of some fatal accident in the course of resistance, perhaps, or in the efforts at escape. For, as you will easily see, the Hermione Street group had to be actually and completely taken unawares, as I was sure they would be by the real police before very long. The informer was amongst them, and Horne alone could be let into the secret of my plan.

'I will not enter into the detail of my preparations. It was not very easy to arrange but it was done very well, with a really convincing effect. The sham police invaded the restaurant, whose shutters were immediately put up. The surprise was perfect. Most of the Hermione Street party was found in the second cellar, enlarging the hole communicating with the vaults of the great public building. At the first alarm, several comrades bolted through impulsively into the aforesaid vault where, of course, had this been a genuine raid, they would have been hopelessly trapped. We did not bother about them for the moment. They were harmless enough. The top floor caused considerable anxiety to Horne and myself. There, surrounded by tins of Stone's Dried Soup, a comrade, nicknamed the Professor (he was an ex-science student), was engaged in perfecting some new detonators. He was an abstracted, self-confident, sallow little man, armed with large round spectacles, and we were afraid that under a mistaken impression he would blow himself up and wreck the house about our ears. I rushed upstairs and found him already at the door, on the alert, listening, as he said, to "suspicious noises down below". Before I had quite finished explaining to him what was going on he shrugged his shoulders disdainfully and turned away to his balances and test-tubes. His was the true spirit of an extreme revolutionist. Explosives were his faith, his hope, his weapon and his shield. He perished a couple of years afterwards in a secret laboratory through the premature explosion of one of his improved detonators.

'Hurrying down again, I found an impressive scene in the gloom of the big cellar. The man who personated the inspector (he was no stranger to the part) was speaking harshly and giving bogus orders to his bogus subordinates for the removal of his prisoners. Evidently nothing enlightening had happened so far. Horne, saturnine and swarthy, waited with folded arm, and his patient, moody expectation had an air of stoicism well in keeping with the situation. I detected in the shadows one of the Hermione Street group surreptitiously chewing up and swallowing a small piece of paper. Some compromising scrap, I suppose; perhaps just a note of a few names and addresses. He was a true and faithful "companion". But the fund of secret malice which lurks at the bottom of our sympathies caused me to feel amused at that perfectly uncalled-for performance.

In every other respect the risky experiment, the theatrical coup, if you like to call it so, seemed to have failed. The deception could not be kept up much longer; the explanation would bring about a very embarrassing and even grave situation. The man who had eaten the paper would be furious. The fellows who bolted away would be angry, too.

'To add to my vexation, the door communicating with the other cellar, where the printing-presses were, flew open, and our young lady revolutionist appeared, a black silhouette in a close-fitting dress and a large hat, with the blaze of gas flaring in there at her back. Over her shoulder I perceived the arched eyebrows and the red necktie of her brother.

'The last people in the world I wanted to see then! They had gone that evening to some amateur concert for the delectation of the poor people, you know; but she had insisted on leaving early, on purpose to call in at Hermione Street on the way home, under the pretext of having some work to do. Her usual task was to correct the proofs of the Italian and French editions of the *Alarm Bell* and the *Firebrand*.'

'Heavens!' I murmured. I had been shown once a few copies of these publications. Nothing, in my opinion, could have been less fit for the eyes of a young lady. They were the most advanced things of the sort; advanced, I mean, beyond all bounds of reason and decency. One of them preached the dissolution of all social and domestic ties; the other advocated systematic murder. To think of a young girl calmly tracking printers' errors all along the sort of abominable sentences I remembered was intolerable to my sentiment of womanhood. Mr X, after giving me a glance, pursued steadily.

'I think, however, that she came mostly to exercise her fascinations upon Sevrin and to receive his homage in her queenly and condescending way. She was aware of both – her power and his homage – and enjoyed them with, I dare say, complete innocence. We have no ground in expediency or morals to quarrel with her on that account. Charm in woman and exceptional intelligence in man are a law unto themselves. Is it not so?'

I refrained from expressing my abhorrence of that licentious doctrine because of my curiosity.

'But what happened then?' I hastened to ask. X went on crumbling slowly a small piece of bread with a careless left hand.

'What happened, in effect,' he confessed, 'is that she saved the situation.'

'She gave you an opportunity to end your rather sinister farce,' I suggested.

'Yes,' he said, preserving his impassive bearing. 'The farce was bound to end soon. And it ended in a very few minutes. And it ended well. Had she not come in, it might have ended badly. Her brother, of course, did not count. They had slipped into the house quietly some time before. The printing-cellar had an entrance of its own. Not finding any one there, she sat down to her proofs, expecting Sevrin to return to his work at any moment. He did not do so. She grew impatient, heard through the door the sounds of a disturbance in the other cellar and naturally came in to see what was the matter.

'Sevrin had been with us. At first he had seemed to me the most amazed of the whole raided lot. He appeared for an instant as if paralyzed with astonishment. He stood rooted to the spot. He never moved a limb. A solitary gas-jet flared near his head; all the other lights had been put out at the first alarm. And presently, from my dark corner, I observed on his shaven actor's face an expression of puzzled, vexed watchfulness. He knitted his heavy eyebrows. The corners of his mouth dropped scornfully. He was angry. Most likely he had seen through the game and I regretted I had not taken him, from the first, into my complete confidence.

'But with the appearance of the girl he became obviously alarmed. It was plain. I could see it grow. The change of his expression was swift and startling. And I did not know why. The reason never occurred to me. I was merely astonished at the extreme alteration of the man's face. Of course he had not been aware of her presence in the other cellar; but that did not explain the shock her advent had given him. For a moment he seemed to have been reduced to imbecility. He opened his mouth as if to shout, or perhaps only to gasp. At any rate, it was somebody else who shouted. This somebody else was the heroic comrade whom I had detected swallowing a piece of paper. With laudable presence of mind he let out a warning yell.

"It's the police! Back! Back! Run back, and bolt the door behind you."

'It was an excellent hint; but, instead of retreating, the girl continued to advance, followed by her long-faced brother in his knickerbocker suit in which he had been singing comic songs for the entertainment of a joyless proletariat. She advanced not as if she had failed to understand – the word 'police' has an unmistakable sound – but rather as if she could not help herself. She did not advance with the free gait and expanding presence of a distinguished amateur anarchic amongst poor, struggling professionals, but with slightly raised shoulders and her elbows pressed close to her body, as if trying to shrink within herself. Her eyes were fixed immovably upon Sevrin. Sevrin the man, I fancy; not Sevrin the anarchist. But she advanced. And that was natural. For all their assumption of independence, girls of that class are used to the feeling of being specially protected as, in fact, they are. This feeling accounts for nine tenths of their audacious gestures. Her face had gone completely colourless. Ghastly. Fancy having it brought home to her so brutally that she was the sort of person who must run away from the police! I believe she was pale with indignation, mostly, though there was, of course, also the concern for her intact personality, a vague dread of some sort of rudeness. And, naturally, she turned to a man, to the man on whom she had a claim of fascination and homage – the man who could not conceivably fail her at any juncture.'

'But,' I cried, amazed at this analysis, 'if it had been serious, real, I mean – as she thought it was – what could she expect him to do for her?'

X never moved a muscle of his face.

'Goodness knows. I imagine that this charming, generous and independent creature had never known in her life a single genuine thought; I mean a single thought detached from small human vanities, or whose source was not in some conventional perception. All I know is that, after advancing a few steps, she extended her hand towards the motionless Sevrin. And that at least was no gesture. It was a natural movement. As to what she expected him to do, who can tell? The impossible. But whatever she expected, it could not have come up, I am safe to say, to what he had made up his mind to do, even before that entreating hand had appealed to him so directly. It had not been necessary. From the moment he had seen her enter that cellar, he had made up his mind to sacrifice his future usefulness, to throw off the impenetrable, solidly fastened mask it had been his pride to wear—'

'What do you mean?' I interrupted, puzzled. 'Was it Sevrin, then, who was—'

'He was. The most persistent, the most dangerous, the craftiest, the most systematic of informers. A genius amongst betrayers.

Fortunately for us, he was unique. The man was a fanatic, I have told you. Fortunately, again, for us, he had fallen in love with the accomplished and innocent gestures of that girl. An actor in desperate earnest himself, he must have believed in the absolute value of conventional signs. As to the grossness of the trap into which he fell, the explanation must be that two sentiments of such absorbing magnitude cannot exist simultaneously in one heart. The danger of that other and unconscious comedian robbed him of his vision, of his perspicacity, of his judgement. Indeed, it did at first rob him of his self-possession. But he regained that through the necessity – as it appeared to him imperiously – to do something at once. To do what? Why, to get her out of the house as quickly as possible. He was desperately anxious to do that. I have told you he was terrified. It could not be about himself. He had been surprised and annoyed at a move quite unforeseen and premature. I may even say he had been furious. He was accustomed to arrange the last scene of his betrayals with a deep, subtle art which left his revolutionist reputation untouched. But it seems clear to me that, at the same time, he had resolved to make the best of it, to keep his mask resolutely on. It was only with the discovery of her being in the house that everything – the forced calm, the restraint of his fanaticism, the mask – all came off together in a kind of panic. Why panic, do you ask? The answer is very simple. He remembered – or, I dare say, he had never forgotten – the Professor alone at the top of the house, pursuing his researches, surrounded by tins upon tins of Stone's Dried Soup. There was enough in some few of them to bury us all where we stood under a heap of bricks. Sevrin, of course, was aware of that. And we must believe, also, that he knew the exact character of the man. He had gauged so many such characters! Or perhaps he only gave the Professor credit for what he himself was capable of. But, in any case, the effect was produced. And suddenly he raised his voice in authority.

'"Get the lady away at once."'

'It turned out that he was as hoarse as a crow; result, no doubt, of the intense emotion. It passed off in a moment. But these fateful words issued forth from his contracted throat in a discordant, ridiculous croak. They required no answer. The thing was done. However, the man personating the inspector judged it expedient to say roughly:

'"She shall go soon enough, together with the rest of you."'

'These were the last words belonging to the comedy part of this affair.

'Oblivious of everything and everybody, Sevrin strode towards him and seized the lapels of his coat. Under his thin bluish cheeks one could see his jaws working with passion.

'"You have men posted outside. Get the lady taken home at once. Do you hear? Now. Before you try to get hold of the man upstairs."'

'"Oh! There is a man upstairs,"' scoffed the other, openly. "Well, he shall be brought down in time to see the end of this."'

'But Sevrin, beside himself, took no heed of the tone.

"Who's the imbecile meddler who sent you blundering here? Didn't you understand your instructions? Don't you know anything? It's incredible. Here—"

'He dropped the lapels of the coat and, plunging his hand into his breast, jerked feverishly at something under his shirt. At last he produced a small square pocket of soft leather which must have been hanging like a scapulary from his neck by the tape whose broken ends dangled from his fist.

'"Look inside,"' he spluttered, flinging it in the other's face. And instantly he turned round towards the girl. She stood just behind him, perfectly still and silent. Her set, white face gave an illusion of placidity. Only her staring eyes seemed bigger and darker.

'He spoke rapidly, with nervous assurance. I heard him distinctly promise her to make everything as clear as daylight presently. But that was all I caught. He stood close to her, never attempting to touch her even with the tip of his little finger – and she stared at him stupidly. For a moment, however, her eyelids descended slowly, pathetically, and then, with the long black eyelashes lying on her white cheeks, she looked ready to fall down in a swoon. But she never even swayed where she stood. He urged her loudly to follow him at once and walked towards the door at the bottom of the cellar stairs without looking behind him. And, as a matter of fact, she did move after him a pace or two. But, of course, he was not allowed to reach the door. There were angry exclamations, a short, fierce scuffle. Flung away violently, he came flying backwards upon her, and fell. She threw out her arms in a gesture of dismay and stepped aside, just clear of his head, which struck the ground heavily near her shoe.

'He grunted with the shock. By the time he had picked himself up, slowly, dazedly, he was awake to the reality of things. The man into whose hands he had thrust the leather case had extracted therefrom a narrow strip of bluish paper. He held it up above his head and, as after the scuffle an expectant uneasy stillness reigned once more, he threw it down disdainfully with the words, "I think, comrades, that this proof was hardly necessary."'

'Quick as thought, the girl stooped after the fluttering slip. Holding it spread out in both hands, she looked at it; then, without raising her eyes, opened her fingers slowly and let it fall.

'I examined that curious document afterwards. It was signed by a very high personage, and stamped and countersigned by other high officials in various countries of Europe. In his trade – or shall I say, in his mission? – that sort of talisman might have been necessary, no doubt. Even to the police itself – all but the heads – he had been known only as Sevrin the noted anarchist.

'He hung his head, biting his lower lip. A change had come over him, a sort of thoughtful, absorbed calmness. Nevertheless, he panted. His sides worked visibly, and his nostrils expanded and collapsed in weird contrast with his sombre aspect of a fanatical monk in a meditative attitude, but with something, too, in his face of an actor intent upon the terrible exigencies of his part. Before him Horne declaimed, haggard and bearded, like an inspired denunciatory prophet from a wilderness. Two fanatics. They were made to understand each other. Does this surprise you? I suppose you think that such people would be foaming at the month and snarling at each other?'

I protested hastily that I was not surprised in the least; that I thought nothing of the kind; that anarchists in general were simply inconceivable to me mentally, morally, logically, sentimentally, and even physically. He received this declaration with his usual woodenness and went on.

'Horne had burst out into eloquence. While pouring out scornful invective, he let tears escape from his eyes and roll down his black beard unheeded. Sevrin panted quicker and quicker. When he opened his mouth to speak, everyone hung on his words.

'"Don't be a fool, Horne," he began. "You know very well that I have done this for none of the reasons you are throwing at me." And in a moment he became outwardly as steady as a rock under the other's lurid stare. "I have been thwarting, deceiving and betraying you – from conviction."'

'He turned his back on Horne, and, addressing the girl, repeated the words: "From conviction."'

'It's extraordinary how cold she looked. I suppose she could not think of any appropriate gesture. There may have been few precedents indeed for such a situation.

'"Clear as daylight," he added. "Do you understand what that means? From conviction."'

'And still she did not stir. She did not know what to do. But the luckless wretch was about to give her the opportunity for a beautiful and correct gesture.

'"I have felt in me the power to make you share this conviction,"' he protested, ardently. He had forgotten himself; he made a step towards her – perhaps he stumbled. To me he seemed to be stooping low as if to touch the hem of her garment. And then the appropriate gesture came. She snatched her skirt away from his polluting contact and averted her head with an upward tilt. It was magnificently done, this gesture of conventionally unstained honour, of an unblemished high-minded amateur.

'Nothing could have been better. And he seemed to think so, too, for once more he turned away. But this time he faced no one. He was again panting frightfully, while he fumbled hurriedly in his waistcoat pocket and then raised his hand to his lips. There was something furtive in this movement, but directly afterwards his bearing changed. His laboured breathing gave him a resemblance to a man who had just run a desperate race; but a curious air of detachment, of sudden and profound indifference, replaced the strain of the striving effort. The race was over. I did not want to see what would happen next. I was only too well aware. I tucked the young lady's arm under mine, without a word, and made my way with her to the stairs.

'Her brother walked behind us. Halfway up the short flight she seemed unable to lift her feet high enough for the steps, and we had to pull and push to get her to the top. In the passage she dragged herself along, hanging on my arm, helplessly bent like an old woman. We issued into an empty street through a half-open door, staggering like besotted revellers. At the corner we stopped a four-wheeler and the ancient driver looked round from his box with morose scorn at our efforts to get her in. Twice during the drive I felt her collapse on my shoulder in a half faint. Facing us, the youth in knickerbockers remained as mute as a fish and, till he jumped out with the latch-key, sat more still than I would have believed it possible.

'At the door of their drawing-room she left my arm and walked in first, catching at the chairs and tables. She unpinned her hat, then, exhausted with the effort, her cloak still hanging from her shoulders, flung herself into a deep armchair, sideways, her face half buried in a cushion. The good brother appeared silently before her with a glass of water. She motioned it away. He drank it himself and walked off to a distant corner – behind the grand piano, somewhere. All was still in this room where I had seen, for the first time, Sevrin, the anti-anarchist, captivated and spellbound by the consummate and hereditary grimaces that, in a certain sphere of life, take the place of feelings with an excellent effect. I suppose her thoughts were busy with the same memory. Her shoulders shook violently. A pure attack of nerves. When it quieted down she affected firmness, '"What is done to a man of that sort? What will they do to him?"'

'"Nothing. They can do nothing to him," I assured her, with perfect truth. I was pretty certain he had died in less than twenty minutes from the moment his hand had gone to his lips. For if his fanatical anti-anarchism went even as far as carrying poison in his pocket, only to rob his adversaries of legitimate vengeance, I knew he would take care to provide something that would not fail him when required.

'She drew an angry breath. There were red spots on her cheeks and a feverish brilliance in her eyes.

'"Has ever any one been exposed to such a terrible experience? To think that he had held my hand! That man!" Her face twitched, she gulped down a pathetic sob. "If I ever felt sure of anything, it was of Sevrin's high-minded motives."'

'Then she began to weep quietly, which was good for her. Then through her flood of tears, half resentful, "What was it he said to me? 'From conviction.' It seemed a vile mockery. What could he mean by it?"

'"That, my dear young lady," I said, gently, "is more than I or anybody else can ever explain to you."'

Mr X flicked a crumb off the front of his coat.

'And that was strictly true as to her. Though Horne, for instance, understood very well, and so did I, especially after we had been to Sevrin's lodging in a dismal back street of an intensely respectable quarter. Horne was known there as a friend and we had no difficulty in being admitted, the slatternly maid merely remarking, as she let us in, that "Mr Sevrin had not be home that night." We forced open a couple of drawers in the way of duty and found a little useful information. The most interesting part was his diary; for this man engaged in such deadly work, had the weakness to keep a record of the most damnatory kind. There were his acts and also his thoughts laid bare to us. But the dead don't mind that. They don't mind anything.

'"From conviction." Yes. A vague but ardent humanitarianism had urged him in his first youth into the bitterest extremity of negation and revolt. Afterwards his optimism flinched. He doubted and became lost. You have heard of converted atheists. These turn often into dangerous fanatics, but the soul remains the same. After he had got acquainted with the girl, there are to be met in that diary of his very queer politico-amorous rhapsodies. He took her sovereign grimaces with deadly seriousness. He longed to convert her. But all this cannot interest you. For the rest, I don't know if you remember – it is a good many years ago now – the journalistic sensation of the Hermione Street Mystery; the finding of a man's body in the cellar of an empty house; the inquest, some arrests, many surmises – then silence – the usual end for many obscure martyrs and confessors. The fact is, he was not enough of an optimist. You must be a savage, tyrannical, pitiless, thick-and-thin optimist, like Horne, for instance, to make a good social rebel of the extreme type.'

He rose from the table. A waiter hurried up with his overcoat; another held his hat in readiness.

'But what became of the young lady?' I asked.

'Do you really want to know?' he said, buttoning himself in his fur coat carefully. 'I confess to the small malice of sending her Sevrin's diary. She went into retirement; then she went to Florence; then she went into retreat in a convent. I can't tell where she will go next. What does it matter? Gestures! Gestures! Mere gestures of her class.'

He fitted on his glossy high hat with extreme precision and, casting a rapid glance round the room full of well-dressed people, innocently dining, muttered between his teeth:

'And nothing else! That is why their kind is fated to perish.'

I never met Mr X again after that evening. I took to dining at my club. On my next visit to Paris I found my friend all impatience to hear of the effect produced on me by this rare item of his collection. I told him all the story and he beamed on me with the pride of his distinguished specimen.

'Isn't X well worth knowing?' he bubbled over in great delight. 'He's unique, amazing, absolutely terrific.'

His enthusiasm grated upon my finer feelings. I told him curtly that the man's cynicism was simply abominable.

'Oh, abominable! Abominable!' assented my friend, effusively. 'And then, you know, he likes to have his little joke sometimes,' he added in a confidential tone.

I fail to understand the connection of this last remark. I have been utterly unable to discover where, in all this, the joke comes in.

from *A Set Of Six*, Joseph Conrad

The Secret of the Fox Hunter

It happened three winters ago. Having just returned from Stuttgart, where I had spent some weeks at the Marquardt in the guise I so often assumed, that of Monsieur Gustav Dreux, commercial traveller of Paris, and where I had been engaged in watching the movements of two persons staying in the hotel, a man and a woman, I was glad to be back again in Bloomsbury to enjoy the ease of my armchair and pipe.

I was much gratified that I had concluded a very difficult piece of espionage and, having obtained the information I sought, had been able to place certain facts before my Chief, the Marquess of Macclesfield, which had very materially strengthened his hands in some very delicate diplomatic negotiations with Germany. Perhaps the most exacting position in the whole of British diplomacy is the post of Ambassador at Berlin, for the Germans are at once our foes, as well as our friends, and are at this moment only too ready to pick a quarrel with us from motives of jealousy which may have serious results.

The war cloud was still hovering over Europe; hence a swarm of spies, male and female, were plotting, scheming and working in secret in our very midst. The reader would be amazed if he could but glance at a certain red-bound book, kept under lock and key at the Foreign Office, in which are registered the names, personal descriptions and other facts concerning all the known foreign spies living in London and in other towns in England.

But active as are the agents of our enemies, so also are we active in the opposition camp. Our Empire has such tremendous responsibilities that we cannot now depend upon mere birth, wealth and honest dealing, but must call in shrewdness, tact, subterfuge and the employment of secret agents in order to combat the plots of those ever seeking to accomplish England's overthrow.

Careful student of international affairs that I was, I knew that trouble was brewing in China. Certain confidential dispatches from our Minister in Peking had been shown to me by the Marquess who, on occasion, flattered me by placing implicit trust in me, and from them I gathered that Russia was at work in secret to undermine our influence in the Far East.

I knew that the grave, kindly old statesman was greatly perturbed by the grim shadows that were slowly rising but, when we consulted on the day after my return from Stuttgart, his lordship was of the opinion that, at present, I had not sufficient ground upon which to institute inquiries.

'For the present, Drew,' he said, 'we must watch and wait. There is war in the air – first at Peking, and then in Europe. But we must prevent it at all costs. Huntley leaves for Peking tonight with dispatches in which I have fully explained the line which Sir Henry is to follow. Hold yourself in readiness, for you may have to return to Germany or Russia tomorrow. We cannot afford to remain long in the dark. We must crush any alliance between Petersburg and Berlin.'

'A telegram to my rooms will bring me to your lordship at any moment,' was my answer.

'Ready to go anywhere – eh, Drew?' he smiled; and then, after a further chat, I left Downing Street and returned to Bloomsbury.

Knowing that for at least a week or two I should be free, I left my address with Boyd and went down to Cotterstock, in Northamptonshire, to stay with my old friend of college days, George Hamilton, who rented a hunting-box and rode with the Fitzwilliam pack.

I had had a long-standing engagement with him to go down and get a few runs with the hounds, but my constant absence abroad had always prevented it until then. Of course, none of my friends knew my real position at the Foreign Office. I was believed to be an attaché.

Personally, I am extremely fond of riding to hounds; therefore, when that night I sat at dinner with George, his wife, and the latter's cousin, Beatrice Graham, I was full of expectation of some good runs. An English country house, with its old oak, old silver and air of solidity, is always delightful to me after the flimsy gimcracks of Continental life. The evening proved a very pleasant one. Never having met Beatrice Graham before, I was much attracted by her striking beauty. She was tall and dark, about twenty-two, with a remarkable figure which was shown to advantage by her dinner-gown of turquoise blue. So well did she talk, so splendidly did she sing Dupont's 'Jeune Fille', and so enthusiastic was she regarding hunting, that, before I had been an hour with her, I found myself thoroughly entranced.

The meet, three days afterwards, was at Wansford, that old-time hunting centre by the Nene, about six miles distant, and, as I rode at her side along the road through historic Fotheringay and Nassington, I noticed what a splendid horsewoman she was. Her dark hair was coiled tightly behind, and her bowler hat suited her face admirably, while her habit fitted as though it had been moulded to her figure. In her mare's tail was a tiny piece of scarlet silk to warn others that she was a kicker.

At Wansford, opposite the old Haycock, once a hunting inn in the old coaching days but now Lord Chesham's hunting-box, the gathering was a large one. From the great rambling old house servants carried glasses of sloe gin to all who cared to partake of his lordship's hospitality, while every moment the meet grew larger and the crowd of horses and vehicles more congested.

George had crossed to chat with the Master, Mr George Fitzwilliam, who had just driven up and was still in his overcoat; therefore, I found myself alone with my handsome companion who appeared to be most popular everywhere. Dozens of men and women rode up to her and exchanged greetings, the men morre especially, until at last Barnard, the huntsman, drew his hounds together, the word was given and they went leisurely up the hill to draw the first covert.

The morning was one of those damp cold ones of mid-February; the frost had given and everyone expected a good run, for the scent would be excellent. Riding side by side with my fair companion, we chatted and laughed as we went along until, on reaching the covert, we drew up with the others and halted while hounds went in.

The first covert was, however, drawn blank, but from the second a fox went away straight for Elton, and soon the hounds were in full cry after him and we followed at a gallop. After a couple of miles more than half the field was left behind; still we kept on until, of a sudden and without effort, my companion took a high hedge and was cutting across the pastures ere I knew that she had left the road. That she was a straight rider I at once saw, and I must confess that I preferred the gate to the hedge and ditch which she had taken so easily.

Half an hour later the kill took place near Haddon Hall and, of the half dozen in at the death, Beatrice Graham was one.

When I rode up, five minutes afterwards, she smiled at me. Her face was a trifle flushed by hard riding, yet her hair was in no way awry and she declared that she had thoroughly enjoyed that tearing gallop.

Just, however, as we sat watching Barnard cut off the brush, a tall, rather good-looking man rode up, having apparently been left just as I had. As he approached I noticed that he gave my pretty friend a strange look, almost as of warning, while she, on her part, refrained from acknowledging him. It was as though he had made her some secret sign which she had understood.

But there was a further fact that puzzled me greatly.

I had recognized in that well-turned-out hunting man someone whom I had had distinct occasion to recollect. At first I failed to recall the man's identity but, when I did, a few moments later, I sat regarding his retreating figure like one in a dream. The horseman who rode with such military bearing was none other than the renowned spy, one of the cleverest secret agents in the world, Otto Krempelstein, Chief of the German Secret Service.

That my charming little friend knew him was apparent. The

slightest quiver in his eyelids and the almost imperceptible curl of his lip had not passed me unnoticed. There was some secret between them, of what nature I, of course, knew not. But all through that day my eyes were ever open to re-discover the man whose ingenuity and cunning had so often been in competition with my own. Twice I saw him again, once riding with a big dark-haired man in pink, on a splendid bay and followed by a groom with a second horse, and on the second occasion, at the edge of Stockhill Wood while we were waiting together, he galloped past us but without the slightest look of recognition.

'I wonder who that man is?' I remarked casually, as soon as he was out of hearing.

'I don't know,' was her prompt reply. 'He's often out with the hounds – a foreigner, I believe. Probably he's one of those who come to England for the hunting season. Since the late Empress of Austria came here to hunt, the Fitzwilliam has always been a favourite pack with the foreigners.'

I saw that she did not intend to admit that she had any knowledge of him. Like all women, she was a clever diplomatist. But he had made a sign to her – a sign of secrecy.

Did Krempelstein recognize me, I wondered? I could not think so, because we had never met face to face. He had once been pointed out to me in the Wilhelmstrasse in Berlin by one of our secret agents who knew him, and his features had ever since been graven on my memory.

That night, when I sat alone with my friend George, I learned from him that Mr Graham, his wife's uncle, had lived a long time on the Continent as manager to a large commercial firm, and that Beatrice had been born in France and had lived there a good many years. I made inquiries regarding the foreigners who were hunting that season with the Fitzwilliam but he, with an Englishman's prejudice, declared that he knew none of them and didn't want to know them.

The days passed and we went to several meets together – at Apethorpe, at Castor Hanglands, at Laxton Park and other places, but I saw no more of Krempelstein. His distinguished-looking friend, however, I met on several occasions, and discovered that his name was Baron Stern, a wealthy Viennese who had taken a hunting-box near Stoke Doyle, and had, as friend, a young man named Percival who was frequently out with the hounds.

But the discovery there of Krempelstein had thoroughly aroused my curiosity. He had been there for some distinct purpose, without a doubt. Therefore I made inquiry of Kersch, one of our secret agents in Berlin, a man employed in the Ministry of Foreign Affairs, and from him received word that Krempelstein was back in Berlin, and further warning me that something unusual was on foot in England.

This aroused me at once to activity. I knew that Krempelstein and his agents were ever endeavouring to obtain the secrets of our guns, our ships and our diplomacy with other nations, and I therefore determined that on this occasion he should not succeed. However much I admired Beatrice Graham, I now knew that she had lied to me and that she was in all probability his associate. So I watched her carefully and when she went out for a stroll or a ride, as she often did, I followed her.

How far I was justified in this action does not concern me. I had quite unexpectedly alighted upon certain suspicious facts and was determined to elucidate them. The only stranger she met was Percival. Late one afternoon, just as dusk was deepening into night, she pulled up her mare beneath the bare black trees while crossing Burghley Park and, after a few minutes, was joined by the young foreigner who, having greeted her, chatted for a long time in a low, earnest tone, as though giving her directions. She seemed to remonstrate with him but, at the place I was concealed, I was unable to distinguish what was said. I saw him, however, hand her something and then, raising his hat, he turned his horse and galloped away down the avenue in the opposite direction.

I did not meet her again until I sat beside her at the dinner-table that night, and then I noticed how pale and anxious she was, entirely changed from her usual sweet, light-hearted self.

She told me that she had ridden into Stamford for exercise, but told me nothing of the clandestine meeting. How I longed to know what the young foreigner had given her. Whatever it was, she kept it a close secret to herself.

More than once I felt impelled to go to her room in her absence and search her cupboards, drawers and travelling trunks. My attitude towards her was that of a man fallen entirely in love, for I had discovered that she was easily flattered by a little attention.

I was searching for some excuse to know Baron Stern, but often for a week he never went to the meets. It was as though he purposely avoided me. He was still at Weldon Lodge, near Stoke Doyle, for George told me that he had met him in Oundle only two days before.

Three whole weeks went by and I remained just as puzzled as ever. Beatrice Graham was, after all, a most delightful companion and, although she was to me a mystery, yet we had become excellent friends.

One afternoon, just as I entered the drawing-room where she stood alone, she hurriedly tore up a note and threw the pieces on the great log fire. I noticed one tiny piece, about an inch square, remained unconsumed and managed, half an hour later, to get possession of it.

The writing upon it was, I found, in German, four words in all which, without context, conveyed to me no meaning.

On the following night Mrs Hamilton and Beatrice remained with us in the smoking-room till nearly eleven o'clock and, at midnight, I bade my host goodnight and ascended the stairs to retire. I had been in my room about half an hour when I heard stealthy footsteps. In an instant the truth flashed upon me. It was Beatrice on her way downstairs.

Quickly I slipped on some things and noiselessly followed my pretty fellow-guest through the drawing-room out across the lawn and into the lane beyond. White mists had risen from the river and the low roaring of the weir prevented her hearing my footsteps behind her. Fearing lest I should lose her I kept close behind, following her across several grass fields until she came to Southwick Wood, a dark, deserted spot, away from road or habitation.

Her intention was evidently to meet someone so when, presently, she halted beneath a clump of high black firs I also took shelter a short distance away.

She sat on a fallen trunk of a tree and waited in patience. Time went on and so cold was it that I became chilled to the bones. I longed for a pipe but feared that the smell of tobacco or the light might attract her. Therefore I was compelled to crouch and await the clandestine meeting.

She remained very quiet. Not a dead leaf stirred; not a sound came from her direction. I wondered why she waited in such complete silence.

Nearly two hours passed when, at last, cramped and half frozen, I raised myself in order to peer into the darkness in her direction.

At first I could see no one but, on straining my eyes, I saw, to my dismay, that she had fallen from the tree trunk and was lying motionless in a heap upon the ground.

I called to her, but received no reply. Then rising, I walked to the spot and, in dismay, threw myself on my knees and tried to raise her. My hand touched her white cheek. It was as cold as stone.

Next instant I undid her fur cape and bodice, and placed my hand upon her heart. There was no movement.

Beatrice Graham was dead.

The shock of the discovery held me spellbound. But when, a few moments later, I aroused myself to action, a difficult problem presented itself. Should I creep back to my room and say nothing, or should I raise the alarm and admit that I had been watching her? My first care was to search the unfortunate girl's pocket, but I found nothing save a handkerchief and purse.

Then I walked back and, regardless of the consequences, gave the alarm.

It is unnecessary here to describe the sensation caused by the discovery, or of how we carried the body back to the house. Suffice it to say that we called the doctor who could find no mark of violence, or anything to account for death.

And yet she had expired suddenly, without a cry.

One feature, however, puzzled the doctor – namely, that her left hand and arm were much swollen and had turned almost black, while the spine was curved – a fact which aroused a suspicion of some poison akin to strychnia.

From the very first, I held a theory that she had been secretly poisoned, but with what motive I could not imagine.

A post-mortem examination was made by three doctors on the following day but, beyond confirming the theory I held, they discovered nothing.

On the day following, a few hours before the inquest, I was recalled to the Foreign Office by telegraph and, that same afternoon, sat with the Marquess of Macclesfield in his private room receiving his instructions.

An urgent dispatch from Lord Rockingham, our Ambassador at Petersburg, made it plain that an alliance had been proposed by Russia to Germany, the effect of which would be to break British power in the Far East. His Excellency knew that the terms of the secret agreement had been settled, and all that remained was its signature. Indeed, it would have already been signed save for opposition in some quarters unknown, and, while that opposition existed, I might gain time to ascertain the exact terms of the proposed alliance – no light task in Russia, be it said, for police spies exist there in thousands, and my disguise had always to be very carefully thought out whenever I passed the frontier at Wirballen.

The Marquess urged me to put all our secret machinery in motion in order to discover the terms of the proposed agreement, and more particularly as regards the extension of Russian influence in Manchuria.

'I know well the enormous difficulties of the inquiry,' his lordship said; 'but recollect, Drew, that in this matter you may be the means of saving the situation in the Far East. If we gain knowledge of the truth, we may be able to act promptly and effectively. If not – well—' and the grey-headed statesman shrugged his shoulders expressively without concluding the sentence.

Full of regret that I was unable to remain at Cotterstock and sift the mystery surrounding Beatrice Graham's death, I left London that night for Berlin where, on the following evening, I called upon our secret agent, Kersch, who lived in a small but comfortable house at Teltow, one of the suburbs of the German capital. He occupied a responsible position in the German Foreign Office but, having expensive tastes and a penchant for cards, was not averse to receiving British gold in exchange for the confidential information with which he furnished us from time to time.

I sat with him, discussing the situation for a long time. It was true, he said, that a draft agreement had been prepared and placed before the Czar and the Kaiser, but it had not yet been signed. He knew nothing of the clauses, however, as they had been prepared in secret by the Minister's own hand, neither could he suggest any means of obtaining knowledge of them.

My impulse was to go on next day to Petersburg. Yet somehow I felt that I might be more successful in Germany than in Russia, so resolved to continue my inquiries.

'By the way,' the German said, 'you wrote me about Krempelstein. He has been absent a great deal lately, but I had no idea he had been to England. Can he be interested in the same matter on which you are now engaged?'

'Is he now in Berlin?' I inquired eagerly.

'I met him at Boxhagen three days ago. He seems extremely active just now.'

'Three days ago!' I echoed. 'You are quite certain of the day?' I asked him this because, if his statement were true, it was proved beyond doubt, that the German spy had no hand in the unfortunate girl's death.

'I am quite certain,' was his reply. 'I saw him entering the station on Monday morning.'

At eleven o'clock that same night I called at the British Embassy and sat for a long time with the Ambassador in his private room. His Excellency told me all he knew regarding the international complication which the Marquess, sitting in Downing Street, had foreseen weeks ago, but could make no suggestion as to my course of action. The war clouds had gathered undoubtedly, and the signing of the agreement between our enemies would cause it at once to burst over Europe. The crisis was one of the most serious in English history.

One fact puzzled us both, just as it puzzled our Chief at home – namely, if the agreement had been seen and approved by both Emperors, why was it not signed? Whatever hitch had occurred, it was more potent than the will of the two most powerful monarchs in Europe.

On my return to the hotel I scribbled a hasty note and sent it by messenger to the house of the Imperial Chancellor's son in Charlottenburg. It was addressed to Miss Maud Baines, the English governess of the Count's children, who, I may as well admit, was in our employ. She was a young, ingenuous and fascinating little woman. She had, at my direction, acted as governess in many of the great families in France, Russia and Germany, and was now in the employ of the Chancellor's son, in order to have an opportunity of keeping a watchful eye on the great statesman himself.

She kept the appointment next morning at an obscure café near the Behrenstrasse. She was a neatly dressed, rather petite person, with a face that entirely concealed her keen intelligence and marvellous cunning.

As she sat at the little table with me, I told her in low tones of the object of my visit to Berlin, and sought her aid.

'A serious complication has arisen. I was about to report to you through the Embassy,' was her answer. 'Last night the Chancellor dined with us and I overheard him discussing the affair with his son as they sat alone smoking after the ladies had left. I listened at the door and heard the Chancellor distinctly say that the draft treaty had been stolen.'

'Stolen!' I gasped. 'By whom?'

'Ah! That's evidently the mystery – a mystery for us to fathom. But the fact that somebody else is in possession of the intentions of Germany and Russia against England, believed to be a secret, is no doubt the reason why the agreement has not been signed.'

'Because it is no longer secret!' I suggested. 'Are you quite certain you've made no mistake?'

'Quite,' was her prompt answer. 'You can surely trust me after the intricate little affairs which I have assisted you in unravelling? When may I return to Gloucester to see my friends?'

'Soon, Miss Baines – as soon as this affair is cleared up. But tell me, does the Chancellor betray any fear of awkward complications when the secret of the proposed plot against England is exposed?'

'Yes. The Prince told his son in confidence that his only fear was of England's retaliation. He explained that, as far as was known, the secret document, after being put before the Czar and approved, mysteriously disappeared. Every inquiry was being made by the confidential agents of Russia and Germany and, further, he added that even his trusted Krempelstein was utterly nonplussed.'

Mention of Krempelstein brought back to me the recollection of the tragedy in rural England.

'You've done us a great service, Miss Baines,' I said. 'This information is of the highest importance. I shall telegraph in cipher at once to Lord Macclesfield. Do you, by any chance, happen to know a young lady named Graham?' I inquired, recollecting that the deceased woman had lived in Germany for several years.

She responded in the negative, whereupon I drew from my pocket a snapshot photograph, which I had taken of one of the meets of hounds at Wansford, and handing it to her inquired if she recognized any of the persons in it.

Having carefully examined it, she pointed to Baron Stern, whom I had taken in the act of lighting a cigarette, and exclaimed—

'Why! That's Colonel Davidoff who was secretary to Prince Obolenski when I was in his service. Do you know him?'

'No,' I answered. 'But he has been hunting in England as Baron Stern, of Vienna. This man is his friend,' I added, indicating Percival.

'And that's undoubtedly a man whom you know well by repute – Moore, Chief of the Russian Secret Service in England. He came to Prince Obolenski's once, when he was in Petersburg, and the Princess told me who he was.'

Unfortunately, I had not been able to include Beatrice in the group; therefore, I had only her description to place before the clever young woman who had, on so many occasions, gained knowledge of secrets where I and my agents had failed. Her part was always a difficult one to play, but she was well paid, was a marvellous linguist, and for patience and cunning was unequalled.

I described her as minutely as I could, but still she had no knowledge of her. She remained thoughtful a long time and then observed:

'You have said that she apparently knew Moore? He has, I know, recently been back in Petersburg, therefore they may have met there. She may be known. Why not seek for traces of her in Russia?'

It seemed something of a wild-goose chase yet, with the whole affair shrouded in mystery and tragedy as it was, I was glad to adopt any suggestion that might lead to a solution of the enigma. The reticence of Mrs Hamilton regarding her cousin, and the apparent secret association of the dead girl with those two notorious spies, had formed a problem which puzzled me almost to the point of madness.

The English governess told me where in Petersburg I should be likely to find either of the two Russian agents, Davidoff or Moore, who had been posing in England for some unknown purpose as hunting men of means; therefore, I left by the night mail for the Russian capital. I put up at a small, and not overclean hotel, in preference to the Europe, and compelled carefully to conceal my identity, I at once set about making inquiries in various quarters, whether the two men had returned to Russia. They had, and had both had long interviews, two days before, with General Zouboff, Chief of the Secret Service, and with the Russian Foreign Minister.

At the Embassy, and in various English quarters, I sought trace of the woman whose death was such a profound mystery, but all in vain. At last I suddenly thought of another source of information as yet untried – namely, the register of the English Charity in Petersburg. On searching it I found, to my complete satisfaction, that about six weeks before Beatrice Graham applied to the administration and was granted money to take her back to England. She was the daughter, it was registered, of a Mr Charles Graham, the English manager of a cotton mill in Moscow, who had been killed by an accident and had left her penniless. For some months she had tried to earn her own living, in a costumier's shop in the Newski, and, not knowing Russian sufficiently well, had been discharged. Before her father's death she had been engaged to marry a young Englishman, whose name was not given but who was said to be tutor to the children of General Vraski, Governor General of Warsaw.

The information was interesting, but carried me no further; therefore, I set myself to watch the two men who had travelled from England to consult the Czar's chief adviser. Aided by two Russians, who were in British pay, I shadowed them day and night for six days until, one evening, I followed Davidoff down to the railway station where he took a ticket for the frontier. Without baggage I followed him, for his movements were of a man who was escaping from the country. He passed out across the frontier and went on to Vienna and then direct to Paris where he put up at the Hotel Terminus, Gare St Lazare.

Until our arrival at the hotel he had never detected that I was following him but, on the second day in Paris, we came face to face in the large central hall, used as a reading room. He glanced at me quickly, but whether he recognized me as the companion of Beatrice Graham in the hunting field I have no idea. All I know is that his movements were extremely suspicious and that I invoked the aid of all three of our secret agents in Paris to keep watch on him, just as had been done in Petersburg.

On the fourth night of our arrival in the French capital I returned to the hotel about midnight, having dined at the Café Americain with Greville, the naval attaché at the Embassy. In washing my hands prior to turning in, I received a nasty scratch on my left wrist from a pin which a careless laundress had left in the towel. There was a little blood, but I tied my handkerchief around it and, tired out, lay down and was soon asleep.

Half an hour afterwards, however, I was aroused by an excruciating pain over my whole left side, a strange twitching of the muscles of my face and hands, and a contraction of the throat which prevented me from breathing or crying out.

I tried to press the electric bell for assistance, but could not. My whole body seemed entirely paralyzed. Then the ghastly truth flashed upon me, causing me to break out into a cold sweat.

That pin had been placed there purposely. I had been poisoned and in the same manner as Beatrice Graham!

I recollect that my heart seemed to stop and my nails clenched themselves in the palms in agony. Then, next moment, I knew no more.

When I recovered consciousness Ted Greville, together with a tall, black-bearded man named Delisle, who was in the confidential department of the Quai d'Orsay and who often furnished us with information – at a very high figure, be it said – were standing by my beside while a French doctor was leaning over the foot rail watching me.

'Thank heaven you're better, old chap!' Greville exclaimed. 'They thought you were dead. You've had a narrow squeak. How did it happen?'

'That pin!' I cried, pointing to the towel.

'What pin?' he asked.

'Mind! Don't touch the towel,' I cried. 'There's a pin in it – a pin that's poisoned! That Russian evidently came here in my absence and very cunningly laid a deathtrap for me.'

'You mean Davidoff,' chimed in the Frenchman. 'When, m'sieur, the doctor has left the room I can tell you something in confidence.'

The doctor discreetly withdrew and then our spy said, 'Davidoff has turned traitor to his own country. I have discovered that the reason of his visit here is because he has in his possession the original draft of a proposed secret agreement between Russia and Germany against England, and is negotiating for its sale to us for 100,000 francs. He had a secret interview with our Chief last night at his private house in the Avenue des Champs Elysées.'

'Then it is he who stole it, after it had the Czar's approval!' I cried, starting up in bed, aroused at once to action by the information. 'Has he disposed of it to France?'

'Not yet. It is still in his possession.'

'And he is here?'

'No. He has hidden himself in lodgings in the Rue Lafayette, No. 247, until the Foreign Minister decides whether he shall buy the document.'

'And the name by which he is known there?'

'He is passing as a Greek named Guenadios.'

'Keep a strict watch on him. He must not escape,' I said. 'He has endeavoured to murder me.'

'A watch is being kept,' was the Frenchman's answer as, exhausted, I sank again upon the pillow.

Just before midnight I entered the traitor's room in the Rue Lafayette and, when he saw me, he fell back with blanched face and trembling hands.

'No doubt my presence here surprises you,' I said, 'but I may as well at once state my reason for coming here. I want a certain document which concerns Germany and your own country – the document which you have stolen to sell to France.'

'What do you mean, m'sieur?' he asked, with an attempted hauteur.

'My meaning is simple. I require that document, otherwise I shall give you into the hands of the police for attempted murder. The Paris police will detain you until the police of Petersburg apply for your extradition as a traitor. You know what that means – Schusselburg.'

Mention of that terrible island fortress, dreaded by every Russian, caused him to quiver. He looked me straight in the face and saw determination written there, yet he was unyielding and refused for a long time to give the precious document into my hands. I referred to his stay at Stoke Doyle and spoke of his friendship with the spy Moore, so that he should know that I was aware of the truth, until at last he suggested a bargain with me, namely, that in exchange for the draft agreement against England I should preserve silence and permit him to return to Russia.

To this course I acceded, and then the fellow took from a secret cavity of his travelling bag a long official envelope which contained the innocent-looking paper which would, if signed, have destroyed England's prestige in the Far East. He handed it to me, the document for which he hoped to obtain 100,000 francs, and, in return, I gave him his liberty to go back to Russia unmolested.

Our parting was the reverse of cordial for, undoubtedly, he had placed in my towel the pin which had been steeped in some subtle and deadly poison, and then escaped from the hotel in the knowledge that I must sooner or later become scratched and fall a victim.

I had had a very narrow escape it was true, but I did not think so much of my good fortune in regaining my life as the rapid delivery of the all-important document into Lord Macclesfield's hands, which I effected at noon next day.

My life had been at stake for I afterwards found that a second man had been his accomplice, but happily I had succeeded in obtaining possession of the actual document, the result being that England acted so promptly and vigorously that the situation was saved and the way was, as you know, opened for the Anglo-Japanese Treaty which, to the discomfiture of Germany, was effected a few months later.

Nearly two years have gone by since then and it was only the other day, by mere accident, that I made a further discovery which explained the death of the unfortunate Beatrice Graham.

A young infantry lieutenant, named Bellingham, having passed in Russian, had some four years before entered our Secret Service and been employed in Russia on certain missions. A few days ago, on his return to London, after performing a perilous piece of espionage on the Russo-German frontier, he called upon me in Bloomsbury and, in course of conversation, mentioned that about two years ago, in order to get access to certain documents relating to the Russian mobilization scheme for her western frontier, he acted as tutor to the sons of the Governor-General of Warsaw.

In an instant a strange conjecture flashed across my mind.

'Am I correct in assuming that you knew a young English lady in Russia named Graham – Beatrice Graham?'

He looked me straight in the face, open-mouthed in astonishment, yet I saw that a cloud of sadness overshadowed him instantly.

'Yes,' he said. 'I knew her. Our meeting resulted in a terrible tragedy. Owing to the position I hold I have been compelled to keep the details to myself – although it is the tragedy of my life.'

'How? Tell me,' I urged sympathetically.

'Ah' he signed, 'it is a strange story. We met in Petersburg, where she was employed in a shop in the Newski. I loved her and we became engaged. Withholding nothing from her I told her who I was and the reason I was in the service of the Governor-General.

At once, instead of despising me as a spy, she became enthusiastic as an Englishwoman and declared her readiness to assist me. She was looking forward to our marriage and saw that, if I could effect a big coup, my position would at once be improved and we could then be united.'

He broke off and remained silent for a few moments, looking blankly down into the grey London street. Then he said,

'I explained to her the suspicion that Germany and Russia were conspiring in the Far East, and told her that a draft treaty was probably in existence and that it was a document of supreme importance to British interests. Judge my utter surprise when, a week later, she came to me with the actual document which she said she had managed to secure from the private cabinet of Prince Korolkoff, director of the private Chancellerie of the Emperor, to whose house she had gone on a commission to the Princess. Truly she had acted with a boldness and cleverness that were amazing. Knowing the supreme importance of that document, I urged her to leave Russia at once and conceal herself with friends in England, taking care always that the draft treaty never left her possession. This plan she adopted, first, however, placing herself under the protection of the English Charity, thus allaying any suspicions that the police might entertain.

'Poor Beatrice went to stay with her cousin, a lady named Hamilton, in Northamptonshire, but the instant the document was missed the Secret Services of Germany and Russia were at once agog, and the whole machinery was set in motion, with the result that two Russian agents – an Englishman named Moore, and a Russian named Davidoff – as well as Krempelstein, chief of the German Service, had suspicions, and followed her to England with the purpose of obtaining repossession of the precious document. For some weeks they plotted in vain, although both the German and the Englishman succeeded in getting on friendly terms with her.

'She telegraphed to me, asking how she should dispose of the document, fearing to keep it long in her possession; but not being aware of the desperate character of the game, I replied that there was nothing to be feared. I was wrong,' he cried, bitterly. 'I did not recognize the vital importance of the information; I did not know that Empires were at stake. The man Davidoff, who posed as a wealthy Austrian Baron, had by some means discovered that she always carried the precious draft concealed in the bodice of her dress, therefore he had recourse to a dastardly ruse. From what I have since discovered he one day succeeded in concealing in the fur of her cape a pin impregnated with a certain deadly arrow poison unknown to toxicologists. Then he caused to be dispatched from London a telegram purporting to come from me, urging her to meet me in secret at a certain spot on that same night. In eager expectation the poor girl went forth to meet me, believing I had returned unexpectedly from Russia, but, in putting on her cape, she tore her finger with the poisoned pin. While waiting for me the fatal paralysis seized her and she expired, after which Davidoff crept up, secured the missing document and escaped. His anxiety to get hold of it was in order to sell it at a high price to a foreign country; nevertheless, he was compelled first to return to Russia and report. No one knew that he actually held the draft for to Krempelstein, as well as to Moore, my poor love's death was believed to be due to natural causes, while Davidoff, on his part, took care so to arrange matters that his presence at the spot where poor Beatrice expired could never be proved. The spies therefore left England reluctantly after the tragedy, believing that the document, if ever possessed by my unfortunate love, had passed out of her possession into unknown hands.'

'And what of the assassin Davidoff now?' I inquired.

'I have avenged her death,' answered Bellingham with set teeth. 'I gave information to General Zouboff of the traitor's attempted sale of the draft treaty to France, with the result that the court martial has condemned him to incarceration for life in the cells below the lake at Schusselburg.'

The Secret of the Fox Hunter, William Le Queux

The Adventure of the Bruce-Partington Plans

In the third week of November, in the year 1895, a dense yellow fog settled down upon London. From the Monday to the Thursday I doubt whether it was ever possible from our windows in Baker Street to see the loom of the opposite houses. The first day Holmes had spent in cross-indexing his huge book of references. The second and third had been patiently occupied upon a subject which he had recently made his hobby – the music of the Middle Ages. But when, for the fourth time, after pushing back our chairs from breakfast we saw the greasy, heavy brown swirl still drifting past us and condensing in oily drops upon the window-panes, my comrade's impatient and active nature could endure this drab existence no longer. He paced restlessly about our sitting-room in a fever of suppressed energy, biting his nails, tapping the furniture and chafing against inaction.

'Nothing of interest in the paper, Watson?' he said.

I was aware that, by anything of interest, Holmes meant anything of criminal interest. There was the news of a revolution, of a possible war and of an impending change of Government; but these did not come within the horizon of my companion. I could see nothing recorded in the shape of crime which was not commonplace and futile. Holmes groaned and resumed his restless meanderings.

'The London criminal is certainly a dull fellow,' said he, in the querulous voice of the sportsman whose game has failed him. 'Look out of this window, Watson. See how the figures loom up, are dimly seen and then blend once more into the cloud-bank. The thief or the murderer could roam London on such a day as the tiger does the jungle, unseen until he pounces, and then evident only to his victim.'

'There have,' said I, 'been numerous petty thefts.'

Holmes snorted his contempt.

'This great and sombre stage is set for something more worthy than that,' said he. 'It is fortunate for this community that I am not a criminal.'

'It is, indeed!' said I, heartily.

'Suppose that I were Brooks or Woodhouse, or any of the fifty men who have good reason for taking my life, how long could I survive against my own pursuit? A summons, a bogus appointment, and all would be over. It is well they don't have days of fog in the Latin countries – the countries of assassination. By Jove! Here comes something at last to break our dead monotony.'

It was the maid with a telegram. Holmes tore it open and burst out laughing.

'Well, well! What next?' said he. 'Brother Mycroft is coming round.'

'Why not?' I asked.

'Why not? It is as if you met a tram-car coming down a country lane. Mycroft has his rails and he runs on them. His Pall Mall lodgings, the Diogenes Club, Whitehall – that is his cycle. Once, and only once, he has been here. What upheaval can possibly have derailed him?'

'Does he not explain?'

Holmes handed me his brother's telegram.

'Must see you over Cadogan West. Coming at once. Mycroft.'

'Cadogan West? I have heard the name.'

'It recalls nothing to my mind. But that Mycroft should break out in this erratic fashion! A planet might as well leave its orbit. By the way, do you know what Mycroft is?'

I had some vague recollection of an explanation at the time of the Adventure of the Greek Interpreter.

'You told me that he had some small office under the British Government.'

Holmes chuckled.

'I did not know you quite so well in those days. One has to be discreet when one talks of high matters of state. You are right in thinking that he is under the British Government. You would also be right in a sense if you said that occasionally he *is* the British Government.'

'My dear Holmes!'

'I thought I might surprise you. Mycroft draws £450 a year, remains a subordinate, has no ambitions of any kind, will receive neither honour nor title, but remains the most indispensable man in the country.'

'But how?'

'Well, his position is unique. He has made it for himself. There has never been anything like it before, nor will be again. He has the tidiest and most orderly brain, with the greatest capacity for storing facts, of any man living. The same great powers which I have turned to the detection of crime he has used for this particular business. The conclusions of every department are passed to him and he is the central exchange, the clearing-house, which makes out the balance. All other men are specialists, but his specialism is omniscience. We will suppose that a Minister needs information as to a point which involves the Navy, India, Canada and the bimetallic question; he could get his separate advices from various departments upon each, but only Mycroft can focus them all and say offhand how each factor would affect the other. They began by using him as a short-cut, a convenience; now he has made himself an essential. In that great brain of his everything is pigeon-holed and can be handed out in an instant. Again and again his word has decided the national policy. He lives in it. He thinks of nothing else save when, as an intellectual exercise, he unbends if I call upon him and ask him to advise me on one of my little problems. But Jupiter is descending today. What on earth can it mean? Who is Cadogan West and what is he to Mycroft?'

'I have it,' I cried and plunged among the litter of papers upon the sofa. 'Yes, yes, here he is, sure enough! Cadogan West was the young man who was found dead on the Underground on Tuesday morning.'

Holmes sat up at attention, his pipe halfway to his lips.

'This must be serious, Watson. A death which has caused my

brother to alter his habits can be no ordinary one. What in the world can he have to do with it? The case was featureless as I remember it. The young man had apparently fallen out of the train and killed himself. He had not been robbed and there was no particular reason to suspect violence. Is that not so?'

'There has been an inquest,' said I, 'and a good many fresh facts have come out. Looked at more closely, I should certainly say that it was a curious case.'

'Judging by its effect upon my brother, I should think it must be a most extraordinary one.' He snuggled down in his armchair. 'Now, Watson, let us have the facts.'

'The man's name was Arthur Cadogan West. He was twenty-seven years of age, unmarried, and a clerk at Woolwich Arsenal.'

'Government employ. Behold the link with brother Mycroft!'

'He left Woolwich suddenly on Monday night. Was last seen by his fiancée, Miss Violet Westbury, whom he left abruptly in the fog about 7.30 that evening. There was no quarrel between them and she can give no motive for his action. The next thing heard of him was when his dead body was discovered by a plate-layer named Mason, just outside Aldgate Station on the Underground system in London.'

'When?'

'The body was found at six on the Tuesday morning. It was lying wide of the metals upon the left hand of the track as one goes eastward, at a point close to the station where the line emerges from the tunnel in which it runs. The head was badly crushed – an injury which might well have been caused by a fall from the train. The body could only have come on the line in that way. Had it been carried down from any neighbouring street it must have passed the station barriers where a collector is always standing. This point seems absolutely certain.'

'Very good. The case is definite enough. The man, dead or alive, either fell or was precipitated from a train. So much is clear to me. Continue.'

'The trains which traverse the lines of rail beside which the body was found are those which run from west to east, some being purely Metropolitan, and some from Willesden and outlying junctions. It can be stated for certain that this young man, when he met his death, was travelling in this direction at some late hour of the night, but at what point he entered the train it is impossible to state.'

'His ticket, of course, would show that.'

'There was no ticket in his pockets.'

'No ticket! Dear me, Watson, this is really very singular. According to my experience it is not possible to reach the platform of a Metropolitan train without exhibiting one's ticket. Presumably, then, the young man had one. Was it taken from him in order to conceal the station from which he came? It is possible. Or did he drop it in the carriage? That also is possible. But the point is of curious interest. I understand that there was no sign of robbery?'

'Apparently not. There is a list here of his possessions. His purse contained £2.15s. He had also a cheque-book on the Woolwich branch of the Capital and Counties Bank. Through this his identity was established. There were also two dress-circle tickets for the Woolwich Theatre, dated for that very evening. Also a small packet of technical papers.'

Holmes gave an exclamation of satisfaction.

'There we have it at last, Watson! British Government – Woolwich Arsenal – technical papers – brother Mycroft, the chain is complete. But here he comes, if I am not mistaken, to speak for himself.'

A moment later the tall and portly form of Mycroft Holmes was ushered into the room. Heavily built and massive, there was a suggestion of uncouth physical inertia in the figure but, above this unwieldy frame, there was perched a head so masterful in its brow, so alert in its steel-grey, deep-set eyes, so firm in its lips, and so subtle in its play of expression, that after the first glance one forgot the gross body and remembered only the dominant mind.

At his heels came our old friend Lestrade, of Scotland Yard – thin and austere. The gravity of both their faces foretold some weighty quest. The detective shook hands without a word. Mycroft Holmes struggled out of his overcoat and subsided into an armchair.

'A most annoying business, Sherlock,' said he. 'I extremely dislike altering my habits but the powers that be would take no denial. In the present state of Siam it is most awkward that I should be away from the office. But it is a real crisis. I have never seen the Prime Minister so upset. As to the Admiralty – it is buzzing like an overturned beehive. Have you read up the case?'

'We have just done so. What were the technical papers?'

'Ah, there's the point! Fortunately, it has not come out. The press would be furious if it did. The papers which this wretched youth had in his pocket were the plans of the Bruce-Partington submarine.'

Mycroft Holmes spoke with a solemnity which showed his sense of the importance of the subject. His brother and I sat expectant.

'Surely you have heard of it? I thought everyone had heard of it.'

'Only as a name.'

'Its importance can hardly be exaggerated. It has been the most jealously guarded of all Government secrets. You may take it from me that naval warfare becomes impossible within the radius of a Bruce-Partington's operation. Two years ago a very large sum was smuggled through the Estimates and was expended in acquiring a monopoly of the invention. Every effort has been made to keep the secret. The plans, which are exceedingly intricate, comprising some thirty separate patents, each essential to the working of the whole, are kept in an elaborate safe in a confidential office adjoining the Arsenal, with burglar-proof doors and windows. Under no conceivable circumstances were the plans to be taken from the office. If the Chief Constructor of the Navy desired to consult them, even he was forced to go to the Woolwich office for the purpose. And yet here we find them in the pockets of a dead junior clerk in the heart of London. From an official point of view it's simply awful.'

'But you have recovered them?'

'No, Sherlock, no! That's the pinch. We have not. Ten papers were taken from Woolwich. There were seven in the pockets of Cadogan West. The three most essential are gone – stolen, vanished. You must drop everything, Sherlock. Never mind your usual petty puzzles of the police-court. It's a vital international problem that you have to solve. Why did Cadogan West take the papers, where are the missing ones, how did he die, how came his body where it was found, how can the evil be set right? Find an answer to all these questions and you will have done good service for your country.'

'Why do you not solve it yourself, Mycroft? You can see as far as I.'

'Possibly, Sherlock. But it is a question of getting details. Give me your details and, from an armchair, I will return you an excellent expert opinion. But to run here and run there, to cross-question railway guards and lie on my face with a lens to my eye – it is not my métier. No, you are the one man who can clear the matter up. If you have a fancy to see your name in the next honours list—'

My friend smiled and shook his head.

'I play the game for the game's own sake,' said he. 'But the problem certainly presents some points of interest and I shall be very pleased to look into it. Some more facts, please.'

'I have jotted down the more essential ones upon this sheet of paper, together with a few addresses which you will find of service. The actual official guardian of the papers is the famous Government expert, Sir James Walter, whose decorations and sub-titles fill two lines of a book of reference. He has grown grey in the service, is a gentleman, a favoured guest in the most exalted houses and, above all, a man whose patriotism is beyond suspicion. He is one of two who have a key of the safe. I may add that the papers were undoubtedly in the office during working hours on Monday, and that Sir James left for London about three o'clock taking his key with him. He was at the house of Admiral Sinclair at Barclay Square during the whole of the evening when this incident occurred.'

'Has the fact been verified?'

'Yes; his brother, Colonel Valentine Walter, has testified to his departure from Woolwich, and Admiral Sinclair to his arrival in London; so Sir James is no longer a direct factor in the problem.'

'Who was the other man with a key?'

'The senior clerk and draughtsman, Mr Sidney Johnson. He is a man of forty, married, with five children. He is a silent, morose man, but he has, on the whole, an excellent record in the public service. He is unpopular with his colleagues, but a hard worker. According to his own account, corroborated only by the word of his wife, he was at home the whole of Monday evening after office hours and his key has never left the watch-chain upon which it hangs.'

'Tell us about Cadogan West.'

'He has been ten years in the service and has done good work. He has the reputation of being hot-headed and impetuous, but a straight, honest man. We have nothing against him. He was next Sidney Johnson in the office. His duties brought him into daily, personal contact with the plans. No one else had the handling of them.'

'Who locked the plans up that night?'

'Mr Sidney Johnson, the senior clerk.'

'Well, it is surely perfectly clear who took them away. They are actually found upon the person of this junior clerk, Cadogan West. That seems final, does it not?'

'It does, Sherlock, and yet it leaves so much unexplained. In the first place, why did he take them?'

'I presume they were of value?'

'He could have got several thousands for them very easily.'

'Can you suggest any possible motive for taking the papers to London except to sell them?'

'No, I cannot.'

'Then we must take that as our working hypothesis. Young West took the papers. Now this could only be done by having a false key—'

'Several false keys. He had to open the building and the room.'

'He had, then, several false keys. He took the papers to London to sell the secret, intending, no doubt, to have the plans themselves back in the safe next morning before they were missed. While in London on this treasonable mission he met his end.'

'How?'

'We will suppose that he was travelling back to Woolwich when he was killed and thrown out of the compartment.'

'Aldgate, where the body was found, is considerably past the station for London Bridge, which would be his route to Woolwich.'

'Many circumstances could be imagined under which he would pass London Bridge. There was someone in the carriage, for example, with whom he was having an absorbing interview. This interview led to a violent scene in which he lost his life. Possibly he tried to leave the carriage, fell out on the line and so met his end. The other closed the door. There was a thick fog and nothing could be seen.'

'No better explanation can be given with our present knowledge; and yet consider, Sherlock, how much you leave untouched. We will suppose, for argument's sake, that young Cadogan West *had* determined to convey these papers to London. He would naturally have made an appointment with the foreign agent and kept his evening clear. Instead of that he took two tickets for the theatre, escorted his fiancée halfway there and then suddenly disappeared.'

'A blind,' said Lestrade, who had sat listening with some impatience to the conversation.

'A very singular one. That is objection No. 1. Objection No. 2: we will suppose that he reaches London and sees the foreign agent. He must bring back the papers before morning or the loss will be discovered. He took away ten. Only seven were in his pocket. What had become of the other three? He certainly would not leave them of his own free will. Then, again, where is the price of his treason? One would have expected to find a large sum of money in his pocket.'

'It seems to me perfectly clear,' said Lestrade. 'I have no doubt at all as to what occurred. He took the papers to sell them. He saw the agent. They could not agree as to price. He started home again, but the agent went with him. In the train the agent murdered him, took the more essential papers and threw his body from the carriage. That would account for everything, would it not?'

'Why had he no ticket?'

'The ticket would have shown which station was nearest the agent's house. Therefore he took it from the murdered man's pocket.'

'Good, Lestrade, very good,' said Holmes. 'Your theory holds together. But if this is true, then the case is at an end. On the one hand the traitor is dead. On the other the plans of the Bruce-Partington submarine are presumably already on the Continent. What is there for us to do?'

'To act, Sherlock – to act!' cried Mycroft, springing to his feet. 'All my instincts are against this explanation. Use your powers! Go to the scene of the crime! See the people concerned! Leave no stone unturned! In all your career you have never had so great a chance of serving your country.'

'Well, well!' said Holmes, shrugging his shoulders. 'Come, Watson! And you, Lestrade, could you favour us with your company for an hour or two? We will begin our investigation by a visit to Aldgate Station. Goodbye, Mycroft. I shall let you have a report before evening, but I warn you in advance that you have little to expect.'

An hour later, Holmes, Lestrade and I stood upon the Underground railroad at the point where it emerges from the tunnel immediately before Aldgate Station. A courteous red-faced old gentleman represented the railway company.

'This is where the young man's body lay,' Said he, indicating a spot about three feet from the metals. 'It could not have fallen from above, for these, as you see, are all blank walls. Therefore, it could only have come from a train, and that train, so far as we can trace it, must have passed about midnight on Monday.'

'Have the carriages been examined for any sign of violence?'

'There are no such signs and no ticket has been found.'

'No record of a door being found open?'

'None.'

'We have had some fresh evidence this morning,' said Lestrade. 'A passenger who passed Aldgate in an ordinary Metropolitan train about 11.40 on Monday night declares that he heard a heavy thud, as of a body striking the line, just before the train reached the station. There was dense fog, however, and nothing could be seen. He made no report of it at the time. Why, whatever is the matter with Mr Holmes?'

My friend was standing with an expression of strained intensity upon his face, staring at the railway metals where they curved out of the tunnel. Aldgate is a junction and there was a network of points. On these his eager, questioning eyes were fixed, and I saw on his keen, alert face that tightening of the lips, that quiver of the nostrils and concentration of the heavy tufted brows which I knew so well.

'Points,' he muttered; 'the points.'

'What of it? What do you mean?'

'I suppose there are no great number of points on a system such as this?'

'No; there are very few.'

'And a curve, too. Points, and a curve. By Jove! If it were only so.'

'What is it, Mr Holmes? Have you a clue?'

'An idea – an indication, no more. But the case certainly grows in interest. Unique, perfectly unique, and yet why not? I do not see any indications of bleeding on the line.'

'There were hardly any.'

'But I understand that there was a considerable wound.'

'The bone was crushed, but there was no great external injury.'

'And yet one would have expected some bleeding. Would it be possible for me to inspect the train which contained the passenger who heard the thud of a fall in the fog?'

'I fear not, Mr Holmes. The train has been broken up before now, and the carriages redistributed.'

'I can assure you, Mr Holmes,' said Lestrade, 'that every carriage has been carefully examined. I saw to it myself.'

It was one of my friend's most obvious weaknesses that he was impatient with less alert intelligences than his own.

'Very likely,' said he, turning away. 'As it happens, it was not the carriages which I desired to examine. Watson, we have done all we can here. We need not trouble you any further, Mr Lestrade. I think our investigations must now carry us to Woolwich.'

At London Bridge, Holmes wrote a telegram to his brother which he handed to me before dispatching it. It ran thus:

See some light in the darkness, but it may possibly flicker out. Meanwhile, please send by messenger, to await return at Baker Street, a complete list of all foreign spies or international agents known to be in England, with full address.
Sherlock.

'That should be helpful, Watson,' he remarked, as we took our seats in the Woolwich train. 'We certainly owe brother Mycroft a debt for having introduced us to what promises to be a really very remarkable case.'

His eager face still wore that expression of intense and high-strung energy which showed me that some novel and suggestive circumstance had opened up a stimulating line of thought. See the foxhound with hanging ears and drooping tail as it lolls about the kennels, and compare it with the same hound as, with gleaming eyes and straining muscles, it runs upon a breast-high scent – such was the change in Holmes since the morning. He was a different man to the limp and lounging figure in the mouse-coloured dressing-gown who had prowled so restlessly only a few hours before round the fog-girt room.

'There is material here. There is scope,' said he. 'I am dull indeed not to have understood its possibilities.'

'Even now they are dark to me.'

'The end is dark to me also, but I have hold of one idea which may lead us far. The man met his death elsewhere, and his body was on the *roof* of a carriage.'

'On the roof!'

'Remarkable, is it not? But consider the facts. Is it a coincidence that it is found at the very point where the train pitches and sways as it comes round on the points? Is not that the place where an object upon the roof might be expected to fall off? The points would affect no object inside the train. Either the body fell from the roof or a very curious coincidence has occurred. But now consider the question of the blood. Of course there was no bleeding on the line if the body had bled elsewhere. Each fact is suggestive in itself. Together they have a cumulative force.'

'And the ticket, too!' I cried.

'Exactly. We could not explain the absence of a ticket. This would explain it. Everything fits together.'

'But suppose it were so, we are still as far as ever from unravelling the mystery of his death. Indeed, it becomes not simpler, but stranger.'

'Perhaps,' said Holmes, thoughtfully; 'perhaps.' He relapsed into a silent reverie which lasted until the slow train drew up at last in Woolwich Station. There he called a cab and drew Mycroft's paper from his pocket.

'We have quite a little round of afternoon calls to make,' said he. 'I think that Sir James Walter claims our first attention.'

The house of the famous official was a fine villa with green lawns stretching down to the Thames. As we reached it the fog was lifting and a thin, watery sunshine was breaking through. A butler answered our ring.

'Sir James, sir!' said he, with solemn face. 'Sir James died this morning.'

'Good heavens!' cried Holmes, in amazement. 'How did he die?'

'Perhaps you would care to step in, sir, and see his brother, Colonel Valentine?'

'Yes, we had best do so.'

We were ushered into a dim-lit drawing-room where, an instant later, we were joined by a very tall, handsome, light-bearded man of fifty, the younger brother of the dead scientist. His wild eyes, stained cheeks and unkempt hair all spoke of the sudden blow which had fallen upon the household. He was hardly articulate as he spoke of it.

'It was this horrible scandal,' said he. 'My brother, Sir James, was a man of very sensitive honour and he could not survive such an affair. It broke his heart. He was always so proud of the efficiency of his department and this was a crushing blow.'

'We had hoped that he might have given us some indications which would have helped us to clear the matter up.'

'I assure you that it was all a mystery to him as it is to you and to all of us. He had already put all his knowledge at the disposal of the police. Naturally, he had no doubt that Cadogan West was guilty. But all the rest was inconceivable.'

'You cannot throw any new light upon the affair?'

'I know nothing myself save what I have read or heard. I have no desire to be discourteous, but you can understand, Mr Holmes, that we are much disturbed at present and I must ask you to hasten this interview to an end.'

'This is indeed an unexpected development,' said my friend when we had regained the cab. 'I wonder if the death was natural or whether the poor old fellow killed himself! If the latter, may it be taken as some sign of self-reproach for duty neglected? We must leave that question to the future. Now we shall turn to the Cadogan Wests.'

A small but well-kept house in the outskirts of the town sheltered the bereaved mother. The old lady was too dazed with grief to be of any use to us but, at her side, was a white-faced young lady who introduced herself as Miss Violet Westbury, the fiancée of the dead man, and the last to see him upon that fatal night.

'I cannot explain it, Mr Holmes,' she said. 'I have not shut an eye since the tragedy, thinking, thinking, thinking, night and day, what the true meaning of it can be. Arthur was the most single-minded, chivalrous, patriotic man upon earth. He would have cut his right hand off before he would sell a state secret confided to his keeping. It is absurd, impossible, preposterous to anyone who knew him.'

'But the facts, Miss Westbury?'

'Yes, yes; I admit I cannot explain them.'

'Was he in any want of money?'

'No; his needs were very simple and his salary ample. He had saved a few hundreds and we were to marry at the New Year.'

'No signs of any mental excitement? Come, Miss Westbury, be absolutely frank with us.'

The quick eye of my companion had noted some change in her manner. She coloured and hesitated.

'Yes,' she said, at last. 'I had a feeling that there was something on his mind.'

'For long?'

'Only for the last week or so. He was thoughtful and worried. Once I pressed him about it. He admitted that there was something and that it was concerned with his official life. "It is too serious for me to speak about, even to you," said he. I could get nothing more.'

Holmes looked grave.

'Go on, Miss Westbury. Even if it seems to tell against him, go on. We cannot say what it may lead to.'

'Indeed I have nothing more to tell. Once or twice it seemed to me that he was on the point of telling me something. He spoke one evening of the importance of the secret, and I have some recollection that he said that no doubt foreign spies would pay a great deal to have it.'

My friend's face grew graver still.

'Anything else?'

'He said that we were slack about such matters – that it would be easy for a traitor to get the plans.'

'Was it only recently that he made such remarks?'

'Yes, quite recently.'

'Now tell us of that last evening.'

'We were to go to the theatre. The fog was so thick that a cab was useless. We walked, and our way took us close to the office. Suddenly he darted away into the fog.'

'Without a word?'

'He gave an exclamation; that was all. I waited but he never returned. Then I walked home. Next morning, after the office opened, they came to inquire. About twelve o'clock we heard the terrible news. Oh, Mr Holmes, if you could only, only save his honour! It was so much to him.'

Holmes shook his head sadly.

'Come, Watson,' said he, 'our ways lie elsewhere. Our next station must be the office from which the papers were taken.

'It was black enough before against this young man, but our inquiries make it blacker,' he remarked, as the cab lumbered off. 'His coming marriage gives a motive for the crime. He naturally wanted money. The idea was in his head, since he spoke about it. He nearly made the girl an accomplice in the treason by telling her his plans. It is all very bad.'

'But surely, Holmes, character goes for something? Then, again, why should he leave the girl in the street and dart away to commit a felony?'

'Exactly! There are certainly objections. But it is a formidable case which they have to meet.'

Mr Sidney Johnson, the senior clerk, met us at the office and received us with that respect which my companion's card always commanded. He was a thin, gruff, bespectacled man of middle age, his cheeks haggard and his hands twitching from the nervous strain to which he had been subjected.

'It is bad, Mr Holmes, very bad! Have you heard of the death of the Chief?'

'We have just come from his house.'

'The place is disorganized. The Chief dead, Cadogan West dead, our papers stolen. And yet, when we closed our door on Monday evening, we were as efficient an office as any in the Government service. Good God, it's dreadful to think of! That West, of all men, should have done such a thing!'

'You are sure of his guilt, then?'

'I can see no other way out of it. And yet I would have trusted him as I trust myself.'

'At what hour was the office closed on Monday?'

'At five.'

'Did you close it?'

'I am always the last man out.'

'Where were the plans?'

'In that safe. I put them there myself.'

'Is there no watchman to the building?'

'There is; but he has other departments to look after as well. He is an old soldier and a most trustworthy man. He saw nothing that evening. Of course, the fog was very thick.'

'Suppose that Cadogan West wished to make his way into the building after hours; he would need three keys, would he not, before he could reach the papers?'

'Yes, he would. The key of the outer door, the key of the office and the key of the safe.'

'Only Sir James Walter and you had those keys?'

'I had no keys of the doors – only of the safe.'

'Was Sir James a man who was orderly in his habits?'

'Yes, I think he was. I know that so far as those three keys are concerned he kept them on the same ring. I have often seen them there.'

'And that ring went with him to London?'

'He said so.'

'And your key never left your possession?'

'Never.'

'Then West, if he is the culprit, must have had a duplicate. And yet none was found upon his body. One other point: if a clerk in this office desired to sell the plans, would it not be simpler to copy the plans for himself than to take the originals, as was actually done?'

'It would take considerable technical knowledge to copy the plans in an effective way.'

'But I suppose either Sir James, or you, or West had that technical knowledge?'

'No doubt we had, but I beg you won't try to drag me into the matter, Mr Holmes. What is the use of our speculating in this way when the original plans were actually found on West?'

'Well, it is certainly singular that he should run the risk of taking originals if he could safely have taken copies, which would have equally served his turn.'

'Singular, no doubt – and yet he did so.'

'Every inquiry in this case reveals something inexplicable. Now, there are three papers still missing. They are, as I understand, the vital ones.'

'Yes, that is so.'

'Do you mean to say that anyone holding these three papers, and without the seven others, could construct a Bruce-Partington submarine?'

'I reported to that effect to the Admiralty. But today I have been over the drawings again, and I am not so sure of it. The double valves with the automatic self-adjusting slots are drawn in one of the papers which have been returned. Until the foreigners had invented that for themselves they could not make the boat. Of course, they might soon get over the difficulty.'

'But the three missing drawings are the most important?'

'Undoubtedly.'

'I think, with your permission, I will now take a stroll round the premises. I do not recall any other question which I desired to ask.'

He examined the lock of the safe, the door of the room and, finally, the iron shutters of the window. It was only when we were on the lawn outside that his interest was strongly excited. There was a laurel bush outside the window and several of the branches bore signs of having been twisted or snapped. He examined them carefully with his lens, and then some dim and vague marks upon the earth beneath. Finally he asked the chief clerk to close the iron shutters, and he pointed out to me that they hardly met in the centre and that it would be possible for anyone outside to see what was going on within the room.

'The indications are ruined by the three days' delay. They may mean something or nothing. Well, Watson, I do not think that Woolwich can help us further. It is a small crop which we have gathered. Let us see if we can do better in London.'

Yet we added one more sheaf to our harvest before we left Woolwich Station. The clerk in the ticket office was able to say with confidence that he saw Cadogan West – whom he knew well by sight – upon the Monday night, and that he went to London by the 8.15 to London Bridge. He was alone and took a single third-class ticket. The clerk was struck at the time by his excited and nervous manner. So shaky was he that he could hardly pick up his change, and the clerk had helped him with it. A reference to the timetable showed that the 8.15 was the first train which it was possible for West to take after he had left the lady about 7.30.

'Let us reconstruct, Watson,' said Holmes, after half an hour of silence. 'I am not aware that in all our joint researches we have ever had a case which was more difficult to get at. Every fresh advance which we make only reveals a fresh ridge beyond. And yet we have surely made some appreciable progress.

'The effect of our inquiries at Woolwich has, in the main, been against young Cadogan West; but the indications at the window would lend themselves to a more favourable hypothesis. Let us suppose, for example, that he had been approached by some foreign agent. It might have been done under such pledges as would have prevented him from speaking of it, and yet would have affected his thoughts in the direction indicated by his remarks to his fiancée. Very good. We will now suppose that, as he went to the theatre with the young lady, he suddenly, in the fog, caught a glimpse of this same agent going in the direction of the office. He was an impetuous man, quick in his decisions. Everything gave way to his duty. He followed the man, reached the window, saw the abstraction of the documents and pursued the thief. In this way we get over the objection that no one would take originals when he could make copies. This outsider had to take originals. So far it holds together.'

'What is the next step?'

'Then we come into difficulties. One would imagine that, under such circumstances, the first act of young Cadogan West would be to seize the villain and raise the alarm. Why did he not do so? Could it have been an official superior who took the papers? That would explain West's conduct. Or could the Chief have given West the slip in the fog and West started at once to London to head him off from his own rooms, presuming that he knew where the rooms were? The call must have been very pressing, since he left his girl standing in the fog and made no effort to communicate with her. Our scent runs cold here, and there is a vast gap between either hypothesis and the laying of West's body, with seven papers in his pocket, on the roof of a Metropolitan train. My instinct now is to work from the other end. If Mycroft has given us the list of addresses we may be able to pick our man and follow two tracks instead of one.'

Surely enough, a note awaited us at Baker Street. A Government messenger had brought it post-haste. Holmes glanced at it and threw it over to me.

> There are numerous small fry, but few who would handle so big an affair. The only men worth considering are Adolph Meyer, of 13 Great George Street, Westminster; Louis La Rothière, of Campden Mansions, Notting Hill; and Hugo Oberstein, 13 Caulfield Gardens, Kensington. The latter was known to be in town on Monday and is now reported as having left. Glad to hear you have seen some light. The Cabinet awaits your final report with the utmost anxiety. Urgent representations have arrived from the very highest quarter. The whole force of the State is at your back if you should need it. Mycroft.

'I'm afraid,' said Holmes, smiling, 'that all the Queen's horses and all the Queen's men cannot avail in this matter.' He had spread out his big map of London and leaned eagerly over it. 'Well, well' said he presently, with an exclamation of satisfaction, 'things are turning a little in our direction at last. Why, Watson, I do honestly believe that we are going to pull it off, after all.' He slapped me on the shoulder with a sudden burst of hilarity. 'I am going out now. It is only a reconnaissance. I will do nothing serious without my trusted comrade and biographer at my elbow. Do you stay here, and the odds are that you will see me again in an hour or two. If time hangs heavy get foolscap and a pen, and begin your narrative of how we saved the state.'

I felt some reflection of his elation in my own mind, for I knew well that he would not depart so far from his usual austerity of demeanour unless there was good cause for exultation. All the long November evening I waited, filled with impatience for his return. At last, shortly after nine o'clock, there arrived a messenger with a note:

Am dining at Goldini's Restaurant, Gloucester Road, Kensington. Please come at once and join me there. Bring with you a jemmy, a dark lantern, a chisel and a revolver. S. H.

It was a nice equipment for a respectable citizen to carry through the dim, fog-draped streets. I stowed them all discreetly away in my overcoat and drove straight to the address given. There sat my friend at a little round table near the door of the garish Italian restaurant.

'Have you had something to eat? Then join me in a coffee and curaçao. Try one of the proprietor's cigars. They are less poisonous than one would expect. Have you the tools?'

'They are here, in my overcoat.'

'Excellent. Let me give you a short sketch of what I have done, with some indication of what we are about to do. Now it must be evident to you, Watson, that this young man's body was *placed* on the roof of the train. That was clear from the instant that I determined the fact that it was from the roof, and not from a carriage, that he had fallen.'

'Could it not have been dropped from a bridge?'

'I should say it was impossible. If you examine the roofs you will find that they are slightly rounded and there is no railing round them. Therefore, we can say for certain that young Cadogan West was placed on it.'

'How could he be placed there?'

'That was the question which we had to answer. There is only one possible way. You are aware that the Underground runs clear of tunnels at some points in the West End. I had a vague memory that, as I have travelled by it, I have occasionally seen windows just above my head. Now, suppose that a train halted under such a window, would there be any difficulty in laying a body upon the roof?'

'It seems most improbable.'

'We must fall back upon the old axiom that, when all other contingencies fail, whatever remains, however improbable, must be the truth. Here all other contigencies *have* failed. When I found that the leading international agent, who had just left London, lived in a row of houses which abutted upon the Underground, I was so pleased that you were a little astonished at my sudden frivolity.'

'Oh, that was it, was it?'

'Yes, that was it. Mr Hugo Oberstein, of 13 Caulfield Gardens, had become my objective. I began my operations at Gloucester Road Station, where a very helpful official walked with me along the track, and allowed me to satisfy myself, not only that the backstair windows of Caulfield Gardens open on the line but the even more essential fact that, owing to the intersection of one of the larger railways, the Underground trains are frequently held motionless for some minutes at that very spot.'

'Splendid, Holmes! You have got it!'

'So far – so far, Watson. We advance, but the goal is afar. Well, having seen the back of Caulfield Gardens I visited the front and satisfied myself that the bird was indeed flown. It is a considerable house, unfurnished, so far as I could judge, in the upper rooms. Oberstein lived there with a single valet who was probably a confederate, entirely in his confidence. We must bear in mind that Oberstein has gone to the Continent to dispose of his booty, but not with any idea of flight; for he had no reason to fear a warrant, and the idea of an amateur domiciliary visit would certainly never occur to him. Yet that is precisely what we are about to make.'

'Could we not get a warrant and legalize it?'

'Hardly on the evidence.'

'What can we hope to do?'

'We cannot tell what correspondence may be there.'

'I don't like it, Holmes.'

'My dear fellow, you shall keep watch in the street. I'll do the criminal part. It's not a time to stick at trifles. Think of Mycroft's note, of the Admiralty, the Cabinet, the exalted person who waits for news. We are bound to go.'

My answer was to rise from the table.

'You are right, Holmes. We are bound to go.'

He sprang up and shook me by the hand.

'I knew you would not shrink at the last.' said he, and for a moment I saw something in his eyes which was nearer to tenderness than I had ever seen. The next instant he was his masterful, practical self once more.

'It is nearly half a mile, but there is no hurry. Let us walk,' said he. 'Don't drop the instruments, I beg. Your arrest as a suspicious character would be a most unfortunate complication.'

Caulfield Gardens was one of those lines of flat-faced, pillared and porticoed houses which are so prominent a product of the middle Victorian epoch in the West End of London. Next door there appeared to be a children's party, for the merry buzz of young voices and the clatter of a piano resounded through the night. The fog still hung about and screened us with its friendly shade. Holmes had lit his lantern and flashed it upon the massive door.

'This is a serious proposition,' said he. 'It is certainly bolted as well as locked. We would do better in the area. There is an excellent archway down yonder in case a too zealous policeman should intrude. Give me a hand, Watson, and I'll do the same for you.'

A minute later we were both in the area. Hardly had we reached the dark shadows before the step of the policeman was heard in the fog above. As its soft rhythm died away, Holmes set to work upon the lower door. I saw him stoop and strain until, with a sharp crash, it flew open. We sprang through into the dark passage, closing the area door behind us. Holmes led the way up the curving, uncarpeted stair. His little fan of yellow light shone upon a low window.

'Here we are, Watson – this must be the one.' He threw it open and, as he did so, there was a low, harsh murmur, growing steadily into a loud roar as a train dashed past us in the darkness. Holmes swept his light along the window-sill. It was thickly coated with soot from the passing engines, but the black surface was blurred and rubbed in places.

'You can see where they rested the body. Halloa, Watson! What is this? There can be no doubt that it is a blood mark.' He was pointing to faint discolorations along the woodwork of the window. 'Here it is on the stone of the stair also. The demonstration is complete. Let us stay here until a train stops.'

We had not long to wait. The very next train roared from the tunnel as before, but slowed in the open and then, with a creaking of brakes, pulled up immediately beneath us. It was not four feet from the window-ledge to the roof of the carriages. Holmes softly closed the window.

'So far we are justified,' said he. 'What do you think of it, Watson?'

'A masterpiece. You have never risen to a greater height.'

'I cannot agree with you there. From the moment that I conceived the idea of the body being upon the roof, which surely was not a very abstruse one, all the rest was inevitable. If it were not for the grave interests involved the affair up to this point would be insignificant. Our difficulties are still before us. But perhaps we may find something here which may help us.'

We had ascended the kitchen stair and entered the suite of rooms upon the first floor. One was a dining-room, severely furnished and containing nothing of interest. A second was a bedroom, which also drew blank. The remaining room appeared more promising and my companion settled down to a systematic examination. It was littered with books and papers, and was evidently used as a study. Swiftly and methodically Holmes turned over the contents of drawer after drawer and cupboard after cupboard, but no gleam of success came to brighten his austere face. At the end of an hour he was no further than when he started.

'The cunning dog has covered his tracks,' said he. 'He has left nothing to incriminate him. His dangerous correspondence has been destroyed or removed. This is our last chance.'

It was a small tin cash-box which stood upon the writing-desk. Holmes prised it open with his chisel. Several rolls of paper were within, covered with figures and calculations, without any note to show to what they referred. The recurring words, 'water pressure' and 'pressure to the square inch', suggested some possible relation to a submarine. Holmes tossed them all impatiently aside. There only remained an envelope with some small newspaper slips inside it. He shook them out on the table and, at once, I saw by his eager face that his hopes had been raised.

'What's this, Watson? Eh? What's this? Record of a series of messages in the advertisements of a paper. *Daily Telegraph* agony column by the print and paper. Right-hand top corner of a page. No dates – but messages arrange themselves. This must be the first.

'"Hoped to hear sooner. Terms agreed to. Write fully to address given on card. Pierrot."

'Next comes:' "Too complex for description. Must have full report. Stuff awaits you when goods delivered. Pierrot."

'Then comes "Matter presses. Must withdraw offer unless contract completed. Make appointment by letter. Will confirm by advertisement. Pierrot."

'Finally: "Monday night after nine. Two taps. Only ourselves. Do not be so suspicious. Payment in hard cash when goods delivered. Pierrot."

'A fairly complete record, Watson! If we could only get at the man at the other end!' He sat lost in thought, tapping his fingers on the table. Finally he sprang to his feet.

'Well, perhaps it won't be so difficult after all. There is nothing more to be done here, Watson. I think we might drive round to the offices of the *Daily Telegraph* and so bring a good day's work to a conclusion.'

Mycroft Holmes and Lestrade had come round by appointment after breakfast next day and Sherlock Holmes had recounted to them our proceedings of the day before. The professional shook his head over our confessed burglary.

'We can't do these things in the force, Mr Holmes,' said he. 'No wonder you get results that are beyond us. But some of these days you'll go too far, and you'll find yourself and your friend in trouble.'

'For England, home and beauty – eh, Watson? Martyrs on the altar of our country. But what do you think of it, Mycroft?'

'Excellent, Sherlock! Admirable! But what use will you make of it?'

Holmes picked up the *Daily Telegraph* which lay upon the table.

'Have you seen Pierrot's advertisement today?'

'What! Another one?'

'Yes, here it is: "Tonight. Same hour. Same place. Two taps. Most vitally important. Your own safety at stake. Pierrot."'

'By George!' cried Lestrade. 'If he answers that we've got him!'

'That was my idea when I put it in. I think if you could both make it convenient to come with us about eight o'clock to Caulfield Gardens we might possibly get a little nearer to a solution.'

One of the most remarkable characteristics of Sherlock Holmes was his power of throwing his brain out of action and switching all his thoughts on to lighter things whenever he had convinced himself that he could no longer work to advantage. I remember that during the whole of that memorable day he lost himself in a monograph which he had undertaken upon the Polyphonic Motets of Lassus. For my own part I had none of this power of detachment and the day, in consequence, appeared to be interminable. The great national importance of the issue, the suspense in high quarters, the direct nature of the experiment which we were trying – all combined to work upon my nerve. It was a relief to me when at last, after a light dinner, we set out upon our expedition. Lestrade and Mycroft met us by appointment at the outside of Gloucester Road Station. The area door of Oberstein's house had been left open the night before and it was necessary for me, as Mycroft Holmes absolutely and indignantly declined to climb the railings, to pass in and open the hall door. By nine o'clock we were all seated in the study, waiting patiently for our man.

An hour passed and yet another. When eleven struck, the measured beat of the great church clock seemed to sound the dirge of our hopes. Lestrade and Mycroft were fidgeting in their seats and looking twice a minute at their watches. Holmes sat silent and composed, his eyelids half shut, but every sense on the alert. He raised his head with a sudden jerk.

'He is coming,' said he.

There had been a furtive step past the door. Now it returned. We heard a shuffling sound outside and then two sharp taps with the knocker. Holmes rose, motioning to us to remain seated. The gas in the hall was a mere point of light. He opened the outer door and then, as a dark figure slipped past him, he closed and fastened it. 'This way!' we heard him say, and a moment later our man stood before us. Holmes had followed him closely and, as the man turned with a cry of surprise and alarm, he caught him by the collar and threw him back into the room. Before our prisoner had recovered his balance the door was shut and Holmes standing with his back against it. The man glared round him, staggered and fell senseless upon the floor. With the shock, his broad-brimmed hat flew from his head, his cravat slipped down from his lips, and there was the long light beard and the soft, handsome delicate features of Colonel Valentine Walter.

Holmes gave a whistle of surprise.

'You can write me down an ass this time, Watson,' said he. 'This was not the bird that I was looking for.'

'Who is he?' asked Mycroft eagerly.

'The younger brother of the late Sir James Walter, the head of the Submarine Department. Yes, yes; I see the fall of the cards. He is coming to. I think that you had best leave his examination to me.'

We had carried the prostrate body to the sofa. Now our prisoner sat up, looked round him with a horror-stricken face and passed his hand over his forehead, like one who cannot believe his own senses.

'What is this?' he asked. 'I came here to visit Mr Oberstein.'

'Everything is known, Colonel Walter,' said Holmes. 'How an English gentleman could behave in such a manner is beyond my comprehension. But your whole correspondence and relations with Oberstein are within our knowledge. So also are the circumstances connected with the death of young Cadogan West. Let me advise you to gain at least the small credit for repentance and confession, since there are still some details which we can only learn from your lips.'

The man groaned and sank his face in his hands. We waited, but he was silent.

'I can assure you,' said Holmes, 'that every essential is already known. We know that you were pressed for money; that you took an impress of the keys which your brother held; and that you entered into a correspondence with Oberstein who answered your letters through the advertisement columns of the *Daily Telegraph*. We are aware that you went down to the office in the fog on Monday night, but that you were seen and followed by young Cadogan West who had probably some previous reason to suspect you. He saw your theft, but could not give the alarm as it was just possible that you were taking the papers to your brother in London. Leaving all his private concerns, like the good citizen that he was, he followed you closely in the fog and kept at your heels until you reached this very house. There he intervened and then it was, Colonel Walter, that to treason you added the more terrible crime of murder.'

'I did not! I did not! Before God I swear that I did not!' cried our wretched prisoner.

'Tell us then, how Cadogan West met his end before you laid him upon the roof of a railway carriage.'

'I will. I swear to you that I will. I did the rest. I confess it. It was just as you say. A Stock Exchange debt had to be paid. I needed the money badly. Oberstein offered me 5000. It was to save myself from ruin. But as to murder, I am as innocent as you.'

'What happened then?'

'He had his suspicions before, and he followed me as you describe. I never knew it until I was at the very door. It was thick fog and one could not see three yards. I had given two taps and Oberstein had come to the door. The young man rushed up and demanded to know what we were about to do with the papers. Oberstein had a short life-preserver. He always carried it with him. As West forced his way after us into the house Oberstein struck him on the head. The blow was a fatal one. He was dead within five minutes. There he lay in the hall and we were at our wits' end what to do. Then Oberstein had this idea about the trains which halted under his back window. But first he examined the papers which I had brought. He said that three of them were essential and that he must keep them. "You cannot keep them," said I. "There will be a dreadful row at Woolwich if they are not returned." "I must keep them," said he, "for they are so technical that it is impossible in the time to make copies." "Then they must all go back together tonight," said I. He thought for a little and then he cried out that he had it. "Three I will keep," said he. "The others we will stuff into the pocket of this young man. When he is found the whole business will assuredly be put to his account." I could see no other way out of it, so we did as he suggested. We waited half an hour at the window before a train stopped. It was so thick that nothing could be seen, and we had no difficulty in lowering West's body on to the train. That was the end of the matter so far as I was concerned.'

'And your brother?'

'He said nothing, but he had caught me once with his keys and I think that he suspected. I read in his eyes that he suspected. As you know, he never held up his head again.'

There was silence in the room. It was broken by Mycroft Holmes.

'Can you not make reparation? It would ease your conscience and possibly your punishment.'

'What reparation can I make?'

'Where is Oberstein with the papers?'

'I do not know.'

'Did he give you no address?'

'He said that letters to the Hôtel du Louvre, Paris, would eventually read him.'

'Then reparation is still within your power,' said Sherlock Holmes.

'I will do anything I can. I owe this fellow no particular good-will. He has been my ruin and my downfall.'

'Here are paper and pen. Sit at this desk and write to my dictation. Direct the envelope to the address given. That is right. Now the letter.

> Dear Sir, With regard to our transaction, you will no doubt have observed by now that one essential detail is missing. I have a tracing which will make it complete. This has involved me in extra trouble, however, and I must ask you for a further advance of £500. I will not trust it to the post, nor will I take anything but gold or notes. I would come to you abroad, but it would excite remark if I left the country at present. Therefore I shall expect to meet you in the smoking-room of the Charing Cross Hotel at noon on Saturday. Remember that only English notes, or gold, will be taken.

That will do very well. I shall be very much surprised if it does not fetch our man.'

And it did! It is a matter of history — that secret history of a nation which is often so much more intimate and interesting than its public chronicles — that Oberstein, eager to complete the coup of his lifetime, came to the lure and was safely engulfed for fifteen years in a British prison. In his trunk were found the invaluable Bruce-Partington plans which he had put up for auction in all the naval centres of Europe.

Colonel Walter died in prison towards the end of the second year of his sentence. As to Holmes, he returned refreshed to his monograph upon the Polyphonic Motets of Lassus, which has since been printed for private circulation and is said by experts to be the last word upon the subject. Some weeks afterwards I learned, incidentally, that my friend spent a day at Windsor, whence he returned with a remarkably fine emerald tiepin. When I asked him if he had bought it, he answered that it was a present from a certain gracious lady in whose interests he had once been fortunate enough to carry out a small commission. He said no mote but I fancy that I could guess at that lady's august name, and I have little doubt that the emerald pin will for ever recall to my friend's memory the adventure of the Bruce-Partington plans.

The Adventure of the Bruce-Partington Plans, Arthur Conan Doyle

Eavesdropping

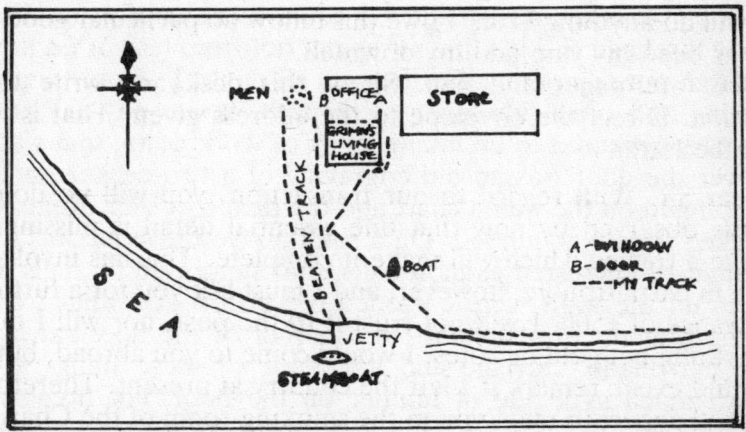

My geography was clear now in one respect. That window belonged to the same room as the banging door (B); for I distinctly heard the latter open and shut again, opposite me on the other side of the building. It struck me that it might be interesting to see into that room. 'Play the game,' I reminded myself, and retreated a few yards back on tiptoe, then turned and sauntered coolly past the window, puffing my villainous pipe and taking a long deliberate look into the interior as I passed – the more deliberate that, at the first instant, I realized that nobody inside was disturbing himself about me. As I had expected (in view of the fog and the time) there was artificial light within. My mental photograph was as follows: a small room with varnished deal walls and furnished like an office; in the far right-hand corner a counting-house desk, Grimm sitting at it on a high stool, side-face to me, counting money; opposite him in an awkward attitude a burly fellow in seaman's dress holding a diver's helmet. In the middle of the room a deal table and on it something big and black. Lolling on chairs near it, their backs to me and their faces turned towards the desk and the diver, two men – von Brüning and an older man with a bald yellow head (Dollmann's companion on the steamer, beyond a doubt). On another chair, with its back actually tilted against the window, Dollmann.

Such were the principal features of the scene; for detail I had to make another inspection. Stooping low I crept back, quiet as a cat, till I was beneath the window and, as I calculated, directly behind Dollmann's chair. Then with great caution I raised my head. There was only one pair of eyes in the room that I feared in the least, and that was Grimm's, who sat in profile to me, furthest away. I instantly put Dollmann's back between Grimm and me, and then made my scrutiny. As I made it I could feel a cold sweat distilling on my forehead and tickling my spine; not from fear or excitement, but from pure ignominy. For beyond all doubt I was present at the meeting of a bona fide salvage company. It was pay-day, and the directors appeared to be taking stock of work done; that was all.

Over the door was an old engraving of a two-decker under full sail; pinned on the wall a chart and the plan of a ship. Relics of the wrecked frigate abounded. On a shelf above the stove was a small pyramid of encrusted cannon-balls, and supported on nails at odd places on the walls were corroded old pistols and what I took to be the remains of a sextant. In a corner of the floor sat a hoary little carronade, carriage and all. None of these things affected me so much as a pile of lumber on the floor, not firewood but unmistakable wreck-wood, black as bog-oak, still caked in places with the mud of ages. Nor was it the mere sight of this lumber that dumbfounded me. It was the fact that a fragment of it, a balk of curved timber garnished with some massive bolts, lay on the table, and was evidently an object of earnest interest. The diver had turned and was arguing with gestures over it; von Brüning and Grimm were pressing another view. The diver shook his head frequently, finally shrugged his shoulders, made a salutation and left the room.

Their movements had kept me ducking my head pretty frequently, but I now grew almost reckless as to whether I was seen or not. All the weaknesses of my theory crowded on me – the arguments Davies had used at Bensersiel; Fräulein Dollmann's thoughtless talk; the ease (comparatively) with which I had reached this spot, not a barrier to cross or a lock to force; the publicity of their passage to Memmert by Dollmann, his friend and Grimm; and now this glimpse of business-like routine. In a few moments I sank from depth to depth of scepticism. Where were my mines, torpedoes and submarine boats, and where my imperial conspirators? Was gold after all at the bottom of this sordid mystery? Dollmann, after all, a commonplace criminal? The ladder of proof I had mounted tottered and shook beneath me. 'Don't be a fool,' said the faint voice of reason. 'There are your four men. Wait.'

Two more *employés* came into the room in quick succession and received wages; one, looking like a fireman, the other of a superior type, the skipper of a tug, say. There was another discussion with this latter over the balk of wreck-wood and this man, too, shrugged his shoulders. His departure appeared to end the meeting. Grimm shut up a ledger and I shrank down on my knees, for a general shifting of chairs began. At the same time, from the other side of the building, I heard my knot of men retreating beachwards, spitting and chatting as they went. Presently someone walked across the room towards my window. I sidled away on all fours, rose and flattened myself erect against the wall, a sickening despondency on me; my intention to slink away south-east as soon as the coast was clear. But the sound that came next pricked me like an electric shock; it was the tinkle and scrape of curtain-rings.

Quick as thought I was back in my old position, to find my view barred by a cretonne curtain. It was in one piece, with no chink for my benefit, but it did not hang straight, bulging towards me under the pressure of something – human shoulders by the shape. Dollmann, I concluded, was still in his old place. I now was exasperated to find that I could scarcely hear a word that was said, not even by pressing my ear against the glass. It was not that the speakers were of set purpose hushing their voices – they used an ordinary tone for intimate discussion – but the glass and curtain deadened the actual words. Still, I was soon able to distinguish general characteristics. Von Brüning's voice – the only one I had ever heard before – I recognized at once; he was on the left of the table, and Dollmann's I knew from his position. The third was a harsh croak, belonging to the old gentleman whom, for convenience, I shall prematurely begin to call Herr Böhme. It was too old a voice to be Grimm's; besides, it had the ring of authority, and was dealing at the moment in sharp interrogations. Three of its sentences I caught in their entirety. 'When was that?' 'They went no further?' and 'Too long; out of the question.' Dollmann's voice, though nearest to me, was the least audible of all. It was a dogged monotone, and what was that odd movement of the curtain at his back? Yes, his hands were behind him clutching and kneading a fold of the cretonne. 'You are feeling uncomfortable, my friend,' was my comment. Suddenly he threw back his head – I saw the dent of it – and spoke up so that I could not miss a word. 'Very well, sir, you shall see them at supper tonight; I will ask them both.'

(You will not be surprised to learn that I instantly looked at my watch – though it takes long to write what I have described – but the time was only a quarter to four.) He added something about the fog, and his chair creaked. Ducking promptly I heard the curtain-rings jar, and: 'Thick as ever.'

'Your report, Herr Dollmann,' said Böhme, curtly. Dollmann left the window and moved his chair up to the table; the other two drew in theirs and settled themselves.

'*Chatham*,' said Dollmann, as if announcing a heading. It was an easy word to catch, rapped out sharp, and you can imagine how it startled me. 'That's where you've been for the last month!' I said to myself. A map crackled and I knew they were bending over it, while Dollmann explained something. But now my exasperation became acute, for not a syllable more reached me. Squatting back on my heels, I cast about for expedients. Should I steal round and try the door? Too dangerous. Climb to the roof and listen down the stove-pipe? Too noisy, and generally hopeless. I tried for a downward purchase on the upper half of the window, which was of the simple sort in two sections, working vertically. No use; it resisted gentle pressure, would start with a sudden jar if I forced it. I pulled out Davies's knife and worked the point of the blade between sash and frame to give it play – no result; but the knife was a nautical one, with a marling-spike as well as a big blade.

Just now the door within opened and shut again, and I heard steps approaching round the corner to my right. I had the presence of mind not to lose a moment, but moved silently away (blessing the deep Frisian sand) round the corner of the big parallel building. Someone whom I could not see walked past till his boots clattered on tiles, next resounded on boards. 'Grimm in his living-room,' I inferred. The precious minutes ebbed away – five, ten, fifteen. Had he gone for good? I dared not return otherwise. Eighteen – he was coming out! This time I stole forward boldly when the man had just passed, dimly saw a figure and, clearly enough, the glint of a white paper he was holding. He made his circuit and re-entered the room.

Here I felt and conquered a relapse to scepticism. 'If this is an important conclave why don't they set guards?' Answer, the only possible one, 'Because they stand alone. Their *employés*, like *everyone* we had met hitherto, know nothing. The real object of this salvage company (a poor speculation, I opined) is solely to afford a pretext for the conclave. Why the curtain, even? Because there are maps, stupid!'

I was back again at the window but as impotent as ever against that even stream of low confidential talk. But I would not give up. Fate and the fog had brought me here, the one solitary soul perhaps who, by the chain of circumstances, had both the will and the opportunity to wrest their secret from these four men.

The marling-spike! Where the lower half of the window met the sill it sank into a shallow groove. I thrust the point of the spike down into the interstice between sash and frame and heaved with a slowly increasing force, which I could regulate to the fraction of an ounce on this powerful lever. The sash gave, with the faintest possible protest, and by imperceptible degrees I lifted it to the top of the groove and the least bit above it, say half an inch in all; but it made an appreciable difference to the sounds within, as when you remove your foot from a piano's soft pedal. I could do no more for there was no further fulcrum for the spike and I dared not gamble away what I had won by using my hands.

Hope sank again when I placed my cheek on the damp sill and my ear to the chink. My men were close round the table referring to papers which I heard rustle. Dollmann's 'report' was evidently over and I rarely heard his voice; Grimm's occasionally, von Brüning's and Böhme's frequently; but, as before, it was the latter only that I could ever count on for an intelligible word. For, unfortunately, the villains of the piece plotted without any regard to dramatic fitness or to my interests. Immersed in a subject with which they were all familiar, they were allusive, elliptic and persistently technical. Many of the words I did catch were unknown to me. The rest were, for the most part, either letters of the alphabet or statistical figures, of depth, distance and, once or twice, of time. The letters of the alphabet recurred often and seemed, as far as I could make out, to represent the key to the cipher. The numbers clustering round them were mostly very small, with decimals. What maddened me most was the scarcity of plain nouns.

To report what I heard to the reader would be impossible, so chaotic was most of it that it left no impression on my own memory. All I can do is to tell him what fragments stuck and what nebulous classification I involved. The letters ran from A to G, and my best continuous chance came when Böhme, reading rapidly from a paper, I think, went through the letters, backwards, from G, adding remarks to each; thus: 'G . . . completed. F . . . bad . . . 1.3 (metres?) . . . 2.5 (kilometres?). E . . . thirty-two . . . 1.2. D . . . 3 weeks . . . thirty. C . . .' and so on.

Another time he went through this list again, only naming each letter himself and receiving laconic answers from Grimm – answers which seemed to be numbers, but I could not be sure. For minutes together I caught nothing but the scratching of pens and inarticulate mutterings. But out of the muck-heap. I picked five pearls – four

sibilant nouns and a name that I knew before. The nouns were
'*Schleppboote*' (tugs); '*Wassertiefe*' (depth of water); '*Eisenbahn*'
(railway); '*Lotsen*' (pilots). The name, also sibilant and thus easier
to hear, was 'Esens'.

Two or three times I had to stand back and ease my cramped neck
and, on each occasion, I looked at my watch, for I was listening
against time, just as we had rowed against time. We were going to
be asked to supper and must be back aboard the yacht in time to
receive the invitation. The fog still brooded heavily and the light,
always bad, was growing worse. How would *they* get back? How
had they come from Juist? Could we forestall them? Questions of
time, tide, distance – just the odious sort of sums I was unfit to
cope with – were distracting my attention when it should have
been wholly elsewhere. 4.20 – 4.25 – now it was past 4.30 when
Davies said the bank would cover. I should have to make for the
beacon; but it was fatally near that steamboat path, etc., and I still
at intervals heard voices from there. It must have been about 4.35
when there was another shifting of chairs within. Then someone
rose, collected papers and went out; someone else, *without* rising
(therefore Grimm), followed him.

There was silence in the room for a minute, and after that, for
the first time, I heard some plain colloquial German, with no
accompaniment of scratching or rustling. 'I must wait for this,' I
thought, and waited.

'He insists on coming,' said Böhme.

'Ach!' (an ejaculation of surprise and protest from von Brüning).

'I said the 25th.'

'Why?'

'The tide serves well. The night-train, of course. Tell Grimm to
be ready—' (An inaudible question from von Brüning.) 'No, any
weather.' A laugh from von Brüning and some words I could
not catch.

'Only one, with half a load.'

'. . . meet?'

'At the station.'

'So – how's the fog?'

This appeared to be really the end. Both men rose and steps
came towards the window. I leapt aside as I heard it thrown up
and, covered by the noise, backed into safety. Von Brüning called
'Grimm!' and that, and the open window, decided me that my line of
advance was now too dangerous to retreat by. The only alternative
was to make a circuit round the bigger of the two buildings –
and an interminable circuit it seemed – and all the while I knew

my compass-course 'south-east' was growing nugatory. I passed a padlocked door, two corners and faced the void of fog. Out came the compass and I steadied myself for the sun. 'South-east before – I'm further to the eastward now – east will about do;' and off I went, with an error of four whole points, over tussocks and deep sand. The beach seemed much farther off than I had thought and I began to get alarmed, puzzled over the compass several times, and finally realized that I had lost my way. I had the sense not to make matters worse by trying to find it again and, as the lesser of two evils, blew my whistle, softly at first, then louder. The bray of a foghorn sounded right *behind* me. I whistled again and then ran for my life, the horn sounding at intervals. In three or four minutes I was on the beach and in the dinghy.

from *The Riddle of the Sands*, Erskine Childers

The greatest traitor and masterspy in history – Kim Philby – was a devotee of Kipling's novel Kim; *he took his nickname from the eponymous hero of the book whose author, more or less, invented the phrase, 'The Great Game'. Others like Napoleon, have described it as 'a profession unworthy of a man of honour'.*

The Great Game

> Unto whose use the pregnant suns are poised
> With idiot moons and stars retracting stars?
> Creep thou betweene – thy coming's all unnoised.
> Heaven hath her high as earth her baser wars.
> Heir to these tumults, this affright, that fraye
> (By Adam's fathers' own sin bound alway);
> Peer up, draw out thy horoscope and say
> Which planet mends thy threadbare fate or mars!
>
> Sir John Christie

In the afternoon the red-faced schoolmaster told Kim that he had been 'struck off the strength', which conveyed no meaning to him till he was ordered to go away and play. Then he ran to the bazaar and found the young letter-writer to whom he owed a stamp.

'Now I pay,' said Kim royally, 'and now I need another letter to be written.'

'Mahbub Ali is in Umballa,' said the writer jauntily. He was, by virtue of his office, a bureau of general misinformation.

'This is not to Mahbub, but to a priest. Take thy pen and write quickly.'

'To Teshoo Lama, the holy one from Bhotiyal seeking for a River, who is now in the Temple of the Tirthankers at Benares.

'Take more ink!

'In three days I am to go down to Nucklao to the school at Nucklao. The name of the school is Xavier. I do not know where that school is, but it is at Nucklao.'

'But I know Nucklao,' the writer interrupted. 'I know the school.'

'Tell him where it is, and I give half an anna.'

The reed pen scratched busily. 'He cannot mistake.' The man lifted his head. 'Who watches us across the street?'

Kim looked up hurriedly and saw Colonel Creighton in tennis flannels.

'Oh, that is some Sahib who knows the fat priest in the barracks. He is beckoning me.'

'What dost thou?' said the Colonel, when Kim trotted up.

'I – I am not running away. I send a letter to my Holy One at Benares.'

'I had not thought of that. Hast thou said that I take thee to Lucknow?'

'Nay, I have not. Read the letter, if there be a doubt.'

'Then why hast thou left out my name in writing to that Holy One?' The Colonel smiled a queer smile. Kim took his courage in both hands.

'It was said once to me that it is inexpedient to write the names of strangers concerned in any matter, because by the naming of names many good plans are brought to confusion.'

'Thou hast been well taught,' the Colonel replied, and Kim flushed. 'I have left my cheroot-case in the Padre's verandah. Bring it to my house this even.'

'Where is the house?' said Kim. His quick wit told him that he was being tested in some fashion or another, and he stood on guard.

'Ask anyone in the big bazaar.' The Colonel walked on.

'He has forgotten his cheroot-case,' said Kim, returning. 'I must bring it to him this evening. That is all my letter except, thrice over, *Come to me! Come to me! Come to me!* Now I will pay for a stamp and put it in the post.' He rose to go and, as an after-thought, asked: 'Who is that angry-faced Sahid who lost the cheroot-case?'

'Oh, he is only Creighton Sahib – a very foolish Sahib, who is a Colonel Sahib without a regiment.'

'What is his business?'

'God knows. He is always buying horses which he cannot ride, and asking riddles about the works of God – such as plants and stones and the customs of people. The dealers call him the father of fools because he is so easily cheated about a horse. Mahbub Ali says he is madder than all other Sahibs.'

'Oh!' said Kim, and departed. His training had given him some small knowledge of character, and he argued that fools are not given information which leads to calling out 8000 men besides guns. The Commander-in-Chief of all India does not talk, as Kim had heard him talk, to fools. Nor would Mahbub Ali's tone have changed, as it did every time he mentioned the Colonel's name, if the Colonel had been a fool. Consequently – and this set Kim to skipping – there was a mystery somewhere, and Mahbub Ali probably spied for the Colonel much as Kim had spied for Mahbub. And, like the horse-dealer, the Colonel evidently respected people who did not show themselves to be too clever.

He rejoiced that he had not betrayed his knowledge of the Colonel's house; and when, on his return to barracks, he discovered that no cheroot-case had been left behind, he beamed with delight. Here was a man after his own heart – a tortuous and indirect person playing a hidden game. Well, if he could be a fool, so could Kim.

He showed nothing of his mind when Father Victor, for three long mornings, discoursed to him of an entirely new set of gods and godlings – notably of a goddess called Mary who, he gathered, was one with Bibi Miriam of Mahbub Ali's theology. He betrayed no emotion when, after the lecture, Father Victor dragged him from shop to shop buying articles of outfit, nor when envious drummer-boys kicked him because he was going to a superior school did he complain, but awaited the play of circumstances with an interested soul. Father Victor, good man, took him to the station, put him into an empty second-class next to Colonel Creighton's first, and bade him farewell with genuine feeling.

'They'll make a man o' you, O'Hara, at St Xavier's – a white man, an', I hope, a good man. They know all about your comin', an' the Colonel will see that ye're not lost or mislaid anywhere on the road. I've given you a notion of religious matters – at least I hope so – and you'll remember, when they ask you your religion, that you're a Cath'lic. Better say Roman Cath'lic, tho' I'm not fond of the word.'

Kim lit a rank cigarette – he had been careful to buy a stock in the bazaar – and lay down to think. This solitary passage was very different from that joyful down-journey in the third-class with the lama. 'Sahibs get little pleasure of travel,' he reflected. *'Hai mai!* I go from one place to another as it might be a kick-ball. It is my Kismet. No man can escape his Kismet. But I am to pray to Bibi Miriam, and I am a Sahib' – he looked at his boots ruefully. 'No; I am Kim. This is the great world, and I am only Kim. Who is Kim?' He considered his own identity, a thing he had never done before, till his head swam. He was one insignificant person in all this roaring whirl of India, going southward to he knew not what fate.

Presently the Colonel sent for him and talked for a long time. So far as Kim could gather, he was to be diligent and enter the Survey of India as a chain-man. If he were very good, and passed the proper examinations, he would be earning thirty rupees a month at seventeen years old, and Colonel Creighton would see that he found suitable employment.

Kim pretended at first to understand perhaps one word in three of this talk. Then the Colonel, seeing his mistake, turned to fluent and picturesque Urdu and Kim was contented. No man could be a fool who knew the language so intimately, who moved so gently and silently, and whose eyes were so different from the dull fat eyes of other Sahibs.

'Yes, and thou must learn how to make pictures of roads and mountains and rivers – to carry these pictures in thy eye till a suitable time comes to set them upon paper. Perhaps some day, when thou art a chain-man, I may say to thee when we are working together: "Go across those hills and see what lies beyond." Then one will say: "There are bad people living in those hills who will slay the chain-man if he be seen to look like a Sahib." What then?'

Kim thought. Would it be safe to return the Colonel's lead?

'I would tell what that other man had said.'

'But if I answered: "I will give thee a hundred rupees for knowledge of what is behind those hills – for a picture of a river and a little news of what the people say in the villages there"?'

'How can I tell? I am only a boy. Wait till I am a man.' Then, seeing the Colonel's brow clouded, he went on: 'But I think I should in a few days earn the hundred rupees.'

'By what road?'

Kim shook his head resolutely. 'If I said how I would earn them, another man might hear and forestall me. It is no good to sell knowledge for nothing.'

'Tell now.' The Colonel held up a rupee. Kim's hand half reached towards it, and dropped.

'Nay, Sahib, nay. I know the price that will be paid for the answer, but I do not know why the question is asked.'

'Take it for a gift, then,' said Creighton, tossing it over. 'There is a good spirit in thee. Do not let it be blunted at St Xavier's. There are many boys there who despise the black men.'

'Their mothers were bazaar-women,' said Kim. He knew well there is no hatred like that of the half-caste for his brother-in-law.

'True; but thou art a Sahib and the son of a Sahib. Therefore, do not at any time be led to contemn the black men. I have known boys newly entered into the service of the Government who feigned not to understand the talk or the customs of black men. Their pay was cut for ignorance. There is no sin so great as ignorance. Remember this.'

Several times in the course of the long twenty-four hours' run south did the Colonel send for Kim, always developing this latter text.

'We be all on one lead-rope, then,' said Kim at last, 'the Colonel, Mahbub Ali and I – when I become a chain-man. He will use me as Mahbub Ali employed me, I think. That is good, if it allows me to return to the road again. This clothing grows no easier by wear.'

When they came to the crowded Lucknow station there was no sign of the lama. He swallowed his disappointment while the Colonel bundled him into a *ticca-garri* with his neat belongings – and dispatched him alone to St Xavier's.

'I do not say farewell, because we shall meet again,' he cried. 'Again, and many times, if thou art one of good spirit. But thou art not yet tried.'

'Not when I brought thee' – Kim actually dared to use the *tum* of equals – 'a white stallion's pedigree that night?'

'Much is gained by forgetting, little brother,' said the Colonel, with a look that pierced through Kim's shoulder-blades as he scuttled into the carriage.

It took him nearly five minutes to recover. Then he sniffed the new air appreciatively. 'A rich city,' he said. 'Richer than Lahore. How good the bazaars must be. Coachman, drive me a little through the bazaars here.'

'My order is to take thee to the school.' The driver used the 'thou', which is rudeness when applied to a white man. In the clearest and most fluent vernacular Kim pointed out his error, climbed on to the box-seat and, perfect understanding established, drove for a couple of hours up and down, estimating, comparing and enjoying. There is no city – except Bombay, the queen of all – more beautiful in her garish style than Lucknow, whether you see her from the bridge over the river, or from the top of the Imambara looking down on the gilt umbrellas of the Chutter Munzil and the trees in which the town is bedded. Kings have adorned her with fantastic buildings, endowed her with charities, crammed her with pensioners and drenched her with blood. She is the centre of all idleness, intrigue and luxury, and shares with Delhi the claim to talk the only pure Urdu.

'A fair city – a beautiful city.' The driver, as a Lucknow man, was pleased with the compliment, and told Kim many astounding things where an English guide would have talked of the Mutiny.

'Now we will go to the school,' said Kim at last. The great old school of St Xavier's in Partibus, block on block of low white buildings, stands in vast grounds over against the Gumti River, at some distance from the city.

'What like of folk are they within?' said Kim.

'Young Sahibs – all devils; but to speak truth, and I drive many of them to and fro from the railway station, I have never seen one that had in him the making of a more perfect devil than thou – this young Sahib whom I am now driving.'

Naturally, for he was never trained to consider them in any way improper, Kim had passed the time of day with one or two frivolous ladies at upper windows in a certain street, and naturally, in the exchange of compliments, had acquitted himself well. He was about to acknowledge the driver's last insolence when his eye – it was growing dusk – caught a figure sitting by one of the white plaster gate-pillars in the long sweep of wall.

'Stop!' he cried. 'Stay here. I do not go to the school at once.'

'But what is to pay me for this coming and recoming?' said the driver petulantly. 'Is the boy mad? Last time it was a dancing-girl. This time it is a priest.'

Kim was in the road headlong, patting the dusty feet beneath the dirty yellow robe.

'I have waited here a day and a half,' the lama's level voice began. 'Nay, I had a disciple with me. He that was my friend at the Temple of the Tirthankers gave me a guide for this journey. I came from Benares in the train when thy letter was given me. Yes, I am well fed. I need nothing.'

'But why didst thou not stay with the Kulu woman, O Holy One? In what way didst thou get to Benares? My heart has been heavy since we parted.'

'The woman wearied me by constant flux of talk and requiring charms for children. I separated myself from that company, permitting her to acquire merit by gifts. She is at least a woman of open hands and I made a promise to return to her house if need arose. Then, perceiving myself alone in this great and terrible world, I bethought me of the *ter-rain* to Benares, where I knew one abode in the Tirthankers' Temple who was a Seeker, even as I.'

'Ah! Thy River,' said Kim. 'I had forgotten the River.'

'So soon, my *chela*? I have never forgotten it; but when I had left thee it seemed better that I should go to the temple and take counsel for, look you, India is very large and it may be that wise men before us, some two or three, have left a record of the place of our River. There is debate in the Temple of the Tirthankers on this matter; some saying one thing, and some another. They are courteous folk.'

'So be it; but what dost thou do now?'

'I acquire merit in that I help thee, my *chela*, to wisdom. The priest of that body of men who serve the Red Bull wrote me that all should be as I desired for thee. I sent the money to suffice for one year, and then I came, as thou seest me, to watch for thee going up into the Gates of Learning. A day and a half have I waited – not because I was led by any affection towards thee – that is no part of the Way – but, as they said at the Tirthankers' Temple, because, money having been paid for learning, it was right that I should oversee the end of the matter. They resolved my doubts most clearly. I had a fear that, perhaps, I came because I wished to see thee – misguided by the red mist of affection. It is not so . . . Moreover, I am troubled by a dream.'

'But surely, Holy One, thou hast not forgotten the road and all that befell on it. Surely it was a little to see me that thou didst come?'

'The horses are cold and it is past their feeding-time,' whined the driver.

'Go to Jehannum and abide there with thy reputationless aunt!' Kim snarled over his shoulder. 'I am all alone in this land; I know not where I go nor what shall befall me. My heart was in that letter I sent thee. Except for Mahbub Ali, and he is a Pathan, I have no friend save thee, Holy One. Do not altogether go away.'

'I have considered that also,' the lama replied, in a shaking voice. 'It is manifest that from time to time I shall acquire merit – if before that I have not found my River – by assuring myself that thy feet are set on wisdom. What they will teach thee I do not know, but the priest wrote me that no son of a Sahib in all India will be better taught than thou. So from time to time, therefore, I will come again. Maybe thou wilt be such a Sahib as he who gave me these spectacles' – the lama wiped them elaborately – 'in the Wonder House at Lahore. That is my hope, for he was a Fountain of Wisdom – wiser than many abbots . . . Again, maybe thou wilt forget me and our meetings.'

'If I eat thy bread,' cried Kim passionately, 'how shall I ever forget thee?'

'No – no.' He put the boy aside. 'I must go back to Benares. From time to time, now that I know the customs of letter-writers in this land, I will send thee a letter and, from time to time, I will come and see thee.'

'But whither shall I send my letters?' wailed Kim, clutching at the robe, all forgetful that he was a Sahib.

'To the Temple of the Tirthankers at Benares. That is the place I have chosen till I find my River. Do not weep; for, look you, all Desire is illusion and a new binding upon the Wheel. Go up to the Gates of Learning. Let me see thee go . . . Dost thou love me? Then go, or my heart cracks . . . I will come again. Surely I will come again.'

The lama watched the *ticca-garri* rumble into the compound, and strode off, snuffing between each long stride.

'The Gates of Learning' shut with a clang.

The country-born and bred boy has his own manners and customs, which do not resemble those of any other land; and his teachers approach him by roads which an English master would not understand. Therefore, you would scarcely be interested in Kim's experiences as a St Xavier's boy among two or three hundred precocious youths, most of whom had never seen the sea. He suffered the usual penalties for breaking out of bounds when there was cholera in the city. This was before he had learned to write fair English, and so was obliged to find a bazaar letter-writer. He was, of course, indicted for smoking and for the use of abuse more full flavoured than even St Xavier's had ever heard. He learned to wash himself with the Levitical scrupulosity of the native-born who, in his heart, considers the Englishman rather dirty. He played the usual tricks on the patient coolies pulling the punkahs in the sleeping-rooms where the boys thrashed through the hot nights telling tales till the dawn; and quietly he measured himself against his self-reliant mates.

They were sons of subordinate officials in the railway, telegraph and canal services; of warrant-officers, sometimes retired and sometimes acting as commanders-in-chief to a feudatory rajah's army; of captains of the Indian marine, Government pensioners, planters, presidency shopkeepers and missionaries. A few were cadets of the old Eurasian houses that have taken strong root in Dhurrumtollah – Pereiras, De Souzas and D'Silvas. Their parents could well have educated them in England, but they loved the school that had served their own youth, and generation followed sallow-hued generation at St Xavier's. Their homes ranged from Howrah of the railway people to abandoned cantonments like Monghyr and Chunar; lost tea-gardens Shillong-way; villages where their fathers were large landholders in Oudh or the Deccan; mission-stations a week from the nearest railway line; seaports a thousand miles south, facing the brazen Indian surf; and cinchona plantations south of all.

The mere story of their adventures, which to them were no adventures, on their road to and from school would have crisped a western boy's hair. They were used to jogging off alone through a hundred miles of jungle, where there was always the delightful chance of being delayed by tigers; but they would no more have bathed in the English Channel in an English August than their brothers across the world would have lain still while a leopard snuffed at their palanquin. There were boys of fifteen who had spent a day and a half on an islet in the middle of a flooded river, taking charge, as by right, of a camp of frantic pilgrims returning from a shrine; there were seniors who had requisitioned a chance-met rajah's elephant, in the name of St Francis Xavier, when the rains once blotted out the cart-track that led to their father's estate, and had all but lost the huge beast in a quicksand There was a boy who, he said, and none doubted, had helped his father to beat off with rifles from the verandah a rush of Akas in the days when those head-hunters were bold against lonely plantations.

And every tale was told in the even, passionless voice of the native-born, mixed with quaint reflections, borrowed unconsciously from native foster-mothers, and turns of speech that showed they had been that instant translated from the vernacular. Kim watched, listened and approved. This was not insipid, single-word talk of drummer-boys. It dealt with a life he knew and in part understood. The atmosphere suited him and he throve by inches. They gave him a white drill suit as the weather warmed and he rejoiced in the new-found bodily comforts as he rejoiced to use his sharpened mind over the tasks they set him. His quickness would have delighted an English master; but at St Xavier's they know the first rush of minds, developed by sun and surroundings, as they know the half-collapse that sets in at twenty-two or twenty-three.

None the less he remembered to hold himself lowly. When tales were told of hot nights, Kim did not sweep the board with his reminiscences; for St Xavier's looks down on boys who 'go native altogether'. One must never forget that one is a Sahib and that some day, when examinations are passed, one will command natives. Kim made a note of this, for he began to understand where examinations led.

Then came the holidays from August to October – the long holidays imposed by the heat and the rain. Kim was informed that he would go north to some station in the hills behind Umballa, where Father Victor would arrange for him.

'A barrack school?' said Kim, who had asked many questions and thought more.

'Yes, I suppose so,' said the master. 'It will not do you any harm to keep you out of mischief. You can go up with young De Castro as far as Delhi.'

Kim considered it in every possible light. He had been diligent, even as the Colonel advised. A boy's holiday was his own property – of so much the talk of his companions had advised him – and a barrack school would be torment after St Xavier's. Moreover – this was magic worth anything else – he could write. In three months he had discovered how men can speak to each other without a third party, at the cost of half an anna and a little knowledge. No word had come from the lama, but there remained the Road. Kim yearned for the caress of soft mud squishing up between the toes, as his mouth watered for mutton stewed with butter and cabbages, for rice speckled with strong-scented cardamoms, for the saffron-tinted rice, garlic and onions, and the forbidden greasy sweetmeats of the bazaars. They would feed him raw beef on a platter at the barrack school, and he must smoke by stealth. But again, he was a Sahib and was at St Xavier's, and that pig Mahbub Ali . . . No, he would not test Mahbub's hospitality – and yet . . . He thought it out alone in the dormitory and came to the conclusion he had been unjust to Mahbub.

The school was empty; nearly all the masters had gone away; Colonel Creighton's railway pass lay in his hand, and Kim puffed himself that he had not spent Colonel Creighton's or Mahbub's money in riotous living. He was still lord of two rupees seven annas. His new bullock-trunk, marked 'K. O'H'., and bedding-roll lay in the empty sleeping-room. 'Sahibs are always tied to their baggage,' said Kim, nodding at them. 'You will stay here.' He went out into the warm rain, smiling sinfully, and sought a certain house whose outside he had noted down some time before . . .

'Arré! Dost thou know what manner of women we be in this quarter? O shame!'

'Was I born yesterday?' Kim squatted native fashion on the cushions of that upper room. 'A little dye-stuff and three yards of cloth to help out a jest. Is it much to ask?'

'Who is *she*? Thou art full young, as Sahibs go, for this devilry.'

'Oh, she? She is the daughter of a certain schoolmaster of a regiment in the cantonments. He has beaten me twice because I went over their wall in these clothes. Now I would go as a gardener's boy. Old men are very jealous.'

'That is true. Hold thy face still while I dab on the juice.'

'Not too black, Naikan. I would not appear to her as a *hubshi* [nigger].'

'Oh, love makes nought of these things. And how old is she?'

'Twelve years, I think,' said the shameless Kim. 'Spread it also on the breast. It may be her father will tear my clothes off me and if I am piebald—' he laughed.

The girl worked busily, dabbing a twist of cloth into a little saucer of brown dye that holds longer than any walnut juice.

'Now send out and get me a cloth for the turban. Woe is me, my head is all unshaved! And he will surely knock off my turban.'

'I am not a barber, but I will make shift. Thou wast born to be a breaker of hearts! All this disguise for one evening? Remember, the stuff does not wash away.' She shook with laughter till her bracelets and anklets jingled. 'But who is to pay me for this? Huneefa herself could not have given thee better stuff.'

'Trust in the Gods, my sister,' said Kim gravely, screwing his face round as the stain dried. 'Besides, hast thou ever helped to paint a Sahib thus before?'

'Never indeed. But a jest is not money.'

'It is worth much more.'

'Child, thou art beyond all dispute the most shameless son of Shaitan that I have ever known to take up a poor girl's time with this play, and then to say: "Is not the jest enough?" Thou wilt go very far in this world.' She gave the dancing-girls' salutation in mockery.

'All one. Make haste and rough-cut my head.'

Kim shifted from foot to foot, his eyes ablaze with mirth as he thought of the fat days before him. He gave the girl four annas and ran down the stairs in the likeness of a low-caste Hindu boy – perfect in every detail. A cookshop was his next point of call where he feasted in extravagance and greasy luxury.

On Lucknow Station platform he watched young De Castro, all covered with prickly heat, get into a second-class compartment. Kim patronized a third, and was the life and soul of it. He explained to the company that he was assistant to a juggler who had left him behind sick with fever, and that he would pick up his master at Umballa. As the occupants of the carriage changed he varied this tale, or adorned it with all the shoots of a budding fancy, the more rampant for being held off native speech so long. In all India that night was no human being so joyful as Kim. At Umballa he got out and headed eastward, plashing over the sodden fields to the village where the old soldier lived.

About this time Colonel Creighton at Simla was advised from Lucknow by wire that young O'Hara had disappeared. Mahbub Ali was in town selling horses, and to him the Colonel confided the affair one morning cantering round Annandale race-course.

'Oh, that is nothing,' said the horse-dealer.

'Men are like horses. At certain times they need salt and, if that salt is not in the manger, they will lick it up from the earth. He has gone back to the Road again for a while. The *madrissah* wearied him. I knew it would. Another time, I will take him upon the Road myself. Do not be troubled, Creighton Sahib. It is as though a polo-pony, breaking loose ran out to learn the game alone.'

'Then he is not dead, think you?'

'Fever might kill him. I do not fear for the boy otherwise. A monkey does not fall among trees.'

Next morning, on the same course, Mahbub's stallion ranged alongside the Colonel.

'It is as I had thought,' said the horse-dealer.

'He has come through Umballa at least, and there he has written a letter to me, having learned in the bazaar that I was here.'

'Read,' said the Colonel, with a sigh of relief.

It was absurd that a man of his position should take an interest in a little country-bred vagabond; but the Colonel remembered the conversation in the train and often, in the past few months, had caught himself thinking of the queer, silent, self-possessed boy. His evasion, of course, was the height of insolence, but it argued some resource and nerve.

Mahbub's eyes twinkled as he reined out into the centre of the cramped little plain where none could come near unseen.

'The Friend of the Stars, who is the Friend of all the World—'

'What is this?'

'A name we give him in Lahore city.

The Friend of all the World takes leave to go to his own places. He will come back upon the appointed day. Let the box and the bedding-roll be sent for; and if there has been a fault, let the Hand of Friendship turn aside the Whip of Calamity.

'There is yet a little more, but—'

'No matter, read.'

'Certain things are not known to those who eat with forks. It is better to eat with both hands for a while. Speak soft words to those who do not understand this that the return may be propitious.

Now the manner in which that was cast is, of course the work of the letter-writer, but see how wisely the boy has devised the matter of it so that no hint is given except to those who know!'

'Is this the Hand of Friendship to avert the Whip of Calamity?' laughed the Colonel.

'See how wise is the boy. He would go back to the Road again, as I said. Not knowing yet thy trade—'

'I am not quite sure of that,' the Colonel muttered.

'He turns to me to make a peace between you. Is he not wise? He says he will return. He is but perfecting his knowledge. Think, Sahib! He has been three months at the school. And he is not mouthed to that bit. For my part, I rejoice; the pony learns the game.'

'Ay, but another time he must not go alone.'

'Why? He went alone before he came under the Colonel Sahib's protection. When he comes to the Great Game he must go alone – alone, and at peril of his head. *Then*, if he spits, or sneezes, or sits down other than as the people do whom he watches, he may be slain. Why hinder him now? Remember how the Persians say: the jackal that lives in the wilds of Mazanderan can only be caught by the hounds of Mazanderan.'

'True. It is true, Mahbub Ali. And if he comes to no harm, I do not desire anything better. But it is great insolence on his part.'

'He does not tell me, even, whither he goes,' said Mahbub. 'He is no fool. When his time is accomplished he will come to me. It is time the healer of pearls took him in hand. He ripens too quickly – as Sahibs reckon.'

This prophecy was fulfilled to the letter a month late. Mahbub had gone down to Umballa to bring up a fresh consignment of horses, and Kim met him on the Kalka road at dusk riding alone, begged an alms of him, was sworn at and replied in English. There was nobody within earshot to hear Mahbub's gasp of amazement.

'Oho! And where hast thou been?'

'Up and down – down and up.'

'Come under a tree, out of the wet, and tell.'

'I stayed for a while with an old man near Umballa; anon with a household of my acquaintance in Umballa. With one of these I went as far as Delhi to the southward. That is a wondrous city. Then I drove a bullock for a *teli* (an oilman) coming north; but I heard of a great feast forward in Puttiala, and thither went I in the company of a firework-maker. It was a great feast (Kim rubbed his stomach). I saw Rajahs, and elephants with gold and silver trappings; and they lit all the fireworks at once, whereby eleven men were killed, my firework-maker among them, and I was blown across a tent but took no harm. Then I came back to the *rêl* with a Sikh horseman, to whom I was groom for my bread; and so here.'

'*Shabash!*' said Mahbub Ali.

'But what does the Colonel Sahib say? I do not wish to be beaten.'

'The Hand of Friendship has averted the Whip of Calamity; but another time, when thou takest the Road, it will be with me. This is too early.'

'Late enough for me. I have learned to read and to write English a little at the *madrissah*. I shall soon be altogether a Sahib.'

'Hear him!' laughed Mahbub, looking at the little drenched figure dancing in the wet. 'Salaam – Sahib,' and he saluted ironically. 'Well, art tired of the Road, or wilt thou come on to Umballa with me and work back with the horses?'

'I come with thee, Mahbub Ali.'

from *Kim*, Rudyard Kipling

PREMATURE DEMISES OF 'KIM' PHILBY

And it is with Philby that we end. A real character so extraordinary and outrageous that, while no respectable writer would dare invent him, several (including myself) have introduced him into their works of fiction, usually allowing themselves the satisfaction of killing him off. Here are two examples. The real Kim Philby died in his Moscow bed, of natural causes, in May 1988.

Stop Press, 1981

He put the book down and picked up the damp *Evening Standard* to read while the coffee cooled.

The front page, like all Saturday editions, was devoted entirely to sport. A big photograph of Botham and a headline that said, 'Arsenal squad ready for new season'. There was little news in the rest of the paper and a few minutes later he tossed it on to the table. As he leaned forward to pick up his coffee he saw the 'Stop Press' column on the back page. In heavy type it said 'Philby Dead'. There were a few lines of smudged copy.

> Soviet super-spy 'Kim' Philby died suddenly of a heart attack at his flat in Moscow today. A brief report from the Soviet Tass Agency said that Philby had been in ill health for some months. Agency reports suggest that Moscow will be giving the British traitor a state funeral.

He sat in the darkness for almost an hour. The telephone rang several times but he made no move to answer it. He tried hard not to care, and not to think; but he knew that there must have been one awful, bowel-loosening moment when Philby knew that his 'friends' had decided which way it would be. A moment when he would realize that all those heart-to-heart talks with Malik had been a waste of time. Those tired eyes would have looked with disbelief at the hypodermic as they held him in the chair. And then that bomb exploding in his heart that meant oblivion, and an entry on a death certificate that would quite correctly be inscribed as 'cardiac failure'.

                      from *The Other Side of Silence*, Ted Allbeury

Or, alternatively . . .

Cut off in Mid-Flow

Philby had been talking for just over ten minutes, without a trace of stammer, his soft voice amplified across the hall where the only movement was the scribble of shorthand and the occasional swing of a sound-boom.

  He looked tired and rather small under the lights. He spoke without notes, gazing out across the rows of faces, and sweating slightly.

  'Now I come to what I believe is a matter of some historical importance. As I have already said, my motives in appearing before you remain my own concern. I know that many will criticize me, many will condemn me. But I wish to go on record as stating that, in what I did, I was not alone. I was never alone. While I was working for the interests of the Soviet Union, there were others in my job – others far more important, far more powerful than I ever was – who were working with me in the same interests, for the same cause. Some of them are still working for that cause.' He paused and closed his eyes against the lights; then, with what looked to some of the audience like a wince of pain, he reached inside his jacket. He stood for several seconds very still, then opened his eyes and slowly drew out a crumpled sheet of paper.

  'Gentlemen—' he steadied himself against the table. 'Ladies and gentlemen,' he began again, 'I am now going to read you the names of five men. They all hold high positions in Britain today, and three of them are still Her Majesty's principal civil servants – who are, and have been, to my certain knowledge, for more than thirty years – in the employment of the Soviet State Security Organization.' He jerked his head down to the paper in his hand, dropped on to his knees and rolled over on the floor.

  In the ensuing uproar, van der Byl called for calm. The two plain-clothes men in the wings were already leaning over Philby. He was breathing in quick gasps. They were joined by a leading British television reporter. One of the plain-clothes men stood up and shouted for a doctor. Philby's eyes showed only slits and his face was the texture of greaseproof paper. One hand was still locked round the sheet of paper; the other fluttered beside him, then lay still.

'Get a bloody doctor, for Christ's sake!' the plain-clothes man shouted again.

The television journalist was down on his knees, trying to prise the paper out of Philby's fingers. He turned and saw Philby looking at him. There were bubbles of spit on his bloodless lips, and his fingers released the crumpled piece of paper. The journalist grabbed it and stared at him in astonishment.

Above the noise, Philby managed a few words. The journalist had to lean close to hear. 'You don't think I'd be fool enough to put it in writing, do you?'

The television man stumbled back to his crew on the floor of the hall. 'Well?' said one of them. 'What the hell went wrong?'

'Heart attack, it looks like. And what a time to choose.' He opened the piece of paper in his hand. It was blank. 'He conned us all again. The bastard.'

from *Gentleman Traitor*, Alan Williams